Praise for G

'He has never los...
for the stories ...
The Sunday Times on *The Crocodile Hunter*

'Compelling novel . . . Seymour's feel for the Kent
landscape and his realisation of minor characters, such as
Cameron's heart-hardened mother, are almost Dickensian'
The Times on *The Crocodile Hunter*

'Another fine spy story with an offbeat protagonist'
Peterborough Telegraph on *The Crocodile Hunter*

'Ask aficionados who is Britain's finest thriller writer,
and many would answer the veteran Gerald Seymour'
Guardian on *Beyond Recall*

'The three British masters of suspense, Graham
Greene, Eric Ambler, and John le Carré, have
been joined by a fourth – Gerald Seymour'
New York Times on *The Outsiders*

'Seymour produces the most intelligent
writing in the thriller genre'
Financial Times on *Beyond Recall*

About the Author

Gerald Seymour spent fifteen years as an international television news reporter with ITN, covering Vietnam and the Middle East, and specialising in the subject of terrorism across the world. Seymour was on the streets of Londonderry on the afternoon of Bloody Sunday, and was a witness to the massacre of Israeli athletes at the Munich Olympics. Gerald Seymour exploded onto the literary scene with the massive bestseller *Harry's Game*, that has since been picked by the *Sunday Times* as one of the 100 best thrillers written since 1945. He has been a full-time writer since 1978, and six of his novels have been filmed for television in the UK and US. *The Crocodile Hunter* is his thirty-seventh novel.

Also by Gerald Seymour

Harry's Game	Holding the Zero
The Glory Boys	The Untouchable
Kingfisher	Traitor's Kiss
Red Fox	The Unknown Soldier
The Contract	Rat Run
Archangel	The Walking Dead
In Honour Bound	Timebomb
Field of Blood	The Collaborator
A Song in the Morning	The Dealer and the Dead
At Close Quarters	A Deniable Death
Home Run	The Outsiders
Condition Black	The Corporal's Wife
The Journeyman Tailor	Vagabond
The Fighting Man	No Mortal Thing
The Heart of Danger	Jericho's War
Killing Ground	A Damned Serious Business
The Waiting Time	Battle Sight Zero
A Line in the Sand	Beyond Recall

THE
CROCODILE
HUNTER

Gerald Seymour

HODDER

First published in Great Britain in 2021 by Hodder & Stoughton
An Hachette UK company

This paperback edition published in 2021

2

A CIP catalogue record for this title is available from the British Library

Paperback ISBN 978 1 529 38604 2

Typeset in Plantin Light by Hewer Text UK Ltd, Edinburgh
Printed and bound in Great Britain by Clays Ltd, Elcograf S.p.A.

Hodder & Stoughton policy is to use papers that are natural, renewable
and recyclable products and made from wood grown in sustainable
forests. The logging and manufacturing processes are expected to
conform to the environmental regulations of the country of origin.

Hodder & Stoughton Ltd
Carmelite House
50 Victoria Embankment
London EC4Y 0DZ

www.hodder.co.uk

For Harriet and Georgia and Alfie.

PROLOGUE

Many others were celebrating, but not Jonas Merrick. Yelling and shouting behind him were groups heading for the bars on Horseferry Road, and ahead was the cacophony of laughter and singing from the office parties on the booze boats navigating the Thames. It was, that damp evening, a hint of frost in the air, a date that Jonas could well have decided was worth celebrating: his birthday, his sixtieth. Not so . . . the least welcome, dreaded in fact. Retirement beckoned, and later that evening his identification for entry into Thames House would be wiped. He would be a creature from the past, unmissed and forgotten. They called him Eternal Flame in A Branch, not with love or respect, but with a sneer: he never went out, was desk-bound, an encyclopaedia of names and faces, and long redundant because computers did the same job.

He had slipped away through the side door, had walked towards the floodlit face of the Houses of Parliament, had crossed the lawns, sparkling from the afternoon's rain, and not cared that his shoes, always highly polished, would be muddied when he went back for the reception planned for him in the atrium. He felt the spit of drizzle on his cheeks, and the wind ruffled his sparse hair. The party, in name only, was a bare half-hour away. In the open-plan area used by the A4 Branch he had heard a woman complain, "God, do we have to go to that pillock's goodbye?" and a young man had said, not caring to lower his voice, "Just so boring, and never achieves anything . . ." and another had murmured, "There's a war out there, and he's the only passenger in A4 who doesn't know what the front line looks like or feels like – good riddance." The Assistant Deputy Director General would make an appearance, stay ten minutes, mouth platitudes, and be on his way.

A formality. He had escaped in order to kill time before he was expected for the humiliation and the chuckling, and the insincerity of it.

Jonas headed for a bench near the river wall, mostly in shadow. His wife, Vera, was not invited, security and all that. He skirted the sculpture, the Burghers of Calais, in the centre of the small park, reached the bench and sat down, felt the moisture seep into his trousers, uttered a mild oath, and became aware he was not alone. There was a slight movement in the gloom beside him. He apologised, was not acknowledged.

He had been in A4 for 35 years, a dinosaur. Knew the targets and the addresses that the surveillance people tracked, just did not do the tracking himself, and his stomach bulged and he felt rheumatism in his knees and hips. He took little exercise, only the walk from home to the station, and from the London terminus to Thames House, and the daily reverse. He had no idea how his life, and Vera's, would shape after the weekend, all those identities and locations no longer relevant ... There would be a minimum number of *prosecco* bottles provided, or *cava*, and the AssDepDG would smile limply and thank him for loyal service. Beside Jonas, a crisp packet was crumpled and dropped, and it blew against his foot. Another wriggling movement, and an arm reached across him, and he saw the face of a young man, and the litter was picked up and there was a faint grated apology. Not to worry ... those he worked with were that evening on a high because there had been a good eyeball on the target's meeting with an additional Tango, and that seemed to link two surveillance targets, a big step forward, and it had been a difficult "follow" with both subjects employing intelligent tradecraft procedures. The team had thought themselves – he did not mind mild vulgarity – the "bee's bollocks". He had twenty minutes to kill. Beside him the crisp packet was pocketed and a wristwatch studied as if the boy with whom he shared the bench was also checking a schedule.

None of them coming back into the work area after the successful eyeball, and photographs to go with it, had acknowledged Jonas's part in the good outcome ... The AssDepDG's appearance would be token. His colleagues would be there a bare minimum of time. He was hurt, bruised . . . Did he make a difference? Not in anyone else's eyes. Would he be missed? No. Was credit ever given him? No . . .

He had only seen the face of the boy beside him for a moment, but he had started to plumb deep into that mine of facial features and biographies that his memory carried. They had been Irish when he had started, then Cold War diplomats and couriers from eastern Europe, but now the operations of A4 were almost exclusively aimed at the *jihadis*.

Originally it had been intended to give him a self-assembly greenhouse. But he'd heard a rumour that such a purchase would outstrip the budget available: he would be presented with a John Lewis voucher as reward for a lifetime at the Security Service.

He knew the face, recognised him. Could put a name to it, and a mother's address, and an age.

"It's Winston, yes?"

He heard the suck of breath beside him, and a head that had been held low jerked up. The moment coincided with headlights U-turning in the traffic and catching the Burghers on their plinth, lingering on the boy's face, then moving on. Quite an interesting moment for Jonas . . . Back where he worked, where just a few more minutes of employment existed, the sight of Winston Gunn – son of Ben Gunn, a Caucasian lorry driver, and Farida, Quetta born of solid Pakistani stock, and a very fractured family as a result of a pregnancy with a white-skinned Briton – would register interest. Dad was long gone. Mum had brought up the boy – listed as resentful, hostile to the world around him, excellent recruiting material. Jonas doubted that any of the other analysts in the work area would have identified the boy's olive-coloured features without rifling through a laptop's archive.

"Bit off your beaten track, Winston?"

And back there, in that work area, if they knew, there would have been an organisational stampede at the presence of young Winston – supposedly drawn into the activist net while serving eighteen months' imprisonment, theft with violence, in HMP

Pentonville – within a stone's throw, or a hand grenade's, from the Palace of Westminster, Mother of Parliaments, the beating heart of democracy . . . all that crap. Ringed now with dragons' teeth, and barricades of concrete and police clutching H&K machine pistols, the illuminated edifices represented the High Value Target of the nation's government . . . No chance Winston's presence was innocent. They'd be calling up additional firearms units, alerting the ambulance service, warning ministers, planning evacuations, and demanding the immediate presence of the psychology team and behavioural experts. How to proceed? It would be batted around, as the clock ticked. Jonas was not a policeman, nor a paramedic, nor an elected Secretary, nor a psychologist or psychiatrist; he was the little man with an ugly mole on his chin and pebble-lens spectacles who was now getting out from A4 Branch, surplus to requirements. Seemed pretty damned obvious. The team would have been gripped by a fear of "getting it wrong": he could remember those days in the aftermath of an atrocity when it had been plain as a pikestaff that a *jihadi* who had reached a target and done his suicide had been fully signed up to a blip on the radar. They would be passing the parcel, hoping the decision – whatever it might be – would be made by someone else. Damned obvious, what to do, and he'd get on with it.

"Don't worry about me, Winston, I'm just the original nobody."

The boy wore a big anorak but, as Jonas remembered him from the surveillance snaps, he would have been spare built, no flesh on his bones. The jacket, black and with a couple of paint smears on it, seemed worn and ready for disposal – as was intended. But the boy shivered as if the cold wind off the river reached inside it and hugged him. His breath came in little spurts. No one there to hold his hand. Young and frightened, and the words of encouragement they'd have used would be draining fast from his head.

"Did they volunteer you, Winston? Tell you that your name would be remembered year after year? That one day a plaque would go up on a wall for you, and crowds would say prayers on this day?"

His calm matter-of-fact questions were not answered: he did not expect them to be and did not want them to be. Jonas thought it best to keep a drip-feed in the boy's ear, to smother his resolve. He was intrigued that Winston had not reacted angrily, exasperated at the use of his old name. The file said he was now called Salah, had been since his recruitment. Pretty much everyone else who came into and went out of the A4 area had experienced being close to those they tracked, had the chance – sometimes for continuous hours – to watch their movements. Not Jonas. He had never made the time to slip out of Thames House, take a bus down to Ludgate Circus, wander into the public gallery at the Old Bailey and sit in on a trial: he maintained the letter of his job description. Now with new-found mischief he shed familiar manacles. His knowledge of Winston, and any of the rest of them, was from what he absorbed from his screen and then stored in the paper files he alone maintained. The breathing next to him accelerated and eyes flashed at him in the gloom, and twice more the wristwatch was checked. To be expected. Just a few minutes to seven o'clock, and the traffic around Westminster was near solid, and the boats were doing good noisy trade. Jonas should be in the atrium with the smattering of colleagues and standing smartly for the arrival of AssDepDG . . . Also on the hour the shift of armed police around Westminster changed. It had been learned from phone intercepts that the perceived *jihadi* wisdom was to attack a protected target just before the relief team showed up, and when the guards' concentration was drifting.

"I suppose you did a video, Winston. Usually takes several attempts to get it word-perfect. I suppose they wrote it for you? Treating you like a pack animal really. Just a donkey, there to carry the load. Did you wonder, Winston, when they were coaching you for the video, why their own kids and their own nephews never seemed to be asked to wear the vest? Look after their own, don't they? Sometimes, they don't think the donkey will go the whole mile, and might bug out, so then they sit a little distance away and watch and have their own electronic firing trigger. Unlikely they'll have put real trust in you, Winston. Could be observing us now, could be about to . . . Don't mind me."

He reached across the shadow shape, slipped a fist inside the Velcro fastening of the anorak, felt the boy squirm away from him. It was a moment of maximum risk. The boy would have had his hand on a button deep in his pocket. Might press it, might not. Jonas's fingers found a mess of wires and his grip closed on them. It would not have been part of the boy's induction to martyrdom to receive a lesson in defusing the beast. The back of Jonas's hand brushed against metal builders' nails, ball-bearings and assorted junk for shrapnel wounds, and worse. The boy did not resist, not yet . . . If Jonas had not chosen that bench Winston would now be walking, like a trance had trapped him, towards an entrance to the Palace of Westminster where the public milled and officials and politicians would be leaving and the armed police were stationed. But he had unwittingly chosen that bench. The boy did not fight him, did not detonate, did not flash a blade at him, just wriggled, his breath coming faster. Jonas had not an idea in his head as to the detail of the potential wiring, and whether it would blow when he tugged.

"I'm thinking how it was, Winston, when they dropped you off. Driven you up from Peckham or wherever they had you in the countdown. A few words of encouragement, but not many. A little slap on the back and a bit of a lecture on the evils of the Crusaders. The door opened for you and you step out, and it slams behind you, and you might just have seen the tail-lights disappearing . . . But one of them might still be watching – getting agitated now because you're running late. Except the scattering of your body parts here, and mine, is hardly a big deal. But a bit of a waste after all the time and resources invested in you, Winston."

He had a tension on the wires, and gulped. Jonas had never attempted anything that ticked the box marked Danger, had never considered an action labelled as Extreme Danger, and the last time he had witnessed a fight outside Waterloo station he had not thought of intervening but had crossed the road, looked the other way . . . They would be, by now, in the atrium. The *prosecco* would be uncorked, nibbles laid out, and the chorus would have started, and the AssDepDG would be coming down in the elevator carrying an envelope with the voucher in it, and a piece of paper with something anodyne written on it . . . A blur of conversations and impatience. "Little sod, he's buggered off home . . . I'm not hanging about, not kicking my heels here . . . A waste of space, no idea of the reality of keeping the streets safe . . . Just a cursor pusher . . . We had a result today, brilliant eyeball . . . you might have noticed there was nothing from him, sitting at his bloody desk – no praise, no *cojones*, nothing – how rude can a guy get?" His fault that he had no friend there? Their fault that he was outside the loop? But, whatever Vera said, past caring.

"I'm wondering, Winston, if you had the chance to call your mum, or didn't they allow that? An opportunity for a little cuddle before you went off to Paradise and all those virgins waiting for you. I think your mum would have been properly upset when the police came to break down her front door, tell her what you'd done, show her the video. Better this way, lad. What I always say, rather be safe than sorry. So we don't have an accident."

Believe that? Not really . . . He pulled. His mouth sagged open. Nothing happened except that the motion dragged the boy half across his lap. The wires came away, and a small household battery with them. His hands shook and the boy gasped, and there was no flash and no thunder roar and no spiralling up of body parts. Horns trumpeted in the traffic and a party on a boat was raucous.

"Just lift your arms up, Winston, please. Don't think of bolting back where you came from, because they won't love you. They'll speak badly of you. Yes, arms up."

Docile, obedient. It was how, long ago out on the Surrey hills on a sunny Sunday, he might have worked a cardigan from Vera's shoulders – without much hope of action to follow. The boy raised his arms and Jonas eased off his anorak. The rain had come on harder and the air was chilled and the boy's shiver was worse. A length of knotted string tied the vest around the boy's chest. Took a bit of fiddling to loosen it. Then Jonas lifted clear the vest, and heard the nails rattle and the ball-bearings tinkle, and he smelled the explosive and choked on it. Because he had never been out in a siege or stand-off he did not know the weight of a bulletproof vest loaded with Kevlar plates. Unthinking, a natural gesture, he tapped the boy's frail shoulder, as if he were a pupil who had done well. He stood and walked towards the low embankment wall. He trembled, thought he might faint, raised it, chucked it. He heard the splash, peered over the parapet and saw the disturbed water.

"Come on, Winston, let's be on our way."

No children had blessed the marriage of Jonas and Vera Merrick, but he supposed he spoke with the tone and charity that parents used on an errant child. He felt sympathy for the boy. They walked together, the two of them, as if leaving a bad place where neither knew true loyalty. Something a schoolmaster way back had read to the class, the words of a wartime pilot. *Those that I fight I do not hate, Those that I guard I do not love* . . . The boy, in trust, held Jonas's hand. He did not hate the boy, nor love the revellers on the river. They walked over the sodden grass and reached a pavement and crossed a main road and left the target area behind them, and the loaded weapons of the police, and negotiated a roundabout.

Many evenings on reaching home, he would complain to Vera of the way he was distanced by those he worked with, ignored and seldom praised, and she might cock her head, grimace, and tell him that "The problem is, Jonas, you're not, never have been, won't ever be, a team player, and you're never in before dawn in crisis time, and you catch the 5.49 back regardless of whether the ceiling is collapsing on the streets of London. You don't give enough back. Always the victim, never to blame, Jonas, but go look in the mirror. They want to be heroes, do something special. And you? Your tea's ready." Ahead of them was the facade of Thames House.

He took Winston to a café in a neighbouring street, left him there and went back to his one-time workplace. The atrium was empty but a few empty bottles stood on a table. There was a sealed envelope on his desk: that would be his retirement gift. He called a duty officer, identified himself, and briskly reported an explosive device that could be found on a mud spit at the next low tide, and told of Winston Gunn, alone, frightened, sitting in a nearby café nursing a coffee and needing immediate attention, and kindness . . . A barrage of questions assaulted Jonas, but he put the phone down and went to the side door. His access ID would be electronically shredded when he passed through, like a flame being snuffed, even an Eternal Flame. A hero? He laughed, rare for him, and stepped on to the pavement.

I

He stepped out on to his front path.

He passed the rose bed, only three bushes, then walked between the parked car and the caravan, and reached the pavement. He ducked his head without looking back but the gesture would have been enough for Vera to know that he was grateful for the sandwiches she had prepared for him, in a plastic box at the bottom of his briefcase, wedged between paper files. He bent the Thames House rules about taking documents outside the building and bringing them home, but few rules at his place of work seemed now to apply to him. The caravan looked well and had come through the winter in reasonable shape, the paintwork in fair condition. He and Vera had been talking only the previous evening about whether to splash out and buy a new cooker or whether to make do for another year with the current one which had been in use for the last eighteen years ... If he had retired when it was intended he should, 34 months ago, then a new cooker would have been at the top of their shopping list.

A neighbour was leaving from two doors down: Derbyshire, who sold double glazing for conservatories.

"Morning, Jonas."

"And a good morning to you."

He smiled, perfunctory, and walked on. Other front gates along this south London suburban street were clicking open and shut. Jonas Merrick knew most of his neighbours by sight and could exchange banalities: the rising cost of fuel, the number of potholes in the road, the increasingly erratic attendance of the refuse carts, or the weather forecasts for the coming weekend. They knew little, next to nothing, of him. They would have reckoned to have known

Vera, been on something better than nodding terms with her, but not been close. Easy to imagine the gossip in the street when Christmas drinks were being served or summer barbecues pitched smoke and fumes over the back fences. "Funny old cove, never know what he's thinking . . . Perhaps not thinking of anything, perhaps as dull as he looks . . . Never been in his house with him there, no invites, never accepted one from us . . . She's all right, quiet and decent, but he's a proper wet rag . . . I feel for her, don't know why she sticks with him . . . Do you know what he does? No, I don't – pushes paper in Whitehall, but that's only a guess . . . God fucking help us if the likes of Jonas Merrick are looking after our pensions or whatever . . ." He remained an enigma to them and supposed they regarded him as a source of mild amusement. It was good that they knew little of him and the nature of his employment, and Vera was always disciplined and coy when other wives pestered her for details of where he worked and what he did. It was that time of year when the gardens in front of the mock-Tudor semi-detached homes in the street were starting to sprout daffodils and in some the crocuses were pushing up, and at Number 49, the snowdrops still held their shape and colour. He always walked the length of the street, through all the seasons, leaving home each weekday morning at the same time, 48 minutes past six. It could be snowing, raining, blowing a gale or balmy, and he would be on foot, never suggesting that Vera drive him to the station. And whatever the conditions he would adopt the same dress code – neither smart nor casual, not formal and not dressed down. This early spring morning he wore grey flannel trousers and dark brown shoes, his shirt had a soft check on it and his tie was a wool weave, and his jacket had a quiet fleck in it, and enveloping him was a heavy mackintosh, old-fashioned but still with plenty of wear in it, and with a fastened belt, and on his sparse hair was a trilby that was losing its shape but was good enough to keep his cheeks dry or his face in shadow. He walked briskly because he had a schedule and would not deviate from it.

Because the raincoat was a size too large for him, the sleeves amply covered his wrists. They hid the watch on his left wrist, and also the metal attachment fastened on his right wrist from which a fine chain ran to the handle of his briefcase. The concession that he should be permitted to take home sensitive documents had been made on the very strict guarantee that the chain would always be in place when he travelled. The practice was frowned upon by those of senior rank but was allowed and none of the rest of the hordes who packed into Thames House each morning were afforded a matching privilege, except perhaps the Assistant Deputy Director General, AssDepDG, and the handful of men and women at the heart of authority in the building. He had owned that briefcase – a present from Vera, then his fiancée – for 34 of the 38 years he had worked for the Security Service, which had the Latin title of *Regnum Defende*. The task of defending the kingdom was, generally accepted by those who cared to know of such matters, about as bloody difficult – that day, yesterday, tomorrow, each hour of each week in each month – as it had been at any time since he had joined the Service with the rank of a junior clerk. As he turned out of his own street, left behind the last of the trees that were coming into bud and might if the cold eased soon be in blossom, Vera would be closing the front door behind her, leaving her with only the presence of their mutually beloved youngster – a Norwegian Forest cat asleep on a kitchen chair. Vera worked in a small gallery in Motspur Park that sold water-colour paintings from the previous century. She, also, those months ago, had expected to retire, had rescinded her notice, had stayed on.

Jonas had a season ticket. He would catch a train from Raynes Park that would take him to Waterloo in 26 minutes. The journey would take the same time as it had more than three decades earlier when he and Vera had scraped together the deposit on their home: they had not moved since and the train timetable had not altered. He could usually rely on getting a seat on that train, in the fifth carriage, and might have to use his elbows, but most mornings he could squirm through the waiting passengers on the platform. There were at least half a dozen other commuters from his street arriving at the station at the same time but he acknowledged none of them. Familiar faces would be in the carriage, some of whom he had travelled alongside for a quarter of a century, but he would keep his head down and rely on the journey to provide an opportunity for reflection. He knew the developing landmarks along the route, through Wimbledon where the stampede started, and then Clapham, knew every new building sandwiched into minimal space, and although the carriage was always overheated he would keep his mackintosh on and the right sleeve would mask the wrist attachment to the chain of tempered steel and the old frayed briefcase that carried no label and most certainly not the insignia of EII in faded gold. He was anonymous, unknown. Jonas Merrick carried huge responsibility on his rather bowed shoulders, and he wore no uniform and none of those squashed around him would have realised that they were pressed close to an individual on whom responsibilities and burdens weighed heavily . . . His job was to keep them safe, and the threat was greater each day and never diminished . . . It was good to have some quiet time to think, put himself in their minds, anticipate their moves.

He pulled up, parked the van on the grass verge.

Behind him he heard whispers, nervous giggles and gasps of anticipation. He switched off the engine, opened his window. Silence nestled around them.

On the files he was Cameron Jilkes, aged 25. The photographs would include ones of him as a child, then as a teenager at school, and one captured almost four years before at an airport departure gate. To his one-time friends, he had been Kami al-Britani. To his mum, whom he had loved, who had been a source of comfort in the years he had been away, to whom he had not spoken nor written since he had taken the plane out, he was Cammy.

He took a cigarette from the pack in his breast-pocket. The packet showed images of rampant cancers that were supposed to deter smokers. Where Cammy had been and what he had seen and what he had done, and the price he had paid, the ravages of terminal illness were a low priority. Behind him, the group he had driven from

Bordeaux were climbing down from the van and were stretching; they seemed to have caught his mood and their voices were stifled and the children were hushed. Cammy had an old lighter, one that produced a surge of flame when the fuel was high but now the supply was near exhausted. He had to cup his free hand around the flame against the wind and hold the lighter close to his chest, risk singeing his anorak and the stubble around his mouth, and the places where the sun had burned patches where the hair barely grew, and places where the cold had scraped the growth further. He dragged on the cigarette and then spat the nicotine fumes clear. He imagined that behind him they clustered close to each other, their hair riffling and their clothing tugged by the wind. They might have realised then that the sum of their journey was nothing in comparison with what they now faced; it was the same for Cammy.

He had been travelling almost a year. They had been on the move – so they had told him – half of that time. Cammy had come from a point on the Euphrates, where it marked the border between Syrian and Iraqi territory. They had started out from the Iranian city of Tabriz, far to the north and to the east of Tehran. They both had a goal.

He smoked and gazed out. They were a little beyond first light. It was common sense to travel at night. They were 500 miles from Bordeaux, and he had done the journey in three legs. They were attached to him, could have been chained to him, seemed terrified they would suddenly lose sight of him and he would be gone. It had started in a café down by the docks, across the Garonne, and his money was used up and he had no documentation. He had been in the café because it was warm, and he was chilled, hungry. The *patron* had been making noises about throwing him out. If a hand had been laid on him by the heavily built, middle-aged manager, if an attempt had been made to propel him to the door and chuck him into the street then he would probably have resisted: had Cammy resisted then there was a strong prospect that he would have chopped the heel of his right hand into the man's neck and paralysed him, probably killed him. It was not difficult for him to take a life if he was minded to.

They had pushed through the door. They were Iranians. Two men, two women, two children. Migrants who had reached France and needed help in edging closer to what would have been a "jump off point". When the café man had challenged him, the Iranians had been sitting at an adjacent table and the kids had been given the menu, and a wad of euros was on the table. He was challenged . . . Was he ordering coffee, alcohol, food? No response from Cammy. The café was not a tram-stop shelter he was told . . . He had spat back, not loud but distinct, in English, that the man could "Go fuck yourself". One of the Iranian men had spoken up. Cammy was to be included on their tab . . . Why? He had spoken in English. Did he drive? He could drive: could have driven a motorcycle, a car, a pick-up, an armoured personnel carrier, could have driven a tractor around which half-inch-thick steel plating had been welded. Yes, he could drive.

He noted the wind and sensed that the children shivered, and fear might be competing with the cold. They had taken a chance. It would have been something to do with his appearance: rugged, uncomplicated, ravaged, and something to do with the clarity of his eyes and the fact he did not blink and did not look away but held their gaze and stared right back into their own eyes, and something to do with the slow and steady and winning smile. The proposition had been made. Would he take them north? He had said yes, that was where he, too, was headed.

One of the men had said, "But we have to go across by subterfuge, not through any legal route, and . . ."

Cammy had said softly, no drama, "And me."

Puzzlement. "But you are going back to your own country. Why do you need to go as we do?"

A little shrug, not necessary for them to know the answer. He was told they had a contact name in the north, on the coast, a man who would facilitate a crossing if he were paid sufficiently. Cammy had eaten with them. He had told them that they should be on the street corner in 25 minutes, had left them. Had gone to a parking lot, had done a hot wire, had come back with a van that had sliding doors and two rows of seats behind the driver. Had driven them away from Bordeaux and had taken the minor roads where any vehicle recognition plate system was unlikely.

The wind was bad. And the wind's force mattered.

For that moment, Cammy ignored his Iranian fellow travellers. They were useful to him. They had money, were headed in the same direction. But he denied them affection or friendship ... They knew nothing of him, unless they had made educated guesses, but were obviously in awe of him. They suited his purpose. They hung behind him. He was alone. The only people in his recent life to whom he had given his loyalty, his love and his respect, were all gone. There had been six of them, all taken. When his anger was hot it exploded in his head and when it was cold then he could plan what he would do, think through the programme of it and comprehend the mayhem. It might have been the force of the wind that came off the sea and flattened the dune grass and blew sand in his eyes, or it might have been the anger and the loss that wet his cheeks. He threw down the cigarette. There had been himself and his six friends, and there had been the *emir* who was their nominal commander but gave them free rein. He had gone first in the break-out after it was clear that the battle was lost.

The six of them, and Cammy, were due to go on the next evening, but their emir was off and away by dusk.

He was Ruhan, an Iraqi, sophisticated and worldly, he had taken this flotsam group under his wing.

There was talk now, among the foreign fighters, of a last stand. An Alamo sited on the west bank of the great Euphrates river, or a bit of Custer. Men boasted of how they would fall in combat and their black-cloaked women egged them on with declarations of the glory of dying in the name of the cause and, between the incessant air strikes, the children ran wild, and screamed in fear or in hunger. Common to all of them in the group was an adoration of the thrill of combat, a delight in their new freedom, a brotherhood, and a belief set in hard, old stone that it was only "others" who would be hurt.

They were Tomas and Pieter and Mikki and Dwayne and Stanislau and Ulrike – and the unspoken first among equals was Cammy. They

*had drifted away from homes as far away from each other as Canada's
Algonquin lakes and the northern extremities of Estonia, had come to
fight under the black flag. At first it had been a series of victories, almost
in the realms of amusement, then had come the serious fighting which
had tested each of them, then the defeats and the retreats. Like an alarm
on a wristwatch, it seemed the right time to find another corner in
which to fight . . . leave the zealots and the bigots to martyrdom or the
shame of surrender. Ruhan moved amongst them and there were kisses
and hugs and slapped backs, and talk of a reunion but not where.
Yemen, Afghanistan, Libya? Anywhere that brothers were welcome.*

The tide had turned. The aircraft came again and again, went back
to a carrier or an airstrip to refuel and rearm, and came again. There
was no food in the enclave, and no medical capability, and the wounded
screamed and cried in the night . . . Time to move on. They would be
together, could depend on each other, were brothers.

They regarded Ruhan as the ultimate fighter, trusted and believed in
him. He was older than they were, had taught Cammy everything he
knew of small unit warfare, and of security, and staying safe from both
the bombers and the internal security bastards who patrolled to prevent
desertion but were never in the front line. Ruhan said, that "sometime"
there would be a meet-up in a bar, "someplace", and it could be in the
Gulf, a five-star joint with Chivas Regal or old malt . . . He had been a
hard man in his time. Now, he was only interested in winning and had
no time for being herded into the enclave by the river. Tells others to fight
on, tells his young brothers to ship out. Himself, he would be going home,
back to the town in Anbar to his wife and his kids. He was indestructible, since winning a place on Saddam Hussein's protection detail, had
once been a colonel in air force intelligence. Had been an emir with
control of a battalion of foreign fighters. He told them where they should
go the next evening, how it was safe in that sector of the perimeter. How
he loved them, told them also that they were shit and without him would
not have known how to wipe their arses, and Ulrike laughed as much as
the boys, and big bombs lasered down, and the bombardment of artillery
was constant. They watched him go.

Another night. Another day. Another stack of confirmation signals
that the little corner by the river was doomed. Another hopeless hunt for

*food and water. Another clutch of hours waiting for the wounded to die
and shut the fuck up.*

They would take all the ammunition they could carry ... Might just
move on into the Syrian desert and fight there alongside the clever boys
who had ditched the women, the kids and the camp followers, and
would start it again but in a lower key. Might ... Ruhan had been
specific on the route they should take out through the front line, and
where the intelligence guys said the enemy were sparse.

Edging through bunkers and foxholes and craters and keeping clear
of the fires burning. Worse than anything before. The right time to go.
That part of a dream lost.

Cammy was in the centre of the line, and Mikki was in front of him
and Ulrike was behind, and Pieter, Tomas led and Stanislau was back-
marker. They followed a route given them by Ruhan, drifted forward in
the darkness. Stepped around a child, silent and beseeching who was
not yet dead but was disembowelled, and passed a woman who clung to
a baby and both were dead but unmarked. An officer in the dying caliphate screamed at them to go to the left where the trenches needed
shoring, and another cried for more ammunition to be taken forward.
All ignored ... they went where Ruhan had instructed them.

And they came to him, recognised him.

Ruhan had been quality at cruelty but had liked and trusted this
gang of misfits. Years before he had cheated death on the scaffold at Abu
Graib gaol because his beaten-up Peugeot had had a flat front tyre. He
had fixed it at the side of a dirt track and then driven along an avenue
of palms. The Black Hawk helicopters had been loading up, preparing
for the lift, and he had caught a fleeting glimpse of the big man, the man
he was supposed to protect. Another of the fugitive President's body-
guards had been captured, had gone through harsh interrogation, had
coughed up Saddam's hiding place in the dirt. If the tyre had not
emptied Ruhan would likely have been trapped in the net himself: he
liked to tell that story. He had not cheated again.

Once he had owned a powerful and impressive face, a jutting chin
and strong bones and a trimmed beard and deep eyes. Always he
carried the webbing slots that could take eight, even ten, loaded magazines for his rifle. The weapon and the ammunition had not helped him

and his face was distorted because of what had been shoved into his mouth ... His camouflage trousers were at his ankles and his grey underpants were at his knees and his groin was a mess of dried blood and already insects were feasting.

Cammy said, a hoarse whisper and passed on ahead by Mikki and behind by Ulrike, "But he was not us. We go forward, we stay strong. We are together. We have each other."

They were a typical family living in the estate high on the hill above the village of Sturry, looking out over the Kent countryside, with a landmark view of the tower of Canterbury Cathedral. It was that time in the morning when they all headed for work or college. Dad was an accountant's gofer, did the heavy lifting that the partners avoided. Mum did the cash till at a pet food outlet on the way into the city and had once been judged Employee of the Month. Bradley was their elder child and had a job on a building site while he waited to hear whether the Royal Navy would accept him and train him in weapons electronics, and their youngest was Karen, who was at sixth form college and wanted to be a dental nurse. They were out all day, came home knackered, but tried to manage a family event at the weekend. They were the Hunters, and financially ahead of the Just About Managing households in the brick semi-detached homes below them, going down the hill. Nothing to be complacent about but coping well with the difficult times.

Trace would drive and drop Bradley at the builder's yard where he learned about scaffolding then Karen at college, and last would be Dave, letting him off at the bus-stop on the main drag into the city, and then she would go to the pet food store's parking lot. Always late, always a bit frantic – and Dave delaying them today because he couldn't find his phone, and . . . then he was in the car, and Trace pulled out of the carport, but had to brake sharply because the neighbour over the road pulling her shopping basket behind her, didn't see them. Trace braked. They all stared out. Sadie might have been a mile away, or might have been half asleep, or might have been . . . What Trace always said, in her youth Sadie must have been a great looking girl and had the relic of a lovely face but, God, time had not treated her well. What Dave always said, they should have made a bigger effort with Sadie because, years before, she had been the best and most popular and reliable childminder or babysitter they'd ever had.

Dave had his window down. "Morning, Sadie, don't seem to have seen much of you. You doing all right?"

Trace leaned across him. "Bit hectic at the moment, Sadie, but when we straighten up you must come round for a coffee . . . Late, sorry – see you soon, Sadie."

They were rewarded with a distant smile that gave little away of her thoughts, and a bit of a shrug. Then they were accelerating and their neighbour was trudging the last steps to her front door, negotiating the long grass. They always called her Sadie. Did not know whether she was Mrs Jilkes or Miss Jilkes, did not know much more than her name, Sadie, and that her life was tough, tougher by a long mile than anything the Hunters had experienced. She always looked as if she had been put through a mangle, the colour gone from her face, and the flesh squeezed off her body, and a vacant stare in her eyes.

"We should make a bigger effort," Karen said.

"One son banged up, her daughter gone on an overdose," Bradley said. "I don't know what we used to talk about . . . As for Cameron, well, he's . . ."

"We'll try and be a bit more sociable – not a bed of roses, her life. That kid, what he's done to her . . ." Dave said.

The talk moved on and the view of Sadie Jilkes lugging her shopping bag up the road was pushed back, out of sight and out of mind. Plenty of everything else to talk about. Hadn't been at the time, not when her youngest – Cameron – had brought the full apparatus of the Security Service and the Counter Terrorism Command crammed into their little road.

" . . . as for that kid, little Cameron – excuse my language – bloody good riddance. What he did to his Ma, it was shameful."

Thames House, on the north side of the Thames, had been built 90 years ago, constructed of clean Portland stone and granite.

Now, the lower windows have reinforced glass, proof against explosives and high-velocity gunfire, and are shuttered; higher windows have blinds through which dull light filters, but the faces of those inside are never visible. It is a building protected by Acts of Parliament and is heavily guarded. It is the workplace of those charged with being in the front line of the defence of the realm. Good days have been seen there and bad ones ... There have been the numbing reactions when the "enemy" has won and bombers have attacked underground trains, concerts, buses, restaurants and bistros and the mayhem has been brutal and the inquests open and savage; and there have also been successes, of which few are trumpeted, when catastrophe has been averted. It is said among the psychologists who patrol the corridors and give counsel, welcome or not, that stress levels inside the fortress are as acute as those found in any military front line where direct combat is joined. The defenders have their own private army offering a separate layer of security around Thames House ...

Kev and Leroy had been newcomers to the police protection detail assigned to the headquarters building of the Security Service on a particular wintry evening three years before. Easy for them to remember it. Should have been an underwhelming leaver's drink in the atrium with one glass of cheap Spanish or Italian bubbles, maximum two, and a parting gift handed over, and a speech of gracious thanks that would have been hustled through. Except that the leaver had not shown, and the press-ganged guests had gone on their way and the atrium had emptied; was silent, deserted, when the guy himself had turned up, a little tongue-tied by way of explanations, and had dumped a job on them. A miserable little wretch was sitting in a café around the corner, and they were to get there soonest and take him into custody. They had watched him hawk-like and their index fingers had never been further than a centimetre off the triggers of their H&Ks. The guy had left the building and the would-be *jihadi* boy had covered his face with his handcuffed arms, might have wept, crumpled and defeated, and no explanation was given to Kev and Leroy, except that it was "all being sorted". The guy had left through the internal gates, had fed in his access ID, and the red light had flashed and a buzzer had warbled – the sign that the card had been electronically destroyed – and he'd gone into the night. A duty officer had shown up, flustered, and that was hardly going to be forgotten. And – the guy's ID had been cancelled, he had no access to the building, but he was back a few hours later, just before their shift ended, and . . . never an explanation. They had learned, Kev and Leroy, that they could set their watches by the time this guy came into work. Not long now, about fourteen minutes, rain or shine, never varied.

An unremarkable guy, hardly a bag of laughs. About once a week they had a smile off him. Had never heard his name, and had never seen anyone greet him – with the one exception of that first morning after the ID cancellation, then Deidre on Reception had picked up a phone as soon as he was through the outer door and buzzed upstairs, and one of the officer toffs from an upper floor had come scrambling out of a lift to greet him, and had done a big charm bit – and the guy had seemed barely grateful. Not easily forgotten but they still knew nothing of him, nor what section he worked in. Kev had been a corporal in the Parachute Regiment, and Leroy had risen to sergeant in a fusilier battalion, and both had done Afghanistan tours and each reckoned himself a good judge of a man: neither could make head nor tail of this fellow . . .

He was always in early, beat the main rush: if he was late then that would have been the fault of the signals or the points on the track. And another thing that distinguished him was the attachment on his right wrist and the chain to his briefcase that played bloody havoc with the metal detector arch. Always good to see that rather familiar face, though neither had any idea of what he did inside the building.

That day, the points were good and the signals worked, and the train was on time. Jonas Merrick was swept out of the carriage, and planted on the platform and needed to walk briskly or he would have been knocked flat in the crush to get clear of Waterloo. No one gave him a glance. He hurried, keeping a tight hold on the fraying handle of his briefcase, and the chain hung sleek inside his shirtsleeve.

The same route was taken every working day. If the pavements had not been made of weathered concrete, and the roads he crossed not of hammered down tarmacadam, there would have been a pattern of his footprints ... down the steps of the main entrance to the station, past the place where the train robber once ran a flower stall, down Lambeth Palace Road, head down and with purpose, too concerned with his thoughts to glance at the A&E structures of St Thomas' hospital. He did not concern himself with health matters, seemed to be lasting well, and Vera had no problems that she'd bothered to broach with him. By the time he was in sight of Lambeth Palace he could smell the river, unique and pungent, then over Lambeth Bridge.

The wind cut across him. There was rain in the air and it stung his cheeks. With his free hand he held his trilby, had no wish to see it cartwheel from his head and be swallowed by the river or fall onto a barge's deck. He was thinking of his day and was oblivious to the presence of those around him who also headed for Thames House: Jonas knew very few of them. He kept to himself. The building was ahead of him; his desk was on the third floor, next to a masked window.

If it had not been for the events of that night, he would have been consigned to retirement and this trek from the station would have been part of his past. Not that Jonas would have attended any of those Christmas lunches for retired staff where the Director General gave a résumé of the problems faced by the Service in the previous year. Nothing classified, of course.

His memory was powerful with clear recall of that night. He had gone home. Had sat on the train, later than usual. Had walked up his street, past the Derbyshires' house from which a TV blared, had unlocked his own door. Had gone inside. Had faced his wife.

How had it gone? Jonas had shrugged.

Was there a good turnout? He'd grimaced.

A decent speech from the big man? Gave a gesture that meant he could not answer directly.

Were the right things said? Just a lift of the eyebrows.

What had they given him? Thirty-five years' work, what was the present? He had muttered that he didn't know what the retirement gift was, had not been there when it should have been presented, then had turned away from her as if the interrogation irritated him.

What had happened? Where had he been? Was there a "difficulty"? Raincoat off and on the hook, and the wrist bracelet unlocked and the briefcase, empty but for his sandwich box, stowed away under the hall table, and his hat slotted above his coat. No explanation offered. Except that he was rather tired, and needed a lie down, and a cup of tea would be welcome. Halfway up the stairs he had stopped. He had not turned to face her but had spoken from the side of his mouth. "It was a funny old evening, dear. An unpredictable one, and sort of made a bit of a nonsense of the timetable. What was planned didn't happen. I'll tell you what occurred, but that'll be 'one day', not tomorrow. Think the best place for me is bed." She had not pestered him. He'd undressed, put on his pyjamas, had brushed his teeth, and flopped on the bed, had stared at the ceiling, had reflected on the evening and his contact with Winston Gunn. The events had played in his mind and he'd remembered each of the heartbeats in his chest when he'd taken the vest and lobbed it over the retaining wall and heard it plummet into the water. Still awake when Vera had come up, he'd seen her shadow movements as she laid her clothes on the chair and put on her usual long nightdress, and she'd slipped into bed and had turned away and had seemed to sleep, or try to. No conversation, nothing said.

There was a clock in a church over to the west from the centre of Raynes Park that struck the hour. Her pretence at sleep was poor . . . she was a good wife for a man working in the Service, did not expect to be briefed on the classified work he carried out at Thames House. Trouble was that he was wider awake than he had been when getting into bed, and the latest worry was whether the alarm had been switched off. He did not have to be up at ten minutes to six the next morning, and Vera would not need to be in the kitchen, making his sandwiches and filling his flask . . . A car crawled along the road. He thought it stopped outside the Derbyshires', then nudged forward, then dawdled. He heard a door open and a murmur of voices. He was good at recognising speech. He switched on the bedside light, told Vera to stay upstairs, went down and unlocked and opened the front door. The Assistant Deputy Director General was coming up his path. It was past four. Jonas felt foul, limp, and without energy. He had always reckoned that the AssDepDG rather despised him, might have been the originator of the Eternal Flame jibe, and the speech in the atrium would have been short, the minimum that courtesy demanded.

On the doormat, he was told, "You have my very sincere congratulations, Jonas. You are something of an example to us all, we are in your debt. What is particularly impressive is that you made a device safe when normal procedure would have called for a mass evacuation of Westminster, Parliament, all those jokers who mill about there. And on top of that would have been a lockdown while little Master Gunn would have been surrounded by marksmen and have the chance to go to God like any good martyr. Instead he is alive and singing with a canary's full vocal strength . . . Would there be any chance of a cup of tea for me and Harry? I've underestimated you, Jonas, and I feel ashamed to admit it. You showed tonight an instinct of how to react that very few in that great heap of a building could have matched. I'm making a rather humble request, Jonas. These are stark times, as you know damn well – I want you there. Want you back at your desk. Sorry, too valuable to be retired . . . Put it another way: if that little beggar had detonated, then the reputation of the Service would have been shredded, credibility gone. A generation of officers would have been damaged. Back at your desk, Jonas – please. Sorry to ask again, but a cup of tea if that's possible for Harry and me." It was then that Jonas had realised that Vera was at the bottom of the stairs, and she'd said something about him being rude in not inviting his guests inside.

They'd sat around the kitchen table. Vera had made tea and put some biscuits on a plate. Harry was a pool driver and had stayed silent, and Vera had only queried whether milk and sugar went with the tea, and Jonas had bitten his lower lip, and remembered sneers and mocking insults, but – of course – had accepted.

Jonas had said later, "They want me to go back, to cancel retirement. It's because of something that happened tonight. They want me to keep working."

Vera had said, "Thank God for that."

They were still talking and the cat had come in through the flap, and the alarm *had* gone off upstairs. He had showered and shaved, and dressed, and Vera had done toast and cereal for them all, and Jonas had talked about his filing system, its value, and what he looked for ... At that time in the morning it was a fast run into London, and it was comfortable in the car and smooth with Harry at the wheel. But Jonas Merrick, true to form, had played contrary and allowed them to take him only as far as the station. Had travelled to Waterloo in his own style and in his own time, with his briefcase and with a filled sandwich box. Inside the building, at the outer desk, a fresh ID card awaited him.

Now, nearly three year, later, Jonas Merrick slipped into the café by the side door of Thames House, and had his *latte* and a Danish. He'd savour them, and perhaps take a turn around the garden further down Horseferry Road before presenting his card and going to work. The agenda said nothing about when he might expect that belated retirement ... His own opinion, the threat level was the highest he could remember in all his years with the Service.

It would have been his third cigarette. He flicked it away, had only smoked half of it.

Be thou my guardian and my guide.

The look on his face, if they could have seen it, was sour, resentful, brimming with hatred. Cammy grinned, rueful. He thought it was the younger man who had started to sing.

And hear me when I call.

Cammy had sung to himself; on the first night as they had navigated the minor roads going north from Bordeaux.

Let not my slippery footsteps slide.

The relaxation on his features was momentary. The group had joined in.

And hold me lest I fall.

Beyond the dunes, a ferry was crossing the Channel, France to Britain. To have boarded a ferry Cammy would have needed a passport and a ticket; his group would have needed the same, and also valid visas. He did not have either; nor did they. He had, sort of, taken it on himself to get them across, get them over the Channel. So different to when he had gone in the reverse direction. He had raided his mother's biscuit tin, kept under her bed, where she kept cash for "dire emergencies", had gone to Gatwick, had taken a flight to Vienna. Would have been around 10,000 feet over the white cliffs and the narrow channel, and then the French beaches and the dunes – where he stood now. There was no joy in coming to this point and staring out at the sea and knowing that home, the final stage of his journey, was within touching distance.

The world, the flesh, and Satan dwell.

All of them sang. He supposed it was his favourite hymn. Isaac Williams, 1802–1865, had died young by today's standards of expectation, except where Cammy had been – when he was Kami al-Britani. There, at the Kobane assault, the expectation could have been a few hours. It had become a meat grinder for the foreign boys, as it was shaping up at Barghuz before they, he and his blood brothers, had done the bug out. Cammy had a good voice, not good enough for the standards set earlier in his life, but pleasant. Isaac Williams' words were from *Hymns Ancient and Modern*, number 116. He liked it best of all the ones he had once known by heart.

Around the path I tread.

He had sung softly to himself driving north from Bordeaux and the voices behind him had picked up the hymn. Nervous to start, and then gaining confidence, and singing firmly – though not in tune – but finally in a chorus. And explained . . . they were Christians. They had felt the isolation of persecution. They had run from their country, believed that the men among them faced harassment, arrest, torture in physical and psychological form, then imprisonment, and the kids would be denied higher education, and the women would face arrest, perhaps, or being turfed out of their homes and facing hunger. Astonishingly they had known the words of the hymn . . . if he had not hummed that tune and mouthed those words then they would have not admitted their faith. A chorus now and the wind whipped the grasses of the dunes.

O save me from the snares of hell.

Cammy had sung when he was with the brothers, when the small unit was indestructible, untouchable and safe; when they were far from the ears and reach of the masked security police, dressed in black, those who did not do the fighting, as he had and those with him. It was a good tune and the words were important, and summed up their existence as they had been pushed back and finally had become lodged on the banks of the Euphrates. The big word was "snares", like a fine wire tightening around an ankle, intended to strangle a rabbit coming clear of its warren. The village of Barghuz and the enclave was a "snare", and it had become "hell" as the bombers had lazily circled in impunity then dumped the payload, and the drones had criss-crossed the skies, and the artillery had plastered shells on them, as it had been on the evening they had left, and had found the body of their mentor, the *emir*, killed by the perimeter guards as punishment for desertion. They had all been jolted that this man, strong and a fighter, had been caught and killed, his testicles and penis shoved into his mouth so that his cheeks bulged, been trapped in the "snares of hell".

Thou quickener of the dead.

He bit on his lip and killed his voice. They started another verse behind him, but he did not lead and by the third line their voices had stuttered and died.

And if I tempted am to sin,
And outwards things are strong . . .

Cammy had no education achievements. Sitting behind him, were a high school teacher and a man who had worked as a psychologist in the principal hospital of Tabriz. The women were not shrunken violets, they spoke good English and seemed aware of the basic tenets of international politics, and the kids were bright, chirpy, and perpetually queried him. He had said nothing of his role as a platoon commander in an international battalion under the black flag, nor said where his home was nor why he would try to cross the Channel with them, and what he intended once he had arrived. They were clever people and he thought them gentle and dignified. Cammy did not regard himself as clever, nor gentle, and had no dignity that he knew of ... He thought that when they looked at him the black mood settled on his face; they were frightened of him and went quiet.

He walked away from them. They hung back. He went into the dunes and the ground ducked down and they would have lost sight of him. They did not follow him and would have feared annoying, irritating, angering him, would also have known that without him they would not cross the Channel. His anger was bad and he was alone.

Jonas nodded the briefest of recognition to the pair of armed police on the pavement, then wiped his face and satisfied himself that no crumbs were stuck around his lips.

He passed through the security gate and walked down the corridor that led into the atrium, where he should have been on his farewell night ... Had he been there then he would have been handed a department store voucher: he had never received it, instead a week later a flat-pack greenhouse had been delivered and Vera valued it. Harry had brought it to Raynes Park and assembled it on flagstones collected from a garden centre. Jonas went up in the elevator. He was good at standing in a crowded space and avoiding eye contact, let alone the need to speak. Down a corridor and into the work area – third floor, south side, 3/S/12.

A favoured corner had been allocated him. He had a window with a view over the river, one prefabricated wall of frosted glass, his own bank of secure filing cabinets, and his own desk. The distorted screen separated him from the dozen or so who shared the space. Nominally this end of the corridor – Rooms 12, 13 and

14 – were the territory of A Branch, who did surveillance . . . Jonas had space inside his personal fiefdom for his work chair, also for a foldaway canvas seat in which he could doze of an afternoon. The electric kettle was used more often than the Service issue laptop. He drank coffee continuously when at work, but preferred paper to electronics and his bank of knowledge was stored in the filing cabinets.

Jonas was often the first into Room 12, and was usually first out, hurrying to make the 5.49 train when the evening had barely started . . . it was under cover of darkness in autumn and winter and spring that much of the team's work was deployed. The individuals, those of High Interest, whom they watched, followed, plotted against, preferred the cover of the hours between dusk and dawn. Not a difficulty for Jonas Merrick: he was in early and went home at an appointed hour and fulfilled his allocated weekly hours.

A swoop was planned for that evening. Those working out of 3/S/12 would be involved, at the front line.

If the suspect was in his home, among the nineteenth-century terraced streets to the east of the railway station, there would be uniforms, dogs and firearms in support, and a fair excess of excitement for the 3/S/12 people on site. He supposed it felt similar to the adrenaline rush his cat, huge and powerful, might experience when it tracked a vole or a shrew or a mouse and closed in for a kill: it would not get a meal from the prey but a drift of satisfaction from decapitating the little creature, crunching its skull, then abandoning the corpse and returning to the back door and being lifted by Vera onto the kitchen units to scoff supermarket cat food. The man they were going after that evening, of mixed Somali and Eritrean origin, would let their excitement burn off. They would go in at a rush but leave the laying on of hands to the uniforms, and the shouts would be deafening and the lights would illuminate the street and the guns would add to the drama and the dogs would be straining on their leashes. A good show, but not for much return.

Jonas knew few policemen. His choice. He was not familiar with detective or investigator culture. He had once heard a phrase used about a Branch man who had worked against the early activists of the Provisional IRA, five decades earlier. The man had been physically unimpressive, with round shoulders and thin claw-like hands and a nose shaped like a parrot's beak, and wore thick-lensed spectacles: the detective inspector had been brought into Special Branch, it was said, because he was an incomparable "thief taker". Nice phrase, useful description. Would have had that sense of where to go and where to look, when to act and when to stand back and allow a target to run: a man who could sense the locations and contacts used by the target.

An American who came into Thames House, open and frank and who seldom shot the party line, had spoken of the massive electronic surveillance effort put into hunting down Zarqawi, the top target of Al-Qaeda in Iraq. US intelligence had put a $25 million reward on his head, dead or alive. A Jordanian spook had won the Americans' trust; he had been invited in, had walked up to the big wall map and had poked his finger at a city that was nowhere near the province being quartered by the drones and their cameras: it was where they had killed Zarqawi, put a 500lb Paveway bomb down his chimney. All about instinct and a nose . . .

The one they were going after that evening, in Luton, had been fingered by Jonas. Only three weeks out of gaol, had done a minimal sentence for radicalisation and courier work, and now might, or might not, be into shifting bomb-making precursors across the Bedfordshire town. The decision had been taken, on high, to lift him, hassle him, question him, allow him to sweat and cringe and maybe spit out some useful detail. If Jonas Merrick had declined to endorse the swoop then it would not have taken place. He had shrugged: the man they would lift was a minor player.

There were others who mattered more.

There were the ones that he knew of, ones that he had an inkling of, and there were the ones on whom he had scant information and did not know where they were or what they planned, or how great were their networks; those were the ones who frightened him . . . not that Jonas Merrick ever showed personal fear. Because the team who worked at the round table with screens in the centre would be out into the small hours, their line manager would have permitted them to come to work late. Jonas appreciated the quiet around him. He thought well on the train in and on the return journey, and could marshal ideas as he walked from Waterloo and across Lambeth Bridge, and he was good at home when the cat lay on his lap, half buried by files and covert photographs. The boy they would lift tonight was of scant importance; the arrest would make a headline and shake the cage and further clog up the judicial process . . .

More important were the young men coming home. They were on the move, drifting back to what they knew. Consumed with hatred and anger, comfortable with brutal violence.

Too many whom he could not name, and far too many that he had no location to pin them to. He had files out and the drawers of his cabinets gaped. He was old-fashioned and used the practices that had long been consigned to the trash bin, but he believed he had the nose and would back his own judgement. That was why the AssDepDG now supported him, stood his corner. He thought outside the loop, was unconventional, and needed the support of a protector, the senior man. They had no common traits, were chalk and cheese, but Jonas was now blessed by his back being watched. Each fed from the other but the link was never spoken of by either of them. Jonas Merrick would not have thought himself unique in his skills, and there were others scattered through the building who gnawed away at similar problems and who might have a better success rate and might not. He could only support himself and hope he was right in the conclusions drawn. If he were wrong, and the others, then their opponents would be under the radar and the results would be catastrophic . . . Each day worse than the last, and each week and month more desperate than those that had gone before.

He heard footsteps.

A measured tread, a door opening and closing and then a gentle rap on the glass and a grunt from Jonas. His protector had sought him out, often did, and wanted it frank, no soft soap.

"Morning, Jonas."

A ducked head as a reply.

"Anything fresh, anything I should have?"

"Not yet."

"Out of a clear blue sky?"

"Where it always comes from."

"And attempting the impossible – to be lucky every time. Which cannot happen. How's that cat?"

"The cat's fine . . . It's always out of the clear blue sky. And then we have to be running, and running fast."

"Pleased about the cat, Jonas . . ."

And he was gone, and Jonas was back in his files and the quiet settled around him again, and only an idiot would believe quiet meant that peace cloaked the streets around the building, and in their principal cities and across the country. Jonas Merrick was no idiot.

2

Time for the lunch hour that Jonas Merrick awarded himself.

No requirement to go to the canteen and queue. Vera would have cooked for him by the time he was home in the early evening, and for now there were the sandwiches she had made, and the flask she had filled.

Slivers of impatience filtered around and over his partition. They were a disciplined crowd, after a fashion, in that section of A Branch, but that afternoon time was moving slowly, and they wanted the hands of the wall clock to shift faster . . . There were cold pork slices with a smear of pickle on them, and he munched and contemplated and nibbled at a tomato grown early in the greenhouse that Vera supervised, and afterwards he would have his flask and a small chocolate bar, and an apple that he would fastidiously peel. Outside his immediate orbit, beyond the partition, as they shrugged into protective vests or checked the comms links (on the basis that communications failures screwed more operations than any other single cause) they would have known there was not a chance of him coming out of his den and wishing them well, telling them what to look for. He had a new name. Among them he was now known as Wobby. The old one, attached to him with contempt, Eternal Flame, had been ditched.

He knew he was Wobby, had heard it when he was sitting at his desk and taking a short, sweet, doze, and they would have assumed, outside the partition, that he slept. He was Wobby because of a description given him by the AssDepDG. It would have been the morning after he had been brought back to Thames House, retirement day cancelled. The big man, unshaven, same shirt as the night before and tie askew, had apparently come into 3/S/12, before the commuter crawl had reached Waterloo or while he was still walking past Lambeth Palace, later than usual, had flicked his fingers for attention. There was a woman who fixed defective computers on that floor, and she'd been there, and was similarly addicted to caravan holidays. She'd told him. Rare for that sort of exchange in Thames House, but the love of caravan sites had proved a clincher. The team had been told that Jonas Merrick had been brought back and would rejoin the team. There had been frowns and pulled faces and snorts, but the big man had ploughed on. "What happened last night is not for gossip and will not be shared, but it was significant. Jonas was missing from his retirement party for a very good reason. Truth is that my impression of his work is that he is superior at getting under the skin of targets, better than any of the rest of us. It is a talent that cannot be taught, is inbred. I have reassessed his value, and I'll hear no more shit about a dull little creep who knows nothing of what's around the corner. He'll have more responsibility and more input. He's a wise old bird." Which had stuck. A Wise Old Bird, a Wobby.

A matter of common sense and understanding the opponent. His card index system told him more than the banks of computers on which the Service depended ... A doubter had once challenged him. Nothing contrite about Jonas's answer because he was averse to giving ground: he had told of a junior army officer in the early Ulster days who had made a name for himself as an expert at uncovering the enemy's arms caches. Just common sense, just a matter of lining up the markers that would aid a courier coming for a pick-up ... a farm gate off a lane, a dead tree left in a field, and a line between the two would reach a hedgerow where it appeared a fox had dug a den – excavate further and find two Armalite rifles and half a dozen filled magazines. A semi-detached house in the heart of a virulently nationalist housing estate on a windswept hill above the town of Newry and a section of a street where there were telephone poles and lamp posts, and there was one place where they were exactly opposite each other. Stand on one side of the street, line up the poles and posts, and follow that line to a house with a concrete slab in front of the doorstep. The officer had been there, a grudging guest of the Parachute Regiment, had stood on the slab, had moved his hips rhythmically and had found the slab rocked under his weight, had told the squaddies to lift it ... more Armalites and more magazines and the best find that Para Regiment had achieved in a four-month posting. Common sense, what Jonas dispensed.

The swoop for which the team beyond his frosted screen were heading was down to him. A breakthrough of sorts. A sweet paper dropped. The wrapping for a type of humbug. That variety of sweet sold at a confectioner, a particular one, and not from a supermarket. Next door to that shop was a café. He told them it was where they should mount surveillance. Foot watchers, and two vehicles, and a camera above the awning of a shop opposite, and a target of medium value had come into the café and had bought time, and the guy was skilled in anti-surveillance procedures – but the humbugs had screwed him. No need for the one-time Eternal Flame to leave Thames House. He was not praised, did not expect to be ... For well over a decade he had provided his small insights to the teams working around him. Often enough they were acted on, and success had beamed down on to the team, and individuals had taken the credit for a suggestion and not spoken of him as the source. He had not complained, not argued his corner, had accepted it. Now that he had the support of the AssDepDG he was, at least, listened to.

There was a knock on his partition. A young man's voice. Was it convenient to speak to him?

"No, it is not. I am having my lunch. I will have finished my lunch at two o'clock and will see you then."

Jonas had good hearing. A male voice: "Daft old beggar, why did he have to be so rude, on about his fucking lunch?" A female voice: "He's never changed, everyone says, will never change, and getting to work for him is a serious shit moment." The male voice said, loud and with too much irony, that he was deeply sorry to disturb the lunch break and he'd be back at two o'clock. With the keen hearing was a refusal to care about either courtesies or kicked feelings. He was paid to think, to peer through the cloud and mist in the crystal ball, to anticipate ... Failure would be devastating – and a few bruised egos were a minor complication. Responsibility, not that he would show it, weighed heavy on him.

A medium-ranked player would be lifted that evening. Maybe, afterwards, if the team were back before "closing" there would be a short session in a bar adjacent to the building. Jonas looked for more important players, and the search for them burdened him. He wiped crumbs off his lap. Impossible to be a Wise Old Bird every day, to be a Wobby every week and every month, and the responsibility seemed to weigh heavier each hour. Not the "lone wolves" from the home counties or the West Midlands or the North West, not the locally grown incompetents from the British cities; no, the ones Jonas Merrick feared were those boys, and girls coming back from war, hardened by what they had seen and where they had been. He poured coffee from his flask and closed his eyes and it was 38 minutes until two o'clock, and he might sleep ... and not forget the picture in his briefcase.

Cammy said to them, "I'll be right back."

If any of them believed it, he would have been surprised. He had driven the van to the edge of a parking area for a Nature Park; there was undergrowth there and the sort of privacy that was intended for the campers to watch the multitude of gulls that flocked to the dunes and the beaches. They were huddled close to the vehicle. The light had lifted and thin sun shone through.

Cammy said, "Don't talk to people, don't move away. I'll get milk and some bread and some cheese."

He held out his hand and some euros were pushed into his palm. Given enough cash to buy a restaurant meal and a litre of house wine to go with it. He had been scrupulous on each stop-over to show what he had bought in their name and give them their change. Taking the money and saying what he would buy was probably insufficient to calm their fear that he was quitting on them. They had details of 'a contact' who would have made deep inroads into the wads of cash they carried and who would get them into a dinghy for the Channel crossing.

"You speak with your contact, but I vet them and I decide on them. I'll be back."

He had not been in Bordeaux by chance. Had been told to be there. Cammy was now a valued commodity. He was moved forward with the same foresight that an expert at a game of checkers would have employed when sending a piece further into "enemy" territory on a board. That division of the old security system, now controlling him, was *Amaiyet al-Kharji* – deep sleepers in European cities, who showed no sign of waking. They gathered intelligence far from the war zones of Syria and Iraq, moved players, looked for new weaknesses to exploit, and required willing bodies. They had Kami al-Britani, and recognised the depth of his hatred. The networks would not have known his name, or the target that he would launch against. When he had arrived in Bordeaux his journey was further plotted.

Cammy thought it inevitable that the Iranian family would now believe he planned to abandon them; already they had learned to depend on him.

"I will come back. You have my promise."

He would come back to them because he was alone. Before, he had been with Tomas who valued the strength of their section of foreigners: *Better to hang together, not separately* – his catchphrase and he was loved for it. Pieter, unfailingly cheerful when there was no justification: *Never look back, never chase the past*, however grim the outlook, and the line buckling and the air attacks screaming closer. Had been with Mikki, dour but strong: *Life is short, live it*, never taking a step back in a fire fight. Dwayne, Canadian, droll and dry, who used a quote from the Marx gang: *Things are going to get a lot worse before they get worse*, and once with small arms fire crackling around them, and American rangers as opposition, they had all pealed with laughter when he'd said it from the shallow bottom of a make-do foxhole. Stanislau, the dreamer, the sensitive guy who could make them pause and think: *I want to snatch the sunset and hold it*, and they would all, however awful the day, look to the west and see the sun drop, the sky become crimson, and see beauty. And had been with Ulrike who was the woman who fought with them, killed with them, messed with them and brought what they all said was a German's logic to the party: *Stay calm, it is never a crisis*, and had been worshipped by all of them. Had been with them all, one battle after another, one retreat following hard on the last, and all of them surviving together, as if their arms were linked. He was alone. Had never been alone before, wherever he had been, whatever queued in front of him as a challenge, whatever smacked him down.

Being alone was like being trapped by the hymn's "snares of hell".

He had the pocket full of phones that had been given him in Bordeaux. Use and ditch was the instruction. The guy had refused him more money but had given him phones. A meeting off the rue des Etrangers, close to the old German submarine pens. He had waited by the indestructible concrete walls and the guy had pitched up on a shiny new Peugeot scooter. Had told Cammy where he had to be and when, given him a schedule to be back in England, and had implied that the hardware was already on the move. How was he to get there without travel documents or cash? The guy had shrugged, not his problem. Cammy had thought the guy probably knew his life expectancy, calculated he was not worth more money, and that he would have the skills and the resources to get himself where he had been tasked to be and hold to the timetable.

He could not see the sea but the wind tousled his hair and blew cold across his face, and in his nose was its smell as the tide turned and carried it further up the beach and nearer the dunes. He had seen people in dips in the sand, small groups of men who eyed him with suspicion, and he had not made eye contact, and behind some of the men crouched their women and small children. He thought it would be a sellers' market for the people who had the boats, small dinghies . . . He would go into the water along with the Iranians he had befriended. He was alone; he needed them.

The number he called was locked inside the phone; he had only to press one key. He would aim to cross the Channel by small boat because it was said that the lorry and ferry routes, and the tunnel, were now too heavily policed for him to have a chance of success.

The call rang out. It was also said that since the collapse of the caliphate's structure, the forgery of passports was no longer of the standard required for the checks at Calais or at Dover, at Ostend or Zeebrugge, Felixstowe or Portsmouth.

The call was answered, a woman's voice, hesitant and cautious. He gave his name, Kami al-Britani. Said where he was, and what he hoped for, what time schedule . . . She interrupted him, gabbled a reply, then snapped off the connection . . . He had a postcode now and a time to be there. He did not know where she had spoken from, in what city or what country. By the roadside he found an overflowing rubbish bin, rummaged a hand inside it and buried the phone near the bottom. In the distance ahead of him was a convenience store. He went to buy milk and bread and cheese for his group. The good times were behind him and only the hunger of his hatred and the thirst of his anger sustained him, gave him purpose.

Victoria's 24th birthday was in a fortnight. Materially, she had little to concern her as her husband, Gavin, worked most of the hours that God gave at a car showroom on the north side of the city. Her home was a three-bedroom semi-detached in a quiet close in a decent part of Canterbury. As a peace gesture and so that acrimony did not fester at home, she would collect their child from the nursery and then walk to her mother-in-law's, take a sandwich there and a cup of tea, and then go to their own home. It was a concession she had made, a compromise.

Much of life was a compromise for Vicky.

She wore boutique clothes. Sensible shoes for that time of year and weather, a decent skirt, a warm pullover and an anorak, from a quality brand, that was proof against rain and cold. She had signed up to the conventions of being married to a car showroom salesman, was not with the boy who had no fixed job, no marketable assets that anyone had recognised, no place to live other than a room at his mother's house up on the hill above the village of Sturry. He had said to her once that they should go together, get the hell out. Where to? Should get the hell out and go and it did not matter where they ended up. Do what? It wouldn't matter if they did "something" or did "nothing"; they would take on the world, make it work for them – like, together, they could ride a rainbow. Her husband's aim was to "better himself and make a good home for her".

He had gone a few years before.

She reached the nursery. Other mothers were gathering and the crèche was about to empty. She wondered how many of the women around her – some already bulging with another on the way – were happy with their lot: how many of them had a memory of a boy from the past who had excited and entranced. How many, like her, had not quite had the courage to take what was on offer, had compromised instead and turned their back on an opportunity.

He had shrugged, had said that he'd see her sometime, like they'd cross paths again.

The wedding had been on the bounce. Gavin was a nice enough man. Came to collect her from her part-time lifeguard shift on his way home from work or on his way there, and always wore a suit, tie, and polished lace-up shoes, and often had a rose in his button-hole. Her own family were indifferent to him other than to express relief that he wasn't that boy from up the hill who was trouble and who she was well clear of. Her husband's mother had made it plain that Victoria was not good enough for her son. She had married. She had a child and a pleasant enough house, and she yearned each day to hold again the laughter and the excitement of the boy who had challenged her.

She had her little one, strapped him carefully into the buggy. Did not stop for chat and gossip. Headed for her mother-in-law's home and would hear a bucket of praise for Gavin, and keep her eyes on the china ducks on the wall so that she betrayed nothing.

It had been two weeks before the wedding that the Counter Terrorism police had come to see her. Had he ever talked about where he was going? No. Had he ever expressed interest in the Islamic faith? No. Had he ever spoken in admiration of a terrorist army in the Middle East? No. Had Cameron Jilkes been in contact with her in the last three years? No. She went to her mother-in-law's home, would have a sandwich and a cup of tea, would make polite small talk, would bite her lip to stifle the screams . . . Loved him and yearned for him more each day.

Tristram, staring at Jonas Merrick's cubicle, said, "I'm not intending to be early, and get that sour response – how long?"

Izzy said, "It's three minutes to the hour, and was four minutes last time you asked."

"Is this drawing the short straw big time?"

The team had gone and Tristram and Izzy were alone in the 3/S/12 work area. They were newcomers, just assigned, on probation. What had attracted them to the A Branch of the Service was the variety of the work, and the front line experience they would be totting up. He was three years younger than her, fresh from graduating; her route in had been through a social services care centre. He had looked as miserable as a kennelled dog when the rest of the unit had charged off into the corridor, the vests heavy on their shoulders and the comms draped on lanyards, and the hiss of nervous excitement. Action beckoned. Not for Tristram and Izzy who waited for a clock's hands to straighten up and the hour to be reached.

"They say he's the sharpest mind on the corridor." She pulled a face.

Tristram was independent school educated, had an Upper Second in Economics, reckoned he had been head-hunted by a tutor. He'd done a charity stint in Africa and Meals on Wheels in a deprived borough, Tipton in the West Midlands, which ticked good CV boxes. He had seen himself as a certain candidate for fast tracking, but had whacked into what he called a "leaden atmosphere" in his first days at Thames House: no ultimate victory possible, a war without end . . . They were allocated to "a creep", a guy who was "like a tick from the Remove", and the pimple on his chin itched.

"Funny way of showing it – we are on countdown."

She said, "How it was put to me, it's a good opportunity to be given."

Izzy's childhood home had been a council tower block. She was the first member of her family to go to a recognised university, might have been the first from that tower to go to any university, then had become a social worker. Her father was long gone, her mother was trapped on a high floor with agoraphobia, her sister worked in a fast food takeaway and her brother drove a mini-cab. She reckoned herself, going into the Security Service, pretty much a celebrity. But actually the place was quite boring ... She had arrived, on her first day, making a statement with a purple flash in her hair; had been told by a sour-faced old bitch to get it washed out that lunch-time or expect to work in the canteen. Her social network had not included any boy remotely similar to Tristram and she rather liked him, and sensed some reciprocation ... and sensed also that both were finding it hard to settle. And they had been given Jonas Merrick as their mentor.

"And sit inside all day – Eternal Flame stuff?"

She said, "Afraid that's getting repetitive, Tris ..."

"Sorry." It was a sincere apology, and a ducked head to go with it. Tristram had no intention of burning boats where Izzy was concerned. Rather fancied her. Different upbringing, different advantages, different ambitions, and a freckle field over her cheeks, short gold hair and a Yorkshire accent, all attracted him. Done anything about it? God forbid. "Up and ready to go."

The hour was reached. He took a half pace forward, but her hand was on his arm and held him back.

Her voice dropped. "Did you hear about the post lady coming by, a couple of months back?"

"No?"

"Internal mail, something about his pension. It was about the way the envelope was addressed."

"How?"

"Had the floor, the corridor, the room, his name. And after 'Jonas Merrick' were the initials, QGM. Know what that means?"

"Is it a decoration? What, long service?"

"Bit off the mark, Tris. QGM is Queen's Gallantry Medal. Act of considerable bravery ... Not Other Bugger's Efforts nor Many

Bugger's Efforts. It's for excessive courage. I was having a moan, but had my card marked. No one seems to know what he did, but he did something ... Doesn't make him liked, he doesn't climb the popularity ladder. Hardly fits with Eternal Flame, but it was there on the envelope, the Queen's Gallantry Medal. Funny old world, Tris ... Let's go and see what awaits."

He knocked. An exaggerated wait, then they were told to come past the partition. Tristram thought him ugly, unimpressive, and without any cheerful or welcoming gaze. There were no chairs, so he and Izzy would stand. He gestured, almost snapped his fingers at Izzy, pointed to a picture on his desk and a roll of Sellotape, then indicated a place on the wall behind him.

"Just up there, please – where the space is."

Jonas pointed. Where he wanted the picture to go was beside a large image of a caravan, above a portrait of a cat, large and pale coloured and with a serious scowl, and below an Ordnance Survey map that showed a section of the Dorset coast and which had colour-topped pins that indicated favoured camping sites.

A couple of evenings before, Vera had been leafing through a magazine – an old edition of *National Geographic* picked up from a charity shop – and he'd heard her chuckle and had looked up to see her showing him, whole-page, a photograph of a crocodile. He saw its nostril cavities, its lines of teeth protruding from the upper and lower jaws, uneven in length and looking wickedly sharp, and there was a dark eye that bulged from heavy lids that hid the mood of the creature. He had stared at it and scratched the thin hair at the back of his head and blinked, and a hiss of breath had been sucked between his lips. He had told her what he wanted and she had gone and done it, had reproduced the picture on the printer in the dining-room, and doubled its size. It had gone into his briefcase the next morning. She had not asked him to explain his interest, made a habit of not prying into his mind and his ideas, let him carry the weight of his work without needless interrogation. No one, looking at the picture, could fail to note the creature's savagery, its ability and intention to kill if irritated or hungry, the danger it posed.

Izzy stretched up, held the picture in place, tore off the necessary pieces of Sellotape, fastened it to the wall.

He said, "A crocodile. Might be African, might be Australian, not important. If you were to see that beast in such a posture, out of the water and exposed, you'd identify its threat. I chose that image because I am aware of the scale of those teeth, successful weaponry, and if let loose among innocents – those we are paid to protect – then the results are catastrophic. It can summon up a killing zone. See the crocodile in that guise and the chances are that you can go and get a man with a rifle: end of problem. Or call up a chap who is adroit at dealing with it and he'll know how to subdue it by subterfuge and then bind up that lethal jaw and negate the effects of those teeth . . . What does the crocodile do when annoyed?"

Neither of them spoke. Jonas was new to mentoring, did not take kindly to the business of having probationer recruits dumped on his lap, but the upside was his own personal screened space and the opportunity to think, search for guidance in a crystal ball, be listened to, respected. Both might have imagined that they had entered an asylum. He was not interrupted.

"There is space for another image. You will find it for me this afternoon. Quite a busy afternoon actually because I have an appointment arranged for you. The picture you will find will show an expanse of water. Somewhere hot and the water is stagnant and reflects undergrowth on a bank, drifting weed floating on a current. A deer might come to drink, or a wading bird flop down from a branch and look to spear a fish. The predator remains unseen, but the fact that he, or she, is not seen does not mean that the hunger or irritation has lessened: on the contrary, it has increased. Perhaps the sharp-eyed man, the crocodile hunter, will identify the killer. If he does not, then the deer or the bird, the innocent, will die – or the tourist swimmer, or the farmer. The predator has great patience, especially when an empty belly or irritation governs behaviour. It is submerged . . . a body that is ten feet long, or fifteen feet, could be twenty, is below the water. It will use all the natural aids available to stay concealed, it can employ the debris in the river. The water is dark, impenetrable, and no outline of its body is visible. So, it cannot be seen and therefore cannot be thwarted? No . . . not true."

No response, except that both gazed up at the picture and he thought they concentrated on the mouthful of heavy, sharp, white teeth and imagined their ability to take off a leg or an arm as surely as the shrapnel from any home-prepared explosive device.

"It has to breathe. It needs air. It has lungs that are serviced by nostrils. It cannot breathe unless the nostrils are above the water-line, and, whatever the camouflage employed, the nostrils are visible. They can be seen if the hunter knows what he looks for. It must see. It has eyes set almost at the top of its scaled head that can be mistaken for a waterlogged dead tree, but sometimes there is light coming off an eye, a reflection, and that can be a giveaway of his presence. The nostrils and eyes could be a half-inch or an inch above the surface and you have to search hard to locate them . . . We have to. If we do not, then the innocents are slaughtered and we have failed. Do I make myself clear?"

"I think so."

"Understood."

Jonas said, "I am not interested in those silly girls who flocked to Syria and spread their legs and now want to get back to the comfort and security of our country. They are irrelevant. Nor am I much interested in the boys who dropped out of college, took a crash course in Islamic studies, who might have chopped a few heads off, but then ran as fast as skinny feet would carry them when the real fighting started, surrendered, claim now they want a 'fair trial': tedious little creatures. I care about the crocodiles . . . There were British-born fighters who went to Syria, and they are not entangled with a girl and with brats. They will not surrender, but they are hungry for vengeance, they incubate hatred . . . They have been subject to retreat and failure, they have had their bums bombed from dawn till dusk, have been tracked by drones and by Special Forces military, and now they are coming back and they will have the intention of hurting us . . . We have to look for the nostrils and the eyes. Nearly through . . . Where they've gone this evening, that is not in the league I have been describing. I deal with those coming back, the returnees, the crocodiles we can barely see. Submerged until they strike. We look in what seem to be peaceful waters and have to see the nostrils or the eyes . . ."

He saw the chin of the young man wobble, quiver, like a sentence was planned but he hesitated as to whether to deliver it.

"May I ask a question, Mr Merrick?"

"You may, and I am usually Jonas."

"If it is not out of place – you have the QGM. Can I ask in what circumstances?"

Jonas was dismissive. "They come round by rote, same as a lottery card win, a pin going into a list of names. And not gossiped about. We frown on gossip."

He repeated the image he wanted them to find, then print – nostrils and eyes – and told them where they should be and when. Perhaps they had social engagements but his glance withered them and neither spoke. They stumbled out, could not get away from him fast enough.

It should not have been known, ought to have been an in-house secret. A mistake in the addressing of an envelope had let it out. Vera had the medal at the bottom of her knicker drawer. Had not been to the Palace in a hired suit, but had been invested, in a degree of privacy, at a Royal's country home, no photographs taken. No announcement for internal consumption had been made, nor anything for the general public: the few who had whispered had been isolated, then bollocked, and warned of consequences . . . Nor had criminal charges been brought against Winston Gunn.

He gazed a long time at the crocodile picture. Imagined the beast watching, waiting, drifting with the flow of water and moving closer to a target – clever and deadly.

The tide had turned, the wind had freshened, and the wall of surf pushed closer. Cammy's gaze alternated between the water and the white caps that chased the surf and the far horizon.

He had been in Marseilles, had met a man in a housing estate, dismal towers on the hills above the airport, and the man was the contact that pushed him towards Bordeaux. The talk between them had been of the Channel. A shrug, a cough, a spit on to the pavement as they walked behind the barricades that made the complex defendable against police incursions. A crossing was "probably" possible in a small inflatable craft, the chance of success was "perhaps" likely. The man had known something of small boats, made his living from organising the shipments that came by sea from Morocco, good stuff and sold in the towers that they walked between. The man had said that poor weather was good, that fine weather was bad. The boats were not expected to come with their cargo when the sea's swell ran, and when the authorities dropped their guard. Then there were the days and the nights when the wind stilled and the gales faded and a zephyr breeze left the sea surface calm, and then the patrols were out in force and their radar scans worked well, and it was easy for them to identify the craft that could carry half a ton of cannabis. Bad weather was good, but when the boats came with the stash of class C narcotics they were steered and guided by experienced seamen. From what he had heard, the man said, the people who loaded craft for the Channel crossing would go only a part of the way into the busiest shipping lanes in the world, then they would abandon their customers, transfer to a following boat, would wish them well, wave, turn away ... He had looked at Cammy as if he gazed upon a felon already condemned, and had slapped his shoulder.

And money? Was there money for Cammy? A little laugh, almost a snigger ... and more advice given him in Bordeaux, and the phones, but again a gesture of helplessness when quizzed for money, and a suggestion. "The Iranians are best, go for the Iranians, they have money." He had fought Iranians.

Had fought Iranians and Hezbollah boys, Syrian troops and the paramilitary fighters in régime uniform, and Russians; and there were times when they had been in combat against Special Forces, might have been British or might have been American. Cammy had fought against the world, was unconcerned about the politics of who he supported or who he opposed. All of them were the same. And good at what they did ... a team of brothers. Stanislau, a rifleman, but devastating in movement when clearing a building or a bunker; Tomas, who understood the trajectory of the 81mm mortar bomb when it was launched, and the wind factors, and could have three in the air before the first landed; Mikki, who did explosives and could make crude pressure-plate booby traps and could defuse them; and Pieter who was the sniper and Dwayne who had twice expertly flown Russian-made drones captured from Syrian paratroopers and had put one into the broken window of a defended farmhouse and with a modification that dumped two activated hand grenades; and Ulrike, who was the mother to them, who patched wounds and fortified their morale and who fed a machine-gun belt. He, Kami al-Britani, would be on the big weapon, the 50-calibre with ferocious hitting power. They were all survivors. Had wounds and she stitched them, had foot rot and gut rot and she seemed able to rustle the necessary antidotes, had once sucked out a snake venom implanted in Tomas's leg. Because she was one of them, she also was a brother. Their own *emir*, Ruhan, was jealous for them and rationed their deployment to other units. They hit hard, came back together, showed no fear, were in love with the danger, always close and supporting each other. Cammy had heard the phrase "one for all and all for one" and thought it made for them . . . Now he was alone.

He strained to see better. A shower came in from the south, from above Dunkirk and it would reach where he sat within half an hour. When the shower came, visibility would be lost.

For a few minutes more the sunshine played on the water and caught the brilliance of the white foam and he spotted a tanker on its way north, the light revealing the enormity of its superstructure. But he did not look at the water nor at the shipping, but concentrated on the horizon and was unsure what he saw.

There might have been, between the sealine and the darkening clouds, a smear of shadow. There would not have been white cliffs, but a part of the coast where the sea met shingle beaches, where he had been on school trips.

Might have been just a shadow to show him where the gulls had come to lift cold chips from polystyrene trays, where ice-creams had been sold, and where pretty beach huts lined an esplanade, and where there were bus-stops that displayed the timetables of the service to Canterbury . . . He was unsure if he could see the shadow and it hurt his eyes to gaze into the distance with that intensity. He had flown over where he thought the shadow was, and had finally reached Vienna. From Vienna there had been the road link to Istanbul, and then buses and hitch-hiking, and a man in a café had gone with him under cover of darkness and shown him where he could lift a fence and get down on his hands and knees and crawl under it and pull his rucksack after him. Had not looked back, not at any stage. Had not considered whether he left indifference or hurt behind him.

The wind had altered, came in a surge from the north and the sand flew up and worked its way between the grass stems and blistered against his eyes. He thought, then, that he saw the shadow of land in the long distance. Might have and might not, but wanted to believe he had seen the pencil-thin strip, but his eyes hurt too much for him to look again. The wind's change altered the pitch of the waves and he thought the white caps wider and more persistent.

He pushed himself up, then took the plastic bag with the bread and the cheese and the milk, and started back to the parking area where the Iranians would be . . .

He would be welcomed when he came home, hugs and kisses and probably tears, and would stay a pocketful of time before moving on. He had made the contact and would be met at the final stage of his journey. Good hugs and good kisses and talk of love that would sustain him when he slipped clear of them again, his morale lifted to do the last leg towards his target. He slipped between the dune grasses and heard the rumble of the sea as it spent itself against the sand; the strength of the wind grew.

He would not be expected, not in his home city and not where he would launch his attack; he would be unknown and unseen; was confident of that.

He heard the light rap on the far side of his partition, and saw the distorted outline. Jonas Merrick was shrugging on his raincoat, had his trilby on his head, and was about to buckle the fastening on his briefcase. It had been a quiet day.

A small hiss of annoyance, then he called for the young man to come past the corner that shielded his work area.

In his hand, Tristram held two large photographs. Behind him, the girl, Izzy, hovered. He thought she looked uncertain and hung back. The boy jutted his chin as if that might give him confidence.

It had been a quiet day because no sliver of intelligence had ended up in front of him. He had spent most of it tucked away, delving into the files that he kept locked in his cabinets and two of them were now inside the briefcase along with the emptied sandwich box and the thermos.

He was handed two photographs. Both colour, both showing an expanse of water.

It was the task of Jonas Merrick in his reincarnation at Thames House to sift through the jottings that came in and look for evidence of returning *jihadis*: an army of men and women coming home, with resentment at boiling pitch. He had taken his usual train and come into work on the mornings after the bomb and rifle and knife attacks in Manchester, in Paris, in London, in Brussels. He knew that shared sense of despair that gripped the building, every floor of it, from those on high to the guys who cleaned cars in the depths of the basement, and had seen men and women wilt under the weight of assault from the politicians and media when failure to intercept came calling ... What was left of the fighters in Syria and Iraq tended now to be the hard-core of the black flag's combat teams. They might be in Afghanistan or Libya or south of the Sahara and might be heading for the haven of the Philippine jungles to regroup, or they might be coming home ...

He took the photographs. He thought he read on the young man's face a brief nervous smirk. The girl, Izzy looked away and failed to meet Jonas's eye, as if dissociating herself.

... or they might be dead. In the chaos of the last days of the caliphate there were strong possibilities that fighters had been carbonised by air strikes, ripped to unidentifiable shreds by shrapnel from the drones' missiles, been cut down. Might be buried, might have a commemorative stone hastily placed at the edge of a mound, might have been taken and stripped by foxes and rats and vultures. No one hanging about on the sidelines of the dreg days of the struggle, fishing in a pocket for a notepad, taking a pencil from behind an ear, and wondering if the corpse carried a dog-tag: not a chance.

He glanced at the pictures. Once there had been a couple of hundred names on a list. These were the profiles of those who had gone away, renounced their allegiance to Britain and had fought or cut throats in the name of as false a God as Jonas and Vera Merrick could have conjured up . . . not talked of often, but agreed. In the holding camps, there were now squads of interrogators from the Sixers, from the office block on the other side of the Thames. The original list was locked in his safe and most of the names were now scratched out: some were KIA and some were captured and held by Kurds or Syrians, God help them, or by the Iraqis and had a fair chance of ending up on the trapdoor in a Baghdad gaol. The interrogators sifted those brought before them, and might have threatened and might have cajoled, and might have offered inducements – unlikely to be honoured – and tried to find out about those who were not yet accounted for. Had they been seen dead, had they gone in a cage, had they fled as the bombing had intensified? Those few names on the list were marked UAF: *un-accounted-for*. Those who were UAFs, and this was not just the intelligence of a Wise Old Bird, had the ability to be the cream of his potential opponents: those who had lasted longest after the military collapse of the cause were the most dangerous, the likely crocodiles in the swamp.

He had a train to catch. Always caught the same train.

The photographs were in colour and showed waters that were dark, impenetrable, with no ripples. He looked up into the face of the probationer and stared him out and the boy bit his lower lip, damn near hard enough to draw blood, and it might have seemed an amusing idea half an hour before, now was fraught with risk. He wondered if Tristram had been at the sort of school where japes and wheezes were regarded as amusing. The first picture, a quick scan of it, showed the place where the nostrils protruded, and the lens had caught the gleam of an eye. Hardly difficult – obvious. Jonas tossed it behind him so that it landed on his desk and he'd not have time to clear it away, but the following morning it would go on the wall alongside the beast's head and shoulders, and below the map of Dorset camping sites. The study of the second picture was momentary.

Jonas rarely used profane language; did not say, "And don't waste my fucking time again, you little shit face". Did not need to. The picture showed an expanse of water, could have been from the Amazon forests, or from a wildlife park in the Australian north. A pretty picture, with a multi-coloured butterfly floating on a strand of reed. No nostril and no eye ... A cheap trick; would have raised a laugh among the team when they were in the gardens behind Thames House for a fag break, a taking down of the Wise Old Bird, of Wobby. He tore the picture in half, then tore the halves into more pieces, and then dropped the segments so that they fluttered down to the floor beside Tristram's shoes. The flush was crimson on the boy's cheeks and his wretched spot was highlighted. Jonas accepted unpopularity: was uncertain whether he actively courted it, or whether his character, his demeanour, his limited communication skills, gave him that image.

"Enjoy your evening," he said. Allowed himself a wintry smile at both of them, and was gone. Always took the 5.49 from Waterloo, and would reach Raynes Park 26 minutes later, and then the brisk walk along his street, and home for tea. As he crossed the atrium, he fastened the attachment to his wrist, tugged at the chain to make certain the link was strong, and carried his briefcase out of the building.

It had been a quiet day, and quiet days were those that most unnerved him.

3

The map covered half the table.

One of the several skills Jonas Merrick had perfected during his professional life was to manage a compartmentalisation of his days and his evenings. But that evening he picked at his food, a pie that Vera would have picked up from a local butcher, a bit of a speciality and a favourite, and his concentration on the map was forced. Normally he would have eaten his meal with enthusiasm, and would have pounced on the detail of the map with almost excitement. It showed an area of the south Devon coast, the section along from the promontory of Berry Head, taking in the coastal path that stretched to Kingswear and Dartmouth, and then edged close to the estuary where Salcombe provided a sheltered boat haven.

He was disturbed and his judgement seemed challenged: his own fault.

The attempts she made to cheer him largely failed, but her efforts were sincere and he felt churlish that he could not respond with the enthusiasm she was owed. An old one, that always seemed to lighten him, was his ability to reverse with the caravan hooked to the tow-bar. Always some unhappy man who was suffering family embarrassment who had locked the caravan behind his car and could not manage the manoeuvre; often, then, Jonas would sidle up and quietly offer to do the business. Never triumphant, usually a little excuse about having "just been on a course and managed to get up to speed – pretty difficult – and where that idiot's parked doesn't help", and she would remind him of successes. Managed a laugh, a little chuckle between them ... There had been a caravan site east of Exmouth where the ground was sodden after a fortnight's solid rain and he had reversed six caravans in a row and could have had enough beer from the grateful owners to last him a month – but had not accepted, just shrugged. "Glad to be of help, always tricky when the field's saturated." She had tried to drag him back by mentioning that day, but had been rewarded with no more than a wan smile. They were planning their next excursion. Needed to plan their next excursion because if decisions were not taken soon then the best sites would be fully booked. They liked the possibility of a new place outside Stoke Fleming, and another at Harbertonford, but he was unable to concentrate.

The old adage resonated through Thames House. The Fivers had to be lucky every time, the opposition had to be lucky once. A statement of the Irish Republican Army, the Provisionals. Jonas had no objection to their declaring the obvious, and it was a truth . . . as certain as were death and taxation was also the guarantee that "they" would be lucky once.

He pushed away his plate. Apologised with his eyes and with a little gesture of a hand, and tried to pull the map forward and over his plate, and made a remark about the qualities of a site at Bigbury-on-Sea they had been to four years before. She took the plate, carried it to the food waste bucket, and he lifted his phone from his pocket. He found his contact, the newest on the list, hit the button. Jonas could not remember the last time he had interrupted a meal with Vera. At least the cat would get the meat that he had abandoned. He typed the message, sent it.

He had not seen the nostril, nor the eye.

What if they were there, in the picture, what if he had not spotted them? He had considered that the two young persons, sent to him for mentoring, both probationers, intended to tweak his nose, show a bit of mischief. It was, perhaps, an indication of the pressure he felt – self-imposed – that he had considered their printout of the picture to be between cheek and impertinence. He had made a rare gesture of pique, had torn the image into pieces.

The cat yowled behind him, grateful for the extra rations. What if he had missed both a nostril and a glint of an opened eye? What if the turgid dark water had hidden the uneven mess of upper and lower teeth?

The message had been sent. Nothing he could do until it was answered. She brought water biscuits and a Scandinavian cheese, and he had the map between them, and they talked again about the sites at Stoke Fleming and Harbertonford, and the merits of Bigbury-on-Sea . . .

In old times, before he had relieved Winston Gunn of his vest, he had sent in his reports, expected minimal response, and had felt many times that he had been ignored. Since the AssDepDG had arrived in the night to cancel his retirement he had been listened to and his insights had achieved greater relevance. The sneers had wilted . . . Not that he was more liked, not that he was a part of the team. Responsibility weighed heavier, sometimes almost broke him . . . Two probationers amusing themselves at the expense of a self-proclaimed crocodile hunter. Were there glimpses of a nostril and an eye in a photograph he had dismissed?

Vera seemed to favour Harbertonford and said the views were pleasant there, and it was near to the moor and close enough to Totnes for a half day, and there was a vineyard on the Dart estuary. He did not dissuade her.

He wondered how long it would be before his message was answered and his phone wriggled on the tablecloth.

It was agreed. In his lunch-hour the following day he would telephone the site at Harbertonford, and would try to make a booking, preferably one with a concrete stand and within easy reach of the shop.

She cleared the table, usually his job, and he sat in his chair, and she had the radio quietly playing music, and he had one of the files out. It was the one listing the men and women who had gone away, been with the black flags, and who were now scattered. Deaths unreported, captures not listed, not those who begged for "another chance" and bleated of the mistakes they had made – always the victim and never themselves to blame; they were the ones who had scratched at him that evening. A bad evening, and they came more often. This file had a sticking power, and any of the men whose names were on the single sheet of paper, two columns of them, had only to be lucky once.

In a centuries-old house on the north side of the cathedral, in the heart of Canterbury, bedlam had broken out in a dormitory for small boys. A House Mother, attempting to maintain an expression of outrage and horror, swept in and called for silence, a return to their own beds, and muttered something about a "disgraceful carry-on". A little sheepish, but not seriously so, the boys retreated. They were eleven or twelve, boys who sang treble in the cathedral's choir. The use of such voices had been central to Christian music since the beginning of organised worship. Books littered the dormitory floor, along with clothes and bedding. The House Mother had a fair stab at conveying anger but it was an unconvincing act. They were the stars of each evening's evensong service, so beloved of the adults attached to the cathedral and to visitors. They were the public face of the establishment that stood at the heart of a worldwide religious authority. They had sung beautifully that evening. As they had filed out of the *quire* area, there had been a welling murmur of appreciation from the filled pews alongside them. The performance was outstanding . . . But the boys who appeared in the guise of angels in their purple and white gowns, with scrubbed faces and their hair neatly brushed and parted, were akin to the terminally sick. Their time was coming close. Few of them would have understood the medical detail of the onset of puberty in their bodies, but all knew that a termination point loomed. Their voices would break. They would become surplus to requirements at this level. From being feted, centres of attention, they would fade away and their voices become at best serviceable and at worst unpleasant . . . They were the roses in the cathedral garden that would bloom, then fade. No longer a focus of admiration. The staff at the school that provided the scholarships for the choristers would try to mitigate the inevitable pain. At a predictable date, the voice would change. Some would take it in their stride and go on to sing with amateurs, others would buckle down to more normal school routines, some would collapse mentally and some would take on a rebel streak ... Some would manage better than others – some would fail to absorb the rejection. They would leave the grandeur of the cathedral, where history lurked in each stone, where there were the graves of warrior princes and a decapitated archbishop, where an altar stood with burning candles to mark the stone slab where another archbishop had been hacked to death by the king's knights, where extreme violence had mingled with prayer. For a very few of the boys the consequences of their voices changing would be drastic.

The gulls were calling and wheeling and the wind was stronger as Cammy arrived back at the parking area. He could hear the sea, could not escape its sound. He found them, sensed their relief. They started their picnic.

The teacher quizzed him. "We almost believed you had left us."

"I had not left you. I promised to come back."

"It is a matter of trust. You did not say where you were going."

"Always a matter of trust. I went to get food. I told you that."

"You took a long time. That is why we thought you were leaving us. Do you know much of trust?"

"What I know of trust is that it should only rarely be given – and then for a purpose."

"Why should we trust you? We do not have your name. Please, why?"

Cammy said, "Because you have no one else to trust. No one."

Not what they wanted to hear. The adults eating and exchanging glances ... the kids had found a football among the dunes. Deflated but still serviceable. They had put down stones to make a goal. Cammy saw that, and saw also that there were new tyre marks beside their vehicle, and saw also that there were cigarette ends there, extinguished, but recent ... With his life he would have trusted Stanislau and Mikki and Tomas, Dwayne and Pieter, and Ulrike: had given them all his trust ... He stared at the butts, let them see him looking at them. The glances between themselves betrayed guilt. He tore off bread from the loaf and broke clear an untidy corner of cheese.

The psychologist was kicked on his ankle by his wife.

"What is your commitment to us?"

"The commitment is convenience. I brought you here."

"We had a contact name, number, to help us go across."

Cammy said quietly, mouth full, "I do not. You do. I would look to go with you."

Did they know now that he was a fighter going home? Know that or think him a criminal? Whether a fighter or a criminal, did they consider what violence he may have done? On who . . .? He thought them decent people . . .

The psychologist blinked, breathed hard, prepared for confession. "We had a contact, we met a man. He came with associates."

"You should have waited until I was back."

The teacher said, "We did not know you were coming back."

The psychologist said, "We had a number and we called it."

"The man came?"

"Came with hard men," the teacher said.

They were decent people and had no defence. Regarded them as innocents, felt no particular loyalty, would help them each step of the way as long as the journey helped him, Cammy Jilkes.

Cammy asked, "What deal did you do?"

The men took turns to answer. "You have to understand that it was difficult to bring money from Iran."

"Most of everything we had remains there."

"We could not tell friends or relatives that we planned to leave."

"We brought some jewels but have left our homes behind, everything in them. Just locked the doors and put the keys in the garbage."

"There was a cat, we all loved the cat. We put food out and it had a hatch at the back to go through. When it finished the food it might have gone to a neighbour, might have gone feral, might have been run over in the street. We left it, try not to think about it."

"My wife's mother, we left her. We could not tell her. She has no sense of preservation. We left her as they left the cat."

"Left those students I was still permitted to teach."

"Left the patients they allowed me to treat – there was never a better time nor a worse time. We have little money left, maybe enough and maybe not. Everybody we meet takes our money . . . I apologise. You do not."

"We doubted your kindness, thought you had left us. For that, I apologise."

In the last months, before the final break-out from Barghuz, Cammy and his brothers had been with columns of refugees, all on the move to the next location billed as that of the "final stand", or the destination for the martyrs. Women, children, supposed fighters with their nerves shredded by the bombing, the wounded who hobbled along with the slowest. But the brothers were a fighting unit, an élite, and were supposed to hold up the advance of the Syrian infantry or plug a perimeter gap when there was a chance the Kurds would break through. They did not waste their time worrying about the prospects of the girls who had come from Europe, and did not help them or their kids. He had no responsibility to these people, the Iranian Christians, and yet . . . The cheese was finished, and the bread.

Cammy asked, "The man who came here, how much did he want?"

"He is a Chechen."

"Is that important?"

"The Chechens have a reputation."

"What is the reputation?" Cammy could have answered his own question. He had not fought, himself, under the instructions of al-Sistani the fighter from Chechnya who was known for his brutality, for his cruelty, for using more deluded kids as martyr material than any other commander. "How much did he ask for?"

The silence hung. The psychologist turned away and the teacher hung his head and the two women fidgeted but stayed silent. It was the youngest of the kids, bored with football who gazed back at Cammy and his jaw quivered, then came the blurting reply.

"They asked for four thousand dollars for each of us, four thousand American dollars. That is from the sale of each piece of jewellery my mother has, and our friends, and their mothers. It is gold and rings and necklaces. It is everything. If they take twenty-four thousand dollars then we have only the clothes we stand in when we reach the far side. They say they have the boat, that we can go, and that is the price and they say they will not argue on the price. It is a fixed price. We cannot go back. We can only go forward . . . Are you the same as us?"

Cammy put out his hand. The kid did not flinch. He let his palm rest on the kid's head, then worked his fingers into the hair, tugged at it. He said he was the same, said he too could only go forward. He said that he would talk with the Chechen man, and with his associates. There was a little ripple of applause, touching almost. He climbed into the vehicle, sat in the driver's seat and pulled his cap down, closed his eyes, and would try to sleep. He had no money, could not pay for his own place in a boat. Sometimes the wind brought surges of sand up over the dune and on to the windscreen; he could hear the sea and thought it had become angrier.

"Hell of a good guy, your Jonas, brave as a cornered she-cat. Not that I've ever met him, but we talk on the phone. Working for him, you're lucky. I'm to give you a crash course: who they are, why they are coming back, what we have to fear – and it's plenty."

In a drab upper-floor corridor of a block of King's College, where the Department of War Studies was located, Tristram and Izzy had looked for the door's number. Most of the students had left for the day and only a few staff remained as the evening settled on London.

"You're not the first he's sent to me, and won't be the last. There's a reason . . . Jonas would say that your gang are unlikely to think out of the loop, prefer to stay in a comfort zone. What that means is that the kids who are hiking home were recruited as foreign fighters after getting a dose of Islam from a local mosque preacher, and bought big into the religion. Wanted to be martyrs, stop off in the orchards where the virgins waited – too trite and too convenient – and the ones who fit that bill, the majority, are not those who concern us.

"The kids with religion dripping out of their minds are going to make a noise and might be responsible for occasional atrocities, but they are not clever and rarely have the motivation to push far forward. The ones who frighten me, and I suspect are top of the blips on whatever radar Jonas uses, are those who are shorn of religion and have a different motivation . . . Let me put a thought to you. While we had the war in Afghanistan bubbling along, and regular processions of hearses through Wootton Bassett, and TV programmes about all the maimed soldiers trying to get their lives back after being blown up by IEDs, the recruitment figures for the army drifted nicely along. Then we pulled out of Afghanistan and recruitment nosedived. I'm saying that the young men worth worrying about are those who joined without an idea of the Muslim faith's core principles. They went for the fight. Got me?"

They had knocked, heard a distant call to enter. Opened the door and seen a backside and part of a torso hanging out of a window, then a billow of smoke. A face had materialised, and a half-finished fag was stubbed out on the window-sill. This was Doug.

"Some would have gone for the sheer excitement of getting their hands on a Barrett 50 calibre sniper's rifle which kills at a range of well over two klicks – it could be a machine-gun, could be an ability, latent before this, to lob mortars. With that excitement comes camaraderie. We're talking about fish in a river that gravitate towards the same species. Like school, like college. Similar minds and similar motives . . . Musketeers or any desperado gang. Each man in such a group, fighting in the front line of the *katibas* – those are the battalions of foreign recruits – is now élite rated, valued, and thinks himself a bit above the level of bee's bollocks. He is a star . . . I doubt he slits throats and doubt too that he helps to chuck homosexuals off rooftops, and I reckon it unlikely he'll be hammering in the nails for the crucifixion of an alleged informer. As a fighter, in my opinion, he is a street length more expert than those who just went along and mostly were in the way of the Kurd troops on the other side. I rate him, and I fear him."

Younger than Izzy, the same sort of age as Tristram, and oozing confidence. Had found a way to beat the anti-smoking technology in the ceiling. A small room with loaded shelves and a desk covered in papers that circled his keyboard and screen. He hadn't shaved and his shirt seemed worn . . . He'd waved them to two hard chairs, but first they had to dump more paper on the floor. No apologies, no coffee, no biscuits, and the water in the bottle looked rancid.

"This man is alone. He's faced some rejection – family, emotional, academic. Sees the world against him, but in Syria had found – amongst all the shit there – something he values. He has his own team, and believes them to be invincible. That's good. He's not jacking it in while the team holds together, but he's moving on. They will be motley, disparate, but they will sustain each other. That's how it will be, contained as far as we are concerned, until the roof falls in . . . or I can put it another way. A man comes and pumps poison into a wasps' nest. Massacres them. You pay him and reckon it's safe to have the picnic and the jam sandwiches. Except that one wasp was late getting back to the nest, and is powerfully annoyed and, sure as night, will sting and not give two fucks, excuse me, about the consequences. All good until the roof falls in."

No questions, no interruptions.

"Excitement and drama sustain a restless man in a boring world, and he has his mates around him, and then his world collapses. Don't ask me how. The luck runs out, it always does. The group scatters, is bombed, is droned, doesn't matter why or how. Everything that has held them together has gone out of the window, finished. Where to go?"

Doug paused, rolled his eyes, gestured with his hands. Neither of them needed to answer. Beyond the window, still open to disperse the dregs of the smoke, were the cheerful shouts of pedestrians, and vehicle horns, and the roar of accelerating engines and the scream of wheels braking, and Izzy would have thought it all so normal, and Tristram's phone – on mute – wriggled on his lap.

"We think, for his last hosanna, he wants to come home. He is now outside the comfort zone of his section. No friends, no best buddies, and angry enough to want people – you, me, and the great unwashed – to suffer. Wants to be the hard man, the guy without fear. Which is his contempt for and hatred of the rest of us. Wants to go with a bang so that he will be remembered. All part of their quite dreadful vanity. What I'm saying is that we do not need clever people with top academic qualifications, nor the best of the psychologists, nor the sympathetic *imams* to read him. Just have to know that he is embittered, resentful, like that lone wasp, and he wants to hurt. Quite simple, except for a problem . . . You have to find him."

"Grateful for your opinion . . . Are we winning? Is this the end-game?"

"God, no." Doug laughed. "Of course not – just holding the line. Each one we lower, another stands up. Actually, they're regrouping. Your age – it'll see you to retirement . . . Sorry, you did not expect to hear that."

The session was finished. Tristram and Izzy were left quiet, shell-shocked, had to absorb what was so different from the marginally more positive "Teaching According to the Book of Thames House". All so basic, and from down at the level of the gutter. They did a brief handshake and Doug was already back at the window, leaning out, and there was a flash of his lighter, then smoke, then a muffled voice that echoed back to the room.

"So, only one problem. Good luck to you. You swat the wasp, but first you have to find him."

They went out into the evening. A majestic church in front of them. The river flowing at high tide behind them. Crowded pavements, traffic jams, jostling crowds.

Tristram checked his phone.

"That's Wobby. Wants to see the picture again, the one he tore up. Wants me to mark the necessary on it, the nostril and the eye, what he didn't see first time he looked at it – now doubting his own judgement. Maybe his nerve's going. Maybe."

★   ★   ★

The table had been cleared, the dishwasher churned in the kitchen and the radio played a concert, and their talk drifted. Jonas had a notepad in front of him and wrote the barest of details of what needed checking, and thought . . .

Time to check the caravan's tyres – probably needed changing.

The target the team went after that night was closer to "moderate risk" than "strong risk", but was to go in the net because they were fearful now of letting a potential hazard stay loose on the streets. The men and women who made little secret of their feelings for him would now be deployed in vehicles or on foot, monitoring cameras' images. It was the time when the Subject of Interest, the SoI, usually came from his brother-in-law's home, walked the length of three streets, then returned to his own address. They would be sitting in their vehicles and leaning against shadowed shop doorways, and the pictures would throw a dull light inside the back of a van . . . and the police firearms teams would be readying their kit, the lethal stuff that added to the stress levels.

Time to hustle for reservations because any pleasant site would be booked up, already four months before the summer holiday, high season.

A front door opening, two men – both of Pakistani origin and both with a heritage in the frontier city of Quetta – hugging each other farewell on the doorstep. Engines starting up and the exhausts chucking out fumes, and fags dropped out of open windows, and the foot surveillance people gulping the last of a chocolate bar or spitting clear some well-worked chewing-gum, and the night's "boss" watching the images and holding the microphone button in his hand and the veins showing on his forehead: always the big moment. The messages coming in as to which of them, near the SoI, had a good eyeball.

Time to decide whether this year the cat would go with them or be left with the neighbours; Vera refused to contemplate sending the Norwegian Forest to a kennel.

The cry was for "Go". And repeated. "Go" resonant in a dozen earpieces. Never seemed important to Jonas to be there but the team, each last one of them and every team operating in the

A Branch of Thames House, seemed to get a big kick out of being there: supposed it would be similar to when a fox was flushed out and the hounds started screaming and the horses galloped faster. Immaterial to Jonas but he was the one despised as the Eternal Flame and now grudgingly accepted because of the initials after his name. The SoI would be walking briskly on the pavement, head mostly hidden in a hoodie, hands in his pockets. The team would be closing around him, coming fast, two cars from the front and two from the back, and the guns out. What they all wanted, the adrenaline rush, and it meant little to Jonas.

Time to decide whether Vera could take the tomato plants with them, remove them from the greenhouse, and plan where they would be stored during the journey.

A residential street on the west side of Luton was transformed. The SoI was pitched forward by the first to reach him from the cars. Doors hanging open. Machine pistols aimed. The target flattened and spread-eagled. The air filled with near hysterical shouting because the guns would seek to dominate, and all of them hyper-ventilating and living the moment and believing what they did was "saving the nation". His wrists twisted behind his back and the restraints being tightened. Hands running over his body, feeling in the orifices they could their get gloved fingers into. The target would have great saucer eyes, and would be panting, the reality of his situation not yet fully comprehended: give it ten minutes. Radios crackling, then the scrape of metal on metal as weapons were made safe. Lights coming on in front rooms, and faces peering from behind curtains, and yelling from the team and from the armed cops for them to get the hell out of sight. The target was down to Jonas, the Eternal Flame, who never went out, did not need to, and who could forego the theatricals. Was the guy armed? He was not. Was the guy likely to implode from an explosives vest? Was not . . . but it was a fair statistic to put him in the cage.

The target would be hoisted up, propped upright on his feet. A circle of men and women around him, all huge in their stab-proof or bulletproof vests. The target's rights would be recited in his ear, not that he would understand, not then. The violence of an arrest was partly down to the need to be safe and not let a guy slip away, but also down to the fear lived with by all of the team, and all of the other teams, and the dread of having to crowd around a TV set and watch the carnage played out live, and know that within hours the suits would be probing in the archive looking for who had cocked up, searching for an opportunity to blame. A ferocious world out there ... The cars would scream away with blue lights revolving on the roofs, and the target would be sandwiched on a back seat, and the guns would go back into their cases. Some of the team would have to write up a report on the lift, and the others would head to a pub, and there would be drink taken and importance lived ... and little solved. Another sticking plaster smoothed on.

The motor home was one of the smaller models, a Toyota HiAce with an elevating roof, but was an ideal size for an elderly couple, Baz and Mags, and so much easier to drive than if they had been towing a caravan. It had UK registration plates. They were in a far corner of the parking space behind a fuel station on the north side of Cologne. Loaded into the vehicle satnav were the autobahn routes of the E314 and E40 and, via Aachen and Maastricht, their destination was the ferry port of Zeebrugge. They sat in darkness and waited for the headlights of a car to approach them.

"Don't suppose there's any chance of a pee?"

"Better not, Mags, better to wait and keep them crossed, if you can."

A little chuckle between them. The motor home had been hired for the trip. They had taken possession of it in the north of England, had driven via the ferry link to the German city, had spent two days of sightseeing there – "A bloody boring place this, Baz, not my cup of tea", and a response of "Not disagreeing with you, love". They had done the basic minimum of what the guide-book demanded, and had been told they should play the part fully, keep the cover alive. They had left Cologne in the early evening and had driven slowly, in the heart of the commuter queue on the main route heading north and west, had left the Rhine behind them and had turned off at the fuel station, had filled up, and had parked in this remote corner and waited. It was a comfortable vehicle, one that normally would have been beyond their reach either to rent or to buy . . . But times were looking up and this was a new departure for them and promised to swell their finances.

No lights illuminated them. Other vehicles came and parked but not close.

They were not supposed to smoke in the vehicle but they did, failed to open the windows, smoked and, predictably, tension crackled between them. It was the first time they had done a courier run on this scale and with such a reward dangled in front of them. And the promise of more to come. They had almost clean records, nothing that would have jumped off a charge sheet and bitten them, and it was difficult to see why, back home, the police, or the customs, should be concerned with them: would be the green corridor and a cheery wave to the uniformed officials, and another rendezvous at another car park, and then they'd be on the way home, and a fat brown envelope would be in his hip pocket or at the bottom of her handbag. "Piece of cake", how they'd described it to each other when it had been put to them.

He checked his watch again. "Right, Mags, reckon it's time to get things in place."

He moved into the back of the camper. He lifted the bench which they sat on when the foldaway table was erected. It was where they had placed spare blankets in case the weather turned cold. Below the blankets were sheets of tinfoil, folded neatly, that they had bought in a German hardware shop; it was a precaution, the tinfoil, because of the need to mask the smell, given off by the cargo they now expected. But there was much that Baz and Mags did not know . . . did not know how much of a recognisable smell would be given off by a *Ruchnoy Protivotankoviy Granatomyot* 7 grenade launcher. With it were coming six grenades that could be fired by the RPG-7 launcher, fitted with PG-7 HEAT, all good for anti-tank operations and those against defended buildings. The length of the package they waited for would be a metre, and the combined weight of launcher and grenades would be 40 pounds. They did not know the smell, nor did they know that the weapon had been tracked by Croatian homeland security from the time the package had left Bosnian territory on its first leg from the fought-over city of Mostar. Then it had been watched, on distant "eyeballs", by the Slovenians, then by Austrian domestic intelligence. And they had no idea that the parking lot in which the motor home was now parked was under the surveillance of units of the BfV, the German counter-terror organisation . . . Baz and Mags knew none of this.

Night-sight intensifier lenses were trained on them but their ignorance was blissful . . . Little squeals of excitement as headlights caught the camper, blinded them, then the brilliance was killed. Nothing said. A car slid close. Two men out of it and fast. The side door of the motor home squealed as it was heaved open. The package, in tightly-wrapped greaseproof paper and with adhesive binding wound around it, was tossed inside, only just caught by Baz. The door was slid shut and the car was gone, and darkness reigned. Baz put the package inside the space and smoothed out the tinfoil and covered it, then heaped in the blankets and closed the bench.

Baz said, "What I'm thinking, old girl, is that we might just deserve a drink."

Mags said, "A bloody large one if I'm pouring."

With drink taken, they'd not risk driving, but they had hours to kill before the ferry out of Zeebrugge, and they did not know that camera shutters had hammered through the exchange of the package . . .

The vehicle edged closer. The sound was muffled in the blusters of the wind. The natural light was long gone and Cammy saw the pinprick illumination of side-lights.

The engine noise was harsh, grating. He was reminded of the pick-up trucks that carried him and his brothers around the battlefields of Syria. Might get them to a destination and might not . . . In his hip pocket was the screwdriver that he had taken from the tool bag in the back of the transport he had driven from Bordeaux. His anorak was long enough to cover the handle and the narrow blade. He had not allowed any of the Iranians to see that he had taken it. Nor had he expressed an opinion on the deal they reckoned they had done with their contact ... If he had argued he would have broken their resolve and he would not have been able to launch with them. He could have argued over the cost and over the weather conditions: he had kept quiet.

The vehicle rattled on the pot-holed track. He assumed these guys, the Chechens – not usually praised for their clemency – would not care how far out into the Channel the craft would manage before it would take water ... might capsize in the swell, might be intercepted by a French patrol boat and rescued, or might get tossed and turned in the bow wave of a container ship ... They would not care, would have the money, would charge the same for another craft the next night.

Along with the approach of the vehicle he heard the singing of the wind and the rumble of the breaking waves. Cammy thought it their best chance.

The vehicle's tyres ground into the loose gravel. He thought the Iranian men, the teacher and the psychologist, now looked to him to take the lead, fearful perhaps of what they had agreed. They would have heard the weather. The women held the children close to their skirts.

He knew the reputation of the Chechens. They were feared, loathed by the Kurds fighting them and by the Syrian troops because of their cruelty to those who were captured. But they also had a reputation of buckling when the fighting was against the Hezbollah militiamen, or the Iranians of the Quds force: were the first to run when the enemy's air strikes came in, would abandon their position in the line ... Not for him to tell these good God-fearing people that he had fought against their fellow countrymen. Politics were beyond his remit, and religion. He would define himself by his actions.

The engine was killed. Three men climbed down from the cab of the pick-up. Cammy recognised the tarpaulin-covered shape in the back. He took the psychologist's elbow. Held it, pushed it back. His other hand impeded the teacher. He set the rules, he was in front. A cigarette was lit which was valuable to Cammy. The lighter flame, cupped for protection, showed him a young man's face and then moved on to an older man whose cigarette drooped from his lips, and whose untrimmed beard was grey, then on to a third man who would have been barely beyond teenage years. Likely a father and two sons. Cammy stepped forward.

English would be the common language. He was addressed in a guttural and rasping voice.

"And you are the passenger? The one they take with them. You want to go tonight? Tonight or tomorrow night, or next week? You are going with them? Yes?"

He didn't speak, just nodded, and went closer. He was sure they were sons: one had stubble on his face, designer style, and the other had just fluff. He saw that when they dragged on their cigarettes. The older man's head was shaved smooth but the boys' hair whipped in the wind.

"You want to go on the water tonight? You speak for these people? The price is agreed. The price does not change. You know that?"

He did not answer.

"We brought the craft you will use. We go a little of the way, we see you into the deep water . . . If you get far out then you telephone the British authorities and they send a boat for you, they pick you up. The other side is a formality . . . a few weeks in a hostel, then you are free. They rescue you, they are very kind. You want to go tonight?"

Cammy held his silence and gazed into the shadows of the man's face.

"You have the money – what was agreed – and we give you a good outboard motor, and full tank and spare gas. We do all that."

There might have been a wintry smile on Cammy's face. The smile would have been recognised by his brothers, not by those who had known him as a child.

"I want to see the boat."

"And I want first to see the money I will be paid."

"The boat, first is the boat."

It would have been unusual for the Chechen, the father, to concede in a discussion about the terms of a deal. He flicked his fingers behind him and the boys lifted down an outboard engine and then the collapsed shape of a rib. He said that he needed to see it blown up, then needed to see that the engine worked, then they would talk of money. Perhaps he was humoured . . . perhaps the Chechen doubted that anyone would put to sea in the weather that night. Perhaps he was cold, perhaps hungry, perhaps he had a whore in Dunkirk who waited for his return, perhaps he was merely bored. Another gesture . . . a pump was used and the sides swelled, and the craft took shape. One of the boys had a phone out to illuminate the dinghy. They started the engine, which took time, but finally coughed to life, and they had a plastic fuel container that would have taken two gallons and which seemed full.

"And the money?"

The phone light was shone into his face. But Cammy's hand had already moved to the pocket at his hip, had taken the screwdriver and had slid its handle up his sleeve. Would he pay $24,000 for the privilege of putting to sea in the darkness in a craft that any reasonably well-off tourist would have rejected if charged more than $2,400, inclusive of the fuel and the engine? He would not. Would he bargain, haggle? He would not. Would he listen to the entreaties of the Iranians behind him – who did not understand the power of the sea running the width of the Channel – and who were strangely desperate to reach his country? He would not. The phone's light would have caught his smile; it had none of the previous icy cold, seemed sincere. The Chechen would have made a life's study of suspicion, employed it through most of his waking hours, and when he was with a whore there would have been a loaded pistol, within reach . . . The smile relaxed him and his boys dropped their guard, and Cammy went forward as if to look more closely at the inflated dinghy.

His smile had disappeared, and his teeth ground together and his lips thinned and the screwdriver was at the Chechen's throat, and the other hand had the Chechen's right arm tucked high behind his back, leaving him rocking with the pain. There, for all to see, was the screwdriver blade and the indentation in the skin behind the beard, and also the shock saturating the Chechen's features. All still as statues for the moments it took for the Chechen to absorb his situation, and for his two boys to read it – and for the Iranians, the men and the women and the children, to appreciate it.

He gave crisp orders. The Chechen's boys would have looked into the face of their father, what they could see of it, would have taken a signal from his expression, might also have noticed that he had wet the front of his jeans. The Iranians were Christians, refugees in flight, would have believed in cheek turning, in abstaining from violence. Would have seen that, in their name, a fleck of blood seeped into the beard of a man who would have robbed them of their wealth, and watched them drift away to their deaths. The father spoke, from the side of his mouth, and the boys backed away . . . if they had a weapon it would have been in the father's belt. Cammy called to one of the Iranian kids, told him in clipped English what he should do, was understood. Hands poked around the man's waist, and he shivered, which deepened the cut in his skin. A pistol was found. Not a PPK Walther but a Makarov PM – and a short-bladed knife. He told the kid to run and chuck them both. The school teacher and the psychologist were to lift the craft and the women between them would bring the outboard engine. The children were to bring the bags from their own vehicle.

Cammy led them through the dunes, between the swaying grasses. He told the Chechen that his sons were to stay at their pick-up and told him that if they intervened then they would have no father. His voice discouraged argument. Cammy kept the screwdriver against the Chechen's throat, close to his windpipe.

They crossed the dunes and the long grasses, reached the soft sand beyond the tide's reach. The waves made a drumbeat ahead of him. Much of his time in recent years he had shrugged when the odds stacked badly. Recalled the moments when he had hugged Ulrike or Pieter, Mikki or Tomas – or Dwayne, who used to say that what he dreaded most of all was the "claustrophobia of conformity" – and pushed on with them around him. Now he was alone and tailed by a gang who could barely help him. They crossed the wet sand, and the waves came forward in steady lines. He told the teacher and the psychologist to get the craft into the water and hold it, and told the women to fasten the engine into place . . . It rose and fell, water splashing over them, in their eyes and up their noses, and they were wading.

Cammy manoeuvred the Chechen in front of it, gave him an instruction. Took the screwdriver from his throat. Released the hand holding his arm.

They were up to their waists. Money was passed – $2,400. The kids were in the floor of the dinghy. The women clung to the sides, hitched their skirts and heaved their legs over. Then the men . . . The dinghy bucked and heaved and the waves broke around it, and someone screamed.

The outboard was started and the little propeller thrashed in the water and there was a moment between the waves breaking when it shifted the dinghy forward.

"You'll be back," the Chechen called. "Back here, washed up, drowned. It is certain."

Cammy clung to the ropes at the side, drove the dinghy forward until his feet were no longer on the seabed, then pushed and swung himself aboard. The next wave tossed them and the engine raced when it was clear of the water, and they dropped, and they lost sight of the beach and the rigid white lines where the surf broke.

And, just for a moment, he stretched his neck, tilted his head as if to hear better – force of habit. He heard the noise of the waves and the coughing throb of the engine and he strained to hear that other sound which was the murmur of a drone flying high above him. Where he had come from, the drone and the threat it carried – the missiles slung from its wings. If it were American then it would be flown by a pilot in the far west of the United States, and if it were British then the pilot would be in a Portacabin at a Royal Air Force base in the east of England. The drones and their crews

were the principal enemy . . . he heard them often in Syria or Iraq,
now he heard only the thrash of the waves and the splutter of the
engine, and little squeals of fear.

The Ordnance Survey maps of the west country, featuring the
southern Devon coastline, had been folded away and were back in
the bookcase. Jonas's mug of cocoa was drunk. Vera would be
standing at the kitchen door and the cat would be prowling around
the garden perimeter, sniffing in the flower bed, too lazy to scale
the fence and go further.

The radio was off now and his phone bleeped.

Jonas and Vera Merrick lived in a quiet corner of the outer
London area: a place of peace, of harmony. The normality of the
streets was a mood of calm. He doubted any of his neighbours,
going to work in the morning, taking the kids to school, heading
for the supermarket, working in education or employment or
retired, felt a sense of threat: Jonas did. Was never free of it . . . He
thought they came, the opposition, on a conveyor belt. Mostly sad
and categorised as losers, and the majority of them could be
cauterised. They could, the biggest number of them, be lifted as
the target would have been that evening, but the belt would roll on
and another found to step on to it. They were not the ones who
currently intrigued Jonas, and who frightened him. He inhaled as
if he needed to stiffen his sinews. Reached for his phone. Vera had
the cat back inside and was opening a tin of food for it.

He gazed at the image that Tristram and Izzy had sent him.
Could have been a river or a lagoon, not subject to fast tidal flows,
or a lake in a swampland. He magnified the detail. Two minute
crude circles were marked on his screen. He zoomed closer on
each of them, and closer again. Inside one circle was a strip of
softer silver, perhaps where sunlight penetrated the overhanging
foliage, and there was a dark point in the centre of it. He eased his
focus towards the second circle and the light here was blocked
and the water was dark except for a single point where a jewel
seemed to shine. He was shown a submerged crocodile's single
nostril and one eye.

The back door was now locked and the cat was eating. Vera would have seen the frown indenting his forehead as he took his mug to the sink, then swilled it, and she'd not interrupt him . . .

There were times when the pressure seemed to crush him, to be an intolerable burden, and there were times when he managed it. But, whatever its weight, Jonas was never free from what he saw as his responsibility. She would go up first and he would switch off the lights and follow her, and he doubted he would sleep well that night.

4

Jonas lay on his back, his eyes fixed on the lampshade suspended from the centre of the ceiling, his head resting in his hands.

His role was to think beyond convention. Not to be particularly clever, almost the opposite. To use common sense and trust an instinct: had always done that. The difference in his life had come on a damp evening, funking an embarrassing retirement drink, and going walkabout by the river, a little down Millbank from Thames House, and the chance encounter with Winston Gunn. Beside him, Vera breathed quietly, did not disturb his thoughts. There was a street lamp outside their house and it would have taken blackout quality curtains to put the bedroom into complete darkness. Light filtered through, and he noticed a spider working its slow way across the ceiling towards the light fitting.

For years, as the Eternal Flame, Jonas Merrick had sat at his desk, always apart from the main circular table where the team worked. Had built his card index, a mini-library of biographies, had nurtured them with the same care that Vera lavished on her tomatoes in the greenhouse, and had written reports. It was all about risk assessment. He thought the spider took a chance in the survival stakes by staking out its territory up there on the ceiling. In the morning, if it were still there, Vera would take a duster to it, carry the spider to the bedroom window, and toss it outside ... Jonas did risk assessment, and tried to work inside the priority choices. He watched the spider's progress, upside down, across the ceiling.

Before divesting Winston Gunn of his suicide gear, Jonas had analysed the information crossing his desk, searched for predictions, submitted conclusions ... had barely been noticed. He never challenged the seeming lack of interest in his submissions, did not demand an audience with senior staff when his name and contributions were airbrushed out by his colleagues at times of minor triumph. As with Irish targets, and then Cold War spies, he had identified those who seemed to mount a primary danger: did the same with the *jihadis*. Not that Jonas ever went to the colleges where the young boys supposedly studied, where the radicalisation was rife, nor did he hang around on the pavements outside the mosques where the teaching was fundamentalist. He talked on the phone, and he read. He was voracious in his consumption of information, and from it he made judgements. But the incident with Winston Gunn had changed everything.

The first move, from the AssDepDG, was a trawl through every one of the recommendations posted by Jonas Merrick of 3/S/12. It became obvious that his strike rate was high, and at least one stabbing incident and a vehicle attack could have been prevented if action had been taken on Jonas's thoughts. And they had gone through his Irish stuff, and then his insight into the work practices of East Bloc spies – best on the Czechs and the Hungarians.

Now, notice was taken of his opinions. His judgements were heard. Thames House had access to the most sophisticated computer programs, could achieve breakthrough science in the manipulation of mobile phones, could summon up brilliant brainpower, but the AssDepDG had given a place of importance to a man who seemed without talent, could not hold his own in argument, seemed dull and boring – that was Jonas Merrick's assessment of himself. The role of 3/S/12 was to predict the re-entry of UK recruits who had gone to the black flag, had enlisted, had fought, were now heading home. To track them and neutralise them. Easy? No. If Vera had been awake, if he had confided his worries to her, which would have been a crass breach of security and had never happened, he might have said in the privacy of their bed, "The point is that the ones we're looking for are the most dangerous. They are hardened, have come through a weight of artillery and air bombardment, have been out-gunned on the battlefield, have lost the new family that had embraced them. They have an angry hatred of us who plod to work each day, and watch the soaps in the evenings, and swill beer down at the pub, and to whom the biggest catastrophe in the world is if some bloody football team loses at the weekend, or if the bloke is shagging another woman. They loathe us, only think of getting back and wiping the smugness off our faces. And they are skilled and . . . Do you know much about crocodiles, Vera? No, don't suppose you do . . ." Did not say it, and nursed the anxiety alone.

The emptiness ahead of the dinghy was broken by two faint lights, might have been those of a small boat, a trawler. Cammy was at the back and held the arm of the outboard and tried to steer them forward and they were lifted high by the waves, then pitched down.

When he turned, he could see more lights moving away, deeper into the dunes. The smuggler team, father and sons, had their own vehicle but would have taken the stolen people carrier . . . It would have different plates on it by morning, and within a week would have been spray-painted: might make up for some of the shortfall in the deal. Then those lights were gone and a blackness formed behind them.

The teacher, at the front of the dinghy, used both hands to cling to the slack rope on the sides and seemed to be flung high and then disappear below the water level when they dipped. The women clung to the two children. The psychologist was rigid in fear and crouched as low as he could. Cammy could not have done without them. They were pathetic and terrified and could do nothing to help drive the dinghy forward, yet he needed them. Had he been with his brothers – Stan and Mikki and Ulrike, with Dwayne and Pieter, with Tomas, there would have been laughter and shrieks of excitement and they would have been together and thought themselves untouchable. The Iranians did not know his name, he had been told their names but had forgotten them. They had researched their trip. They had told him basic facts. They had waded to the dinghy, their clothing was drenched, the crossing – if it was successful – would last for a minimum of ten hours. They would already be suffering from "cold water shock", and the wind blew a chill air over them and each wave they broke into spattered them with spray.

It was a surprise to Cammy that they made any progress at all. He'd have thought there was a fair chance they would be pushed straight back and that the spinning propeller blades on the outboard would grind into the sand, then break, and they would be dumped in a couple of feet of water: humiliated, screwed. But the dinghy was going forward.

They were level with the twin lights, and then passed them, faced another wall of darkness. The moon, if it were going to appear, was not yet clear of the dunes behind them. Cammy thought it felt like the buffeting they had been under when artillery was called down on them, or a mortar barrage, and they could be lifted, could be dropped, could feel the impact when they were landing in the troughs. The tiny dinghy was somehow staying afloat and was making a hesitant passage. Sometimes they were high above the swell and pirouetting on the wave crests, and sometime they were far below the water level and the spray came over them and he could barely see the teacher clinging on at the front.

The women had screamed when the first waves broke over them. Now they kept up a sort of keening moan. He knew that sound. The brothers would be with a strike battalion that had surged through a village, had fought past Syrian troops or Iranians who did not have the luxury of air support, would have done their combat and then would have trudged back, through the wrecked buildings, and the follow-up cadres would have come after them and would have had the names of all those who were government supporters or who had a son who had gone to fight on the "wrong" side. Bodies would be in the street . . . The sounds that the women made then were the same as the women now as they clung to the sides of the dinghy. A universal cry for the misery to finish, the same note struck in Syria and Iraq, and in Iran.

The dinghy engine raced and howled when out of the water and then chugged noisily against the din of the breaking waves, but it was moving them. He thought they might have gone a mile, thought that the minimum crossing distance would be 30 miles, and he wondered why these people wanted to come to his, Cammy's, country. They could have walked into Germany, could have stayed in France, could have reached Belgium or Holland. Why were they prepared to put themselves through this terror for a dream of the country that Cammy was now heading back to himself? As the engine thrashed and the dinghy pitched, his mind drifted, and then there was a higher wave and a deeper trough. A shattering impact when the dinghy landed back on the water and it was spun a half-turn. The keening became a scream.

A child had gone over.

The dinghy lurched as one of the women crabbed across the narrow width of the craft. Cammy thought they were about to capsize. Waves hit them and they fell, then rose, and the spray came like an avalanche over them, and if the dinghy was overturned, none of them would get to their promised land. He grabbed her, caught her clothing, felt the seawater wrung out of it from the tightness of his grip. Used his authority, pushed her down. The psychologist had switched on his torch ... Cammy saw the kid; the one who had taken the pistol from the Chechen's belt, had thrown it high and far into the dune grass.

Cammy slipped over the side.

The water entered his nose and his mouth, and swilled in his ears, and he felt the weight of his clothes and trainers dragging him down. He saw the kid, barely heard the screaming behind him, but saw the kid and maybe there was a small amount of air trapped below his anorak that kept him afloat. The distance between them grew, widening with each wave. He used the old discipline, the crawl stroke that he had learned in the Leisure Centre, and Vicky there, and powered away from the dinghy – and caught the kid.

He had once pulled a girl out from the pool at Kingsmead; she had panicked and gone under, he had grabbed her and her costume had torn and exposed her, and her mother had seemed more concerned at the girl's loss of modesty than if she'd drowned. This kid's mouth had been wide open with fear but he must have seen Cammy go into the water and then had shown a strange calm, which was trust. He brought the kid to the side. The motion of the dinghy made it hard to clamber in. The kid was too cold to help himself. Hands came down, caught him, tugged him back over the side.

Cammy struggled, wrenched himself up. Told the psychologist to switch off the torch, not to waste the battery. The cold was a bastard, not just for Cammy and not just for the kid, for all of them – could be a killer. The darkness was a wall around them.

Tristram said, "Am I allowed to say this, but you're not great company."

Izzy said, "Just that it's like a cloud over us, what you said."

"About old Jonas?"

"Because we did it with that picture, played silly buggers, played a trick on him."

"And all about his instincts, and him calling us back – and doubting himself."

They were the sole patrons of that corner of a wine bar; had gone halves on a bottle.

"It would be a hell of something to carry round. Responsibility."

"Like his bits are cut off, losing his instinct."

There had been long silences, as if both were cowed. They had gone through the selection process, and had come out smiling, and most of what they'd reckoned to be the smart-arse crowd of potential recruits had been sidelined, sent home. All fun and all interesting, and all part of the big build-up to "doing something truly useful", and having faith in the system they were now a part of. She had her phone out, checked the screen between their exchanges. He thought it a piss poor evening.

"Know anything about crocodiles?"

"No, Izzy, I don't. Saw one in a zoo when I was a kid. My gran had a crocodile handbag, genuine. That's all."

"Because of where we are, what we're at, I looked them up. Useless facts. The biggest ever is called Gustave. Lives on the Ruzizi River that goes into Lake Tanganyika. He is twenty feet long and he weighs a ton, and he might be a hundred years old – I am not making this shit up – he has plenty of bullet holes, because guys with AKs have blasted at him. He is not too fast now so cannot get deer or antelope, but goes after a hippopotamus if it's close. When he was last seen he was dragging a full-grown bull buffalo off for tea."

"Do I need to know?"

"Only that he's blessed with a good set of teeth. Where he is, people all know about him, are bloody careful, but he still gets them. He's killed three hundred human beings. Just that they don't see him. There but hiding, then the big splash, then it's over."

Both rueful. Time to go home, another day tomorrow.

Tristram said at the door, glasses not emptied but abandoned, "Don't know, Izzy, if I'm up to this . . . Just have that picture in my head, up on Wobby's wall, and what the man said, 'You just have to find him.' Have to."

They went in single file, left their emir behind them, reached the water's bank. They had stayed close as they eased among the reeds that flanked the river. If they had come across a security patrol, watching in the darkness for deserters, they would have killed all of them, done it quietly and without gunfire, managed it at knife-point. As a group they were poor on the discipline demanded by the security for those fighting under the black flag. Stanislau led, Mikki behind him, and Cammy held his usual position in the centre of the line.

An air strike was going on behind them. Cammy could see the navigation lights on the wing tips of the fast jets, and every few minutes a drone would come over and dump some flares to float down on parachutes. They might have hung around too long, might have gone earlier. Behind Cammy was Tomas, then Ulrike and Pieter, and Dwayne was back-marker. He felt nothing for those he left behind, men and women and tiny crazed children, cowering in shallow scrapes or in tunnels they had dug. Enough vehicles burned for the flares to be unnecessary but there would have been a paper-pusher back in some air-conditioned bunker who had decreed how many should be dropped that night, and dropped they would be – even if they lit a hell's inferno. It did not matter what they left behind because they had each other, were brothers . . . and believed it, and had survived too many strata of Hades to worry about anything bar themselves. They were close together when they moved soundlessly through the reeds, and followed the markers left the previous evening. They were headed across the Euphrates – and afterwards?

Not sure. Somewhere, and getting there sometime. Where there was a fight, and where the brothers stayed together. Almost, as if they now formed each other's only meaningful family . . . except that Cammy had his mother, but a long time ago . . . What they had done in the reeds the night before was make a raft from a big builder's pallet and they had carted two emptied oil drums through the reeds, and had lashed the sealed drums under the wood slats. It was big enough to take them all, and a couple of makeshift paddles from planks would give them propulsion. They would get clear of the river, then hunker down, and build a fire, and sit around it and Ulrike would cheer them and they'd talk about where they were headed. He now knew nothing else but fighting, had cleared his mind of "old days", former times, and loved his brothers.

They launched. The current here was slack because it was a deep stretch. There were great orbs of light behind them. Talk was impossible. Communication was by pulling one of them close, mouthing words and being lip-read. The bombs falling on the Barghuz enclave were 500lb each and it seemed little effort was made to differentiate between "hostiles" and camp followers. Tomas was beside Cammy and was paddling.

Tomas was short, fair-haired, always cheerful. Twenty-two years of age. His parents logged in the forest outside a place in Estonia none of them had heard of, Jarve, off the E20 highway running east towards St Petersburg. Tomas hated Russians with a frenzy: a grandfather had been carted off on a one-way ticket to Siberia and his own father had had a bad time before independence. After a few weeks' basic army training as a conscript, Tomas had deserted. Had gone to Syria with no Islamic fervour, just a desire to take the chance offered to kill Russians. Tomas always stayed close to Cammy, a pace and a half behind him, his longing to be there showing in his eyes like a dog did: was always *there except when the time came to blast with the 81mm mortar. They all carried his bombs for him, had enough for him to put three in the air and then they would run, as fast as wild hares, before the retaliation. Before the military, he had done a term and a half at Tartu University in engineering, then had dropped out. Just lived for his brothers, only cared about his brothers. Used to say,* "Better to hang together, not separately" . . .

His paddle might have hit a sunken tree trunk, or the drum under him had collided with any of the shit now submerged in the river from when a pontoon had gone under in an air strike. Tomas went over. Scrabbled for a grip on the pallet slats. Caught at Cammy and seemed to have a grip on him, except that he shifted his hands for a better hold, and was gone.

Cammy dived after him, but they were moving fast in the current. They were in darkness other than from the drone flares, and the fires behind them. He could not use a torch. It was extraordinary, and ridiculous, but Cammy cannoned into him. Arms reached out, and the raft was nearer to toppling than it was to staying afloat. Tomas did not fight his rescuers, nor struggle, nor cry out. On the far side of the river they should have, immediately on landing, hiked away fast. But they did not. Ulrike started the resuscitation. Doing mouth to mouth and heaving Tomas's chest, and losing. All of them trying, none of them succeeding. Must have worked on him for half an hour, until Ulrike pulled them off, until Dwayne, the eldest, announced the unthinkable: a brother down, a brother lost.

Could not hang about, could not do a fancy job. Scratched a shallow grave, and put the Estonian boy into it. None of them said a prayer but they shared a cigarette by the freshly moved earth. Dogs, scavenging and starving, might have him up by the morning, but none of them said it.

The death by drowning of Tomas was like a knife wound, was the first.

"What do you think you saw?"

"Too much rippling in the wave patterns – could have been debris, like an oil drum, or could have been . . ."

"Could it have been an inflatable?"

"Might have been, cannot say."

On the bridge of the container ship – some 380 metres in length, overall weight slightly north of 100,000 tonnes, sped through the Channel lane of 19 knots, registered in Panama, heading for Rotterdam – was a Norwegian skipper, a navigation pilot who had boarded from a west country harbour in the UK, two Filipino watchmen, and a Croatian engineering officer. All had seen something, none was certain what they had seen.

The pilot said, "They're mad enough, some of them, to try to cross in this weather."

The captain said, "I don't think so, not possible. And if we want peace and quiet, we saw nothing."

The Croat officer said, "Broadcast a suspicion, and we are caught up in an inquest, because assuredly they will drown."

The first to have seen something was one of the Filipino watchmen. He said, softly, and made the sign of the cross on his chest, "It was a dinghy, men and women and children . . . I do not think they have long."

They could not have stopped even had they wished to, and there were more vessels behind them in a steady stream, and away to the port side were the lights of ships traversing the Channel in the other direction. It was the busiest set of sea lanes in the world, and not a place for a small craft even in the best of weather conditions.

A monstrous shape went past them, throwing out a crisp bow wave. The lights, seemingly suspended high above them, did not waver. They could hear the thrash of its engines and the turbulence of the propellers and the impact of its front end on the water ahead. Cammy clung to the outboard's arm.

He had not the knowledge of the sea or of boats to know where he should steer, whether to try to divert away from it, even turn and head back towards the French shore where there were now only occasional pinpricks of light. Closer than the engine noise and the roar of the weather, and the slapping of the bottom of the dinghy each time they came down in a trough, was the sound of frantic screaming. Cammy wondered whether any of them, the teacher and the psychologist and their women and the two children, had entertained the slightest idea of how it would be to take an open boat, under-powered, and try to navigate a path across the Channel, whether any of them had an inkling of an idea what it would be like to have a vast cargo vessel sweep past them, whether any of them would still want – not even halfway across – to commit to a journey towards the new Heaven which was Cammy's country.

The bow wave hit them.

He thought they were traumatised. They clung to each other. Shrieks and sobs, and a woman and one of the kids was sick but they could not lean over the side to vomit or they would have been carried away. The sickness was over their clothing and between their legs and sloshed with the rising level of seawater now covering their feet.

He needed to take control, knew it.

Would have been simple enough if he had been with his brothers, all of them together, and the yells would have been of the black gallows humour vintage, what they cracked when times were bad: if they were in the artillery coordinates, or if the air strikes were coming in, or if they were pinned down by a Yank or Brit sniper. Always good then to have a joke, and chat funeral plans.

The bow wave was brutal and came on them with a thunder and the white cresting line of it slapped against them. They were spinning. A different motion to anything before. Pushed sideways, twisting like a dancer's steps. Going through a total revolution, and then the trough deeper than any before. They held on to each other ... He saw the lights of the back end of the bridge of the container ship, and the foam bristled from the screws. It ploughed on, but there would be another because the dinghy now straddled the traffic lanes going north and east. They had taken on too much water and he had concentrated too hard on progress and not enough on the ability of the dinghy to stay afloat.

He yelled instructions. Should cup their hands, and sweep away the water that threatened to swamp them. His fault for not seeing

before that they must be involved, were not merely his passengers . . . Without them he would not have been able to cross; if he
did not have them shivering and crying and puking around him
then his journey would be wasted. A moment's thought: what if he
went into the sea himself? Forget them . . . What if it were Cameron
Jilkes, once part of a community on a hill and near enough to the
cathedral at Canterbury, what if he went into the water and the
cold had him and the water filled his lungs and the will to fight had
gone, and losing strength . . . and all for fuck all of nothing. He
needed them to bale and fast. They started slowly, and he reckoned more water came in than they were managing to get out, and
they were listless and the struggle seemed too great, and . . .

He sang.

There had been another favourite psalm, not as treasured as the
"snares", but loved and always done with gusto.

Cammy led them. *Cast Me Not Away*. Samuel Sebastian Wesley.
The creation of a man who had died nearly 150 years ago, and the
words had lived in Cammy's mind since they were placed there by
a choirmaster.

*Cast me not away from thy presence, and take not thy holy spirit
from me.*

He sang into the night, confronted the drenching spray, let his
voice rip, could not hear himself against the chaos of sound around
him.

*Restore unto me the joy of thy salvation; and uphold me with thy
free spirit.*

Had exchanged the peace, the aching quiet, of the cathedral
with the battle storm of the Channel, the weather and the surge of
the container ship. They joined him. Little voices at first.

*The sacrifices of God are a broken spirit: a broken and a contrite
heart, O God, thou wilt not despise.*

Bellowed it at the night, and a gull came, a big bastard, its wings
tucked to deflect the wind, and hovered for a moment, then maintained a station above them, and might have wondered what in
Hell's name was below its webbed talons when suddenly it was
lifted away. Their voices had started small but grew. He assumed

that the women had picked up on the first line but by the third they were all with him, were his chorus. Like it was a battle statement . . . like with his brothers, a moment of hugging and of heads together and the shared belief in survival, then all moving . . . machine-gun, and mortars, and Ulrike spotting for them, and the crack of the sniper rifle . . . Cammy had needed no other brothers, but they were all gone, and now he needed these refugees – not fighters, not in love with combat – to be with him.

Make me to hear joy and gladness, that the bones which thou hast broken may rejoice.

They sang together. And the psalm, number 51, was repeated. Shrill voices from the kids, soft from the women and deeper from the men, and when Cammy's own voice died on him they kept singing, and he thought the moon had broken thinly through. They were all baling hard, using their hands and a cap and plastic plates.

He thought the wind eased.

No judgement, only luck, and thought that they had a run between the oncoming ships in the reverse traffic lane. Thought the force of the wind softened though the dinghy shook and rocked and swayed, still rose and pitched, and took them back to *Be thou my guardian and my guide*, and kept them singing, in their innocence.

Thought that he could see, very faint, a haze of light ahead, and if he blinked and wiped his eyes might have noted a coastal light, a navigation buoy. Thought it, but said nothing.

"You have no right to be here. It is harassment, simple harassment."

He liked to be called Wolfboy by his closer friends and associates and by his "brothers", but the man and the woman on his doorstep this morning – not yet five o'clock and hardly any natural light filtering into the street – called him Farouk. Upstairs the baby had started to cry, not his baby.

"I can report you, I can get a lawyer to chase you off. You have no right to do this."

The man and the woman were members, so his "brothers" said, of the Security Service, and they referred to the pair and the organisation behind them as "the Box". The man wore jeans and a T-shirt, trainers loosely knotted, and a leather jacket that was a size too small. She wore a shortish skirt that was at the edge of causing offence to Farouk, and a blouse that was unbuttoned one or two holes too many, and her hair fell lazily over her face: he thought she had probably undone those buttons when she came to his doorstep. The proposition was made each time they came and pressed the bell by the front door that rang out in the house where he lodged.

"I will not do as you ask. You want me as an informer, want me to tout, I will not do that – anyway I do not know anyone who engages in criminal acts. You ask me to help you, be an agent for you, I will not. You offer me money, I don't want your money. It is harassment, pure and simple."

What annoyed him at these encounters, always in the hour before dawn and while the street was quiet, before first prayers, was that they would give the invitation and then would decline to argue with him. He was left to shout at them. Most of that part of the street would now know that the anti-terror people had hooks in him. He worked in an internet café and sometimes helped those with no idea of the intricacies of the web, but also made coffees, served soft drinks, washed up, sold skunk to regulars, and the pay was pitiful and this man and the woman offered him the huge sum of £500 every month to inform. He was three years out of prison, HMP Wealstun, north of his home city of Leeds, and had been on B wing, all Category C prisoners, most of them harmless – but he had witnessed at close quarters what was done to two prisoners who had touted: the shit beaten out of them and their faces cut. He would not inform . . . and almost enjoyed the moment.

"Go on, lose yourselves. You have nothing on me. I'll get the lawyers on you. It is bullying and it is harassment."

He stepped back and into the hallway, and the baby's crying was more pitiful. It was a cousin's house. He stared back at the two, and neither argued or tried to persuade. He thought he had bested them, which pleased him. He shut the door. Through the spy hole he could see that both were still on the pavement, in no hurry, and had lit cigarettes, and talked in murmurs ... He supposed that was all part of the intimidation. They knew nothing. He would not have been allowed to stay in the room of his cousin's home if they had known anything of who he was and what was planned, and which role he had been given ... He went upstairs and saw through the landing window the man and the woman walk away. The baby had stopped crying. He had no baby of his own, no women who could have been the mother of his baby, no fiancée. Had once; but no longer. He did not know whether it was that man and that woman, or others from their organisation, who had been to his fiancée's family home and had bad-mouthed him, had called him a Subject of Interest, had warned them. The relationship was broken, she refused to see him again. He would hurt them, they would suffer.

Farouk, or Wolfboy, went to clean himself up before going to work.

A man was coming. A man who would take delivery of a cargo.

A man would use what was given him, would hurt them hard, and he would have helped ... Hurt them hard enough for them to scream.

Cloud was beginning to spread from the east. The wind had dropped, would die away. Or so the weather forecaster had claimed from the bedside radio. Jonas opened the kitchen door to let the cat out.

Most mornings he slept until the alarm began to beep, but he had been waking early since the matter of returning veterans had been dumped on 3/S/12. He stood on the step in his pyjamas and dressing-gown and on his feet were the slippers Vera had bought him four Christmases before, and the sun rested on his face, threw warmth on his cheeks, as he watched the cat.

It was the sort of start to a day that, if he let his imagination run riot, gave him most concern. Not a cloud in the skies, not yet. The cat patrolled the perimeter of the garden as if it were a Border

Force unit. There was a clear blue sky and those days bothered him. Out of a clear blue sky, unwanted and unheralded, came the "incidents" that were the nightmare of his life. Could not call them "unexpected", but they came without warning and without any preannounced target. It had been uneventful, free of atrocities, for several weeks and he fancied that the public would have lapsed towards complacency and that the warnings continually trumpeted on the London Underground and in railway stations were slipping from consciousness. The cat moved, large and menacing, around the flower beds. It was in the nature of any individual practised in the arts of counter-terrorism to loathe those sunshine-bathed days when the collective guard sagged. He whistled shrilly, competed with a robin's call, and the cat turned and came back to him to be fed.

Almost always playing catch-up in the counter-terror trade, always late and seeking to mitigate disaster, rarely in the driving seat but chasing the moments of chaos and mayhem that came from the clear blue sky. He climbed the stairs. He saw that Vera was awake, and that she had left the duster on the window-ledge and there was no longer a spider on the ceiling which meant that the creature's risk assessment had failed it.

He went to shower and shave, then dress ... Always wore a clean shirt and a sober tie, and always wore his jacket of light-weight tweed and polished shoes, and always took the trouble to clean his spectacles ... He would be off and out, keeping to the schedule that gave him enough time for the train.

He thought of the recruits he had been given. They'd have bitched. Would have been in the building long enough to have known of him, his reputation, and wondered why they were assigned to him for mentoring. Might have wondered aloud, either of them when posted, "What the fuck did I do wrong to deserve this?" Not much, and the thought of it was enough for a short-lived smile. He had asked for a pair who had "not yet been washed by the stereotypical thinking of Thames House", and they were both ignorant enough to have retained an innocence, were not yet acclimatised to the system.

There had been a previous pair, nice youngsters, and they had complained to the AssDepDG, "with respect and all that, but he's hardly modern, still pretty much in the steam age", and the big man had given them a welcoming grin and had invited them to his own partitioned office and had unlocked a drawer in his desk – not gone to the computer screen – and had produced half a dozen blown-up photographs, and their monochrome texture had seemed to enhance their quality: a foyer in a concert hall, where kids had gathered, shattered glass and broken lives, body parts, contorted faces in the last moments before pain and life ended – good photographs for the AssDepDG to keep in his drawer because they were guaranteed to shock. He had said to them, "Prefer this?" Jonas had been told, and he had found them excellent learners, and one was now with the Service out-station in Bristol and the other was in Manchester, and he had been sorry to lose them. He thought the current pair might be good; they had not tricked him but had tested him. He had been found wanting – and was concerned.

He lived off his instinct, would be naked without it. The man, next in line, would come out of the clear blue sky and he did not know where, nor what trace would be left of him, nor when.

Dawn had broken. They were in thick mist. No sunshine and nothing visible ahead of them. What concerned Cammy was behind them.

The Iranians would have heard it too: the sound of the high-powered engine of a coastal patrol vessel. Easy to assume that the vessel tracked them but could not see them except as a blip on a screen; would not have wanted to get close because of the risk of capsizing the dinghy, but the engine noise had kept steady with their slow advance through the slackening waves.

The Iranians had not queried Cammy, had not second-guessed him. More gulls materialised out of the fog around them, shrieking and hovering above the dinghy. They were nearer to land: he had noticed weed that would have been dislodged during the overnight storm. They would have known that the authorities now shadowed them, would remember what the Chechen had told them: welcomed by naval personnel only too anxious to help, given care if needed, provided with a hot breakfast of porridge and scrambled eggs, and taken to a hostel that would have beds and satellite TV and then a fast track through refugee status by emphasising persecution back in their homeland, then a decent flat and job opportunities. The teacher had questioned Cammy as first light had come. Cammy had told him that the promises were rubbish.

One moment they were wrapped in a mist blanket, then they were out of it. Nothing to see, then everything.

A woman in a tracksuit threw a ball for a dog to chase.

A man, wrapped against the wind, ran on the sand.

He could see the beach huts, prettily painted in pastel colours, and could see vehicles speeding on an open road behind them, and saw a pensioner couple, each with a stick.

Cammy said, "You never saw me. I was never with you."

His little group were huddled down. They gawped at him, then looked ahead and would have seen the waves rising and falling and heaving; and the crisp white crests and then the broken, foamy water running helplessly up a dark sand incline, and falling back because the power of the storm was past, and the gales had fled. The younger child, probably near unconscious from the cold and the experience in the sea, squealed. Would have seen the people and the huts, and the road and the cars and, away to the south of the shoreline, the dull height of the cliffs. He could not have done it on his own; had brought them to their promised land; had gained strength from the camaraderie of singing the hymn and the psalm. Like it had been a deal between two parties, and both satisfied with the outcome, and nothing much more to be said, except . . .

"Good luck. Don't look back. I was never with you."

A last glance, and everything in front of him was so normal. He thought that in a moment the patrol boat would emerge from the mist. The runner had stopped. The dog ignored the ball and had begun to bark. The older man hooked his stick on his elbow and took out his mobile phone. The dinghy shook as the teacher and the psychologist and their women and their children waved frantically. Cammy cut the engine. He reckoned the fuel tank must have been just about empty. They would drift the rest, be taken by the waves, but not with him.

A last deep, lung-filling breath. He rolled over the side, went into the water with barely a splash. He went under . . . would have been frightened if he were not a swimmer, terrified if he had not done – years before but not forgotten – the lifeguard training. Under the water and flailing with his feet and making distance . . . If they had looked for him they might have seen a dark shape that became fainter, and might have seen a flick of the top of his head and might have seen an arm break the surface, then disappear beneath the water.

He needed to separate himself from them. No more thoughts of homeland, nor of childhood and his mother and all that had once been familiar. Fleetingly, Cammy saw the land and the beach and where the road petered out beyond the huts. He swallowed and he spat. He could not see the place on the beach where the dinghy would ground but imagined that the runner and the dog walker and the pensioners, and all the others who were on their way to work or were out for early exercise, would have been scrambling down the steps from the esplanade. Imagined it, and thought also that the Iranians would wait until the dinghy was stuck and then would begin to climb out and step down into the slight surf. The men would be first, and then the women, and the kids might push past and jump clear.

His knees grazed a rock protruding from the sand. He kept swimming. It would be fully light soon but for the moment he was helped by the unbroken ceiling of cloud. It was the best that he could have hoped for. He swam parallel to the shore, only in four or five feet of water but that was enough. Suddenly the sand shelved steeply. He used his hands and his knees to propel himself forward. His head was out of the water and he was ringed by the surf rolling back and he pulled his shoulders clear, and his hips, then his legs, and the weight of his sodden clothing dragged him down. He lay on the sand and gasped for breath and seawater ran off him and made a puddle around him. Cammy knew where he was . . . There was a small fishing boat beached high on the sand in front of him and below its hull was a shadowed, sheltered place. He was exhausted, had barely the strength to breathe. He had come home.

"Did you hear that?"

"No. Should I have done?"

Babs and Dominic were constables in the Kent police force, Tactical Firearms Unit.

"You know what it was like last night, a hell of a gale. It's a miracle they got across," she said.

"A foul night. Reckoned our roof might come off," he said.

He stood back. Had his H&K in his hands, routinely ready and finger alongside the trigger guard, armed and with the Safety on, and watched them closely . . . A rum little group barely believable that they had made it across. She had the same weapon, and both also sported Glocks in holsters flapping against their upper thighs, and they had all the gear for Tasering, and sprays and gas and cuffs, and their belts sagged under the weight of it all. They were always called out when migrants made it across and up on to a beach.

"Say they're Christians, that God and a love of Jesus kept them safe."

"I believe anything after seeing what they came in, knowing what they came through. Probably believe that pigs were flying overhead."

"They were singing hymns."

"Had good cause to – a wise shout."

They had come with sirens and blue lights from the station at Dover. A member of the public had called in but there had already been a warning from the Border Force vessel people. They were deployed because there was a fear, a mood shoved out from the Security Service in London, that "returnees" could come back in the cover of a migrant trip, be snuggled up close to Iranians or Syrians or any of the others who'd take to the water in the hope of better things to come. Except, the weather the last night had been horrific and it would have needed serious courage, big time, to attempt to cross. Every time they had been deployed they had been confronted with a little huddle of pitiful wretches, shivering, teeth chattering, and looking as threatening to public order as a flock of cowed sheep.

"What I'm saying – just eavesdropping – there was a guy with them, brought them across. Took on the smuggler clan and saw them off, then took them into the water, saved the life of one of the kids who had a ducking. Then started singing, a hymn and a psalm, and sung over and over like an old record with a scratch on it. They called him an angel, an angel of God."

"Which one is he?"

Dominic was single; late twenties, more pounds on his gut than there should have been. Took too little exercise because for the last seven years he had been a part of a small county force firearms team. Looked at the little group that didn't seem to possess the resolution to "take on" a smuggler group – cruel bastards, what their briefings said, and good at handing out rough stuff – nor the sanctity of that elusive angel.

"That's the problem. Not there. That's what they're saying."

"Meaning?"

Babs, married and with a daughter who would now be heading for school, was six years older, wore her looks well. She shrugged.

"He led the singing, kept them afloat, literally and mentally. Brought them through. They had sight of the beach and he called to them, 'I was never with you'. Went over the side . . . They've gone dumb now, you noticed that? Like he was a no go area and shouldn't have been talked of."

"Shit, bloody hell."

"Went over the side. Ditched them. Can you add that one up?"

"Nine marks out of ten for a cluster-fuck . . . and a half-hour start on us. Be a bad boy, wouldn't he?"

She said he would be a bad boy. Gone into the sea to avoid being picked up. It had started out as pretty routine, now was heading into territory beyond their immediate experience. Left them flattened . . . She went back to the car where she would not be overheard by the crowd that had gathered in a half-circle near the migrants. It would set alarm bells pealing when she reported in.

* * *

He'd had his coffee, eaten his pastry.

Jonas was in the garden behind Thames House, sitting on a bench, and the low sunlight came through the canopies of the trees.

A man worked with a rake and tidied where there was nothing to tidy. He saw him often enough, had never spoken with him, and liked the dedication that brought the fellow to these gardens, unchained the gates, kept them in a state of perfection, fulfilling a duty. He had his barrow, and at his waist were secateurs, and after he had raked he would clear the rubbish bins and painstakingly pick up each cigarette butt thrown on the grass or the paths, and if birds had defecated on the historic gravestones then the faces would be wiped clean. A troubled man; the garden would have been his best home . . . Jonas had heard it said that the man had done service for a Five operation in southern Spain. He seemed humble . . .

Jonas was ready to confront his own day. He went to the side entrance. The police were there, close to the end of their own shift.

One said, "Morning, sir, looks like a lovely day."

The other said, "Let's hope, sir, that's what we're in for, clear blue skies."

And Jonas said as he passed them and their loaded firearms, "Have to hope that – yes – that things don't change. Can but hope."

5

Room 3/S/12 was deserted. Almost every day, Jonas was first in. Not that day. Clear evidence that the team had been and gone.

A mess covered the circular table; some of their screens showed the "save" images: dogs, cats, children, beach scenes. There were coffee beakers, single-use, and the wrappings of sandwiches and pastries were stuffed in the bins. In one corner was a pile of lycra, what the joggers and cyclists wore for the journey to work . . . He did not know where they had gone, what had called them out.

He went behind his own partition, unfastened the handcuff and chain at his wrist, and began to unlock his filing cabinets and his desk computer. Next he would remove the sandwiches from his briefcase, and the flask. No note had been left for him, hardly surprising.

He was permitted to beaver away behind his screen, and had the patronage of the AssDepDG, was safe behind his firewall, and his insights and predictions went on a roundabout cruise along the corridor and up the stairs and landed on the desks of more senior managers – and his patron – and then came back down and were slotted into the workload of the team.

He took off his jacket and arranged it on the hanger; another reflex action was to straighten his tie, then to loosen a reef in his belt to make sitting at his desk more comfortable. Other than for comfort breaks, visits down the corridor and near the emergency stairs, he would not move until the scurried departure out of the building, back along the river and into the station for the journey home.

Not something he had looked forward to, but the first task of the day was to transfer an image from his phone and play it through his printer. The machine spluttered into action. The main working area, and Jonas Merrick's space, were expected to be tidied, the desks cleared and the screens locked down, so that the cleaners could come in overnight. They were all vetted and regarded as truly faithful of the security rigours, and they would take out all the overnight paper debris, along with food rubbish and the usual mountain of squashed tissues and water bottles. Discarded paper would be earmarked for shredders or general disposal. Torn segments of a view of a dark stretch of water, location unknown and unimportant, where debris floated and where the surface was undisturbed, would not have been regarded as a security lapse. The cleaners had removed what he had, dismissively, torn up. The new picture was spat out. A pair of circles had been marked on the picture. He took a magnifying glass from the drawer of his desk and used it to scrutinise the two areas of water within the circles; good enough to see the nostril cavity and the brightness of the eye. From the top drawer he found his Sellotape. He stretched up, fastened the picture to the wall.

Dominating his thoughts were not the picture of the crocodile's head and shoulders, not the one that showed the uneven rows of teeth, but the two circles and the signs that he had not recognised.

The quiet built around him. Usually, even if Room 12 on the third floor, on the south side of Thames House, was empty except for him, he would hear the comings and goings in the corridor outside and doors slamming and voices, greetings and laughter – talk of "fucking traffic", of babies shrieking all night, of a restaurant that had been a "total bloody rip-off", and "absolutely off-side, referee a complete wanker", and he heard nothing. Nothing until . . . the sound of footsteps with iron tips at the toes and heels.

The outer door opened. "You about, Jonas?"

"I am."

His protector: the man who provided Jonas Merrick with what was known in the Russian mafia as the "roof", the power in the land that kept him safe. "A bit of a shambles in the night."

"Affecting me? I don't think so or I would have been notified."

"Not affecting you as long as we are not bidding on your behalf at auction."

"All quiet on my front. Nothing that disturbs me except for that. *Nothing* . . . 'nothing' that I know of."

"A bad time, Jonas."

"With respect, a bad time for the last two years. A thumb over the dyke crack."

"I suppose it's what we might call a Churchill moment."

"The Battle of Britain. Churchill asks, 'What reserves do we have?' And the fight in the skies is at a desperate stage, and they are coming in waves, and Keith Park answers, 'There are none.' Is that where we are?"

Jonas had learned in the last three years that the man he knew as AssDepDG had been baptised with the name of Huw Denys, knew that he was state educated, had worked in pretty much every section of the Service, would not rise higher and entertained a lack of correctness . . . his like would not be seen again. Wanted to have the sole of a boot on the throats of the returnees, gave not a damn – however harmless they now might be – for the one-time fighters languishing in Syrian, Iraqi or Kurdish gaols. Talked up Jonas's corner in meetings with the Thames House hierarchy. Was an ally but would also, with ruthlessness, keep Jonas tethered to the treadmill.

"With brass knockers on it, you could say . . . Had to rout this team from out of the pub last night. No clean knickers and no clean socks, unless they had them here, no time to go home, and we've parcelled them off to meet a courier run. Fully involved in North-East, North-West, West Midlands, and South-West is covering from Bristol almost up to Thames Valley. The onus on our surveillance teams, Jonas, length and breadth of the country, is at breaking-point, unsustainable . . . The courier is sailing tonight from Zeebrugge and will dock at Hull. Believe it is a decisive weapon. Don't know about a hand-over point, or a target. Big cock-up because North-East were tasked with it, but they made a case for the full works on a Leeds boy. We are shuffling round the board, Jonas – but not your problem."

"Glad to hear it," he said without warmth. Was regarded as a "miserable old sod" and did little to prove the title wrong.

"Just thought you should know – just thought you should know not to bid at auction, if you know what I mean."

Conversation over, footsteps echoing away. Jonas buried himself in the almost private world of his card index archive and searched for new snippets of information on buoyant *jihadi* fighters gone, fate unknown as the war turned brutally against them, all of them potential returnees if they had survived, and the tantalising scraps offered up by the interrogators doing their business in the holding cages. Flitted between the identities of the fighters he rated as dangerous.

He knew that section of beach because he had been there with his mother and with his elder brother and his sister.

It ran west from the town of Deal. Where he sheltered, the sand had been replaced by an orange carpet of shingle. The boat had been pulled up, high enough to be clear of the surf. He shivered, could not control it. Down the coast was the ferry port of Dover. It would have been twelve years since he had last been on the beach here, and his mum would have taken a day off work, the sun had been shining, and he remembered that she had persuaded his half-brother to come, aged 22 then, and had sat against the low wall at the back of the shingle and had worked his way through a six-pack and had smoked half a packet of fags. And his half-sister had been there and had spent most of the afternoon whining about being bored, alternating the complaints with working on her fingernails. Cammy had stayed on the beach, had hardly spoken, had gazed out on the infinity of the water, and had dreamed of crossing it.

His mum had been burned twice with her failed relationships, had been looking for love after the first guy disappeared, and the second guy had given her what they called in those days "a bun in the oven", and must have raided one of his bank accounts to leave a grand in notes in an envelope. Big crises had never come at convenient times in Cammy's life . . . his GCSE exams had been due to start the next day when the police had called round. His half-sister was dead. She had been part of a TWOC gang – Taking Without Consent – a high-performance Impreza this time, and her chum, the driver, had lost control and the signs were that he'd done so because she'd had her hand inside his flies as he'd come into a hairpin. Had not greatly affected Cammy and his marks had been tolerable. Had done averagely well when the next round of exams had pitched up two years later and they were supposed to determine whether he was "blue collar and crumpled or white collar and starched", and his mum had been in the Crown Court to see his half-brother go down for fourteen years: conspiracy to supply and a bit of choice enforcement. He didn't really miss either of them, but his mum did . . . He'd hung around the village and the estate and the cathedral city for another three years and then had taken the flight that would have climbed away from this beach, this coast, and across the Channel behind him.

Through the haze he could see the group of people several hundred yards away, but the view of them was partly blocked by several more grounded fishing boats.

The weather conditions helped Cammy now. The mist behind him, the brief spell of sunshine had gone and low cloud had drifted in. He was regaining his strength, and could shrug away the sodden cold of his clothes . . . Took him back to the days when they had lain all night in the slight sand scrapes and the rain had come on and the only priority was to keep their weapons dry. Always good to attack when the weather was at its lousiest, when the sentries huddled behind sandbags, when the air strikes were postponed and the pilots would have been comfortable and dry in their Mess building. Made a habit of going forward when no sane beggar wanted to put his nose outside, and the first they'd have known that the assault was coming in would have been the mortars that Tomas launched, three in the air and then shifting, and Pieter shooting with extraordinary accuracy with the sniper rifle, and Stan ducking and weaving and running and putting down suppressive fire. Cammy in with them and the rainwater streaming off his face and hard to keep it out of his eyes and carrying the big machine-gun, Ulrike following him, swathed in belt ammunition, and getting forward far enough to be able to blitz the bastards when they broke and ran; what the manuals called "enfilade fire". Go in fast, and when least expected, and never hesitate until the stop line was reached, and they'd gather and laugh and be panting and swapping tales of how it had been. The adrenaline going into overdrive . . . Times when they had made progress although the weather had been fair, and then it was because their *emir*, Ruhan, had begged, borrowed, demanded, that he be given a "martyr"; better still if he were allocated a martyr who could drive an armour-plated vehicle. Sometimes the kid would have his own press button to send him to Paradise, but most times the martyr had a minder who stayed back, having checked the electronics, said some kind words, and would send the signal when the kid might have panicked and not done the business. They did not talk about the martyrs, kept away from the kids who had the glazed look of the walking dead, and who muttered their invocations of words from the Book. He and his brothers were survivors, believed themselves to be indestructible.

Had allowed himself a few minutes of dream time, which was good because it refuelled his anger.

He wriggled ahead, kept his head and shoulders down, tried to keep his backside low. The orange pebbles crunched as he crossed them and he must have left a trail behind him, and there was a spit of rain in the air. He could see down the beach and towards the castle and the town of Deal but he could no longer make out the blue lights of police or Border people or ambulances. He was under a low wall. Could not see over it and used it as cover, and waited, and listened, and waited . . .

He felt warm breath close to his face, then a tongue slurped across his cheeks. The breath was foul and the tongue was noisy as it cleaned his face of sand. He thought it a spaniel, or a spaniel cross. It seemed satisfied with what it had found, and its breath came faster, and it had cleaned both cheeks and now started on his throat. Cammy had waited and listened and had heard no vehicle approaching. He pushed himself up and his knees took his weight.

A woman sat on a bench. She held an expander lead. She reeled the dog in and gave it a treat from her pocket. She studied him, and he gazed back at her. He thought her middle or late 70s, well wrapped against the chill of the early morning, wearing a long coat that showed only her ankles and the collar was turned up. A fleece hat was tugged down over her head, protecting her ears. He thought that while she studied him she would be considering what to do, and the dog wagged a docked tail. She could pull a mobile out of her pocket and do a treble hit on the 9 button, or she could stand and wave her arms and shout and point to him, or she could run as fast as her legs would carry her, and head back towards the police.

Somewhere in the background of Cammy's life, but curtained off, there must have been a grandmother, his mum's mother, but the rift had come when his mum had gotten pregnant with him: never mentioned, never heard from not even on birthdays or at Christmas. He thought of why he had returned to his homeland, and the target he had there, and of the efforts of many to organise the putting of the weapon in his hands, and of those committed to getting him to within sight of his goal. Thought of what the uniformed men and women in that complex of buildings had done to him and his brothers. Would an old woman with a spaniel be permitted to stand in front of him, block him, undermine the whole effort? Would he hit her? Would he disable her, silence her? Thought of it . . . She stood.

Not much to her. A frail little thing, a sparrow of a woman. A slap from him would have felled her.

She took off her coat, and told him what he should do. He crouched on the shingle, beneath the wall, and he squirmed clear of his socks and shoes, and his trousers, then his coat, his anorak and his shirt and T-shirt, down to his underpants. He gathered them up, except for the footwear, and the wind chilled him and rain flecked his skin. He passed her the pile of clothes, pushed his feet into his wet shoes and put on her coat; it was tight, and barely met at the waist and chest, and the wind lifted the hem. She said what she would do with the clothes, and where he should go in the town and which charity shop had the best to offer. She had the bundle under her arm, and the dog at her feet and he fancied she would hurry now that she was without her coat.

"You've come from the sea – good luck to you. Don't hand yourself in. They'll send you back. You'll not find hostility here, not among Deal folk. Keep walking, don't stop, keep going – and God go with you."

She was, it was claimed, the best informed person in Thames House. She was Lily, and had been, it was said, a useful netball player until a fractured fibula had cut short that sporting career. She was blessed with sufficient common sense on which to float a battleship . . . All the untidy strands came across her desk in the big basement area adjacent to the Archive, and all the little scraps of information, so easily ignored, that might otherwise have had no home. She was adept in finding the right place for apparently orphan information: police, customs, military, and the observations of the general public. The equation between yet another migrant landing on the Kent coast, routine now for the local force and the Border people, and the strange submission from those who had survived an horrendous night crossing. Something of a miracle this one; had spoken of a man who had ushered them across and then had gone overboard and swum away – and then they had clammed . . . Confusing, and probably criminal, and she had in her mind a berth for it in Jonas Merrick, up on the third floor, south facing, in Room 12. The information had been passed on by Kent police from their Dover station and it was stressed that the source had only just returned from the call-out, and their information was sketchy and not yet filtered. She had the names of two officers. Jonas Merrick did fighters coming back from the war. She could not for the life of her comprehend why any "ordinary, decent criminal" would hazard liberty and life by going into the water in a dinghy and crossing 28 miles of congested Channel, and in a storm reported to be of "biblical intensity". Lily could not think of anywhere else to send it, so the report – vague, inconclusive – went to 3/S/12. No acknowledgement, never was. No gratitude, not expected, but she reckoned that if anyone could find a home for what she had sent upstairs, it was him.

She put out the rubbish, clattering the bin out to the front of her house.

Sadie saw the Hunters queuing up for Trace to lock the front door and drive them down the hill. They waved, she waved back. She could not hear them but imagined what they might say. "Poor woman, what a burden she carries." "A really decent human being, and look what's been served up to her.' And might be something patronising: "Holds herself with such dignity, such courage in adversity." And a bit that reeked of complacency. "We do everything we can, can't do more, everything that we ought to do, nothing to blame ourselves for." She was dog-tired. Up in the small hours for a first shift of cleaning, then a bit of the day, and then out again as the evening started and more cleaning, and she was relied upon and her praises were sung by those who employed her. Of course, it was acknowledged that she carried a bloody heavy cross. Sympathy was given her, bucket loads of it. She had one son in High Security, had a daughter in the graveyard at the back of the house, and another son who had disappeared, left no trace, and who was a "person of interest" to the counter-terror people. Lucky to have any jobs at all . . . The Hunters' car drove off. She went to her door, stepped inside. She had the house because Cameron's father, as a peace offering, had left her a brown envelope which was stuffed with fivers, and that had been good enough as a deposit, but it was a lousy house and marked down in price because of the new-build subsidence crack all down the back of it. The mortgage would have been a struggle but her elder boy had known people who could shift money, launder and rinse it, and would have done a good deal and had something spare, and paid off a good chunk of what she owed. She'd make some toast, and probably peel an apple.

And would have the same the next day which was her usual feast on her birthday. She'd have a card from the gaol. Always a pretty one, always the only one.

She ate the toast, could not be bothered to peel an apple. Made a cup of tea with yesterday's teabag. If she sat down and wept then the likelihood was that she'd go into the trees at the back and sling a rope over a branch and find something to stand on and . . . She often took the wastebins' newspapers, and the colour supplements, and brought them home: would never sit down and let the tears come. She kept a shrine to Cameron, the room he had taken over when his half-sister had been killed, mangled and unrecognisable in the crash. Drank the tea and climbed the stairs.

The room was never opened. Was as the counter-terror police had left it.

They had come in, mob-handed. Cold and polite, but with an air of contempt for her, like she was responsible. Behaved correctly until they had reached Cameron's room. Had torn it apart . . . She had sat on the stairs and the front door had been open and she had seen the net curtains flicking across the street, and had noted that the dog-walkers and the buggy-pushers averted their eyes and kept on the move, but would have seen – and would have heard.

Shelves down, cupboards and drawers dismantled, carpet ripped up off its tacks and the floorboards screaming as they were lifted, bed stripped and the mattress slashed open. Some broken glass, might have been the picture frames, and china fragments because they had cracked open a piggy bank. Sadie had not uttered a word that day, did not cry now. Probably they would have been in better humour if they had found some black flag propaganda leaflets or posters, or a heap of books on revolutionary warfare. Nothing there to soften the blow of a failed search, had even slit open the little beggar's bear which had been with him for nearly 20 years and had been hidden away at the back of a wardrobe shelf, had spilled out its guts. They had left shamefaced. A heavy footfall coming down the stairs and she'd not shifted her backside, not an inch, had made them step around her. They had driven away, she had gone up and had looked into his room. Had gazed at the chaos, had been knifed by the humiliation. Damaged furniture, scattered clothes, dumped pictures of a fresh-faced chorister. Had closed the door. Would have locked it if there had been a key. Had closed it and had never opened it again. A sort of sealed shrine. The way it would stay and the anger at what Cameron had inflicted on her would never leave, her promise.

She went into her bedroom. Had a photograph there of her elder son who always wrote cheerfully from his cell block, claimed he was doing well. Had another photograph – of her daughter, and went once a week to talk to her. Had no picture of Cameron.

She lay on the bed, closed her eyes, but did not sleep.

"It's out of a clear blue sky, figuratively that is . . ."

Tristram and Izzy stood at the entrance to Jonas Merrick's work area. Listened. Both would have tried to disguise their inability to fathom the logic of his remark.

"That's the way things are, where they always come from – the juicy ones and the frightening ones – out of a clear blue sky."

Tristram said, "Understood."

Izzy said, "Least expected."

"It comes from a clear blue sky."

On his screen Jonas had the message from Lily, sent up from the bowels of the building. "A clear blue sky is the time when our guard is lowered. Cannot help it, fact of life. It is when our alertness is dulled, and suspicions . . . There was a ferocious storm last night, even rattled the roof-tiles in Raynes Park, but out at sea, in the open Channel, it would have been horrendous. Imagine an open dinghy, a pump-up job, and it has seven passengers on it and it's coming through fierce waves and swell and also crossing the twin shipping lanes. Precautions to intercept migrants are at base-level on the French side, and on ours. Anyone who goes into the water in those circumstances has a pressing reason to get here. When it is close to the beach at Deal, the weather alters and the storm drops and a patrol boat is launched. In these calmer conditions its radar picks up the dinghy. End of story? Not quite. At first light there is a sea mist and the patrol cutter cannot make a positive sighting, has to rely on the electronics. The dinghy runs aground. Local people help ashore six Iranian nationals, and they say they are Christians. Likely to plead persecution and stand a good chance of some sort of permission to stay. Straightforward. End of story. Too easy. They said a man was with them – described him as an 'angel'."

Jonas Merrick's voice was staccato, matter of fact. He never used theatre to emphasise bullet points, his tone did not vary. Nor did he look at them.

"They say without him they would not have crossed. Without him they would have drowned. At the darkest moments, when they might have been swamped, capsized, no life-jackets, he led them in the singing of hymns. They are Christians, know their *Ancient and Modern*. As he did. He brings them within a hundred yards of the shore, then goes overboard. Swims away from them. They are the centre of attention: willing helpers, Border people, armed police, ambulances, the whole circus, and no sight or sound of him ... Chose the worst conditions to attempt the crossing. Would have gauged our door was flapping open. That is 'out of a clear blue sky'. I hope you understand."

Both of them had noted that a new print had been taken of the dark still water in Africa or northern Australia. Both were able to identify the nostril and the beaded eye inside the pair of circles. He told them about a policeman and a policewoman from the firearms unit. About explanations that had been picked up when the Iranians were still chilled and in shock, and gabbling thanks to their God and to the "angel" sent to help them. He had a name and identification number, scribbled it, passed it to Izzy.

"What do we need to do, Jonas?" he asked.

"Dig, find me detail – anything, everything, and ..."

"What's the chance that he is a criminal, a druggie – a fugitive?" she asked.

"Just do it, just get on with it, just find me detail. Go on, hurry up."

The audience terminated, they left his work area. The emptiness of the room echoed.

Tristram said, "Proper narky today, the old boy."

Izzy said, "Because he's frightened."

*   *   *

Jonas heard her verdict. Thought it a fair assessment.

He had his filing cabinet open, was hauling out the cards. He had the list in front of him, all those who had gone on to become fighters; none of the names could be accused of cowering in cellars, all were soldiers of the caliphate. Around a hundred names now. His fingers moved over the cards with the blurring pace of a teller counting bank notes in former times. He had each card in view for the time needed to check the name: enough for him. The library of fighters who had gone away and who were – so far – unaccounted for was fixed in his memory.

What to go on, how to move forward? No description, no accent, only two factors to work on.

A leader, a man who inspired confidence, who stood at the front and did not back off. Could take a dinghy into a storm and had shown the amount of courage required by an extended Iranian family to follow, and who had brought them through. A different courage to that shown by Jonas when he sat beside Winston Gunn who wore an explosives vest which was later reported by the ordnance people to have had a killing zone of 50 metres diameter; he had been unprepared and what he did was impromptu, unrehearsed.

A singer, sufficiently familiar with formal church-based christianity that he knew the words and cadences of hymns and psalms, an area far outside the competence of Jonas Merrick who went to church only for funerals, and had been married in a registry office. And along with the Sunday morning and evensong training was the courage that was intensified by having time to consider the odds that were faced.

A formidable man. A serious man. A man of exceptional danger . . . and a man who had alighted on Jonas Merrick's desk. He was justified in being "narky", and would have been an idiot not to have been "frightened". Outside his window, the storm was already history, clear blue skies had fled, and a dreary day had descended on the Thames and light rain fell.

He looked for a match, anything that would begin the process of identification.

*   *   *

The wind was tangling Cammy's hair, and whipped of his bare legs, revealing the scrapes and the scars and the places where the big blood-sucking flies had bitten and left discoloured spots. There was a scar by his right knee where Ulrike had put in five stitches after probing around for shrapnel.

First he had gone behind the beach huts, had found a path where the autumn's leaves still swirled, then walked down a residential street, where most of the people who lived there would have still been in bed or pottering around in dressing-gowns making the first cup of tea of the day. Past the castle with the old cannon in revetments on the walls and a sign stating that it was closed for the winter. He thought it a God-forsaken place . . . thought Deal held nothing for him. Wanted to get moving. He was able to manage a lurching run, and started to get blood into his legs and wind into his lungs. The town had more charity shops than he'd remembered. With the wind came the rain, which was useful. Kept the pavements near deserted. He stepped aside for a couple of Zimmer frame punters, and avoided a girl pushing a buggy. The only guy who looked at him was opening up a gallery, wearing a jacket and tie. No one else whom he passed seemed surprised that he wore a woman's coat, not long enough to cover his knees and not much more than a cover for what old people would have called his modesty.

He came to the charity shop that the coat's owner had named for him, down at the far end of the main street in Deal and opposite a fine church, now closed to religious worship. He hustled the coat closer to him, and sagged down in the doorway. In the gloom he could see racks of clothing, mostly women's, and a couple of bookcases filled with paperbacks, and tables loaded with bric-à-brac. He owned nothing except for his trainers, his underpants, his wrist-watch which had been taken from a dead Syrian officer and was good quality, and his empty wallet . . . He would hitch to Canterbury, and his mum would give him cash for the journey to his target. Nobody moved him on, nobody challenged him, but a couple of dogs sniffed at him before being yanked away on their leashes, and a child walking reluctantly with a hurrying, smoking mother made a face at him. His stomach growled, but his mum would feed him when he reached home. His mum did great food and he could remember each of the favourites she served up for him, and he'd recall those tastes every time he had eaten the dry hard bread that was available to them in the field, or what they called lamb but was goat. Ulrike had cooked well but would only do it if there was a birthday, or a victory, and if a small store had been liberated and she could sweep up an armful of spices ... A police car went by but the driver did not even glance at him, and ... Two women arrived.

It was two hours since he had crawled ashore, and might have been a full hour since he had had his face washed by the dog and been given the coat, and had undressed under the esplanade wall. One of them unlocked the door. Both stepped around him, and went through to the back of the shop and the lights were switched on.

He heard one say, "Maude said he was a fine young fellow, but he never spoke to her, not a word. There was a landing this morning ..."

The other said, "Was on Facebook, they were Iranians, came through that storm – God, lucky to be alive – and he must have come with them ... but they said he swam away."

"Don't know what language he'll have. What do you think?"

"Wouldn't know ... Syrian, Egyptian, or another Iranian. Not a clue."

"Well, Maude will want her coat back – and he'll need some clothes, and we'll not turn him away. Makes me shudder just thinking where he'll have been and what he must have gone through. Anyway, time to get the show on the road ..." She spoke to him slowly, loudly and accented each syllable, like he was an idiot, but she was not threatening. She was a tall woman, had green streaks in her hair and wore a floppy necklace of large stones, a tight sweater and a modest skirt, and smiled. "Come on in, friend. Let's be having you."

The other was younger, and Cammy noticed the rings near blocking her right nostril. "Don't be worrying, friend. That's what you are, a 'friend', and we don't hold with chasing people like you away. In you come."

Cammy did not have to answer. He shrugged out of the coat. He stood naked except for his trainers, and his underpants that sagged wet on his hips.

One said, "Not a bad start to a morning, but rain forecast. Quite dishy."

The other said, "And look at his body! All those scars and stitches . . . Excuse me, bloody hell, is that a bullet hole?"

"Not anything else I can think of, pet. In and out, and going through flesh, that's real luck. A charmed boy . . . What do you reckon?"

He was beckoned, came forward. He set his eyes to hangdog, pretended that he understood nothing, was a harmless fugitive.

The other said, "I'd guess about the size of the stuff that widow from Walmer brought in last week."

A towel was tossed him. The one with the streaks in her hair made a gesture for him to drop his pants, and to kick off his shoes. They seemed intrigued by his wounds, not by the rest of him . . . The brothers used to see Ulrike in stages of undress, and the boys would not necessarily cover up because of her. He did as he was told and then started to towel himself, did it hard to get the blood flowing. One of them, as an afterthought, went back to the door and lowered the blind and left the sign on Closed. They started to rummage for socks, shoes, underpants, a T-shirt, and a shirt. He started to dress. The shirt was held in front of him, like he was a mannequin.

One said. "A good jacket came in at that time. Sort of tweed. A forty chest be all right?"

"Perfect."

"What would you say for trousers?"

"I'd say a thirty-two waist and a thirty-one inside leg. Have we got that?"

A giggle. "Shall we give him tae tie?"

A chuckle. "Why not?"

He dressed. Hardly a surprise to be kitted out in the clothes of a pensioner: a checked shirt and a jacket with a fleck in it, a sober tie and brogues. He ate a cheese and lettuce sandwich, and had a swig of coffee from a flask, and was given an anorak. They laughed a bit, shy now. Perhaps they feared they patronised him. He wanted to show his appreciation, but did not speak. An extra pair of socks was stuffed in his jacket pocket, and a small bar of soap, and a little plastic razor.

One said, "We're not all bigots and racists here. Get to London and try to find some of your own people there. Don't think he understands a word of what I'm saying."

The other said, "Like to think we're all God's children. You are very welcome."

Cammy ducked his head, hoped they interpreted it as a gesture of appreciation; the street door was opened for him, and he left them using their toes to manoeuvre his underpants towards a waste-paper bin where his trainers had already been dumped. He went out on to the street, shrugged into the anorak and lifted the hood so that much of his face was covered. He knew the route he would take. He walked back up the High Street. They would return the lady's coat. They would talk about their pleasure in performing a basic act of kindness. It would have happened in any small Syrian community where hospitality was an obligation and a welcome always given. It did not fit with his view of his home city up the Dover road. Kindness and generosity had twice been shown him. Not that it would deflect him when he reached his target. Then there would be no kindness, no generosity.

"So, that was the Five lot." Dominic, in their rest room, grimaced.

"Coming up in the world, I'd say," Babs pouted.

The phone was back in his cradle. It had taken fifteen minutes to route the call from London through a secure system, and the area of sofas and easy chairs, with a coffee machine, had been abruptly cleared of every other constable, male or female, who might have been enjoying a few minutes' relaxation. They had been turfed out, and the room given up to Dominic and Babs, their gear still festooned over their uniforms – guns and gas, cuffs and Tasers, spare ammunition, all of it. But had assumed that their initial report, gone into the system, would take a day, maybe a week, to be noticed. No names given, but a man and a woman had shared the grilling down the phone line.

"I don't reckon we over-egged it . . ." Dominic showing apprehension, like they had played their cards too big. "Said it as we saw it, heard it."

"Nothing wrong with what you said, what I said. Swear by it."

A shrug from Babs but pronounced enough to rattle the gear suspended from her shoulders. It was standard procedure for a firearms pair to attend each landing by migrants making it ashore either side of the port city of Dover. Had seemed ridiculous, a waste of time and effort and resources, when confronted with a little huddle of wet, shivering, cringing, people who seemed to think they had made it to some sort of Promised Land. All the firearms units said they felt embarrassed, awkward anyway, to have weapons bouncing on their chests when they tried to help the Border Force unit, or an ambulance crew, and the people who had come off the sea were scared of them and cowering . . . They had come into the rest room and had not yet hooked their boots up on the coffee tables when they had been alerted to the call from London. As if they were both chastened. They had heard from folk on the esplanade that the dinghy had materialised out of a sea mist and then made its final drift to the beach. The Border Force cutter, they'd been told, had never had a visual sighting of the craft, only a radar link had identified it. Must have been the moments before the mist had thinned that the joker had rolled over the side and gone into the water, and would have had to swim hard to get clear of the cluster of well-wishers and supporters and uniforms gathering around the family. Would have gone ashore perhaps 200 yards, or more, further up the shingle, then legged it. They had been up there, had cruised in the car, had not seen a fugitive, then had done their report – had repeated into the phone everything they could remember, done it between them.

It was a sobering moment. The odds were that neither Dominic nor Babs would ever fire a weapon – other than perhaps an incapacitating Taser – in a situation where the intention was to inflict a fatal wound. They were taught that a "disabling shot" was never acceptable, they would fire only to kill – had never done so, nor had any of the other officers who drove the armed response vehicles in that sector of the county. The likelihood was that Dominic and Babs would never be confronted with a situation where the Safety was off, the red laser beam settled on the target, and a finger tightening inside the trigger guard: that was what they had been trained for.

A man who had taken that degree of risk, gone into the sea to avoid being snared in the official net, would have had a powerful reason to avoid them. Would have been a serious player. Would have been a man representing the reason why they were sent on each call out for a migrant landing. Might have been the sort of man that in changed circumstances they would have been required to "take down", might have been the moment which the endless, repetitive training predicted. Did not know how they would be, either of them, if called upon to kill a guy posing a supreme threat, whether they would take it in their stride, whether they would crumble, whether if either of them fired they would then find the urge for "high fives" irresistible.

He had been out on the London road, going south and west from Deal, and had reached a tree that gave some shelter from the increasingly persistent rain. Already his trousers were soaked at the ankles, and his hair would once more have been plastered down. A van had stopped for him.

Where was he going? Canterbury.

Why was he not on a train or a bus? Had been out the previous evening, had been in a bar in Deal, pocket picked, no money and no cards.

What was in Canterbury? His mum was in Canterbury. Was coming back to see her having been "away". The van had the wipers going and the central display showed sharp short showers for the rest of the day, and after the forecast a local radio programme had resumed with saccharine tributes to birthdays – and gave the date. The date was the trigger. He told the van driver that the next day was his mum's birthday. Seemed to give him some credence.

Where had he been? Down on the Mediterranean (which would account for his weathered face). Needed to talk, but only to answer questions. Not being evasive and creating suspicion, but more as someone who was shy. Had worked in bars in the south of France and in Italy at the Adriatic coast resorts. He would have said that it was wise to beware of chatting with strangers; a man could easily be taken into a string of lies that would then trip him. He said the minimum.

The surprise was that the van driver seemed another stranger showing goodwill and generosity. He was not going to Canterbury but would do a short detour – "Not a problem, mate, no problem at all" – then would drop him on the A257, around Shatterling or Durlock, and he'd get a bus from there into Canterbury. The van driver must have felt good that day – like a bond had come up, or a promise was going to be honoured – and had wriggled in his seat and brought a five pound note out of his hip pocket and had palmed it to Cammy – "Think nothing of it, mate, can lose that on expenses and not even be trying". He had come from a world where death came casually and frequently, where suspicion was rampant, where strangers were questioned, interrogated ... He had been dropped off at a bus shelter. A bus had come along in half an hour and his stomach groaned again in hunger, but he had eaten that morning in the charity shop, and going without food or drink, for a day and a night, was not remarkable.

The bus was almost empty; he did not have to talk. He had used most of the £5 on his fare. The cathedral tower was in the distance as they skirted the housing estates on the edge of the city.

He would see his mum, then would move on. He would be in the city in a few hours, had a schedule worked out in his mind, then would move on. He stepped off the bus and kept his head down. It was his own ground, his own territory.

*   *   *

Jonas fidgeted, rapped a pencil on his work surface, was annoyed with himself for displaying his stress.

Tristram said, "They're just two coppers – ordinary, conscientious plods – and this is their valued judgement."

Izzy said, "They were there within a few minutes, no one else had done much of a debrief before they pitched up. The boat people are Iranian and Christian, two adult males, two females and two children – don't have the family alignment yet. They were in Bordeaux, in a café, and a guy who was sheltering there and had no money was going to be slung out by the manager. The family felt some sympathy and it was a deal of convenience. The guy 'borrows' a vehicle, drives them to Dunkirk. They had a smuggler contact there."

"Had a price agreed, complete rip-off. There was a powerful wind over there last evening. Only an idiot would take to the water."

"The guy takes over negotiation, will pay one tenth of the price. Does some 'persuading' on the goons, a weapon at the top goon's throat, and they take the dinghy, an inflatable, and launch."

As he listened, Jonas Merrick played games in his mind: worked up a profile of a man who would go to sea in those conditions, would ally himself to a helpless gaggle of unfortunates who could offer him nothing other than a way of crossing the Channel in secrecy.

Tristram said, "The Iranians called him an angel. He went into the water – mid-channel – when a kid was washed overboard. He brought the kid back . . . If this had happened off the coast here on a Bank Holiday Monday then people would be talking about medals. They're sick, all heaving their guts up."

Izzy said, "Vomiting everywhere, and baling for their lives, and terrified, and they're hit by the bow wave of a monster container ship and they're damn near dodging other craft. He starts to sing."

A frown settled on Jonas's forehead. Slight, but pursued by a twitch of his eyebrows – as if greater concentration was being brought to bear on what they said. He stared into the middle distance and his eyes took in the crocodile's head and the smooth waters of a lagoon. He was hearing little that was new and had not figured in the report directed to him by Lily down in the bowels of the building; he needed flesh on bones, meat on them.

"They all join in. Hymns. In English."

Tristram said, "So, the plods wanted to know who he was – what he called himself and everything they knew about him."

Izzy said, "Who is this guy belting out *Ancient and Modern* into the elements? They seemed to realise they'd spilled too much, had nothing more out of them."

"Like a tap turned off. Like they protected him. Couldn't get another syllable out of them . . . The 'angel' stayed anonymous."

He told them to go down there. Immediately. Felt a cold on his neck and did not know whether he would be lucky, every time lucky. Snapped at them to go, go fast.

6

He spoke to himself, and to the crocodile pinned to the wall. Quietly but not in as measured a tone as he would have wished.

"Not a quitter. Not if he went through that storm."

He glanced down occasionally but not from necessity. He knew the names on the list, and was familiar with their backgrounds and motivations. All of them represented a high degree of risk.

"If he were a quitter he would have taken a look at that storm, turned over in his sleeping-bag and closed his eyes. Waited for another day, or night."

There were three cards that he kept flicking back to, where his eyes would linger momentarily then go back to the beast with the scaled skin and the awkward and uneven teeth.

"He's not coming back because he's missing home, because they don't serve cod and chips in any café along the Euphrates. He's coming back to hit and to hurt."

Jonas usually liked it least when the work space beyond his partition walls buzzed with voices and the squealing of chairs being shunted around, and the odd claps of laughter or peals of humour, and liked it even less when voices were raised in dispute: then, he would permit a slow snarl to drag across his face and he would believe they were beneath his attention ... Not that morning, quiet bounced off his walls.

"He comes back to hit and to hurt. It dominates him, consumes him. No other explanation. Forget anything about him softening, wanting to put it all behind him ... He's spent years out there in rough combat, he's a changed man."

But that day Jonas would have liked to have heard the bustle of the team's voices. Would have killed to have felt that he was not alone ... Of the three cards that he examined there were two that had a few of the necessary markers, and one that stood out. He detested the idea of "rucksack preconceptions", and when he had youngsters under his tutelage he would rail against the idea of a closed mind, fitting facts to the outlines of prejudice and the distortions that came from blinkered thinking. He would continue to stamp on a conclusion, give it every opportunity to wriggle away, and when it was almost crushed – as would have been any living creature that was unfortunate enough to find itself between the jaws of that brute pictured on his wall – then he might accept that the idea held substance. He needed certainty.

"Nothing soft about him. Enveloped in anger. Never going to say, 'Sorry and all that, seemed a good idea at the time. Want to settle down now, have a second chance, drive a delivery van, rear some kids, put it all behind me. Oh, the killing? Someone else did that, I was just a bottle-washer.' Not that sort of man."

There was a youth, second-year computer studies at Westminster University, had done time in Pentonville for credit card fraud and inside had played in a rock band which was thought by the authorities to be helpful and likely to wean him from potential radicalisation. Wrong: he had taken the black flag shilling, and had travelled to Syria ... Another had worked in an uncle's record store in Wolverhampton, and was known for his knowledge of vinyl and had an interest in guitar playing until an *imam* had snared him, and he had gone and there were reports that he had died in an air strike but not confirmed. And there was another ... the card that he most often went back to, and ... The silence was broken by the iron-tipped shoes rattling down the corridor, hesitating momentarily by the door, and the squeak as it opened and closed. The AssDepDG was at his entrance. Jonas did not turn to face his visitor but addressed the wall, the beast.

"Not there yet. But confident that we are close to an identification. Will it come soon enough? Don't know ... If I'm right then you will be told."

The footsteps moved away. The door into the corridor was opened, then closed. He was alone. It would be at least another hour before the pair of them reached the Kent coast where the family were temporarily held. No point in Jonas decrying their ability, their minimal experience: they were what he had. Stretched like a bow string to almost breaking point, reserves committed . . . The three that he had identified for further interest had a common musical background: it was a frail and fine thread with which to work, but the last was more promising. He breathed hard.

"And you are alone. And you may be frightened."

He gazed at a photograph . . . not that the appearance of any young man would be the same now. Would have aged, and the features would have attracted a hardness, and the eyes would have gone as cold as any predator's . . . It was a pleasant face that Jonas looked at.

It was too early in the day. Cammy had no wish, yet, to go through the city.

Time enough later for the indulgence of an old haunt and a place of nostalgia. He had trekked up a hill and had passed the formal main gate of what had been Her Majesty's Prison, Canterbury. He was now hunkered down, behind bushes, and gravestones, like rows of sentinels, shielded him from the few who wandered along the path to the door of St Martin's.

He knew it well. It was dark, shielded by trees, and pretty much as he remembered it. It was a place of his childhood, a refuge. He could sit there, rain or shine, steaming hot days or chilly with frost on the grass between the stones, and he would be hidden. He knew this place because it overlooked the high red-brick outer wall of the gaol. His mother had gone to the prison every Thursday morning, for 11 o' clock visiting. He and his half-sister had been dragged along during school holidays. Once, only once, had Cammy been inside. Had smelt the piss, and the disinfectant, and the stale air, and had heard the clang of iron gates slammed shut, and the rattle of keys. The first time had been the last time and he had sat at the table while his mother had tried to make conversation with her eldest child, and he had seemed indifferent to where he was, and had hardly wanted to talk. His half-sister had cried quietly until his mother had kicked her shin. Cammy had not spoken and had stared at the floor. Going in and coming out, queueing with other families, and seeing the smaller faces and bowed shoulders of the inmates, Cammy had made a decision. Never going back. The next time they had come, he had slipped his mother's hold on his hand and had sprinted up the hill and had gone into the churchyard and made a den for himself and avoided a gardener who tidied and swept, and had been waiting at the prison gate when his mum and his sister had emerged.

His mum had tolerated his defiance. The next year Cammy had won his short-lived scholarship to go to the college high on the hill above the city, and the next year had seen his half-brother come home, loaf and lounge about in the day and disappear at night. The year after the next year, his half-brother had been taken to Maidstone gaol, a Category C offender, another stretch and not the last and his mum had not fought Cammy over attendance. He assumed his mum had hoped that taking him to Canterbury gaol at an impressionable age would turn him away from a life of crime. Truth was, Cammy had rather enjoyed his half-brother's company and lifestyle, everything about him except for the years of imprisonment.

He was hungry but he would be fed when darkness fell on the city, when he would go back to his home on the estate above Sturry on the city's outskirts. He would walk there, had a fast loping stride that could cover ground; was able to trek long distances even when the weight of the heavy machine-gun was biting the flesh on his shoulder . . .

Canterbury prison was now a builders' site. Men worked in high-visibility orange. Far beyond the cranes were the cathedral's towers. He would go there, then home. He thought it would be useful to be still and to watch, and he had time to kill.

Perhaps it was that ability, to assess and make judgements, that had propelled Cammy in his role as Kami al-Britani into the rank where his counsel was accepted by the group. If he said how it would be, then there would be no dispute from any of them: not from Mikki or Tomas, nor from Stan or Dwayne, or Pieter – not from Ulrike. Missed them, missed them so bad. Had made his promise while the hatred burned fiercest. Would get to the target, would have it in his weapon's sight, would shout out all their names – and he would fire. Had nothing without them but for the determination to avenge . . .

Cammy had no idea of the situation affecting his security now that Syria was far behind him. They had lectures from guys representing the *Amn al-Askari* people but that was about the intelligence needed for planning attacks up the road. Once they had been addressed by a plump, bearded man from *Amn al-Kharji* which did foreign intelligence, anything beyond the battlefield. Often enough they were visited, even in the front line, by the more sinister of the organisations, *Amn al-Dawla*, who did the counter-intelligence of tracking down spies and informers, and it was a nightmare for all them around Cammy that they be betrayed. But he knew nothing of the intelligence-gathering systems in place back here, but he was suspicious, cautious. Had slid from the dinghy, and then swum up the shoreline, but had no knowledge of whether his name figured in briefings, whether he was forgotten, whether he was tracked, or whether he was an old file on a dust-covered shelf, deep in a hard drive library, and not looked at. Did not know. But assumed the worst, always good to look for the worst.

Time passed. He was not seen, attracted no attention, and the afternoon came and his stomach hurt, and ahead of him was the cathedral. And in the span of a day and night he would be far from here, and preparing to strike, and the hours slipped by and a man came to shut the gate to the churchyard. When the cranes on the site were still and when the high-visibility jackets were gone, he would move. He had the ability to sustain patience, and would need the rest before the following day came, his reason for living.

"You know what I'm thinking Mags?"

"Sorry, love, not a clue. What are you thinking?"

They were well on the road and the camper was travelling smoothly and within the speed limit, and traffic flowed easily around them. Baz drove carefully, and frequently checked his mirrors, and Mags had kicked off her shoes and had her feet hitched up on the dash in front of her. They were beyond Aachen and short of Maastricht and closing on the internal European frontier. On schedule and going at a speed that matched the habits of an elderly British couple returning home to the UK after a pleasant few days on the Continent – and bringing with them a little cargo.

"I'm thinking that we might have company."

"You sure of that, Baz?"

"Not entirely sure, but almost sure."

"You got the nose for it, love, if we have company."

He explained. There was an Audi in their lane, dark green paintwork. A good colour because it did not stand out. Three back from them. Did not come closer, nor did it drop further behind. Very soon, they would be leaving German territory and going into Dutch jurisdiction . . . which was an opportunity, as he told it. He had her clicking at her i-Pad, checking the map.

"Just sort of need to nail it down."

"Best idea, Baz, just that – nail it down with a bloody great hammer."

He did not have to say that "company", a police tail, would be a severe handicap to their hopes of a better funded lifestyle for their remaining years. Pretty obvious to both that the package they ferried was not cigarettes or cannabis skunk, and the weight of the item was such that there had been a sweat sheen on the forehead of the lad who had slung it toward Baz in the back of the camper. Obvious that it was weapons; weapons, in Baz's limited experience, paid well. Where weapons were used was not a consideration in his mind, and she had dismissed it. "We're just the delivery team, love, and how it's used is not our business." And he had thought she meant that the contents of a package were unlikely to disturb her beauty sleep – well, what there was of her "beauty", and he chuckled. He told her what he wanted, and she started to plot the route for him . . . First he had to make sure.

Still in Germany. Still cruising, and had been holding that central lane for the last 40 klicks. A sudden flick of the wheel as they were coming towards a junction for the centre of Aachen, and they went into the inside lane, and he slowed the camper. He was checking his mirrors, and was rewarded. There were headlights flashing in the middle lane, the reaction of annoyed motorists. The Audi had left its lane and, alongside appeared a BMW 5 series, in the same green, and a guy was yammering into his sleeve. Baz had his confirmation. He went back into the middle lane and the Beamer and the Audi were left to sort themselves out.

"You want to know a bit more about what I'm thinking, Mags?"

"Tell me."

"I'm saying to myself that we have German company. Chance is that soon we will have the Dutch doing the job. And another chance is that we're going to have attention all the way to the Channel. That will be how it works."

"They were too complacent, love?"

"Can't fault that, Mags. We just potter along and they forget their procedures. Except we're not as dumb as they'd like us to be."

"Too right."

What they had never talked about, had not needed to, was a future for the pair of them if they ever went into the net. Talked about the good times and what the money would bring, and where the winters could be spent and where sunshine and cheap booze could be factored in; did not talk about arrest, separation, meeting in the cells below a courtroom, being shipped off to different gaols – no conjugal visits – and big lonely stretches of time and growing old . . . and none of the money safely cached and waiting.

Baz said, "The Germans won't go on to Dutch ground. They'll hand over at the white line and the Dutch will take over. Bet you, if we were still on this road, heading for Zeebrugge, and looking out for them then we'd see the Dutch. Just a couple of old people aren't we, half senile, no wits. Tell you another thing, this will be a special operation, limited access, nothing for general radio alerts. Piece of cake, Mags."

"Go for it then, love."

The last turning off before the frontier, Baz was holding the centre lane. The turn was sudden and the truck behind him was a whisker off a collision. He stabbed across the slow lane and on to the filter road, went on to a roundabout and was accelerating, foot down, took a left turn into a suburban street on the outskirts of Aachen, and past a school where flocks of kids were emerging, and more rights and more lefts, and Mags singing out the direction. Then south, off towards Belgium, her finger tracing roads leading into France.

"Giving them something to think about, Mags."

"More likely thinking about whether they wet themselves, love."

"Can't keep the customer waiting, right?"

Tristram and Izzy were ushered in.

They were sitting around a formica-topped table littered with plastic coffee cups and cardboard plates. They had all – men, women and children – been kitted out in bland grey tracksuits and flip-flops.

The walls were bare but for an old portrait of the Queen, a framed document listing the rights of migrants taken into custody following illegal entry to the United Kingdom, and a No Smoking sign. The room had one window, but any view it might have given of the Port of Dover and harbour area, where intercepted migrants were always brought as a first call, was blocked by a lowered blind. All eyes were turned to the door and the new arrivals.

Maybe they would have expected a warm welcome to the UK, the keys to accommodation and a list of useful phone numbers for schools and employment opportunities ... Maybe they would have expected after half an hour in this place, with escorted trips to a shabby toilet, that they would be confronted with boots and batons and scowling uniformed officers ... Maybe they would not have anticipated the arrival of a young man and a young woman, no uniforms, wearing neutral expressions. Tristram breathed fiercely, not the emotion of the moment but the legacy of Izzy's drive to the coast: there would be a book of speeding tickets awaiting her when she was back in Thames House. They were stared at, warily. Tristram might have revelled in the authority given him by the card he had flashed at the duty officer, and asked, demanded, that their escort peel off. There was a hesitation.

"Meaning *now*, not tomorrow," from Izzy.

A stubborn response: "There are regulations and procedures, and . . ."

"Not with us, there aren't. And, please, close the door after you."

It started well. Names were given, and ages, and the children had started to smile, and they heard the nightmare stories about the crossing, and the force of the storm with interruptions to describe the frantic baling, and the height of the bow wave from a giant cargo ship, and where they had come from, and the reason they had fled Iran . . . All going well, and all irrelevant to Tristram and Izzy. Neither had bothered to take a note. Time to kick on.

"And what did he call himself, your saviour?"

"The chap who brought you across, what name did he give you?"

"He must have had a name . . ."

"If you try and tell us that you let a perfect stranger drive you from Bordeaux to the Channel coast, then confront people traffickers on your behalf, then you put your lives in his hands – and he had no name?"

"Saved the kid, but still had no name?"

No answers given. Heads hanging . . . Tristram and Izzy, trusted with work that was beyond their grade, bottom rung of the ladder were looking down the barrel of having to call Jonas Merrick and tell him that they had failed. First proper test run for each of them and they faced silence.

His voice rising, "I will ask you again . . . What name did he give you?"

And hers, quieter and colder, "Refuse to identify him and it will go badly."

No reply. One of the children had started to cry, little soft sobs.

From Tristram, "Who was he? What did he say about himself?"

From Izzy, "So that we all understand what is at stake – you can be handcuffed, you can be led to a ferry, put on board, held under guard for the crossing and then returned to France. That can all happen . . . Who is he?"

"You set out to come to the UK. You are here. You want to stay a lifetime, or a couple of hours? Which?"

"What name did he give?"

It had dawned on Tristram that their debt to this nameless individual, their saviour, was greater than any momentary loyalty towards the country in whose care they now rested. Was clear to Izzy that they felt a love of him and a regard for him – because of where he had led them and what he had brought them through – that outweighed their future advantage. It was a wall of silence, the stuff that the daily rags used to write about, but this was not East London, not Sicily or Naples or the toe of Calabria . . . They were "decent Christian worshippers" and they did not look down at the table or at the wall, but stared back into the faces of Tristram and Izzy. Seemed not to relish their stubborn response, seemed to have no pleasure in their refusal to cooperate.

He murmured in her ear, "Would some rough stuff work with them?"

She answered, "No idea. Never been taught it."

"Quite rough stuff – slap them around a bit?"

"Don't know. He'll think we fucked up, but we have to call him, tell it like it is."

Tristram, grim, told them: "Your choice. It was all for nothing. What you did, surviving that journey, was just time wasted. You'll go back to France today. Perhaps you can find another trafficker and do a deal with him. Perhaps you can stay there a month or a year, however long you want – and congratulate yourselves that you made the choice not to say anything about the guy who brought you over. Fair exchange?"

They went out into the corridor.

Izzy said she'd do it, report the failure.

*　　　*　　　*

And Jonas remembered.

Thought back to how it had been in the days when he was young, "wet behind the ears". They were the Irish days.

Men sporting tight tweed jackets, regimental ties and twill trousers had walked the corridors of the building then occupied by the Service. They had done the "Irish scene" while Jonas Merrick was a junior, little more than a clerk, and they would have chuckled at the thought of getting any Irish boy into the darkened corner of a cell and administering a beating. The boy would be from the wastelands of Fermanagh or the hillsides of Tyrone, or the farming fields of Antrim, or might have been lifted out of West Belfast: there had been the men in the Service who could pull on leather gloves and "do the necessary". And Jonas remembered that photographs marked "for restricted circulation" used to drop by from time to time, pictures of faces with split lips and missing teeth and closed, bruised eyes, and with them there was often a note that no worthwhile information had been extracted. The story was that, in the majority of cases, the men who inflicted shock and awe on prisoners would step out into the corridor of the cell block, sweating from exertion, and frustrated at wasted effort, and would straighten their ties and walk away and have learned very little. They were gone, had used up their life span in the Service. Where might they be now? Maybe running a pub in Devon or a guesthouse in the Lakes, maybe a garden centre in the Black Country, or on a short-term security contract in Bahrain or anywhere else down the Gulf where "robust methods" were still practised. They did not exist in the current Service. Thumping men and boys seldom delivered the goods.

He might get around to telling Tristram and Izzy that a thrashing in a dark corner rarely produced worthwhile intelligence. Was once thought to be beneficial to the public good. Was the old way . . . Torture did not work.

Not long after the move into Thames House, a gentle-voiced Russian had addressed them. A subdued man, not seeking celebrity status although he had been a colonel in the old KGB and had done two tours in Chechnya . . . He had talked of torture.

Described an assignment in Moscow where he worked against the powerful forces of organised crime. A clan leader was in the cells, refusing to communicate: he had been roughed up, robustly questioned. The colonel had gone into the cell and had sat on the filthy floor, had stayed there for four days, eaten there and slept there, and had won the clan leader's confidence. All they wished to know had become known. They had all thought the colonel interesting and had regarded him as brave, principled: to his own people he was a traitor and they had successfully poisoned him nineteen months after his address to the Service audience ... One man's hero was another man's scum. Still, a useful insight into torture and other alternatives.

Not a matter of him losing his job, exiting in disgrace: nor of the two youngsters ditching their careers. Simply that fists and boots and falls down the cell block steps did not produce information.

He rummaged in his files. It could have been that his eyes were tired, or might have been that the light through his window was dulled by the low cloud and the fine rain. It was hard for him to see the details of the pictures: a white American, a German with snow-blond hair, a Russian national who had been in their military before switching sides and heading to Syria. And the face of a British boy who had been a student, supposedly studying an aspect of computers, and another who had an encyclopaedic knowledge of long-playing records – then found the one of a fresh-faced lad, pleasant looking, with an open and mischievous face, and he marked that picture "CJ" with an indelible pen, then marked all the others. It was not necessary for him to pinch himself for allowing the thought of it to play in his mind. There was no burden of conscience involved. He did not approve of torture in any form – noise, sleep deprivation, pain, abuse – because he did not think it worked well enough or fast enough.

Jonas was not skilled at loading and sending photographs by electronic mail, but he managed it ... was quite pleased with himself when they had been sent, and more so to learn they had been delivered ... There would be a delay. The images would have to be printed and then one of his probationers would have to pop

out and find an ice-cream booth. It would take a few minutes . . .
He had eaten his sandwich and drunk a mug of coffee from the
flask, now flicked crumbs from his work surface, closed his eyes,
and hoped to doze. Believed that soon the opportunities for rest
would be scarce.

He walked on a sward of rough cut grass that stretched away from
the prison wall where the cranes had swung and the lorries
manoeuvred and towards the immediate outskirts of the city.
Cammy had rested, not slept because of the pains in his stomach
and the dryness in his throat, but he could cope with that, and his
mum would feed him.

Parkland and ruins marked the site of St Augustine's Abbey,
now with only a fraction of its walls still standing. It was a familiar
place for him. Every school kid, from the posh end up on the hill
or the college beside the cathedral park down to the overflowing
state schools, was carted around the county's monuments: they
did Roman ruins and Saxon ruins and Norse ruins and Norman
ruins. They all did ruins like it was a staple for breakfast, necessary
for keeping the bowels moving – he had hated ruins. Ahead of him
were three parties of tourists, their guides carrying multi-coloured
umbrellas though the rain had stopped, and gathered among the
sunken stones of an excavated chapel were schoolchildren in neat
blazers and short trousers or gingham frocks. He kept moving, his
chin tucked against his chest. The kids would have been regi-
mented, same as the wannabe "martyrs" that had come to Syria
and were then tucked away in special camps, separated from the
living, breathing, laughing, smoking fighters. Cammy, as Kami
al-Britani, had been a free spirit, and his brothers had been too,
and they had all found friendship, and what they had believed to
be "liberty" when they carried the assault rifles and big mortar
tube and a sniper's rifle, when he had balanced on his shoulder the
weight of the heavy machine-gun. The kids had sheets of paper on
clipboards and would be tested later on what they remembered of
the dirge they had been told about these buildings, and the tour
guides breathed enthusiasm and the tourists snapped

photographs. He could go forward as covertly as a fox at dusk, all of his brothers could. And later that day, when the light fell, his abilities to move unnoticed would be used. For now he was an independent man, alone and isolated, and knew it.

So easy then, those long-ago days, to act outside the loop, and stake big survival cash on the unexpected. The time outside Deir Ezzor. He and the brothers moving in a defile towards a village believed to be deserted. The "empty" village was occupied by at least 100 of the Hezbollah force – hard, squint-eyed bastards from south Lebanon. The laconic Stanislau had been point man. A guy of few words because of his cleft palate; probably the only time in his life that he had prospered was when he'd caught up with Cammy. Came from Belarus, and grunted that when the war was over and no more fighting to be done he would be a poet. Something of a miracle but the shots fired at him had all missed, and their surprise factor was lost. They had been pinned down, multiple fire positions on them. Ulrike, flat on her stomach and surrounded by the mortar bombs she was supposed to be hauling, had started the chorus for them to back off, reverse down the defile, and Cammy had thought it the worst of options. His word counted. Up front, in an alley he had seen a waving radio aerial. An aerial was where the boss was, the top man. Not argued with. No dissension. He led, the brothers followed. Ulrike up close to him and sweating, grunting, under the weight of the bombs. They had charged together and had woven a path between doorways and rubble, any cover available, but had kept going. Dwayne had killed the top man, had done it with a knife: his handset had dropped and he had shrieked, and that was what his people would have heard: their leader in pain, in terror, his scream. And those around the top man had gone down . . . an attack where it was not expected and the pace had been frantic. The Hezbollah boys had done a runner . . . Pieter had said that if they had tried to extricate themselves, gone back and deeper into the defile, then they would have been cut to pieces. There had been a cursory celebration, nothing like "triumphalism", and others had utilised the hole they had made in the line and come through it. Ruhan had told them that the execution of the attack was "brilliant", but Ruhan was dead, and Tomas, and . . . He was alone and strode across the grass and looked neither right or left but kept the tower of the cathedral – the Bell Harry Tower, 250 feet high – in his gaze. Would not let it from his sight, and the afternoon wore on and the guides would soon be finishing their talk, and the kids were already late for the bus to get them back to school.

Here, Cammy thought himself to be near his home, the place where his life had been shaped, more so than in the semi-detached house on the estate above Sturry. He was drawn towards the cathedral. He did not think of caution, went forward and tried to believe he was not alone, was again where – briefly – he could gather comfort.

Ice-creams had been brought in from the town, proper ones with cones and chocolate sticks, and the adults had been separated from the children.

Tristram and Izzy nowhere to be seen, and friendly smiles from the staff at the holding place.

The children alone with a minder, and then the door opening, the attending uniform gone. The boy and the girl were left with Tristram and Izzy. He had a broad smile and she had a grin that said conspiracy and mystery.

The ice-creams were handed over.

The photographs were placed on the table.

They had come through onto Tristram's mobile phone. A room had been found where he could hook up to a printer. They were A4 images. Perhaps the kids when they saw the photographs would have accepted the truth of that old adage, however it was expressed in their culture: no such thing as a free lunch. Good ice-creams but cheap when set against the photo gallery on display. The girl, older, understood. She turned away and looked at the Annigoni portrait of the Queen painted more than 60 years before. The night before the boy had been in the water, his breath seeping away between his lips, darkness and noise all around him, and a hand had grabbed him. His life had been saved, and for a moment he would not have known, confused and open-hearted, that he was about to betray the best man he had ever known.

One by one, the pictures were pushed in front of him by Izzy.

The student from Westminster University, and the shop worker who specialised in vinyl. A shake of the head and another mouthful, the chocolate dribbling from the sides of his mouth. The last picture was marked with the initials "CJ", and the child had rocked and his eyes had bulged and there was a gasp of recognition.

The child bent over the table. Held the ice-cream cone away from his mouth. Kissed the image of the monochrome face. An uninhibited kiss – out of innocence, as they had hoped for and as Jonas Merrick back in London had indicated might happen.

The girl, older, wiser, better able to read the moment, saw what her brother did. She kicked him hard. Her toe, in the flip-flops, careered into his shin. His head came up and he would have seen his sister's contempt . . . Tristram wondered if, in their Christian teaching and whatever equivalent to a Sunday School they had, either of them knew of a Judas kiss . . . The girl dropped her ice-cream on the floor and reached out to grab the picture. Not fast enough. Tristram had it, and palmed it behind him, and Izzy took it.

They left the room.

In the yard, Izzy said, "Sort of leaves me with a bad taste. And you?"

Tristram said, "No sort of taste at all. Wobby had it right. Not known as a Wise Old Bird for nothing. You going to call him? Sorry, we could have beaten three shades of shit out of them and they'd not have done the identification. I don't feel good and I don't feel bad. It's not a fun world, Izzy, but you know that. But didn't know it when you joined."

"Pompous fucker," she said and punched him, grinning. He was looking at the picture, good-looking young man, clean and neat, with the stain of the ice-cream around his lips.

"Heh, old cocker. Fancy . . . bloody hell."

Cammy's way was blocked. He had left the grounds of the ruined abbey, was heading for the Burgate opening in the city walls, sitting close to the cathedral.

"That is you? Cameron? Yes?"

The guy stood in front of him. Joey Pickford, a year ahead of him at the comprehensive, no friend. Had been the kind of guy who could recognise a kid coming down in the world, literally down from the college on the hill overlooking the city and whose scholarship had been binned. Could recognise and milk an opportunity.

"It is you . . .? That's a turn-up. Old Cameron – Shit, thought you had been blown into small pieces. You all right? Look like you're not. And dressed like a bloody pensioner."

He had not examined the possibility of being recognised, identified, had not seen that as being relevant to him . . .

Was in his home city because his mum was there, and it was her birthday tomorrow and that would be her present – to have him back – and she'd pull faces and complain that he had not written, and never a phone call, and he would do the smile that had always won her. She would be in the kitchen and the rings would be lit, and she'd be cooking him something that was a favourite and special, might be chops with chips and mushrooms thrown in, and of course she'd have a can in the fridge, a beer for him, and then he would hug and kiss and smile all over again, and would slip away in the night when she had given him some money. First train of the day out and going to his meeting with the man who had facilitated the hit, then being driven to the target and its fence. Had to be here for his mum, owed it her, and had to be back at the cathedral where there had been big times. There he had been a star, then had been rejected – cut off. Joey Pickford blocked his way.

"Have I got this wrong? Don't think I remember every kid I was at school with, but you're special. Were special at school, got the chop from the private place, and then got more special. All that stuff in the papers . . . everyone said you'd have your arse blown off."

Cammy said, "Don't know who you are. If you'll excuse me?"

"But you're Cameron, Cameron Jilkes. Lived up the hill from Sturry? Had a thing with that Vicky . . . Are you not Cameron Jilkes?"

"No idea what you're talking about."

"Talking about Cameron Jilkes. Brother was a bad one, sister got pranged in a car accident. Cameron Jilkes went off to fight. Cops all over his pad, photo on the front of the paper. Was with those people who slit throats, revolting bastards . . . Are you not Cameron Jilkes? Isn't that who you are?"

He'd always thought Joey Pickford a shit and a bully . . . Doubt was now clouding his face. Cammy saw the shabby trousers and the shirt with a drainage firm logo on the chest. Where he had come from and who he had once been, he would have had Joey Pickford down on his knees and jabbering for mercy and wetting himself and messing himself, but that was then . . . And he remembered Vicky. He showed no hint of recognition.

"Can't help you. Never seen you before."

"Not Cameron Jilkes? Not the guy dating Vicky Wilson, married now, Gavin Davies and a kid . . .? Not the guy who went out to fight, headlines, cop raids, not him?"

"No, excuse me."

He did a sort of wintry smile and walked right through Joey Pickford, and the guy had to stumble aside or would have been knocked over, and confusion was on his face and uncertainty. Cammy kept walking and was through the gate and the wall and he'd have bet that Joey Pickford stared after him all the time he could see him, . . . and if he gossiped and told mates and the news of it went viral in the limited and dead-beat group that Pickford would have moved with, by then Cammy would be well gone, distanced, and would be facing his target. Pickford was forgettable, not Vicky. What he could recall of Gavin Davies was of a keen, neat and tidy lad who had ambitions to wear a tie at work.

Daft of him, but all the time he had been travelling, ever since the break-out and his decision to come home and deal out damage, he had not considered the consequences of his flight, and the reaction. Kept walking towards the entry gate.

*   *   *

Almost enough, but not quite enough.

The photograph taken from his file, JILKES, Cameron (Canterbury), was now on his wall, adjacent to the crocodile's image, and the ice-cream was still visible over the mouth, had shown up well through the print process.

He dialled a number, overseas and on the secure net: always preferred to speak direct, to listen and then weigh information rather than follow the fashion of impersonal email contact. Had to have "enough". The war against the *jihadis*, scaling down, was run out of the al-Sayliyah camp close to the Qatari capital, Doha, where the US had their CentCom operation, and allies sent assets to show the flag and pretended that influence could still be exercised. Some British personnel did it better than others.

He had talked to those girls four times in the last year. They were Sixers and had been relocated as if that were part of a penance and a re-education programme. A section of Six across the river had been closed down after accusations from on high of a cavalier approach. The stables were supposedly in the cleansing process. All a bit childish to Jonas Merrick. Flamboyant, childish and theatrical. He supposed the girls existed in this American hinterland on a diet of air-conditioning, baked beans and peanut butter.

A crisp voice answered. He remembered Alice. Pretty as a chocolate-box picture, might have been standing in front of an old stone wall where roses climbed. Gave the name and also spoke about a voice. Did he wish to hold or should she call back? He would hold. New Orleans jazz was played back to him. Jonas anticipated the answer.

The ice-cream ringing the mouth gave a small distortion but not enough to destroy the complexity of the face . . . He thought it one that he would have trusted, that of a man who would lead, one who would be followed. He could place himself in the minds and in the faith of an Iranian group who had started out on an odyssey, and who were within touching distance of a destination, but needed the spur of a single man's courage to get them there. Deep eyes and an honesty in the chin . . . Jonas Merrick could read a face. Liked this one and was amused by the smear ringing the mouth. But the photograph was not contemporary. His files were packed with the images of those men and women who had returned from Syria, Iraq and any other of those wretched locations, and he knew their faces would have altered – lines indented where there had been smoothness, eyes dulled by what they had seen. All of them would carry the weight of a burden, and the final and undefined factor would be the anger bred from the scale of defeat. It was the anger, the hatred, that most concerned him.

The music stopped in the middle of a trumpet solo.

The voice of Alice. "You still there? Yes . . .? Good. We don't know that name, but there was something marginally similar that we never seemed to get around to analysing. The name was Kami al-Britani, but no one did sufficient work on it. The man wasn't a High Value Target, but had a 'dead or alive' bounty on him. Not a big one. We do have a footprint, something out of the ordinary."

"I'd be grateful for that, the footprint."

"You'd talked about a hymn singer."

"I did. It's what I am trying to identify – a man with knowledge of Christian hymns. Not a fundamentalist, but a young man familiar with the traditional church and its music."

"There is only one footprint – we'd call it 'aural'."

"An aural footprint? Give it me, please."

"It was picked up on a radio intercept. There was a squad opposite some of the US forces. Rated as high level, a bit kamikaze, but also survivors – if that fits. They were monitored. They were talking to their officer, an Iraqi national and a field commander and there was a low voice singing in the background. They ran it through all the filters because it was so strange. This is a crack unit in the black flags, and among them is a guy singing a Christian anthem. It's one we used to do at convent school – *How Great Thou Art*. This is an ISIS crowd, and he was singing a hymn. It's two years ago that it was heard . . . I've nothing else on singing."

Before she rang off she gave Jonas the name of an American combat officer who was seconded into intelligence, and a line that would link to him.

"Thank you, Alice, and thank you for your aural footprint."

It made good enough sense to him. He felt little immediate satisfaction because now they would be running, desperate to catch up, and always so little time. He rang Vera, was fulsome in his apology.

7

Jonas's screen told him that it was nearing the time that he should have been preparing to clear his desk, leave everything tidy behind him and think about getting his coat on and heading off into the evening. That night of the week, Vera usually made a cottage pie for their supper. She had sounded surprised at his message, but had not quizzed him.

He was, he thought, almost at that moment when he could press the button, let loose the sirens and the alarms, and could circulate the photograph and biography of Cameron Jilkes. Others might already have done so. Down by his knee was the cupboard that held his bag. Others would have been fearful that should their world collapse, should an attacker break through the defences, should a bomb detonate, should a vehicle swerve on to a pavement and pile into commuters, tourists, innocents, they would have to explain to a subsequent inquest why they had backed off. Better to pass the parcel and give one's superiors the responsibility of calling the shots . . . A quick and rather guilty smile at the thought of it. His fingers clattered on his keyboard.

In the office space there was still only the emptiness and the rattle of silence. It was why he was prepared to invest a few more hours, at his desk, his screen, his card files. The room beyond his partition was deserted because the men and women who usually milled there were committed. It would be the same in many other parts of the building, where the surveillance teams had their space. Nothing more to throw into the hunt and the chase, the defence of the state and its streets. It was possible that in a week or within two weeks, the pressure on resources would have eased: possible, but unlikely. It would be the same with the numbers of police serving in counter-terror units.

Vera had said to him, "Jonas, you'll not be doing anything stupid?"

He had replied, "No dear, nothing stupid, it's just that we're thin on the ground."

"Don't do anything daft. I'll cook the dinner anyway, and we'll have it whenever."

"Yes, whenever. Anyway, I'd better be getting on with things."

"Nothing idiotic, Jonas."

"And I'm sorry about our dinner, very sorry, and the inconvenience."

He'd rung off. Had he lingered, she would have questioned him about the contents of the bag, would they be creased, a multitude of matters that he could not, at that time, handle. The bag had been brought to the office on the evening before his investiture. If it had to be awarded him, he would have preferred it to have come in the post, but powers beyond the reach of Jonas Merrick, and convention, had demanded that the medal be pinned in person . . .

He had been earnestly asked to give some detail on the circumstances where he had found himself sitting next to young Gunn, but he had been sparse with his answers and the "royal" might have had the impression that security confidences were not to be shared. The bag, as Jonas remembered it, contained socks, a folded shirt, underwear, pyjamas and his shaving stuff, and a toothbrush. He had stayed overnight at a B&B, and been driven there and back, and had been "economical" with anecdotes on getting back to Raynes Park.

He had not known resources to be so stretched, at break-point, in all his time in the Service. And himself? Also stretched. Good at disguising the stress, adept at masking it, most of the time. He could have looked up at the image of the beast with the ferocious teeth, or at the dark pool from a lagoon or a tidal estuary and seen two ringed areas, could have focused his attention on the picture of a young man whose mouth had a smeared and untidy halo around the lips. Could have . . . and then pondered why he, Jonas

Merrick, a low-grade official in a Service with a payroll of thousands, seemed to have so much weight on his shoulders. He allowed that moment of indulgence. Of course, self-inflicted. Had he not been out of the building that evening, and walking in the light rain, had he not sat down next to a prospective suicide bomber, had he not been on a bench adjacent to the Mother of Parliaments where the "great and the good" paraded, and had he not been stupid enough to tug free the cables running from the power pack to the detonator, he would now be in gentle retirement, with abundant time to plan caravanning holidays. He was an oracle. Unloved but now with a basket full of grudging respect, his opinion valued. It was a time of maximum danger. Jonas feared that he would buckle under the weight of those pressures . . . Of course he was not alone. Many men and women in the building endured similar burdens, tried to worry through. He could have said that his reputation, unwanted, damned him.

He called, spoke to Izzy. Told them what he wanted.

The bag was light, would be easy to carry. He called the AssDepDG's office and named a time when he would appreciate a meeting . . . and his screen told him that the team from 3/S/12 was confused because the German counter-terror people had lost a surveillance target, had *lost* it, had lost contact with a lethal weapon being couriered to the ferry port at Hull. But that was another problem, lying across someone else's desk . . . It was a pleasant face, the one on his wall beside the crocodile's head.

The building towered over him.

It was, for Cammy, the end of a pilgrimage. This was the place he had to come to if he were to purge an old life and prepare for his last actions.

The cathedral was, as he knew, a place of death, of violence and of bloody struggles for power. Was also, and this had been dinned into him when he was a valued part of the majesty of it, a symbol of power and of authority. He was outside the gate policed by cathedral constabulary, but he stayed inconspicuous, waited with his head tucked down until a party of schoolchildren, German, were ushered through. A teacher at the front had negotiated the group's entry, and another teacher was at the rear and, as they came past him, he took the necessary half pace to his left and was swept forward.

Inside, he stopped, gazed around him, and above, and drank it in. He had not stood here since the day that he had been dumped off the choir, and his mother had come to collect him – would have taken time off work, and had puffed and reddened eyes and had tried to hurry him away. He had snatched his hand from hers and had paused to look up and into the dark rain clouds and see the height of the Bell Harry Tower, and the glory of the glass, look at it a last time. Then had turnd and walked briskly, never twisted to glance behind him, and his mother had had to chase after him, and they had taken the bus home to Sturry, and his dream had been taken from him. Had often thought of this place, and its effect on his life when he had been with his brothers. Had talked of it. Had sung to them, quiet all around him, or just hummed the tunes, and the only interruption might had been a stray incomer, 110mm or 151mm, from the enemy's artillery.

Could remember the first day, being brought here by his mother, pride creasing her tired face, and him sauntering in with a hand in his shorts pocket. A new blazer, and a tie he barely knew how to knot. They could have gone to the building where the choristers lived but his mother had wanted the taxi – rash expend-iture for her – to drop them at the cathedral. She had struggled with his case, and he had not helped her, and they had gone inside after the rain had spattered them and left diamonds on her hair: he would have liked, that afternoon, to kiss them from her head but had not done so. This was to be his new home, and he was a chosen one. They did scores of auditions, chose only the best, and he wore the black shoes and grey socks and the short trousers and white shirt and tie and the blazer to prove his status.

He went through the doorway into the great cavern of the building. A guide sidled up to welcome the German party. Cammy loitered and listened. A teacher translated. The guide said nothing about the glories of worship, private prayer, or the joys of choral music. He talked of the killing of one archbishop, and the decapitation of another, and of the great, revered and feared, fighting men of their time. He spoke of the looting of the building by a monarch determined to break the power of the Roman church, and the carrying off of 26 cartloads of valuables – gold pieces, silverwork, statues fashioned from rare Italian marble – and the memories were sharpened for Cammy of how it had been in what had seemed to be the pinnacle of his life. And the guide told the kids of the consequence of a Royalist defeat when civil war had split the nation, and how the cold men who were the victors had vandalised the interior – what he called "mindless destruction" – and the great multi-coloured windows had been smashed by men on high ladders, and the glass they could not reach was broken by musket balls ... and mentioned a later war, did not name the nation then arrayed against Britain, and said bombs had fallen on the city but by some intervention, luck or divine, the cathedral had been spared.

The guide began to walk forward, and the kids followed. Cammy had time to lose ... for the first time since he had gone into the water, the matter of his freedom concerned him. It could have been the quiet of the ancient building, or the depth of the shadows thrown down, but he felt a chill on his neck. Cammy had not considered that he might be a hunted man. He would not advertise his presence, of course not, but the matter of whether some official apparatus was actively searching for him had not occurred to him.

He would return, he would come to the cathedral which had shaped so much of his life, he would visit his mother, then move onto his last journey. He had been told where he would meet a facilitator who would have the photographs and maps of the target and who would bring him the weapon that he would use ... All that was clear, but the chill on his skin, under his unfamiliar shirt collar, seemed to warn him of danger.

No one to ask, and no brother from whom he could take confidence. He was alone ... he shivered and the hugeness of the building seemed to close around him. He swayed on his feet, then was aware that he attracted attention. He bit at his lip, scratched the palms of his hands with his nails. He walked towards the nave.

They were moving professionally, not in a cluster but strung out, Mikki somewhere in the middle. There was a moon which gave them enough light. Mikki was from Ukraine.

They walked towards a wilderness. The aim was to get clear of the fighting zone beside the Euphrates river, and to keep away from roads and vehicle tracks, to lie up in daylight in abandoned buildings. They would light no fires, would stay hidden, then, when the light fell, they would move on and use instinct, or a compass, to get them into remote territory where only nomads lived, or others with black flags folded and hidden in rucksacks. Cammy had not told them, nor had there been a discussion amongst them, where they were headed, which frontier they might cross, which conflict they might enter, not yet determined. Stanislau led.

Dwayne was back-marker. Sometimes on the march Cammy would murmur the words and anthem notes of a hymn. That night he was quiet. Ulrike was immediately ahead of him, then Mikki. Pieter was behind Mikki ... Pieter's chest was bad and he had a hacking cough that he tried, with no great success, to stifle. That evening, Cammy had spoken to them all before they had started out, and had caught Mikki's eye as he finished, and had been rewarded with the usual heavy grin, and the mock melancholy.

On the west side of Kiev were the tower block apartments built in the communist era, where Mikki started life. He had military experience, had been in the army and had done front line tours of fighting with the separatists in the east. Hated Russians, had tried to kill them, had tried harder to avoid them killing him, loathed them. The chance had come to fight Russians again and he had joined the black flags. Knew little of Islam, cared for it less, but had an opportunity to do them damage. He was an ordnance expert, did clever booby traps and could get on a workbench and manufacture the improvised bombs for the roadside. Never spoke of parents, had not been married, didn't claim to have fathered any kids, would deny he had ever loved before joining the brothers. "*The Boss*" *was what he called Cammy.* "*The Madonna*" *was his name for Ulrike. Probably, among them, he had found his only worthwhile home.*

They had left the deserted building as soon as darkness came, had not felt happy there, none of them, and Tomas was mightily missed though not talked of. They were heading north and veering a little east. They had no night-sight gear and Stanislau as front-marker had noted a vehicle parked up and abandoned on the reverse slope of an incline. If anything confused them, needed checking for explosives, then Mikki was called up. They were pressing on and needed ground covered . . . Mikki had an accented growl and his big phrase, often repeated, was Life is short. Live it. *He liked to talk about a "bender", a few days of excess alcohol in a five-star place, Muscat or Kuwait, but better if it were Beirut, room service and booze, had that dream for "one day". Mikki was disciplined most times, was safe hands, and all of them trusted him, and his stories of fighting Russians were sexed with diabolical killings and the awesome fate of their wounded and his eyes would be bright in the telling.*

He told his Boss he would look at it. His Madonna, whom he adored; stopped, unhooked her rucksack. Stanislau crouched at the front, and Dwayne at the back faced away and peered out into the darkness. Cammy was checking a bootlace. None of them would actually see it, know what Mikki had done that detonated it. Might have been a trip-wire, might have been a pressure plate. The flash and the blast of scalding air, then the thunder roll, the scouring dirt and grit and the singing of the shrapnel, then the scream.

Mikki lost both legs. Taken clean off immediately below his knees. He had not even reached the vehicle, a desert warhorse, a Toyota pick-up. Mikki screamed into the night and none of them, at first, dared move. Then Ulrike did: she had the limited medical know-how none of the rest of them had learned. She called it . . . two legs gone, blood pumping, and the bitter observation that there would be no Chinook coming in for a "casevac". Pieter yelled at her that she should not go closer for fear of a cluster of the fucking things. Dwayne cocked his rifle. They'd look to Cammy to give them authority. He nodded and Dwayne would have seen the movement of his head.

Good luck to Mikki, and a kindness done him. One shot, one bullet to crack open his forehead and to strangle the screams.

They agreed that to bury him would require a heavy pickaxe to break up parched ground, and there were no stones to make a cairn, and the chance of a few rocks – what they could forage, holding off rats or wild dogs – was minimal. Pieter had gone to him and hooked out his wallet. Empty – no address to which a "sympathy note" could be sent if ever they reached a place where there was paper, an envelope, stamps and a postbox.

Paused, held their silence, allowed their thoughts to run free. No tears but a promise given. Cammy allowed a couple of minutes that followed the crack of the single shot, then said what was needed. Life is short. Live it. *They were on the move.*

The line closed up. They had no gap, no sign of a place where a tooth had just been extracted. Another brother gone.

Washing up dirty plates, used coffee mugs, glasses from which juice had been drunk, Farouk reflected that the schedule was now far advanced.

He stood, suds and warm water dripping from his hands, at the hub of a considerable organisation, and knew it: he believed the self-given name, Wolfboy, was well earned. He would do his full shift that evening, and the next day he might arrive an hour or two hours later than he was expected, but the internet café owner knew him as a good worker, loyal and conscientious, and would excuse him, would not quiz him as to where he had been. He expected to be there when the news broke. His assumption was that it would take an hour, minimum, for the full detail of the attack to be carried on news programmes, and by then – God willing – he would be back in Leeds and would be helping to make coffee, to serve cake, and to give guidance to anyone who found it difficult working with a computer.

He had put much of it in place. The schedule was prepared for the following morning. A ferry would have docked in the night, and the weapon would be brought by the couriers to Grantham in Lincolnshire. Also arriving there would be a young man, British, white-skinned and a veteran fighter . . . That man was the star of the Wolfboy firmament. Farouk could easily find kids who would not be fearful of martyrdom, who might have a great enough love of their religion to seek to paint their names in its legends. What he could not have summoned up in Leeds, in Dewsbury, in the terraced streets of Bradford, or even from Luton, was a fighter who had the skill necessary for the attack, who had the anger to carry it out.

He did not know the man's name, nor had he seen a photograph of him.

The front area of the café, beyond the kitchen where he worked, heaved with the music of the near East, with voices raised in laughter and debate, and money filled the till. It was a good place for him to work, and strangers came and went each day and only a few of them had business with him. He thought the building was probably watched but it was swept regularly and he believed no bugs were planted, and no informers were among the regulars, and he trusted that his own communications were secure. He would see the man, watch him from a distance, would see him slip into the vehicle, and already the package – opened and readied – would be behind the driving seat. He would have liked the opportunity to grip the fighter's hand, even hug him or brush-kiss his cheeks . . . that would not happen. He was assured the man was militarily able, and no longer had a love for life, and had chosen the target himself. More mugs and plates were brought to him.

Excitement gripped him. He thought himself privileged that a man of his reputation would be dependent on the quality of Farouk's planning, might even thank him. A fierce and shivering excitement. Farouk was a believer but did not think he could ever match this man's anger, as described to him . . . And in less than the span of a day it would be over and he would be back here, the sink filled, and the music playing.

As if he were still the child he had been, Cammy walked the length of the nave, and climbed steps, and peered at outer doors, and remembered.

There was the great chair, the cathedra, which had been used by archbishops for 800 years. Once he had parked his own butt on it and had heard a squeal of annoyance from an attendant, and had run. He gazed at the ancient worn Petworth marble.

At the Trinity Chapel he looked at the tomb of Archbishop Simon who had doubled as finance boss to the king of his day, and who the mob had captured, then hacked off his head; all of him buried here, except his head which was on the north side of the Thames estuary.

Paused at the resting place of the Black Prince, Edward, victor against superior numbers of French troops at Crécy, aged sixteen, and in the front line at the heaviest of the hand-to-hand combat, and ten years later at Poitiers, a hero, and dead in middle age and lying in splendour in a tomb topped by a carved likeness of him in full armour, his double-hand fighting sword on his hip. Against the odds, succeeding far from home, recognised and honoured.

Images, romanticised, of the mediaeval combat had stayed with Cammy. By the tomb were the prince's coat of arms, among them the feathers and the message of *Ich Dien*, taken from the shield of John of Bohemia, totally blind, who had ridden, his knights around him, towards the English formation at Crécy, and had been killed.

Kings were here, and cardinals, and archbishops, and the dead were honoured . . . Cammy had passed the old wooden doors that led to the famed cloisters, through which four kinghts had stormed. Archbishop Thomas, expecting them and too proud to flee, had been at prayer. He paused, in front of the altar, stood on the stone slab on which the knights would have pirouetted before raising their swords and slashing the clergyman to death . . . The king had wanted it done, the king's wish was executed, the king had not stood by his knights, had disowned them. Cammy imagined the shouting and the yelling, and the chaos of the moment, and slipped away, overwhelmed by the hugeness of the place where once he had owned a stake.

Plaques on the walls commemorated men fallen in combat in Zulu wars, in India and on the Western Front, in North Africa, and regiments raised from men recruited in Kent's villages and small towns . . . This was where he had been as a boy and where a greater part of his character had been formed. Where the nobility of combat, his interpretation of it, was carved.

He still had time to lose . . . He thought no one had noticed him, no one watched him. He needed to be here to suck in the strength he would require for his final attack; he thought he would be talked of here, and remembered.

"Jonas Merrick?"

He confirmed it.

"How is it in London?"

He said it was raining in London.

"You called my office. They took some time finding me. They reached me on the beach. I'm calling you from the beach. You want to know where my beach is?"

Did not give a toss where the beach was. Where this American army officer, attached to intelligence gathering, was probably drinking beer with his mates and likely had some nurses with them. He said he would be fascinated to learn where the beach was.

"It is the Al-Farkiah beach, Mr Merrick. We have a section of it to ourselves, and I reckon it Qatar's best. It's dark here now but we have a bit of a fire going and the barbecue is stoking up nicely, and . . . I'm told you want to know about an 'aural footprint', that right?"

He had bided his time, had not hurried the man. An aural footprint on a hymn singer was his point of interest.

The officer said, in a laconic voice, "We could always fuck them with our technology, Mr Merrick. The gadgets that we could put into the field against them made it, sort of, an unequal contest. That's good, because these are bad bastards and we had no sympathy for them. The purpose was to get locations on them from tapping into mobiles and radios – I'm talking about front line – and then we could better hit them from the air, get the air force in with heavy ordnance or blast them with the Hellfires from drones. You remember one of our pilots described hitting retreating Iraqi transport, 'like a turkey shoot'? Well, nothing much has changed. Kind of unequal. Anyway . . . the material you're talking about was close to two years ago, could be longer. Our gear was a long way forward, and we reckoned we had struck lucky. There was an officer we were tracking – one of the old Saddam boys and a capable man – and he was right for taking down, but a cunning guy and making plenty of effort to stay alive. He and his people had a tactic that we had not cottoned on to at the beginning. They would only do radio and mobile communications just before they moved. You got me, sir?"

He sat in his partitioned area and felt as if he had been transported far from the river and from Thames House; imagined himself in a desert, or beside a fetid waterway, or among arid concrete buildings or in an alley stinking of mules and goats. Felt the place, and smelt it.

"The Iraqi guy was called Ruhan, a major. He was interesting to us because he seemed to operate primarily with units of foreign fighters. Other times the team I was with was aiming to get inside the security procedures of their paper-pushers running the finance side of the war, and their real bad guys, the ones with knives. This stretch in time we were going after effective fighting teams. He was one we chased a fair amount, but had no positive result. Had a favourite gang . . . what I mean is that when there was a job that needed doing, beyond the general run of the mill troopers, they'd send for this officer and he would bring up his people. Seemed to get things done. They had come off a message and the operator at their end of the radio, the Iraqi, had left the set powered up for a few seconds at the end of the transmission. Brief, tantalising, but clear. With me?"

Jonas said he was.

"Sir I don't know my religious anthems. If my grandparents, up in north Wisconsin, had heard the tracks they would have known the title, the verse, and the writer's name. There was no doubt, though, that it was a hymn that was being sung. One guy with a good voice. I reckon we had three or four lines. Called others in to hear it because it was just extraordinary what we were hearing . . . I mean, in downtown Raqqa, a guy would have been in serious trouble – know what I mean by 'serious'? – for that sort of music. We reckoned these people – this voice in particular – were of the highest quality as fighters and that they believed themselves to be untouchable. Can I add something?"

He could. Jonas listened. He rarely interrupted source material, allowed a story to be told in its own way, in its own time.

"I said, 'the highest quality as fighters'. Most of what they get in are just fodder for our fire-power, but a few of them are dedicated and professional. Fortunately, sir, only a few. The Iraqi officer had an overview of their operations, but on the ground they were led by an English boy. Kami al-Britani, that seemed to be a name that came through. We didn't get him . . . Truth to tell, Mr Merrick, he was not the biggest target for us because he hadn't sliced the throats of any aid workers, not that we knew of. Now, I've lost touch with the state of ground operations in Syria. I don't know whether this guy, the one with the choir voice – must have been taught to sing that heavy stuff – was taken down in an air strike, or went into the cages. You know what happened to him, sir?"

Jonas told the American that it was believed this individual was on his way home, might already be back on his home territory. The line went quiet. He heard voices in the background, and light laughter, and then a hiss for them to be quiet.

The American said, "That sort of guy, sir, if he's headed back to where he started out from will be nursing a powerful anger. We made sure they did not have an easy ride. They were hit every way we could pummel them: bombs, missiles, artillery, Special Forces raids. They had a tough time. They will not be coming home to get work in a factory, or drive a car or fade into the background or peddle dope. They want to give something back, and with interest. You need to take him down, and quick, and forget the niceties. Kill him, Mr Merrick. Right, sir, if that's all, please excuse me. The burgers are about ready. Nice to have spoken to you, sir, and good luck."

"He was rather lovely, Cameron. Am I allowed to say that?"

Tristram said she was. Izzy didn't remark on it.

"You have a class full of ten-year-olds, and they pitch up at the start of the Christmas term and you really don't know what they'll be like. You don't know who is going to become a pain, who is just negative, no ambition to better himself, herself, and who will be the leader. Always one kid, usually a boy, and it's like a herd of any animals and the rest will follow, go the way he takes them. I rather liked him."

They'd had to wait for her to get back to her flat. A living-room and a bedroom, a bathroom and a kitchen, and a very small balcony that was home to a few pot plants. An austere interior, and evidence of a life with few excitements. They had not given her warning, preferred to bounce her, a better route towards frankness, both Tristram and Izzy had been taught.

"If I had little Cameron on my side then the class was usually quite manageable. I suppose I paid him too much attention, but you don't get a star coming through your hands every day. He had a beautiful voice . . . not disciplined, and untrained of course. I tried to get a school choir going, hard work, but when I persuaded him to sing then others flocked to follow. For nearly a year I based the choir around him. Most of the boys would have reckoned that singing was too effeminate for them, but I had Cameron on my side. Not for very long . . . he was too talented to stay at the level. I had a friend who worked with the cathedral's choir, we sang together, indifferently, but she helped with the proper choir, the best.

"Look at it this way. Every cathedral has to have a very competent set of choristers. Think how many there are – then consider the pressure on the cathedral authorities to provide, year in and year out, the best . . . And Canterbury Cathedral is the headquarters of Church of England plc. It is a massive undertaking, it hosts prestige visitors pretty near every day of the week, and it cannot be second rate. I told my friend about this boy, little Cameron Jilkes. The cathedral has scouts, looking for voices, the same as any football team does. I suppose I can say this now, can I? A tough family. A brother in gaol, a sister who was killed in a car crash. A mother working all hours God gave. A father who was long gone. And there is this child with an exceptional voice. I put him up for audition . . . Expected that I would have to cajole him, offer bribes of some sort but I was wrong. Took it in his stride and there was a scholarship built into the agreement. There's a school that provides the academic side. He sailed in there . . . in case you think – sorry, I didn't catch your names – that I am too gushing, there could be a darker side. While he was still with us, an older boy picked on Cameron because he received free school meals, was disadvantaged as we call it now. The boy had a go at him one lunchtime and Cameron was eating and he didn't react. Finished his lunch, then took the fork off his plate and went to where this boy was sitting and came behind him, and held the fork against his tormentor's throat. It was a dramatic moment. It could have ended with the emergency services. The older boy stumbled through an apology and the assault was never again mentioned.

"What do you want me to say? He had a superb natural voice . . . I heard what happened, the Syria business. I'd like to think that he was not responsible for any of the really beastly things that were done there. That's all I can tell you, but I have a name and a number for the choirmaster who took Cameron on, retired now . . . A difficult boy, but in that brief window while his voice was perfect he soared to great heights . . . Did he die out there? Don't misunderstand me, I hope he did. A free spirit. Not one to languish in a cell, behind barred windows."

At the door, they were again asked, "Forgive me, did I ask you? Did you tell me your names?"

The phone rang and the child was crying.

The cot was in front of her, the phone was out in the hall, and the ironing board was between the two, and a pile of washing filled the plastic basket.

It was the time that Gavin had said he'd call to let her know whether the conference would go on through the evening and whether he'd stay overnight.

Vicky did not particularly enjoy the motherhood experience, had not taken to the housewife role chores, did not particularly relish the marriage bit either and him working all the hours God gave him for their "future security". No time left for fun, for excitement, for challenge . . . She picked up the phone.

"Hello, love, just thought I'd check in with you. We're between meetings, so I had the chance to ring, and we don't know yet how it will be later. I think it will be an overnight job but . . . Love, what's wrong?"

What was wrong was that the baby was filling its nappy, and was hungry, and was yelling.

"What I'm saying, we may stay and may not. The talk after lunch was excellent, the new model, electric, really interesting. Sorry, is it not convenient?"

Hardly convenient . . . Put the phone down, skirted the ironing board, caught her ankle in the flex, spilled water out of the iron, swore, picked up the little one . . . God, the stink . . . and shoved the dummy in its mouth, which would, according to her mother-in-law, distort the baby's face.

She retrieved the phone. Her husband was saying, ". . . so that's where we are about this evening but most likely we'll do the over-night, unless . . . Well, I've told you that. Anyway, the new electric model is very exciting, it's incredible. Is it not convenient?"

"Not really, no. Have a nice evening, and don't drink too much. See you tomorrow . . ." She rang off.

The phone was on the hall table beside the wedding picture. On the rebound, and expensive, and she had thought of him all through the first honeymoon night. She took the baby into the kitchen to heat its food. In the kitchen was a framed photograph of the baby in her arms paid for by her mother-in-law. After the rebound wedding the rebound baby had arrived.

He had been a wonderful shag and he was exciting and different but he had gone and had never said anything approaching a fare-well . . . This was her life now, and she fed the baby and had some gurgles in exchange and some wind and some smiles, and then she'd get back to tackling the ironing: the harder she worked the better she was at suppressing the memories.

★　　★　　★

"Hello, Cameron . . . Welcome home."

He was sitting in the middle row: across the aisle were the places that would soon be taken by the choristers. Each of the cushions carried the name of an archbishop and the date he had been elevated to the see of Canterbury. He could have sat on John, 1486–1500 or Simon, 1366–1368, but had chosen William who had been in office from 1375 to 1381. He did not move, did not turn.

"All those years, but faces don't change. Thought it was you."

He had heard the man sit behind him and imagined it was a tourist, a visitor. The voice had startled him and he might have made a poor fist of hiding his reaction.

"Was it that bad there? As bad as we read about?"

The gentle voice was familiar, but he could not put a face to it.

"But all over now? Pretty hellish if you were on the receiving end, yes?"

The voice was little more than a whisper and Cammy had to strain to hear each word and inflexion in the voice. There was no pretence of sympathy in the words. Cammy could have said what he imagined he would say if he were interrogated – not that he would be – about the propaganda being fed into the minds of the wonderful British public and that the black flag guys – with a few exceptions – were nowhere close to matching the atrocities dished out daily by the Syrian régime or its coterie of allies. He thought the voice cold.

"We had the police and the spooks crawling all over us when it was first revealed you'd gone. Dismembering your life history. Caused quite a stir."

Should have considered this, but had not. He had made the journey, had been sent to the recruitment camp where they were kept under close guard while the vetting was done, then to the front line. The group had formed, his brothers, and the war had started to turn and what might have happened here had seemed distant. What sort of men and women would they have been, those who came to pick at the entrails of his life, and his mother's, and who had traipsed around the cathedral and the college, trying to join dots? Boring little people. No respect for them. They would not understand a free spirit, and the excitement of the hammer against the shoulder of the big machine-gun, and the adrenaline pump of the charge across open ground – and the brotherhood, and how strong they had been, all of them together.

"Do not imagine that I make judgements. I see no point in joining the condemning rabble, but your side did seem to take a quite unpleasant approach to conquest. I thought the burning alive of that Jordanian pilot was just horrible. But I am not about to morph into the role of inquisitor, accuser. I just live out my years here and recall good times and some rather lovely young voices."

Knew of it but had not been there. Cammy had been on the front line, trying to hold positions in the effort to take control of Kobane. The bombing had been incessant but the tide had turned. Accepted no responsibility. He wondered if he should turn his head, peer into the face of his accuser, answer him. Wondered if he should stand up and leave, head left towards the presbytery and the Trinity Chapel and find somewhere else to sit and avoid scrutiny. Or turn right and go out past the quire screens and back into the nave . . . But he had come here to relive the past and to go would be to turn his back on his youth and on the choir – a time when he had soared, been proud. He stayed where he was, did not turn.

"I'm not looking for the sanctity of the other crowd's confessional though I am quite practised in discretion. There won't be a price on your head, not here in leafy Kent, but they'll want to talk to you. What I heard, the sort of gossip we get in this place, is that you were regarded as a serious fighting machine. Some of the Scandinavian countries, so I read, have adopted a policy of greeting their *jihadis* and putting them on de-radicalisation programmes. Like nothing ever happened, like it was all a mistake and the sort of jape that youngsters get up to. Not the attitude taken here, Cameron. Is it my duty to go up the Old Dover Road to the police station and report our meeting? Or is that not necessary?"

He stared straight ahead. Spoke from the side of his mouth. The man's head was bent forward the better to hear him and he smelled fresh toothpaste, imagined it a necessary part of the modern cleric's presentation. He said he had made errors and deeply regretted the shame and the pain he had inflicted on those good enough to love him . . . That he planned to go to his home that evening, after the beauty of the evensong service, spend time with his mother, make his peace with her, then go to the police station in the morning . . . Lied fluently.

"Seems satisfactory. I think I can live with that."

And would ask for his mother's forgiveness.

"I hope you've left the hate behind . . . Please, Cameron, give my best regards to her, a fine and decent lady . . . What time will you be at the police station?"

He named the hour, and hung his head, a gesture of his sincerity.

"That is sensible and intelligent. I wish you well."

Cammy heard the priest leave his seat. He did not have to turn because he walked to the front, moving slowly, with the aid of a stick, along the length of the pews where visitors sat for evensong. He thought he had lied with conviction. As he had lied to his mother "Just popping out, Mum" and had not come back. As he had lied to the interrogators who were paranoid about informers and had questioned him at the *jihadi* recruitment camp, told them of his devotion to their cause . . . Cammy had no doubt that the priest would honour their agreement and would not go to the police station before noon. By then he would be far away, heading for his target, working into position for his last attack.

"It is about priorities, Jonas."

He did not reply. Had requested a meeting with the AssDepDG, had heard the clatter of his heavy shoes in the corridor and the internal echo as the outer door opened into the work area, empty still.

"I had priority 'problems' before, a couple of hours back. Now I have priority 'difficulties', and each hour it is harder. We have diminishing resources, as you know, and I have put our maximum effort into the places where we have the maximum danger."

Jonas shrugged.

"You have identified the returnee that you believe crossed the Channel this morning?"

Jonas pointed at the picture that carried, in his own hand-writing, the initials of Cameron Jilkes.

"And he comes from Canterbury, and may return there, but you do not consider him to be the type that will renounce his immediate past? Want to 'start again', accept that the interlude is over? You don't predict that?"

Jonas shook his head. He was reading his screen, absorbing the young people's report of their interview with the retired school teacher. They were now on their way to meet with a choirmaster, retired. He had the intelligence report from the Gulf, and had a call in to a Special Forces veteran, a decorated sergeant. Jonas prided himself on being honest. He did not believe that he should milk short-term opportunity, nor ever gild a threat to get it higher up a ladder of concern. Priorities demanded truths.

"I cannot instruct resources to send a full surveillance team to Canterbury, Jonas. Simply, I do not have those numbers. Your colleagues were sent to Hull to meet a courier returning from the Continent. The courier, and his wife, are carrying – to our best knowledge – an RPG-7 launcher and a number of the bloody things it propels. Capable of penetrating buildings. Effective at well over a quarter of a mile. That is why we have scrambled from here. Except . . ."

Jonas waited to be told. He raised an eyebrow, but his own pitch was all that concerned him.

"It is – and I am sure you know this as well as I do – a devastating weapon. It is being shipped here from the Balkans. From a family on hard times. Most of those unfortunates who endured their civil war would have followed the old Irish advice 'kept a pike in the thatch'. A pike, or a rifle, or an anti-tank missile launcher. Kept it in the event of hostilities flaring again, or kept it for when the family finances faced a rainy day, and they could flog it off. It came from near Mostar. The Croats tracked it, then the Slovenians and then the Austrians. We were very happy with the degree of cooperation extended. The couriers are a couple from the East Midlands, pensioners, looking for a bonanza payday. Pushed into a pick-up at a fuel station outside Cologne, so we were reliant on our esteemed German colleagues . . . God and do those beggars not delight in extolling their virtues . . ."

Jonas felt old, old and weary. He blinked but did not turn to face the AssDepDG. Would have been, for his superior, therapeutic to have a chance of bouncing his frustrations – and fears – onto another's shoulders.

"They lost the vehicle on its way to Zeebrugge. They lost it, Jonas. Fucking lost it. The Germans lost it. We think they showed out and then the old boy at the wheel did some basic procedures and dumped them. It would be nice to report that the Germans then put out a Europe-wide alert, but they sat on their hands. I anticipate that we'll get a string of mealy-mouthed excuses, not their fucking fault. So, I have kept the team from here as a flying column. When, or *if*, we hear of this weapon on the move, I can divert them. But, what if they are able to change vehicles and arrive at another ferry with a different set of wheels? What if they are well enough organised to have a second set of travel documents? What if . . .? That is where I am, Jonas."

He stared at the two faces on his wall: the one of Cameron Jilkes, and the one that showed an unnamed beast, no doubt sunning itself at the time the picture was taken, digesting a previous day's feed, but almost certain in the next few hours to slip back into the dark deep water, and lie sill, patient, beneath the surface. Jonas Merrick never argued his corner, accepted that he could rarely alter decisions taken, would not bicker over it. An alternative strategy was obvious, and he could have recited why it would be rejected. The thought was offered.

"Call in the police? An option, but not one we would like. They crawl over us, Jonas, always anxious to pinch territory, kleptomaniacs for gaining acreage. They bring little to the party beyond heavy boots, rigid rule books. There is faint praise for the Service's efforts in this bloody war. There are those who would restrict us, emasculate us. Not on my watch. You have a Jo who is drifting back to the UK, intentions unknown. I have a lethal weapon freewheeling across the near continent. And we have a list of potential targets as long as your arm and throw in a leg. We'll manage, we have to manage. And we'll have to manage the matter of priorities."

Again the shrug, which was enough.

The footsteps clicked away. He would speak soon to his probationers, and would speak to that section in the building that dealt with access to police support units. Jonas felt older, tired, was dreaming fleetingly of the joys of driving on a crowded west country route with a caravan bumping and swaying behind him. And waited for a call. Cammy looked a pleasant enough lad – but the photograph was not yesterday's and Jonas assumed that many men were changed by the experience of war. The light was slipping outside and the river gleamed and rain dribbled on his window. Thought also of the lost launcher and the projectiles that could penetrate a tank's armour, and what type of man would be skilled in its use. Too much to think of and answers coming that were unwelcome.

8

"They punched above their weight – know what I mean?"

Jonas told him to expand.

"They were a small unit. We'd heard of them but didn't have a contact. Must have been that bad hour, the one before dawn, when we all want to be in bed, and the people that we were training were in their pits, wanting to be anywhere but in that camp. The front line was stable, but the black flag guys had tried to break through, and had failed. Maybe we were complacent, but . . ."

Jonas had a young British officer on the phone. He had taken some tracking, was out on the wastes of Dartmoor, a freshener course in survival with the Marines. Two years before he had been with the Special Boat Service and had been attached to a supposedly "good guys" crowd of anti-régime and anti-*jihadi* fighters.

". . . always difficult when complacency settles. The feeling was that they had made their main effort, had not dislodged us, that we had done our job well. Normally if they attacked they would come in yelling and screaming, fire points from every angle and probably a suicide boy, or two of them, to blast a hole. It's intimidating, but you get notice of them coming. Not this time. Came in the small hours, and there were very few of them. They were quiet, and they took us by surprise. Hit very hard, gave us heavy stick. There were four of us in the training team, in our command building, but one of our sergeants had gone out for a piss, and . . ."

Jonas thought he knew the part of the moor where the officer spoke from. Vera had said that it was not necessary always to have a sea view, and that a break in the shelter of one of the tors – Dartmoor or Bodmin – would be pleasant. He thought he could hear the rattle of rain falling on canvas roofing, not that Vera would have minded rain if she were snug in her caravan. His mind could wander but not his concentration, and most of the time his eyes were on the face on the wall beside the crocodile.

"... caught short at an inconvenient time, as we later reminded him. Odd thing was that we *were* able to remind him. We had bulbs slung from cables, linking the command post to the mess hall and to the latrine pits. Shots were fired. My sergeant was still zipping his flies and groping for his weapon when he's confronted by this guy. Black kit, black mask, black-painted assault rifle. English voice. The barrel is pointed at my sergeant – we're talking half a dozen paces, point-blank range, where your granny couldn't miss. South of England accent. He was dead, effectively, my sergeant. Nowhere to go, illuminated, a weapon on him. This guy says, no lie, just says, 'Get the fuck out of the way, and stay there, out of the way.' He does. Each pace he takes to the command bunker he's expecting to be shot in the back. Funny old world. They don't hit the bunker, but they create five shades of shit amongst the people we're supposed to be indoctrinating into close quarters warfare. They're chucking grenades around, and incendiaries. Blitzing the camp. We're trying to put down suppressive fire but we don't have targets, and I don't have enough assets to leave the protection of that building. They stay clear of us, like we're not important. There was a method to it."

He thought of the comfortable life he and Vera led, and their dreams of short holiday breaks. Thought of the nightmare of being in the darkness of a Syrian night, mortars and grenades exploding, and the jagged lines of red-tipped tracer fire. The shrieks of pain, and the terrifying extent of the chaos. He stared at the photograph of the man with the smear around his mouth.

"We heard other voices in the few minutes it lasted. All in English but we thought there were middle Europeans and Americans and very definitely a South African ... No hanging about. They were gone ... In theory we had held the position, but that sells them short. It all went quiet. They had no casualties and when daylight came there were no blood trails. There were four of us, and some two hundred and fifty recruits in the camp. We reckoned there were half a dozen of them . . . By midday, our place was abandoned. Three of their officers were dead and the rest had legged it. Hardly a score draw. They broke the morale of the men holding the line. More important, my team and others had spent six months in the training programme and it was all negated in about five minutes . . . that's why it was, in my opinion, 'punching above their weight'. Who were they?"

Jonas seemed to see an innocence in the eyes.

"There had been talk about a small special formation. You hear that sort of thing all the time, but believe it only when you're hit and it goes badly. The more élite they are, then the better you feel if your arse is kicked. It was a very committed attack, well planned and well directed. It did the job as intended, and I promise you, Mr Merrick, it takes discipline to retire in good order when that job is done, not to hang about. Singing their praises loudest was that sergeant with the weak bladder."

And saw the cut of the jaw, its power. Not a man who would take a backward step . . . He had a map laid out in front of him, and had drawn a crude circle around the village and the estate off the Margate road.

"That sort of action is not planned by a committee. There will be one of them and the rest are followers. And then intelligence threw in the name of Kami al-Britani as their chief honcho. We find that successive layers of UK military keep bumping into the sort of people that we would like to have had as our senior non-commissioned officers: very able, think on their feet, those who come out on top of any leadership cadre. Just a pity that he was on the wrong side – and best fought when he is respected.

"I have to hack on, Mr Merrick. Been good to speak . . . Oh, and there was a woman with them . . . You'll not be surprised if I say my sergeant spoke well of him. Why was his life spared? Can't say, don't know, except that he'd have had the union flag stitched to his upper arm. What I do say is that we might have hit him at the right time because in the months ahead they were given a heavy battering. When they were pulling back, they were hassled all the way from the air, especially from the drone attacks. It was awesome, Mr Merrick, the force used against them. Did he survive?"

No answer given.

"If you are interested, does that tell me he's come home?"

Jonas chuckled softly, was about to ring off.

"Remember what I said about 'respect', and remember the pounding they've taken. And remember that what they dread most is going in a cage. Good night, Mr Merrick."

The time for evensong was half past five – the central point in the cathedral's daily routine. The choir came in procession.

Cammy had once been part of this magnificence. A chosen one. His appearance had once been as theirs was. Faces scrubbed, and hair – always seemed to be blond – tidily cut, immaculately parted. Fingernails short and polished black shoes. A white surplice over a purple robe, and a starched ruff – also white – at the throat. They filed in, took their places beside the block of seats where Cammy was.

Worshippers and tourists were pressed around Cammy.

A young man led them. In Cammy's day, toward the end of his time, an older man had replaced for a few months the choirmaster who had gone on sick leave, or a sabbatical. The boys called the stand-in "old Fergie".

He listened. He did not need to open the hymn book, *Ancient and Modern*: recalled it. *Cast Me Not Away*, one of his favourites, following only minimally behind the "snares of hell" anthem. A woman beside him, her elbow against his, had closed her eyes, and her lips moved and she had the look on her face of adoration. As Cammy remembered it, reverence and praise were heaped on the young voices, and it was understood that they were unique in the church world of their country, were the best. He had come from the estate on the hill above the village of Sturry, had been pulled out of the local state junior school, had sung in auditions, had heard older men and a woman murmuring, tapping pencils, and scribbling notes, and the letter had dropped through the letterbox. His mother had opened it, had slumped on the stairs, had held the single sheet of paper, half a dozen typed lines on it under the address of the college, and tears had streamed on her face and she had been rendered speechless. His half-brother had cuffed him on the shoulder and had muttered that he had "done well", which was as good as it would get. His half-sister had pulled a face, had hugged him, and then kissed his cheek, left lipstick there. A new school uniform, fitted for his robes, gone with a cheap suitcase to Choir House where he would be a boarding pupil. His accent different to the other new recruits, and his manners rough, and his discipline lax, but as the months had gone by these were tolerated because of his voice, and his ability to learn, and the thing of beauty that he possessed.

He looked at each of their faces. He estimated which were about to feel the weight of failure, pain of rejection. Their voices soared into the upper arches of the great roof ... He had cared not a damn for the religion. The chanting of priests, the rituals, the heads bobbing towards a faraway altar, the kneeling and the devotion, had mattered as nothing to him. He had been noticed and, in the last months, old Fergie would fix an eye on him and draw him out and would seem, with thin and bony fingers, to conduct only Cameron. His mum came when she could. She would bend her hours, and sometimes he would see her, and sometimes only learn that she had been there when he was at home on those weekends when the choir was not required. She would sit in the back row of the pews opposite and would keep her head ducked down so that she would not catch his eye if he glanced around; she would not have wanted to distract him. She told him that the visits to the cathedral to hear him brightened the whole day, or whole week.

He had been cut out of the choir, had known it was coming, and had known that his voice had suffered the first indications of what one of the adult choir members had called "imperfections". Had noticed that old Fergie had begun to take a keener interest in him, and had started, not often, to wince when Cammy hit certain notes.

They were all condemned – Cammy as much as any of the kids he was listening to now, in their white and purple, singing to the rafters far above. Put crudely, "because their balls are going to drop", their voices would deepen. Most would stay on at the college because they had "made a good impression", had shown promise at cricket or rugger, or had taken to a musical instrument, or were doing well in the classroom. Did not harbour what old Fergie called the "rebel streak". It was the way of the estate, for the young'uns, that retaliation should be got in first. In two years, the college had not taken the estate out of Cameron Jilkes. At the last evensong he was no longer allocated a place in the front row and nearest the choirmaster. His mum was not there.

It was expected that he would be leaving both the choir and the college. Surplus to requirements and considered "unsuitable material". Did not have to be done with pain and angst; rough edges would have been planed smooth and scholarship money made available.

They sang *Nunc dimittis*. His lips moved with the words, so well remembered . . . Could remember the day trip, a week before decisions were made for the future of those whose voices were breaking, "changing".

"We went by coach for lunch at Sandwich, a pretty little place, and then on to the Roman fortifications at Richborough."

The pipe smoke filled the room, then was wafted towards an open window. Tristram would have prompted had it been necessary; Izzy had shorthand and took a note.

"I think I was quite popular. They called me 'old Fergie'. I was temporary, a stand-in, just there for a few months. My difficulty came when some of the voices were no longer fit for purpose. I was in the front line for passing on the bad news: and worse news, in a very few cases, was when we were parting company lock, stock and barrel. He knew he was going to take the bullet. I could see a hardening of attitude, a different child, and we are talking of a thirteen-year-old – as if a mask was removed, left the real personality bare."

The former choirmaster lived in a bedsit in a decaying post-war block. The nobility of the great cathedral down the road was far away. He was slouched on a faded settee and Tristram and Izzy were sitting on upright chairs.

"It is an amazing ruin. Probably the best example of the power of Rome's occupation of England. Huge high walls and all still in extraordinary condition, and clear signs of the gatehouse, home for two centuries to the Second Augustinian Legion. Wonderful place. All the boys were spellbound by it, the size, its authority. Except one child. That was Cameron. I was singing its praises. He challenged me. One thing to disagree, another to challenge. Perhaps my language was florid, I'd talked up Roman power. He called out from his usual place at the back of any group, called my remarks, 'Rubbish'. Pushing it a bit, you could say. I told him firmly, slapping him down, these ruins are remarkable, should be admired. He said, voice cracking, gruffness setting in, 'That's rubbish. Look around you. All collapsed. Thought they'd last for ever. Just a heap of stones.' They had had a dose a week or so before of Shelley. This child was no fool. Had made the connection. Quoted back at me: *'My name is Ozymandias, king of kings, Look on my works ye mighty and despair . . .'* "

Tristram recited, "*Nothing beside remains. Round the decay Of that colossal wreck, boundless and bare.* Did it at school."

Izzy said. "*The lone and level sands stretch far away.* Big poetry isn't just for posh kids. He had a point."

"It was a calculated piece of impertinence. What I'm saying is that Cameron had set his face against anything that represented power, discipline, tradition. The choir was acceptable to him because he was its star; not for the glory of God or the beauty of the hymns and responses. He was the centre of attention . . . A week later, after his situation had been thrashed around by the staff at the college, and the decision had been taken, it was my job to break the news to him. 'Sorry, Cameron, but we don't think going on here is in your best interests. We'll do all we can to find you another school, more suitable for your needs.' No tears, no explosion of bad language, just a deadening of the eyes. I had my hand out, to shake his, which I thought the correct gesture. I was ignored. He turned on his heel after a momentary glare of contempt, and left the room. He closed the door carefully, did not slam it, did not make a scene. Never heard of him again until the news of where he'd gone. Did not surprise me."

Tristram said, "Thank you for your time."

Izzy put away her notepad.

Old Fergie said, "I suppose you are here because he's back. I doubt he's changed except that he has probably hardened further. I hazard an opinion: he'll not roll over. You'll have to shoot him. I can hardly believe I am saying that. I doubt I am wrong – shoot him dead."

The Hunters were home.

Trace was in the kitchen, preparing their tea, and Karen was upstairs washing her hair, and Bradley was looking at Royal Navy brochures, still waiting to hear whether he had been accepted for the electronics course, and Dave came down the stairs after changing out of his work suit. The television was on in the front room but nobody was in there so no one was watching. Darkness was gathering. There were not many street lights to illuminate the facades of the houses, the parked cars and the little pocket handkerchiefs of grass by the paths to the front doors. He would always go to the front window, look out and around as if he were some sort of neighbourhood sentry. He'd check there were no vehicles that he could not identify, and no strangers loitering, and his gaze would always linger on the house on the far side and further down, the last in the line.

Dave Hunter felt a soft spot for his neighbour, Sadie Jilkes; they all did. Her curtains weren't drawn, there were no lights on. He knew it was important to Sadie to keep her bills to the minimum. She walked to a bus-stop that was further from her home than the nearest because it cost her less to board and get off there. He thought they did not do enough for her: did not know what else they could do; social invitations were invariably rebuffed. He dragged the curtains across the window.

The television news had reached the weather forecast, and that part of the south-east would have a decent start to the day tomorrow, and there would be a dry night and light winds . . . fact was that the forecast was pretty much the same as most days. Fact also was that life in their road stayed simple, ordered, and that crises seemed not to happen. An unremarkable street, he would have said if describing it "on a hill, looking down on the city, plenty of fields near us and a cemetery where I'll probably get parked. Nice place where nothing much happens." Sadie would be at work somewhere in the city, sweeping and wiping and dusting, emptying waste-paper bins and filling black bags and pushing a vacuum cleaner, and likely she'd have toilets to deal with too. Not his business, that Sadie Jilkes had a son in gaol, had a daughter who was in that cemetery, and another son who was God knows where – if he was still alive.

A wry smile slipped on to the face of Jonas Merrick.

He imagined the reactions of those who worked further down the corridor, because they had not heard him pass their doors at his usual time. The same down in the big front hall where the women sat behind desks and checked out internal staff and external visitors. The same for the police who patrolled the pavement outside. All of them would have said they could set their watch by the time he left. Not that evening.

The traffic was nose to tail and headlights gleamed, and beyond them was the river with slow-moving barges and a single pleasure boat. He now involved himself in the lives of strangers.

It was his skill to insert himself into the existence of people who would have no reason to think they were being examined by a man they knew nothing of. His computer had the power to penetrate their telephone logs, to dig out their mobile numbers, to excavate their bank accounts. Below his picture of the crocodile in the still, dark pool and the photograph of a young man with a pleasant smile, he crouched, frog-like, over his keyboard. Almost caressed the keys, seemed to win favours from it.

He had been, as if with a scalpel, into the life of a one-time girl-friend. Had found her picture, pretty girl, before her wedding. And another with her baby and her husband and her mother-in-law. Had her job references, her bank accounts and her husband's, had her address.

Had passed on the details, to Tristram and Izzy, told them what he needed.

Had gone on a virtual tour of the street at the top of the hill off the main road to Margate. Had used the computerised attachments to walk him along it and then to stop in front of a semi-detached house, the last in the row, a cemetery behind it. It looked in need of repair. A decent home, but uncared for: the paintwork needed attention and weeds grew in what had once been a small shrub bed. He had a list of neighbours. The property next to that of Mrs Sadie Jilkes was in the name of an Asian couple and he had established that they ran a Post Office franchise. There were others; the process was tedious but he preferred to make his own investigations, then hold to his own decisions . . . There was a family that lived diagonally opposite. The man was an accountant . . . the family seemed unremarkable. And remembered . . .

. . . A year and a half before. After his gong had been pinned, and after the detailed debrief of Winston Gunn, a rule had been broken. What rules were for – Jonas did not believe in the inflexible. Young Winston, failed suicider, had been spirited away to a safe house, and a mobile phone was made available so that he could speak to his mother once a week. And the poor boy had shown extraordinary emotion at being permitted to make those calls. Jonas had ramped it, as if rewarding Gunn for his levels of cooperation and his treachery to those once his associates, now in the "chokey", and a visit was arranged. Farida had been controlled, dignified, had wrapped her arms around her errant kid and hugged him. Winston, unsuccessful in his bid for martyrdom, had been in distraught tears and had clung to her. A monitoring psychiatrist had written a few paragraphs for a report about the importance of the image of his mother in the mind of a fighting man. Not a girlfriend but a mother – more important than anyone else for the fighter far from home.

He would be gone within an hour. He had one more call to make then he would be gone. The clock raced and there was no chance of serious reinforcement being granted him. But he preferred to carry his own responsibilities, not share them. It was a lousy night out there that he would soon be going into before improvement in the morning and probably turning into a lousy night where young Cameron was.

A priest had noted the presence of the gaunt young man at the evensong service. Had seen a tough and weathered face and the blemishes on it from acute sunburn and the blisters from insect bites, had been confused by the old man's clothes he wore, but recognised him. Had always rather liked the boy. Had thought he had taken a generous and yet responsible line with him. Would not denounce him, not that evening. Would go in the morning, after Cameron Jilkes had visited his mother, spent a night in his own bed, and had then taken a bus into town to check himself in at the police station. He would go himself, but later. He would make an excuse to justify his delay in reporting the recognition. Had seen the face, had thought it haunted. Believed the experience of that form of warfare would have scarred deeply, and was pleased that the young man would spend time with his mother before surrendering.

It would be his last sight of the cloisters, the water tower, the treasury. He went past the garden where wild flowers grew out of the mortar binding the old stone walls. He had walked through the gravestones of men dead for centuries. Behind him was the building where once he would have been called "a chosen cherubim" or "that little angel".

It had been, for Cammy, a pilgrimage before his main journey. Could not have gone, without it, to the place where he would attack, wreak – he believed – a fearful vengeance and give his name a resonance, would not be forgotten as were the men whose bones were lying beneath him. Other than in school holidays and occasional weekends, for two years the Choir House had been his home. He had worn a school uniform that would have singled him out from every other kid of his age on the estate above the village of Sturry; he would have known music that none of them knew; learned the basics of the Latin language that none of them would recognise. He came to the door of the boarding house and stopped. Why was he there? A fair enough question.

A woman came out. She glanced at him. She would have seen his scarred face and the stubble on his cheeks, and noticed the conservative jacket he wore and the anorak hooked over his shoulders, maybe seen a decent shirt and a sombre tie, and a pair of shoes that would have looked right at a bowls club committee meeting, and he was obviously loitering. She turned to face him, hands on her hips. Cammy turned away from her. He remembered the priest and the easy lie. The last time he had walked this path, around the cathedral's outer walls, the tears had run on his face. His mother had carried his suitcase. Not much in it, a few books, a few games, and pyjamas. His school uniform, his robe and ruff, were left behind, would be allocated to another child. It was the last time he had cried.

Visitors to the cathedral had stopped and turned to stare at the child whose mother carried the case, and who marched him briskly towards an exit. One teacher had said to him that he should not feel any sense of guilt because his voice had suffered the inevitable changes of aging. Another had said that he was not "really cut out for this place, find somewhere that'll make you happier". A younger member of staff had remarked, "You're not, frankly, your own best friend, Cameron, too full of argument." His mother's grip on his hand brooked no argument. They had almost reached the outer Christ Church Gate when she had jerked his arm.

She'd said, "Come on, get a grip and stop that bloody noise. They're not worth it. Put them behind you . . . Those people that look down their long noses at us, they use the same hand as you when they wipe their bums. They're no better than you . . ."

He had smeared an arm across his eyes, had blinked hard. Of course, then, had not known how but had made a promise that a price would be paid, and with interest.

He did not look back as he approached the gate. A price to be paid and a big one . . . would be done the following morning. He had all of them in his mind – Stanislau and Mikki and Tomas,

Dwayne and Pieter, and Ulrike – and his stomach growled in hunger and the rain had come on heavier.

"Oh, for fuck's sake . . ."

Dominic was at his car, a weight of gear dumped at his ankles, and his phone had beeped, and he'd checked the text.

"This is the bloody end . . ."

On the other side of the parking area, Babs had the boot of her car open and everything loaded in it that had not gone back into the armoury, and her phone had gone and she'd read her text.

"This is just bloody unreasonable," he murmured.

"God! Do they not think we have the right to a life?" she snapped.

They walked towards each other.

"I was going to a movie."

"We have a birthday next week and I'm due to make the cake."

"It will be overtime, won't it?"

"Bet your life it will be."

Different ways, and different types, but both were wedded to the job. He had a new girlfriend who worked in a solicitor's office and who was sorely tried by the hours he kept and his devotion to the work, and who just about hung in there, and would get a call in the next five minutes telling her to find a friend to take to the Cineworld. She had a husband, father of their kid, and he joked, pretended to, about being second in place, or third, even fourth, to her job; he'd get a call telling him to shove off down to the Co-op, and buy a cake and make sure he checked the "Use Before" date.

Rain was beating down on the tarmac, and on their kit, and starting to soak them. The call had not come as a surprise. They should have been released hours before but had been asked to hang around, something was in the wind. They were to get up to Canterbury . . . Why them? They were not entitled to see the duty roster, or to know where the armed response vehicles were tasked that evening. They were to get up to Canterbury, were to check in at the station there. Would be contacted by a Mr Merrick.

Dominic rang through to his sergeant. "Are we part of a big team?"

"Don't think so, Dom. They've asked for a bit of muscle for the ride, and we're sending you and Babs, and you take all your artillery. You might be wondering about Merrick? He's the Box. He's a spook. Merrick says that it will all be over by the morning. Part of it is that we are thin as a fag paper, and part of it is that you were on the beach this morning and were in there at the start. Anything more will expose my ignorance . . . Enjoy."

He said to Babs, "I don't want to go rash, like jump off the end of the pier, but this might just be interesting . . ."

Together they went back inside and drew out their firearms and their ammunition and their grenades again. Had enough stuff, the armourer observed, to start a small-scale war.

She said, "Could be a lot better than interesting if it's that guy on the beach. Serious and interesting."

The busker had a traditional guitar and strummed vigorously and sang without amplification. The rain was soaking into his woollen hat and into his sweater and he seemed not to notice. In front of him was a plastic plate with a rim to it that would protect the coins thrown into it. Cammy was his sole audience. Recognised him.

Thought the sweater was the same, and the beanie, but his beard was longer and the flecks of grey more pronounced. Sitting in the same place with his back to a war memorial, topped by a small Celtic cross. He had been there the day Cammy had gone, taken the flight that would lift him into fighting alongside the black flags. He had walked past the war memorial on his way to the bank on the main drag and the busker had been playing. Perhaps he noticed the guy with the weird face and the clothes that did not match his age, and might have wondered whether the attention shown him meant that he was going to get a generous pocketful of loose change. "Out of luck, friend."

He stayed and listened and wondered . . . Cammy had been in Raqqa and in Deir Ezzor and in Kobane and in Barghuz, and plenty of other places that barely figured on most maps. The busker had been here with his guitar; Cammy went on to have his assault rifle and the use of the 81mm mortar tube, and the RPG-7 launcher and had the support of his brothers. The busker still played alone. Cammy had been with the people he loved: and now, he, too, was alone. The busker would be playing through that week, and Cammy would be gone. Their eyes met, a brief exchange . . . The guy finished and realised that he'd get no coins off the man who watched him. Shook his head and flicked the rain off his beanie, and put the guitar into its case. Cammy watched as he started to walk away.

He said to the man's back, "I don't know your name. You don't know mine, but you will tomorrow."

He had been given the number of a psychologist, employed by the military until retirement four months before. Jonas explained why he called, what he needed to know.

"Kami al-Britani. We knew him quite well, able to form a decent profile of him."

He did not interrupt, had no need to. Jonas gazed at the photograph on his wall.

"You've told me about the confrontation with an experienced NCO, a sergeant in SBS. Implied that some sense of nobility, or patriotic sentiment, saved the sergeant's life. You indicated that this young Briton declined to kill a fellow countryman . . . Mr Merrick, from what I hear of you, you are unlikely to be gullible. I would lay odds – my shirt, my vest, my underpants, perhaps even my Marylebone tie – that the weapon jammed. This is not some Robin Hood figure who patrols the desert and seeks to right the wrongs inflicted by the Assad regime, or the Iranians and Hezbollah, or the UK and the Americans, by the rest of the known world. We can assume him and his coterie are in love with the business and pursuit of warfare. Some people play golf, some stand on the end of a platform and jot down the numbers on the sides of locomotives, some want to have a loaded weapon in their hands. He led a group. It was a talisman to other units. They were believed to be invincible. They attacked against ludicrously uneven odds and seemed to come through unscathed. That bit is important."

Jonas seldom took notes, relied on his memory.

"They were survivors, winners. We might have imagined that they had, collectively, no great sense of the burning injustice of the day. Nor would they have concerned themselves with the hideous atrocities that were the daily practice of the black flag movement. They proceeded with the combat, with the killing, and they soaked up the praise. Had a sense of enduring excitement rather than anger . . . But it started to go wrong. Where I started out, Mr Merrick, we go back to a wall. Go back to the bricks that have been removed. The wall is now unstable, its strength is unpredictable. It will create mayhem when it falls. The bricks are the people involved in that group. I was privileged to sit in on security assessments. They were intact when they left the enclave at Barghuz. A coherent unit, but a small one. Keep thinking of the bricks, Mr Merrick."

He thought of them but continued to stare at the mouth of the crocodile, its jaws and its teeth.

"They were multi-national. All significant misfits in the society they came from. Cameron Jilkes – I did not have that name, only that of Kami al-Britani. British. There was a German woman and we had identified a young Estonian boy, and a white South African, a Ukrainian, a Canadian and a Belarus man. They had stayed untouched, were celebrities. Like the fighter aces over the trenches in the First World War. A peculiar irony, but once they quit the main war theatre and were looking to drift away, go to ground, they began to take casualties. What we learned, the Estonian was first. He was followed by the Ukrainian, and more. I suppose that only one is still active . . . From your interest I assume that the one we call Kami al-Britani survived, has returned. He has lost the stability that came from his colleagues. He will be alone. People may seek to use his combat skills but he has no friend to take on the burden of decision making. His mind-set will dictate just one ambition. Maximum havoc and revenge. What he knew has been destroyed, and bloodily. That makes a powerful anger . . . He will want to find a target that he can equate to the value of his colleagues. His weakness? He will need to get his hands on a weapon that can deliver the Valhalla moment, a decent bang for the buck . . ."

Jonas arched an eyebrow. "Meaning . . .?"

"Military explosive, a heavy machine-gun, an 81mm mortar, or an armour-piercing grenade projectile from an RPG . . ."

"He could use that?"

"Of course, yes. Has been at war in a savage theatre for more than two years. This is heavy lifting, continous fighting. He can use anything. An RPG would be difficult to get his hands on but would be an ideal weapon . . . My conclusions, Mr Merrick? Very capable, physically brave, determined to hurt, to avenge those colleagues. If he can find the weapon, then he'll go out with drama. They are one-dimensional people and with a quite colossal sense of grievance. But you know that, Mr Merrick . . . My final observation. You do not get to Valhalla by holding up a handkerchief, waving it at the guns and having your hands high above your head. Much worse than death is the idea of imprisonment. A lifetime in a cell, behind bars, unheard and unknown and uncared for, is a true torture for such people. Hope I have been of help. Good luck."

It was always a matter of having the skill to join the dots, Jonas believed . . . A vehicle had been lost while apparently heading for a ferry port from which regular sailings went to the UK. And the cargo was believed to be a *Ruchnoy Protivotankoviy Granatomyot* weapon, doubtless serviceable.

He cleared his desk, locked everything away other than the file on Cameron Jilkes which he slid into his bag. He left it neat, looked a last time at the crocodile, and a last time at the photograph of a young man, smiling and with a ring of ice-cream smeared around his mouth.

9

He felt he was going to war, not with bands playing and crowds cheering, but in stealth and unheralded. The building seemed deserted as Jonas Merrick locked the outer door of 3/S/12 and set off down the corridor towards the bank of lifts.

He went by rooms that showed no light under their doors, and along silent corridors, passed the coffee machines that did no trade at that time of the evening. The ceiling lights were dimmed because that was the new edict in support of a Save the Climate campaign. He carried his bag, pitifully light because it contained so little . . . and just the one file, the name of "JILKES, Cameron" scrawled across the cardboard in his painful handwriting. In his pocket was that awkward-shaped and necessary item of equipment that he had, last minute, decided he should bring with him.

Jonas reckoned that it was neither family holidays or sickness that had emptied the floors of Thames House. He thought the quiet and the ghostly still of the place was because of the stretch factor. No way around it, and "all hands to the pump" as they would have said in former times. Stretched to snapping point, and any man or woman working there who had even half of the necessary ability was sitting in an unmarked car, loitering in a shop doorway, travelling on a bus or train. Those who were not press-ganged into being on the ground were probably huddled over a desk top, staring at screens and trying to find patterns of behaviour without which the Service might as well accept it was blindfolded.

It had never been this bad before, not even in the dark times when the Irish had tried to bomb the city into political capitulation. Not at any time in his Cold War experience, not during the previous years of the *jihadi* emergency.

He waited for the lift and the shape pressed against his hip, hard and uncomfortable. The lift came.

"All good, Jonas?" he was asked by the AssDepDG. There were lines on his forehead, bags beneath his eyes and damn near a shake in his hands.

"Everything's good," he said, his face impassive.

"If it gets more than you and the allocated resources can manage, then shout and . . ."

They travelled down two floors. "I doubt I will."

"I'll come running with what I can muster, tea ladies and God knows who else."

"I think I understand, thank you."

He was alone again descending to the ground floor. The building operated "a need to know" culture, but few had more need to understand the pressures for the commitment of trained personnel. Jonas assumed that some 500 investigations were underway at any one time. He rarely smiled, not even to himself in private moments of humour, but he enjoyed the image of AssDepDG leading a platoon of the women who used to push the tea and biscuit trolleys, and those who shuffled around delivering and retrieving post items, and chauffeurs, and the sweepings off front desk reception. The doors opened.

He saw Lily. She greeted him, shyly, perhaps admired him and perhaps knew of the gong in Vera's knicker drawer.

"You're late this evening, Mr Merrick."

"Am I? I suppose I am."

He hurried towards the desk. There was an elderly security man there, would have been a company sergeant major from the old Irish days, now eking out time until his pension could be drawn, and a woman – thin as a rake – beside him. Lily, from the Archive, would be whispering to the colleagues around her that it was *extraordinary* for him, quite *bizarre*, for old Jonas still to be in the building this late. He thought he saw a nod and an understanding wink from the pale, thin little creature in her chair and the heavy built man sitting beside her. "Good God, shouldn't he have been long gone? Gone before we came on shift?" Fat chance that he would not be noticed

He reached the internal gate. He was slow going through and his coat caught, and a red light flashed . . . . Struggling with the damn thing did not help free him. Security approached. A button was pressed. The coat came away from the clamp that had held it. And there was a clatter of metal on the hard floor.

Handcuffs shivered on the surface, rattled, then fell still. Shiny ones, looking as new as the day they had come off a production line.

Jonas Merrick had been issued with the handcuffs nineteen years before. They had stayed wrapped in tissue paper from the day he had received them. Astonishment on their faces . . . what in the good Lord's name was Jonas Merrick doing with a pair of handcuffs? Security maintained a poker face, and went down on one knee to pick up the handcuffs and give them to Jonas. Then, bent again and retrieved from the base of the gate a pair of small keys on a split ring, straightened up stiffly and handed them to Jonas.

"Best to be able to open them, Mr Merrick, don't you think? Helps to be able to unlock them if they're not going to be just an ornament. Goodnight, sir."

This time they went into his bag, joining his sponge bag and his pyjamas, his socks, underwear and folded shirt. He went out of the main entrance and stood on the steps. He had mapped out his route, would walk past the open space with the statue of the Burghers of Calais, past the bench he had shared with Winston Gunn, and then the Palace of Westminster – the building he was credited with saving – then would take the underground train north, one change, to get to the mainline station. He hesitated on the pavement. Two armed police faced him. He knew them well enough, and thought them always close to the limits of bonhomie, verging on the impertinent. They should have been gazing up and down the street, watching for a bomber or a gunman or a grenade thrower, but instead they stared at him. Had he been certain of his lip-reading skills, he'd have sworn on the Book that one whispered, "Fuck me, I've seen everything now", and would have been asnwered. "Never thought it, the Eternal Flame gone out." And, "I'm not bloody messing, Kev, but if Eternal Flame goes out, then we face serious times." And, "Too right, Leroy, too right, or times that are more than serious."

Leroy said, "Good evening, Mr Merrick. Difficult old night – I mean the weather."

Kev asked, "Going somewhere nice, Mr Merrick? Not that it's my business?"

"It is not . . . A bit of rain never hurt. I'm off to look for a crocodile . . ."

Cammy meandered.

He passed pubs that he had drunk in, had worked in. And a couple of Italian fast food outlets and he'd washed up in the kitchens of both, and past the stationery shop where his mum had carted him before the start of each school term.

The rain was steady. Shop fronts clattered as grilles were lowered. Nothing seemed to have changed since he had last walked here.

Had been with Vicky then and her holding his hand and him with his secret, and nothing said. One drink, later, when they were in the bar, the Miller's, the place heaving with tourists. He had not slept with her that night, had pleaded tiredness, a headache, a difficult day starting the next morning. No real explanation, because he had a "nothing" job in a builder's yard where being tired or having a headache was immaterial.

Had walked her home to her mother's . . . Had hardly thought of her when he was away. Actually even now he had to blink and screw down his concentration to try to recall her face. Cammy, out with the black flags, had never touched any of the girls that came to Syria from England, who had put on the *burqas* and had the sole ambition of being a *jihadi* bride. Had never touched Ulrike who was like a Wendy to them, whose message was *Stay calm. It is never a crisis.* She came from Rostock, up on the Baltic . . . They had not talked about her city, nor his – nor about the North East Transvaal where Pieter was from, nor Toronto which was the city nearest to Dwayne's family home, no talk of Minsk, nor of Tartu and not of Kiev. A life gone by and holding no value, to any of them.

He drifted on to the main street and the rain settled in his hair and on his collar, and darkness had fallen. Men and women hurried past him. He might have been the only person on the street who had no pressing destination . . . until tomorrow.

And nothing much was altered. A few businesses with different logos, a few windows where trade had changed. Cammy had been far away, had fought in ferocious small arms battles, had been under the terrifying noise and impact of airstrikes, had seen the dead and the dying and the mutilated – and none of it had reached here. He doubted anyone would have cared as they bustled past him.

He thought about Vicky. Sweet, innocent, simple Vicky – would pass her mother's house as he walked north out of the city, left the cathedral behind him, headed away and up the river, climbed out of Sturry and into the estate where his home was. *His* home? Of course, *his*. Where there would be money, and food, and a welcome.

Baz said, "We go through with this?"

He had parked in a lay-by. Had switched off the engine, had gone to the rough grass at the side and had scooped up gravel and dirt and wet earth, had smeared it over both registration plates. She had passed him a roll of cling film from the glove compartment, always kept there – reasonable enough for a couple who are doing picnics out of a camper and needed to keep food fresh. He spread the cling film over both plates, then climbed back in.

"We never welshed before," Mags answered.

"Said we'd do it, didn't we?"

"We don't back down. Not us."

"And not our business who they are, what it's for?"

"Sweet fuck-all to do with us, Baz."

Decision taken. The cling film would act as a reflector off the vehicle plates. The number recognition systems would struggle to read them and the filth spread would make identification even harder. They were out of Germany, were past Namur in Belgium and would soon be in France and close to Lille. He started up the engine. She gave him half of a bar of chocolate, as if that were a reward for keeping going . . .

He asked her to map him a route for Boulogne, which had a ferry route to Folkestone.

He said, if he put his foot down, but kept inside the speed limits, they would get to the French port and beat the alert system of the German authorities. He said that the system did not permit a direct swap of information . . . And at Boulogne, they'd take the cling film off the plates. He finished his chocolate, and put his hand on her thigh, like he used to when they were young, and had a giggle in response.

"We said we'd do it, and took their money."

Mags said, "Which is a good enough reason for me."

Vicky should not have had any complaints. There were precious few of the girls, her contemporaries at school, who – at her age – could boast a modern, well-equipped three-bedroom home, valued at around £300,000, had a healthy baby, a husband who worked all hours – and a mother-in-law with constant advice. Precious few of the girls would have known what it felt like to be suffocating – no shortage of air but a surfeit of boredom. And precious few of the girls would have walked away from the chance of time out with Cammy Jilkes. She went downstairs, and into the kitchen. It was a bad night and one of the gutters was overflowing, and she started to make herself a cup of coffee. There was a microwave meal for two in the fridge, that she would have shared with her husband, except that he was going to be away that night, and she'd not be bothered with the effort of heating it for a half portion for herself. She sat at the table to start the shopping list for the weekend; later, if she stayed awake, she'd flick through the *Kentish Gazette*, see what jobs were on offer . . . didn't have to, made clear to her.

The doorbell rang, a prissy little chime.

She was out of her chair. Let it ring once more, and there would be bawling upstairs. She went to the door. The security light had come on in the porch. A couple were ducking for cover and she saw a car parked half in the driveway and half over the pavement. She did not have a light behind her and they might not have realised she was there.

She heard, "This, Tristram, is a piss awful night. Shall I lead?"

"Doubt it's going to be the crown jewels, Izzy, but you gush the sympathy better than I do . . . Ask her if she's seen Gustave."

They were both laughing as she opened the door. Each flashed a card at her that showed their photographs and had a motif of a crown. He said his name was "John", and she said her name was "Betty". So, that was two lies straight up. But "Betty" said that it was a "security matter", and Vicky doubted that was an untruth. They came in. She had not invited them. She pointed up the stairs, put a finger over her mouth. She thought they both grinned but sheepishly, as if babies weren't part of the world of security. They went into the kitchen and sat themselves at the table.

The guy, who was not "John", admired a print on the wall, a view of an old bridge and the river – given them by her mother-in-law. Personally, Vicky would have binned it. She assumed that was a chat-up line for whatever level of spooks they were. She disliked the pair of them, had not taken long to form her opinion. She did not ask if they would like coffee or tea, anything.

"So? Yes? How can I help?"

The girl who was not "Betty" said, "Don't want to waste your time, Victoria. You used to know a boy called Cameron, Cameron Jilkes . . .?"

She did not answer, did not have to. Nor would she help them.

"You used to be friends with Cameron Jilkes? An item? Boyfriend, girlfriend?"

No response, stared back at them. And remembered.

"Then he went away . . . Counter Terrorism Command interviewed you once it was known that he'd travelled to Syria. I've read the transcript . . . you said that you had no warning that he was leaving the UK, let alone that he intended to enlist in a terrorist army. Correct?"

She supposed them to be Cammy's enemy. Smoother than the mob that had turned up before, had treated her like shit and had reduced her mother to tears and her dad had gone into the garden because otherwise he might have taken a crowbar to them. Then, supercilious and loading contempt on her . . . Now, more polish and more apparent manners, except that it was plain they were dealing in low-life and she'd be just the "totty" they'd have expected him to be sniffing after. She wondered why they'd called Cammy by the name of Gustave – would not ask.

"I understand also, Victoria, that you were visited a year or so after he went. By the way, he was not a stretcher-bearer, was not helping bombed-out refugees, was not driving a taxi. He was a signed up fighting man. In a combat unit. He may be alive and on the run out there; he may be dead – we haven't heard but it's possible because the war area is chaotic. But it is also possible he is alive and coming home. May already have returned to the UK. Whatever your feelings for him in the past, Victoria, I should tell you that he is now regarded as a particularly dangerous individual . . . If he has survived. Is that clear to you?"

Like a game of chicken. What the kids did on the dual carriageway going out to the village from the Leisure Centre. Chicken games between the pavements and the central reservation and drivers going berserk. She stared at them. They stared at her. Neither looked away. She would have been poker-faced but they'd assumed the expressions of those shop assistants who have pulled out a dress in a pricey boutique and were now bored half out of their minds, going through the motions, just needed answers from the customer. They were the enemy.

"I am assuming, Victoria, that you have had no contact with him since he left the UK . . . We'd like an answer though, Victoria . . . Any contact with Cameron Jilkes since he left the UK? Or, Victoria, I can escort you down to the central police station in the city and put you in the cell block and then bring you into an interview room, and can ask you again: 'Any contact with that little fucking animal, Cameron Jilkes?' Which?"

Hated them. Hated their confidence, hated them being in her home, hated the sneer in "Betty's" voice, hated the lies. Imagined having to ring her mother-in-law and ask for emergency baby-minding favours because "Well, I'm being carted off to the slammer for interrogation about Cammy who used to shag me before your son, limp dick Gavin, came on the scene." Spat it through her mind . . . Still the smiles but hard eyes. She supposed it was a code-name they had for him, Gustave. Their eyes bored into her, and then the girl who was not Betty started, ever so gently, to ease her chair back as if playtime were over.

Vicky said, "I've heard nothing from him. No contact. Nothing."

"He may have left Syria a year ago. He's been on the run, if he's still alive, since then. No contact? I am being very serious, Victoria, because an untruth now would involve a criminal offence and probably a prison sentence. Have you heard from Cameron Jilkes in the last fifteen hours, since early this morning?"

She shook her head, was crying quietly. A card was passed her. It showed a crown, and the Latin words *Defendere Regnum*, and she'd no idea what that meant and the guy wrote their names on the card above a printed phone number with a London code. If he did call, *if*, then she should ring that number.

They stood, made their way to the front door and let them-selves out. She heard the car engine start, then its radio starting up, some sort of jazz . . . She took the card off the table, tore it into small pieces and binned it, then made that cup of coffee.

Jonas caught the train at the King's Cross/St Pancras terminal, had never started or finished a journey there before.

The train was a Javelin. Comfortable, clean, fast, and full. A schoolgirl had looked hard at him as he'd stood in the corridor as the carriages lurched out of the station and must have thought him either in poor health or decrepit, had given up her seat . . . had shamed him. They went out past the Olympic site – he had put heavy hours in before and during the competitions, but had not watched any events: had no interest. A quick stop at Stratford International and then at Ebbsfleet, and they were nearing Ashford. He was shamed because he had never – not once – given up his seat on the run to or from Raynes Park. Jonas was skilled at looking after himself. From his seat, he had ducked his head in a closet gratitude to the girl, but she had already forgotten him and had a physics textbook in one hand and steadied herself with the other . . . He imagined her as a potential victim.

It was a familiar mind-game for Jonas Merrick. He would take an individual as they walked towards him and past Lambeth Palace, or on the concourse at Waterloo, or along the pavement at Raynes Park before turning into his own street, and he would imagine where they might face the random danger of a *jihadi* assault. They were the *ordinary* people, the *innocents*, the ones who had no interest in the politics and fault-lines of the Middle East, even less interest in the schisms between Shia and Sunni worship, and yet they were front line cannon fodder. An attack on them was only considered worthwhile if many tens of them were left dead in a station, a shopping mall, or the foyer of a concert hall . . . Could summon up a conversation on the sweet-smelling grass and under an apple orchard's trees, the requisite 72 virgins in place, and two suiciders – and one might have been little Winston Gunn. Questions: "How many did you get, bruv?" Answer: "Only got four, couldn't get into a crush of them." A snort: "What? Only four, bruv? Fuck's sake, I did nineteen. You know what they say?" A shrug, and embarrassment: "What do they say?" Laughter and a cuff on the shoulder, and the girls all over them, "Not worth getting out of bed in the morning for less than ten, bruv . . ." He had a sense of comfort. Jonas did not consider that Cameron Jilkes, Kami al-Britani, posed a threat to the girl who struggled with the physics text, or the guy standing next to her who wore a London bus driver's uniform, or the businessman in his suit and his loosened tie, or the two women who had splurged that afternoon in the Oxford Street stores. Not worth it. Not deserving of his man's anger.

Surrounded by the innocent and the ordinary, Jonas Merrick doubted he attracted the remotest attention . . . He believed he knew Cameron's journey, and had an estimation of the sort of target to be attacked, and reckoned he knew the legacy the man would want to leave. The light had faded and all he saw of the countryside was when headlights speared a passage along narrow hedged roads – funny old place for a battlefield – and a cathedral city, a place of homage and pilgrimage, would make it funnier.

He thought also that he knew what Cameron Jilkes wanted least in the few hours before his intended death. Believed he knew how it would end for a man who was off course, had lost all certainties.

Cammy was halfway down the High Street when he heard shouts and jeering. Shops had closed, some were shuttered, and the first wave of the young boozers was out, marching in phalanx formations. More shouts, and abuse.

The day's litter was not yet cleared, and bin bags were stacked outside the fast food outlets, and the rain was persistent, and there was little that was obvious to drag kids out of their homes or student hostels. He was near the statue of Geoffrey Chaucer, had learned about him at the choirboys' college. Could have recited a few of the lines and . . . He listened.

More shouting up ahead, the bridge where the river flowed under the street. Some around him tucked down their heads and hurried away from the disturbance. Others paused and gawped. Cammy kept going, knew where he was headed and had enough time for it: had assumed that his mum would have the same routines. Something that was locked in him was the belief he had hardly been away and that the world in which he had once existed had stayed constant, petrified, marooned in a time lapse. Him fighting, him the hero, him with his band of brothers and on the front line, and the rest of his old life just plodding along, unchanged. The shouting reached a fevered pitch. Aggressive, hostile. He saw a knot of people by the boarded-up windows of a shut-down Poundland store. He kept walking.

It was a pedestrian street. Cammy walked in its centre. People came towards him, some scuttling home after the last dregs of the city's day, and some could have been heading for the first clubs that would open or the pubs that had a Happy Hour. He kept his position in the centre of the street. People backed away from him. One glance was enough for them . . . a kid might have challenged him, but his mates knew better, would have seen the expression in Cammy's eyes, and had tugged him aside.

He came level with the store and the plywood sheets that covered its windows. The jeering had become abuse which had become anger. Two boys, their backs against the plywood, were hunched over, trying to protect their heads and their stomachs.

He stood. Cammy stopped walking in the centre of the street.

He thought the two boys were gays. There was a shuffling movement in the doorway to the right of them and their tormentor, and a rough sleeper was hurrying to gather up his blanket and the loose shape of a squashed cardboard box. Had a small dog on a length of rope.

Cammy could see one of the boys had smudged lipstick, and the other, as the light caught his face, seemed to be wearing dark eye-shadow. He wondered if they had been holding hands, or had even thought they were unseen and had kissed in the shadows – or might not have cared a damn and could have been in the centre of the street and making their feelings for each other crystal clear. He counted half a dozen in the knot, but Cammy knew about crowds and thought this was only the beginning and if there were a commotion and the chance of amusement then more could come to share the sport.

The boys made no sound, just attempted to protect their bodies. Perhaps their lack of defiance annoyed the gang . . . He remembered a neighbour's cat, a weedy and unlovable beast that would come over the garden fence with a mouse in its mouth, carrying it by a fold of skin at the back of its neck. It would dump the mouse on the patio at the back door. The cat needed the mouse to contribute to the fun, show some spark, attempt a break-out. If the mouse did nothing other than tremble, then the cat would bash it with a paw, try to get a reaction, would be irritated if the mouse did not scamper . . . Now, the gang shouted insults, violent and obscene.

Cammy saw a fist thrown. Heard the hit and the wheeze of breath that followed and a swallowed cry, but no retaliation. And saw a boot go in. No response.

Cammy knew it would get harder for the boys, and one – the boy who wore eye-shadow – was covering his groin and his head and another punch was swung at him. The boy ducked and twisted and he would have seen his assailants, seen the hatred and contempt on their faces, and would have seen all the people scurrying past and looking away and ... The boy's eyes found Cammy's, locked on them. Might have thought that a man who lingered would intervene. Would have seen that he was dressed in a sports jacket and a check shirt and wore a tie and had an anorak against the weather, and was weighing up the situation. Was not too proud ... implored his help, pleaded for aid, and fists came more frequently, and boots and more abuse. The boy, in silence, cried out for his help.

A long way back ... two years ago.

A suburb of Raqqa. A stinking heat, the middle of the day, and stuck in a traffic queue. Dwayne driving the pick-up and a heavy machine-gun mounted behind Cammy's front seat, and Tomas beside him. In the open back were Mikki and Pieter, and Ulrike wearing camouflage and with a *keffiyeh* scarf wrapped around her face: a combat unit and untouchable, almost. The street was blocked and the men in front wore black and had the long beards of the security police. They had brought a guy out of a house, and a woman was shrieking and kids were bawling. The woman was reaching to touch her man and a rifle smacked into her face and she reeled away. He was struggling, and there was a moment when his glance found Cammy. Might have believed he saw a fighting man, and might have believed that a fighting man was different stock to the political police unit whose principal job was to root out spies. If they weren't busy they went after kids who played on the internet, or guys who were shagging the girl next door, and they went after the homosexuals too; but top of their list was hunting spies. Spies would have been recruited by the middlemen who worked for US or UK intelligence agencies, or for the Saudis and the Jordanians and the Gulf rulers. Their main job was locating High Value Targets. HVTs would then be hunted down with air strikes and drone strikes, or even justified the insertion of a Special Forces team for capture. The HVT would come to see his wife, and might want to see his kids, and the bug would be slapped under the vehicle and he could be tracked, then hit from the air. If he was seen but no vehicle identified, then the enemy would put up a drone and fly high over that quarter of the city and their analysts would feast on the feed pictures and dissect that area of the city. Unlikely that a target would hear the approach of a fast jet with a 500lb bomb laser-guided to a matter of inches' accuracy, or the drone above. Spies were feared and detested by the régime. The fate of a spy? Might be tortured to extract information, then crucified. Might be tortured then taken out and filmed as his throat was cut. Might be tortured, then have a breeze-block roped to his ankle and be tossed off a bridge into the Euphrates. A man did not know if he had made it sufficiently high on the pecking order to be targeted. No way that Kami al-Britani would know if he might have been betrayed. Leaders, *emirs*, might assume they were named and that the drones flew slow circles unseen in the sky and that the geeks searched the screens. Not a matter that had then concerned him, nor worried any of the brothers . . .

He did not know why this man fastened his gaze on him, beseeched him. Might have seen something different in his face, thought he might find help. The woman wailed on the threshold and the kids howled and clung to her. Why would he help him? If he had stepped in, caught the guy by the scruff of his neck and hoisted him into the pick-up, Cammy would have brought down on his own neck many layers of Hell. He saw the fear before the guy was heaved into the waiting vehicle. The street was left with the reek of diesel fumes. The woman gone back inside and closed her door. No neighbours would come to her home with food, with flowers, would stay with the children if she went to the authorities to try to discover the fate of her man. She was abandoned. Cammy remembered his face for many days, and the appeal in his eyes.

The two boys were having a bad time. Cammy could have intervened. Could have pushed through, used his presence and the authority in his voice, and the threat he carried when controlled aggression was painted on him. He did nothing. The boy no longer looked for him, would have given up on him. More shoving, more fists and more boots: it would have been close to the time, both boys down, when one kick hit an unprotected head and jolted it hard enough to affect the brain tissue . . .

He had not gone there, travelled over the frontiers, for a cause. Had been purely selfish, had looked for the gratification of fighting, chewing on danger, and feeling the pump of big weapons at his shoulder. And while it had been good, he had loved it. Had saved the child in the Channel crossing because otherwise the Iranians, in their panic, would have capsized the dinghy. He had no need to save these particular victims. Close enough to see that one more kick to the groin would do life changing damage to his organs. Cammy walked away.

Not his business; he felt no shame, too preoccupied. He heard the sirens. A cop car was coming close and the lights were brilliant blue on the West Gate tower. The gang scattered, fled. He turned and saw the two boys helping each other to stand. Not his fight. Had he intervened he would have destroyed the knot of youths, put them to flight, but he had not.

"Boss, I just need to slip out . . . be an hour, not more. That all right, boss?"

It was not all right, and the hour ahead would be busy, but Farouk's employer – the owner of the café – knew him well enough, would not have considered him unreliable, and there was a distant relationship through marriage . . . but only an hour. Plenty came through the café at that time in the evening and the weather made no difference. Farouk asked if he could take the scooter out the back. Would get it back in the hour.

The keys were thrown to him. The café boss might have realised that this employee had attracted interest from the counter-terror people, might have heard that he was hassled by them, was under sporadic surveillance. Might have ... But his work ethic was not to be faulted. He would not ask where Farouk wished to go in mid-shift, why he needed to be gone, no prior warning, what business was so important.

The journey was to the northern outskirts of the city, the Kirkstall area, west of the allotments and sandwiched between the Aire river and the railway tracks. Streets of terraced homes, and the one where he headed had a lock-up garage at its rear. The cinder track was not overlooked. It was probably illegal but the council had better things to do than worry about a cottage industry doing vehicle repairs. Farouk set off. Rode with confidence, heading for the garage, and wearing a crash helmet with a tinted visor.

He felt good, thought himself blessed with power. It was close to a year since he had been granted a meeting, in a car park in the moorlands towards the Pennine hills, and had been allowed to talk with a man of authority, and had explained his idea, and had talked of the qualities of the individual needed if a plan were to become an action. A month before, he had been summoned again, had been told that such an individual had been identified, was on his way; the work had started and he imagined the pace of it was now frantic. A week before he had been told the day it would happen ... tomorrow. He rode fast on the wet roads and at times was showered in spray, and rejoiced.

"Hello, Mum."

"Hello, darling."

"You sound good."

"Not too bad, darling. Nothing to complain about."

"Where are you, Mum?"

"In an accountant's, but there are solicitors on the next two floors. Doing the lavatories. You don't want to know."

"Isn't there other work you could be doing? I worry about you, Mum."

"Staggering actually, that the women's are worse than the men's, how they're left. I manage ... Anyway, what's your news?"

A pleasure for Sadie Jilkes was getting a call from the Category A wing where her elder son was held. His news? Not much actually. Was doing shifts in the gaol laundry, which took him out of his cell. Was enrolled in a reading group and that was positive and meant more time off his landing. They'd had an attempted suicide on the landing the week before last but the guy had screwed it, had failed, seemed cheerier now . . . They chatted a bit. She always wanted to hear from him but there was so little to say because she could not share his life and he had no part of hers. The conversation, as usual, petered out. She didn't visit anymore, saw little point in it and the journey to where he was held now was awful, and expensive, and there would have been even less to say if she was back in an interview room and across a glass screen. He was not a child, was damn near middle-aged, and she dreaded him coming home in a couple of years, feet up on the sofa, dirty plates on every table and leftover pizza, and . . .

"Anyway, good to hear you, darling, but I have to get on."

"Love to you, Mum."

The call was cut. She went back to work. It was a bad night outside and the last few evenings the late buses had been erratic. Worse things had afflicted Sadie Jilkes' life than cleaning toilets and waiting for delayed buses, and she tried not to think of them . . . First time the older boy had gone down, custodial. The night her girl had been in the accident, and the funeral. Cameron leaving that school, and Cameron making a mess of the next place, and Cameron gone and her reporting him missing, and Cameron found and the "filth" – what the older boy called them – crawling over her home. Tried to get rid of the thoughts but it was hard. She flushed a toilet. Her supervisor said she was the most conscientious of all the women on the shift. Was satisfied it was clean. She went out of the cubicle. She stood in front of a mirror, saw her untidy grey hair, no make-up and no jewellery, and tiredness was evident and she could not remember when she had last laughed.

Looked at herself in the mirror and heard herself say, "Of course, no phone call from you. No call. Not even a card. Too busy were you, full-time job killing people – to write or phone? Damn you."

She started to wash down the basins.

The car turned in from the main road and hurried to do so in the face of oncoming traffic, and went through a big puddle by the kerb, drenching him further. He had been about to cross the top of The Avenue, and its significance had not been in his thoughts – more obsessed with his lack of money, lack of food, lack of sleep . . . but then remembered she used to sneak out of her home, slink up the pavement, using the shrubs in a couple of front gardens for cover: Vicky.

The nearside wheels went through the water and the rising wave hit his trousers up to his waist, and splattered his anorak. Cammy glowered at the car, gave a finger, cursed . . . recognised the driver. No change of hairstyle. Same spectacles on the bridge of her nose. Vicky's mother. He stood on the pavement, the water dripping off him and the car moved on, then stopped, and began to reverse into a parking space. Cammy checked his watch. Still too early if he were going to walk to Sturry and then go along the Margate road and take the turn-off, and expect his mum to be home . . . assumed that nothing changed. The cathedral had not, nor the choir – a hymn's music and words played in his mind – *Jesus came when the doors were shut*. No change in the High Street and none on St Peter's Street except that the Poundland store was now boarded up, and nothing different at the Miller's where he and Vicky drank, her usually paying, and nothing seemed to have changed at the Leisure Centre he had been past, or the gardens where the daffodils were in late bloom and the last of the crocuses. The car's lights were killed, but the security system had kicked in. He had one good view of Vicky's mother as she paused by her front door to rummage for the key. Opened the door, went in, closed it. And Cammy felt the aloneness. Felt it bad . . . these were the last hours of his life and he reckoned he did not deserve to be alone.

He turned into The Avenue.

Would go to Cindy Piggot's house, two doors down from

Vicky's mother. She used to have a small dog and Vicky would mind it if she was out for the day and if he was not at work they would use her place. He went to the door and rang Cindy Piggot's bell. He saw movement behind the opaque glass. He straightened his tie, she'd check him through the spy hole. The door was opened, but was on a chain. Eyes peered at him. He'd manage an educated voice, a believable and trustworthy one . . .

Could do as great a deceit as the time they had, him and the brothers, dressed in uniforms filched off the battlefield dead, and gone in the night to a storage depot behind the lines and had conned a couple of sentries at the gate, then had deceived the sergeant in the guardhouse who was watching streamed football from Europe, had taken the talk. They had seemed to be Hezbollah and in need of supplies, and . . . they had loaded two pick-ups with mortar bombs, and the rest of Mikki's devices would not have started to detonate until they were a clear mile out of the arsenal and away across the open sand. They had laughed fit to bust, but they had been together . . .

He explained that he had been to Victoria's old home but her mother was out. It was about renewing a savings policy. Always lied well.

"So sorry to trouble you. We heard she was getting married but the paperwork must have gone astray. Don't have the new address. It's the computers, wouldn't have happened in the old days."

Might be the last time in his life that he was required to lie . . . Vicky lived in the next street, the one beyond The Avenue, The Close. Cindy Piggot gave him the number. He thanked her warmly, and walked away, retreated into the darkness.

Jonas held tight to his bag as he came off the train. He had talked to his probationers, quiet and guarded, and had repeated what he wanted of them. They had told him of another crocodile, Brutus. Did he need to know? Tristram said that Izzy had found it on the internet. Izzy said that Brutus was over sixteen feet long and weighed two tonnes, lived in Australia, and ate sharks. Tristram said that Brutus hated sharks because one had bitten off the front of his left leg, and he was a big attraction for tourists and . . . He crossed the bridge at the station and was carried along in the flow of passengers ending their journey. He passed the tourist posters outside the toilets and the coffee shop and went through the barriers. The rain had eased. He thought it might turn into a reasonable night . . . Was quite certain in his own mind that, by the time those commuters who had shared the carriage with him were back at the station for their morning train into London, the matter would have been resolved. Was confident also that he would not need to call on "the cavalry" to come cantering on to the scene with reinforcements. He walked out into the forecourt. The rheumatism in his right knee was aggravated by the hour in the train, a longer trip than his usual journey, and he winced but then put it out of his mind.

He saw the car. Granite-grey and unmarked, a BMW. The front passenger door opened and a light came on. They were uniformed. He imagined that this rather conventional looking vehicle would be equipped with a highly tuned performance engine and could reach speeds of near to 150 miles an hour. If they imagined they would be pushing those limits then they were due for disappointment.

The man stepped out of the car and the woman was behind the wheel. He reckoned they would regard him as rather under-dressed, might try to foist a bulletproof vest on him that he would decline to wear. The man had a weighed-down belt which carried more gear than would have fitted on a good sized Christmas tree, and he had a Glock in a holster strapped to his thigh. He had a swagger about him. Most of them did, in Jonas's opinion. They carried the guns and the ammunition, and they were as highly trained as any of junior rank in the local police forces. He would have seen a shambling old guy walking towards him, coat open, tie a little askew, and a trilby on his head, not quite straight, and trousers that had lost their crease . . . His face fell. They would have been all excited to be involved in a Security Service operation, and a short elderly man approached them.

"Hello, I'm Jonas."

Doubtful. "Pleased to meet you, sir. I'm Dominic."

"Hope you haven't been waiting too long."

"Haven't, sir. This is my colleague, Babs."

He leaned inside and offered his hand. The rear door was opened for him. He squeezed in, there was a boxed area that separated the seats and a pile of wet weather gear and a couple of large black grips that took some shifting. He assumed they'd enough weapons on board to launch a limited-scale war: none of it would be necessary if his ideas panned out, and it finished well.

He said, "There's an old and apt line for police and military and intelligence work. 'Few plans survive contact with the enemy', and it's one that I like. If the plan works – always *if* – by the time you settle to your breakfast you will be able to walk quite tall . . . *if* . . . Sometimes the plan works and sometimes it does not but we have to give it a stab."

He told them where they needed to be. Jonas settled back and closed his eyes.

10

She drove carefully, correctly. Seemed to observe the speed limit and made the regulation number of mirror checks and did not push to overtake in the flow of cars and vans and lorries leaving the city at the end of the working day. Once or twice there was a sharp hiss of breath from her that meant she was displeased at the driving of another motorist. Jonas assumed they would make a virtue of abiding by every aspect of the laws of the road. He assumed they knew little of their mission, had been poorly briefed – their superiors would have qualified for the mushroom farm: "kept in the dark and fed on shit"; not pleasant but good practice.

A satnav system to guide them. He had been general as to where he wanted to be, a junction of roads. They would have regarded themselves, Jonas believed, as an élite. They'd see themselves as the best of the best, the most highly trained, the guys and girls who had the authority to carry a weapon into a live confrontation, to ignore or countermand the orders of a superior officer, practised each week of each month at the business of killing people . . . existed for that purpose and were paid well for it, little bonus rewards on the side. For the next few minutes, they would be prepared to let him snooze on the back seat but when he was delivered to the location he had requested, he expected a short sharp shock to be administered and a rule book read him, and their terms of reference. He let the smile play on his face – knew what to expect, and knew his response.

They headed up the main road to the seaside town of Margate. Two or three of the fellow members of their Caravan Club in Raynes Park had been to Margate for holidays, had booked into sites outside the town and said that the views over the Channel were impressive, but quite boring. They passed a retail park with the usual big brand names of electrical goods outlets, and he saw the floodlit perimeter fence of the city's sewage treatment works, and there was a Park and Ride place, and a Mercedes dealership. Like anywhere else: new homes going up, crammed close to each other. Nothing exceptional. He had seen the cathedral tower, floodlit, from the station but they drove away from it. An unremarkable road, and a route towards what he assumed would be an unremarkable estate, and in the middle of it would be an unremarkable home. He appreciated being in places that could be accused of unremarkable boredom. It seemed appropriate.

Jonas Merrick, of course, had never been to Syria. But neither had he visited, in his counter-espionage days, the cities of Russia, and in the times of the Troubles it had never been thought necessary to fly him to Ireland. This evening marked something of a first for him, and the road out of Canterbury towards the village of Sturry was suitable, meshed with the traits of his character. Would have been wrong to have cornered a fighter, a man who acted out the part of a wounded, angry big cat, and allow him to get a foothold in that Valhalla place that he no doubt yearned for. Much better that it would be on ground chosen by Jonas Merrick, where there was nothing special – not a place where a doomed hero would have wanted to be. There would be no last stand, courage and bravery to the fore, in an irrigation ditch of a corn or maize field in Syria, and no "down to the last round but keeping one for suicide" in a military bunker, and no weaving between palm trees and attempting to avoid the heat-seeker cameras of a pursuing helicopter. Would be nothing of romance for Cameron Jilkes . . . he would not make it easy for the lad.

With his eyes closed and his breathing regular he would have shown no indication to the two officers in the front of the car that the events of that night and into the early morning would play out – in his opinion – in any extraordinary way. Not for them, Dominic and Babs, nor for Cameron Jilkes who would have been gulping down doses of vengeance – as they all did in their final hours, as they hoped. He would aim to make it, as best he could, a tedious finale, and unremarkable ... Like a balloon when the air was allowed to leak from it, not with a dramatic hiss but a slow subsidence of emotion.

They were in the village, and she swung the wheel. It would be good to see Cameron Jilkes, see his face close-up and register the pain lingering there, and the anger. Would also be good to speak with him ... it had been too long since the conversation he had enjoyed with Winston Gunn. Could recall the monosyllabic statements the boy had uttered, and Jilkes was unlikely to be very different.

No doubts in his mind. There had been stress points when he was alone in his work space, behind the partition. Also, magnified moments of anxiety when the heavy footfall of the AssDepDG had come down the corridor. Now, blissfully, Jonas seemed free of them, the stresses and the anxieties. Not a matter of arrogance, nor of conceit, but an assessment of his own abilities to read and predict an opponent.

He sat up, yawned, stretched. Jonas said, "Very smooth ride, thank you. Just need to check my phone, then we'll get down to talking, and I'll tell you how it will be ... sorry, how I *think* it will be. But to be going on with, the target's name is Cameron Jilkes, and ..."

She said, "Sorry to interrupt. You call him a target?"

"I do. A serious target ... an experienced fighter from Syria. Anyway, more of that in a minute ... but, serious, dedicated, and dangerous."

He had no business there.

The traffic breezed behind him, flowing fast on a main road.

He had come to see his mother, he owed it to her to come – and because he needed to be fed, and needed money – and then he would be moving on, starting out on his final journey. Where he stood now, away from the street lights and sheltered in shadow, was stupid, emotional: Cammy would have declared his contempt for both stupidity and emotion. Never once had any of them been guilty of such barefaced and cardinal sins. If any one of them was behaving like an idiot or being soft, they would have had a sharp kick in the arse and would have been on their way: even if it had been Ulrike on whom they depended, the punishment would have been the same ... Stupidity and emotion weakened a fighting man and stripped him of focus: "focus" was staying alive, fulfilling a mission.

A car turned off the main road and its headlights caught him. The car slowed. Cammy turned on his heel and walked away briskly, enough to satisfy the driver that an unknown man in the side street no longer loitered. The car drove to the far end of The Avenue. By the time that Cammy had turned again, taking more care to hug the shadows, the driver was parking on a forecourt four doors away from the number given him by Cindy Piggot. He stared at the house, the windows and the lights behind poorly drawn curtains.

He saw her.

Did not actually see her face, saw her shadow as she passed the front room window, and the light was turned off. Lights coming on upstairs. He would have expected at this time of the evening that her husband, whatever he did, would be home from work, his car parked on the driveway but the space was empty. Faintly heard a baby yelling, listened to that for a while and the rain pattered on his shoulders and on his head, and his stomach groaned with hunger.

When he was with his brothers, he would never have felt the pain of loneliness. Would have read the riot act at them, any of them, for being soft.

The baby went quiet.

The front door opened. She came out. He saw Vicky ... the first girl he had made a pitch for, first girl he had kissed properly, and first girl he had been on top of and him groping at his clothing and her wriggling with her own, and the first girl that he had walked away from without a kiss or an explanation ... The only girl he had been with because he had never touched any of the scum kids who had come from Europe. She carried a plastic bag. The rubbish bin was at the pavement edge. She wore a blouse and a skirt and her hair was tied clumsily and the light caught it. She dumped the bag in the bin, then jogged back to the door, would have wanted to be out of the rain. The door shut. The light above the door lasted half a minute then went out ... What little did Cammy know of married life: assumed that she would have left the front light on for her husband's return.

He had no business to be there; it was idiocy and emotion that kept him motionless, standing in the gentle rain and in the shadows.

Tristram and Izzy stepped out. Would have seemed – and how they intended it to appear – like any young couple. The sounds around them were of subdued TVs playing behind drawn curtains. Cars were parked up and the residents, young and old, had returned to their homes for the night.

There was a location, east London, in Epping Forest, where there had once been a prisoner of war camp; it had become a police firearms training base, and had also had facilities for Fivers to learn particular skills. They had both been through it, not together but in successive induction courses, had been taken through sessions on self-defence, and the point had been laboured that it was *not* always possible for the backup to be close. Might be, as near as made no difference, on their own. Facing what, on their own? Facing a guy – maybe – pumped up from years of getting the shit bombed out of him in far away Syria, survived – just about – the slaughter inflicted on a defeated rabble, now in a foul mood. Coming where? Here on the say-so of Jonas Merrick, guru of the hour in Thames House. They were at the end of a cul-de-sac, peering its length and looking into the shadows and hearing the patter of rain off leaky gutters. And backup? The cavalry were somewhere behind them, but not identified. The training course in the Forest had given them the basics of self-defence. Hairy big bastards, tattooed arms, moustaches, bald heads, piercing and sneering eyes. Had done simulated attacks on guys and girls in the surveillance teams who were on their own, then had shown out. Just pretend attacks, but both Tristram and Izzy could remember them. They had come with such suddenness, from nowhere, supposed to be warned but still not expected, that Tristram – the first time – had broken wind, gasped, shrieked, then gone down in an armlock, too petrified to fight back. Izzy – not proud of it, bloody embarrassing – had wet herself, had been incapacitated, too shocked to make a response.

A recruit on Tristram's course had queried the action of the instructor: she had asked whether the "ferocity" of the play-acted attack breached Health and Safety regulations. Was there a statute laying down acceptable levels for the effects of the shock inflicted? The rest of them, so Tristram said, had all muttered about "snow-flakes", and anyway that girl had failed to make it through . . . And all of them had said later that "There but for God's grace go I, go each last fucking one of us". But, of course, it never would happen, would it? They were all graduates, all chosen by rigorous selec-tion, all had good brains and above-average awareness and their job would be to analyse, to predict, to turn out the plods to do the heavy lifting . . . Would not be alone, the two of them, in a dark-ened cul-de-sac where some crazy embittered idiot would be coming – according to the Eternal Flame – to visit his mum. No backup. No weapon.

They reached the end of the road and stopped.

Could not have said, either of them, who made the move. Hands close, then touching, then fingers entwined. Not affection but a mutual need for safety. Other than the rain and the TVs and one bloody owl that kept shrieking, they heard nothing. They were under a tree which took some of the rain and there was an ever-green shrub that took some more of it, and a pigeon exploded out of it and broke the quiet. It thrashed in the branches as if in panic flight and she squeaked and he gasped, and they held each other tightly.

She did not let go of his hand, had no weapon to hold instead, said, "Well, come on. Let's get this fucking business moving."

Doing what they did best, getting all the pieces in place.

She did the check-in, and Baz was parked up in the line for vehicles waiting to collect tickets. Not gone for long, not more than five minutes. He watched her walking towards the camper. A lesser woman than his Mags would have waved the tickets at him so that he would see the moment of success, or would have done a high-five for him. Too clever, his Mags. That would have been the behaviour of kids, not of professionals.

He guessed there would be layers of bureaucracy to get through. The German tail would have first done their own search, been unwilling to cry "Failure" too quickly. Then they would have called in their local control. The local people, either in a command car or taking over a police station office in Cologne or Aachen or where-fucking-ever, would then have had to go up to a national level. From national level there would then be a fast sub-committee meeting, when they could get enough people together who were not stuck in traffic, already on their way home, and then a decision would need to be made. Face lost, bucket-sized. Having to explain at an international level that a surveillance team had fouled up – and a British target, and Brits in this day and age were the least favourite chums to have on board. So, reluctantly the bad news would be spread. Given to the Dutch and to the Belgians first because they were on the obvious route the camper would be taking . . . then the French. That would have been a hard pill to get down the gullet. As he had often enough said to Mags, "I may be a complete arsehole but I'm not a complete fool". He reckoned he understood the way the systems worked.

At the French end it would reach – might not have done so yet – an office in Paris. A junior would have fielded it, and he or she would pass the parcel up the ladder and try to contact a relevant duty officer, and that's how it worked . . . Likely as not be a call back to the unhappy Huns asking for more details, and then the British might get a query and it would end up in a labyrinth where pride and national prestige played their part, took centre stage. Reckoned he knew how it worked, and reckoned he had read it well.

She opened the door, shook herself and water cascaded off her. "I done well."

"Would have expected nothing else, not of you."

"Did a bit of negotiation."

"God, you're a cheeky cow."

"A discount for late booking, and a cabin thrown in."

He helped her up and on to the bench seat, and they laughed together. He did not have to ask whether her antennae had twitched. She'd a better sense of cock-up than he did, sharp as a razor's blade. She'd have told him. A peck on his lips, and she handed him the tickets. He powered up, went to get in line. They'd time to kill, would sit it out.

Would say to her, later, "No second thoughts, going on with it?"

Her answer; "None. Doing what we're paid to do. Anyway, I reckon it's all quiet ahead."

"No offence, Mr Merrick, but time for some talking." Dominic had twisted around to face him.

"So that there are no misunderstandings, Mr Merrick." Babs had tilted her mirror so she had a view of him.

"My experience, mistakes happen when matters have not been talked through."

He saw an eyebrow flicker up, regarded the gesture as intentional and impertinent.

"And mine, and the best way, Mr Merrick, to avoid mistakes is to lay down the ground rules and then stick to them."

She noticed him blink but not in any way to acknowledge what she said.

Dominic turned to their passenger. "You've not yet favoured us with an explanation for why you are here, why *we* are here."

Babs had extended her seat belt, was able to gaze into Merrick's face. "When we are assigned to a situation it is because there is an estimate that total force may be required, which is what we have to offer."

"Yourself, Mr Merrick, you described this target, as yet unnamed, as 'serious, dedicated and dangerous', and that means that we have primacy."

"And you, Mr Merrick, whatever your so far unexplained role in the Security Service may be, whatever your responsibilities there, are a civilian."

"We lead and civilians follow our instructions."

"We say what can happen and what cannot happen."

"Say what you can do."

"Where you can go."

"You are not in charge of us, Mr Merrick."

"We call it."

Dominic would have expected that the man from London, foisted on them, elderly and needing to rest though it was not yet night, would have started to offer a series of explanations, guarantees. "I have absolutely no intention of moving outside the orbit of the protection you are able to provide me with." That sort of stuff. The man stayed silent.

"Not that we have been told why it is only us who are assigned when dealing with a man who is – your description, Mr Merrick – 'serious, dedicated and dangerous'. Would have imagined that if it were believed that this individual was on his way to this housing complex then we would have called out all available resources, brought our people in from across the county. Put it at the top of any list. It's like it's a circle that doesn't square."

Babs said, "I can say confidently, Mr Merrick, that you do not appear to me to be a man with a detailed knowledge of political violence, except what is taught in seminars. We have that experience from the training programmes and can deal with pretty much anything thrown at us. Above all, given evidence of a threat, we have the ability to call for a lock-down on an area, we can sanitise it. I'm not hearing you, Mr Merrick."

"Why have you come from London?"

"What is it that you are expecting us to do?"

"Our training is very thorough, all situations are covered."

"If it's the Security Service, then we assume it's a matter of terrorism, likely the Middle East, and it could go along with where we were at dawn this morning – the beach at Deal – and a guy coming ashore having brought in a boatload of migrants. If confronted with such a man then we have a duty . . ."

". . . and not a duty to be taken lightly."

". . . a duty to protect life. What that adds to is us needing a guarantee from you."

"I reckon I know where my colleague is going, Mr Merrick. The guarantee is that you will adhere to our instructions at all times, and once you have accepted that then we can plan what is possible and what is not possible."

"Not a matter of debate, not negotiable. We are looking for your guarantee."

Babs said, "All our training points to these people as being ruthless, very violent and needing to be met with equivalent force."

Dominic said, "Not wanting to scare you off, Mr Merrick, but I could wager you have never come into direct contact with these front line *jihadi* people. We had a lecture only last month from the military about these guys – lunatics of course – and wanting a quick ride to God and Heaven, and not caring who gets in the way."

"I am getting aggravated that you have declined to give us the assurance we have requested."

"I'd call it 'pissed off', how we are feeling."

"So, what is your answer?"

And both drew breath. He was annoyed and she was irritated. They had pulled in by a T junction, where a slip road led to the small car park for a convenience store. They could barely see the man's face. His clothes were those, Dominic would have said, that pensioners wore when they walked along the esplanade at Deal or were on guided tours of the Castle at Dover, went to hear a retelling of the "miracle of Dunkirk", yesterday's man and dressed for yesterday. His appearance, Babs would have said, showed that Five, the Box, had this one as a low priority or they wouldn't have sent someone from the bottom of the talent barrel. No dynamism. A few late shoppers passed, barely gave them a glance. And they waited for their answer, for their guarantee, and were kept waiting. They had tried to make it plain enough, clear to a simpleton, that they were about to run a show and the passenger would do as he was bloody told. He had not yet answered, stared back at them and his mind seemed to be far away. They might have wondered whether a single word they had said, coming at him with their argument and pincer movement logic, had been taken in. Might not have heard a word, might not have listened to anything they'd said. He had a small bag by his feet, and had started to rummage in it. They waited. One certainty, the sergeant back in Dover, at the station on Ladywell, would get a heavy-grade bollocking for letting them loose on this cretin, and both would batter him with their problems. A file was taken out. The guy, Mr Merrick – and they had both been scrupulously polite while their voices dripped sarcasm – extracted a picture, an individual's head and shoulders, what would have been a passport snap blown up. He used a pencil-thin torch to illuminate the picture and Babs saw that the name of a south Devon caravan site was on its side. The beam was shone on the picture. A decent enough looking lad, nice enough hair, no tattoos on his neck, what seemed like a genuine and understated smile – not cocky and not supercilious – but the smile was still hard to gauge because of the smear ringing the mouth.

"Is that him?"

"Is that the target?"

"What's around his mouth?"

They were answered, quietly, and both had to strain to hear. "That's ice-cream. We went out and bought some ice-cream for the kids who came ashore this morning, the Iranians. The adults didn't want to make an identification, but he'd saved one of the kids from drowning during the crossing, brave of him, and that kid did the business for us, kissed it and his mouth was full of ice-cream and a chocolate stick. Always go for the weakest link, the way to break a chain. Know what I mean?"

The voice had a chill to it, like there was no emotion. They looked at the picture until he switched off the torch, and replaced it in the file.

He said where they should go.

* * *

A car was already parked there.

They swore. Jonas, to himself, chuckled.

The car would have been left by Tristram and Izzy, Babs expertly manoeuvred their car into the remaining space. More grumbling from the front and he saw no benefit in disabusing them. No need to explain to them who else was on the plot and what their requirement was.

Jonas looked at his watch. "I think we are a little early. Should have picked up a flask, shouldn't I? Just one thing I'd like you to find me, and . . ."

"All in due course, if you don't mind, Mr Merrick. We still have loose threads," Babs said.

"I think we spelled it out pretty clearly, Mr Merrick, but didn't get an answer."

"The guarantee, sir, and our primacy – and, full respect, you are elderly and may be confronting a motivated and dangerous individual and we'd not want you blundering into our line of sight."

"Into our line of fire."

Jonas said, "No risk of that. I think I understand what you want and I'm sure we'll get along rather well."

"So, that's done and dusted."

"Not a problem," Jonas said.

"Would you mind stepping out, Mr Merrick."

He did. He stood under the tree and let the rain fall, felt comfortable and at ease. Babs unfastened one of the boxes and Dominic started rummaging on its far side and then heaved out two vests. Jonas had never worn one. The surveillance people in 3/S/12 liked to show them off when they were on an arrest operation, and they'd come back into the building and come up the stairs for their debrief, still wearing them, then would dump them on the floor: he'd always thought it was similar to a peacock displaying, letting the corridor know they'd been at the sharp end. He was told they did not have one for him. He answered that it was unlikely he would need such equipment and that he had no intention of going anywhere close to where he might require one. They were satisfied.

Jonas could have trampled all over them, might have suggested that they had never, *not ever*, confronted a living terrorist who was armed and who represented a straightforward and unarguable risk to life: thought for a short moment of Winston Gunn and the quiver in the boy's lower lip and the shake in his hands, and thought of the wires and the detonators and the sticks of commercial explosive – could have rubbished them and spoken of a private investiture and a gong now safe in his wife's knicker drawer. Would not have dreamed of telling them of that faraway and irrelevant event. Nor would he have considered it fair comment to remark on the probably indisputable fact that neither had ever gone with their main armament, to the stage where they eased off the Safety and were ready to fire . . . Would never have fired, would never have known – whatever their training – how they would be if "Christ, it's actually happening" . . . as a body-guard had shouted when the President, "Rawhide", was shot on a Washington DC pavement. Would have been churlish because they might do the business and might freeze – did not know. Vera had once tried to ask him what had been in his mind when he had started yanking clear the wires of the bomb young Gunn had been wearing, and he'd had no decent answer. They had the guns out and locked in the magazines, and armed the weapons, then did the same with the Glock pistols carried in holsters looped to their thighs. They made a harsh noise doing it, but the TVs indoors continued to play and the rain to fall and they attracted no attention.

Jonas watched, then said, "It's what he'd want. His name is Cameron Jilkes and his home is at the bottom of the cul-de-sac that is second on the right of the road we're in. That's where his mother lives. My assumption is, he'll visit tonight, then move on. I've an idea where he's headed but not certainty. Put mildly, I'd be disappointed if you shot him."

"Best place for him, from what you say."

"Out of harm's way."

Jonas said, "What he'd want. The glory moment and the wipe-out of pain and angst. Not suitable for him. A cage is right for him . . . We might not get much sleep later on so another doze would be welcome."

Babs said, "Earlier you told us that you'd like us to find you something, but didn't say what it was that you wanted."

"Well remembered. Thank you. Yes . . . Please go to the nearest house and ask if they can lend you a dog lead. Or the next house, or the one after. Of course, you'll promise to bring it back. Yes, I'd like a dog lead."

Might have stood there half an hour on the opposite side of the road, but Cammy now moved to the pavement in front of the house. Heard nothing saw nothing and the baby was quiet.

Not in years had he known himself so hesitant.

A cat came to see him. A decent looking beast, with long hair plastered down by the rain. Took a liking to Cammy and rubbed against his ankle. It was a madness that intoxicated him. But he did not take the step forward . . .

Remembered when he had not hesitated, not stopped to consider. Their little unit of foreign fighters had been pushed in to plug a gap in the line, and a main force of Syrians was probing for weakness and had brought up three tanks – mean bastards, Russian built T-72s, each with a combat weight of 40 tonnes. They were like the guys out of a comic book, Cammy and Mikki and Pieter, just had one RPG-7 with them, and grenades, and a single sniper rifle. They had done a weaving run forward, having broken clear of their brothers, and then had put themselves into a warren of damaged buildings and all the time had heard the growing clanking thunder of the tanks' tracks. No hesitation. The tanks were in file. They had been level with them, would have had enemy infantry within a handful of yards, and Cammy had called the plan. Took as big a risk as at any time he was in Syria and fighting. An RPG round into the tracks, side-on shot and breaking them apart and halting it, and Pieter's sniper shot taking down the commander in the second one as he stood and gazed out of the turret, and Mikki going like a mad kid in an adventure playground and swarming up the side of the third one and crouching a moment to prise a grenade into the hatch window used by the forward observation guy. Had moved fast. More explosions behind them but the armour was stalled. The line had held . . . If any of them had hesitated it would not have happened.

He stood in front of the door and the rain fell on him and the cat now gave him best friend status. Still could not take the next step forward.

No tanks here, no line to be held and no white heat from fire, and no brothers with him . . . Stood in a residential street and shivered. Easy when there had been tanks and brothers and a front line. Wanted her, and had not wanted her at this same pitch, at any time that she had been available, easy. The cat gave up on him. He was alone.

The wild flowers grew to the height of Dwayne's knees.

He loved flowers, would always wander away from the group when he saw them growing but would never pick them, not even to make a posy for Ulrike. The flowers that seemed to grow well on river banks entranced him. There were red petals and yellows and blues, and it must have been that week when a mass of them came into bloom at the same time.

They heard the aircraft.

The rest of them had gone to a small sand spit where the stream bent sharply and had stripped and all of them were naked except for their privates and there was a pool where they had knelt and scrubbed themselves and had washed their clothing. The stream at that point was little more than 100 yards from the track they had driven down. The vehicle was a luxury. A military type of jeep, with spare filled fuel tanks and small arms weapons, and had been abandoned. The likely scenario was that government troops had dumped it, and probably their uniforms too, and had then hightailed across country and had a dream of getting back to their villages. The jeep was on the track and Dwayne was close to it, his head down as he moved in a state of bliss through the flowers.

At a distance, a strike aircraft, coming low on an attack run was always near impossible to hear as it approached, coming at perhaps 500 klicks.

He came from a ribbon development on the outskirts of the big park of Algonquin, north of Toronto. He'd told them often enough about where he had been raised. To the rest of them the stories of Dwayne's life had seemed almost idyllic and many times they puzzled why anyone should want to walk away from his family and his home and exchange them for fighting in Syria and Iraq, now from running in Syria and Iraq. His father was a retired corporate accountant, and his mother soldiered on as a school teacher: conventional and God-fearing but unhappy to debate politics or morals with their only child; argument upset them. They had a Labrador dog and a Maine Coon cat and the porch from spring to autumn was full of rods and tackle; a couple of powerful four-wheel drives were parked in the front. Dwayne said it was a life lived in "a culture of conformity". If he had not left, had stayed with them, what else might he have done? He'd scratch his bum and deliberate and would talk of writing a book or a poem or the words of a song, and drink beer and fish for walleye – and boredom would have been lethal ... Often enough, since they had welcomed Dwayne into their band, allowed him to be one of the brothers, Cammy had fussed around him like an irritated sheepdog, had rounded him up and bawled abuse because the Canadian was immersed in his thoughts in fields of wild flowers.

Pieter was shouting and pointing, then Cammy saw it: a grey shape against a hazy sky and streaking towards them.

He was the worst military guy amongst them, except that he had the innate skills of a tracker and a woodsman. He could move towards a roadblock position under the cover of growing maize and not a plant would be disturbed and even alert guards would have no warning as he approached. He might then have slit throats with the same detachment as he might earlier in life have cleaned out the innards of a fish. He was the best cook among them and most useful at that time when they were in flight and food was scarce. And he had a philosophy that seemed valuable. Like a vinyl record with a scratch so that it repeated. "Things are going to get a lot worse before they get worse", and he said that was not original to him but came from one of the Marx guys. No fear ever shown ... and unaware in the last seconds of his life. Not hearing and not seeing and probably with the scent of flowers in his nostrils, and in a state of grace.

The bomb careered away from the undercarriage of the aircraft and almost floated before it began to fall.

It would not have happened when they were going forward. Impossible to imagine that Cammy would have shown such dereliction of basic survival procedures. A military vehicle parked up in the open, a tall figure in black clothing easily visible among bright flowers, the rest of them away from their weapons, their clothing scattered. But the heart and the spirit were being torn from them, and their brothers were being taken, and they no longer advanced but tried to make sense of defeat and retreat, and a mistake delivered them into an enemy's hands. No guns within reach, not that a heavy machine-gun could hope to hit a fixed-wing strike aircraft even as it pulled out from the level flight and veered away as its bomb came down. Would have been on a mission and with one bomb left and a target offering itself. They were shrieking at him, but even if he had heeded them and had flattened himself it would have been too late to save his life.

The bomb struck, extraordinary precision, hit the ground close to him and beside the empty vehicle, then the eruption, and the dirt and the dust and the deafening noise and the blast of the gale that it blew. Their cries died. They dressed themselves, which seemed important. Then gathered up their weapons, all except for the German woman, for Ulrike. She ran, wore only skimpy underpants and they hung low on her hips from the weight of the stream's water and her body was white. Dwayne, the big man never swore in her presence, called her "Ma'am" and had liked nothing better than to sit cross-legged in darkness by a guttering fire while she told them stories: little more than nursery tales – witches and dragons and castles and princesses – and would calm them and then in the morning they would go again and fight, and Dwayne would be their point man because he had the best skill in crossing ground, in finding cover.

The aircraft soared to regain altitude and came over them, and Cammy saw the markings. The pilot and his navigator would be back in time for a cup of tea and a biscuit before the debrief on the mission and they'd tell the ground-based RAF officers who controlled them of a little bit of a bonus, taking down a black flag vehicle and at least one of *the "bad boys". Clear from the roundels painted on the fuselage that the aircraft was British and the pilot was Cammy's enemy.*

The vehicle was well fucked, was on its side, the chassis at a twisted angle, and in the field of flowers there was a single dark and messy crater. The debris had fallen, the smoke had cleared, the noise gone. Stanislau had brought along with him the clothes that Ulrike had worn before going into the river. She dressed. Nothing to say. Then they started to search, did it in silence. Pieter was the first to give up on something futile and he went to the toppled jeep and started to wrench free whatever could be retrieved and was not damaged. Some of the weapons and some of the ammunition and some of the food and the medical box, as much as they could carry – as Cammy and Ulrike and Pieter and Stanislau could carry. They found part of an arm. It was taken off at the elbow and Dwayne's watch was still on the wrist and it had been given him by his father on his 21st birthday. They put it in the deepest part of the crater and then covered it with stone and earth.

Cammy looked at the skies. The aircraft was long gone. Its trail had disappeared. There was a hawk high in the sky, nothing else. He blamed himself for their carelessness, was right to. He gazed into the emptiness and cursed the man who had flown the plane, did it silently and with acute anger. And his prayer for Dwayne was of revenge. A promise repeated, and strengthened. Loaded with the kit, they turned their backs on the stream and the crater and the broken jeep, and the flowers.

It was Cammy's style, his defiance, that after they had gone perhaps a mile he started quietly to sing. Something from Henry Francis Lyte. Gave them Praise my soul, the King of Heaven; To his feet thy tribute bring. They trudged away.

All the lights on the ground floor were off.

The baby slept. Cammy saw Vicky's shadow go up the stairs.

A light came on above, peeked between the drawn curtains. The rain fell remorseless and heavy on him.

His mum could by now have been home from work – if it were the same work, same hours, same journey home on the same bus schedule.

He had no doubt as to how it would be when Vicky saw him, when he stood on the step and Vicky faced him from the open doorway.

Where he would go in the morning, alone, it would be as if she came with him, ran by his side, matching him step by step. The light upstairs went off.

Down the street, a porch light lit a forecourt and he imagined that in a moment a door would open and a dog would be pushed out or be coaxed on to grass . . . He had not seen the cat again. There were no tanks here.

He stepped forward, his finger found the button. He felt the shiver in his hand. He pressed the bell.

Jonas had wedged himself again on the back seat, was hard up against the now emptied weapons box. Slept or dozed or dreamed, eyes closed.

"Didn't answer us, did he? Never gave us an answer."

"Did not, Dominic. And what was all that about a cage?"

"Not a clue. You'd have thought that Five could have done better than him."

"A bit pathetic, but I'll not have him getting in our way."

Might have dreamed it, have imagined it. Saw himself and Vera, side by side, heading west towards a Devon site, their Norwegian friend in the wicker cat basket and the caravan bumping along behind them. Filling each mirror, showing the A303's hills and bends, was the build-up of traffic that had no chance of passing, and they would be the source of annoyance, even anger, because the queues had no prospect of getting beyond them, not on the A303 and not the way that Jonas drove . . . Might get away by lunch-time the next day – if all went well. Might be there by dusk tomorrow.

"You heard all that, Babs, about dangerous and serious and he called him 'motivated'. We're not talking about a guy thumping his wife with a knife at her throat."

"Too right, Dom. We're talking about an experienced killer. So I don't understand why this is not a mob-handed job. The place should be flooded, and we have no risk assessment and no mission statement, and old Merrick seems to make it all up as he goes along."

"Weird."

"Worse than weird – except you can look on the bright side."

What had changed in Jonas Merrick's life since he had shared a bench, briefly, with Winston Gunn, was that he now commanded an audience. Reflected that he had the same insights now as before, just that none of his colleagues or superiors had bothered to listen to him. They did now, led by the AssDepDG. Had made his bed, had to lie on it, or was "hoist" as Lily might have put it down in the Archive. Could not yet step back. Would have been entitled, hours earlier to catch his normal train that evening, and eat the cottage pie that Vera had made, but was the victim of a compulsion . . . Had once sat next to a chap, same sort of age and from the Russian monitoring section, in the café outside the side door and the chap had been needing to babble: his son had sent them a photo from New Zealand, and the boy was hanging upside down by the ankle at the end of a bungee jump, had done 140 feet and a few inches. The chap had quoted his boy as saying that he knew he had to do the jump from the moment he had landed on that island, had to – could not evade it. Laid his lofty reputation on the line and could not have backed away. But Jonas felt *nearly* confident of the outcome: had to, or by first light tomorrow he might be face down and breathing, heavily, his last gasps.

"What's the 'bright side', Babs?"

"You'd say 'breaking a duck', I'd say 'losing' what it is that we'll never get back. Cop on, like a first shag. Easy once you've done it, big deal when you haven't. Might get to shoot, Dom."

"Take him down – dangerous and serious and motivated – actually pull the trigger. Myself – and you know it – I've never actually been close to pulling the trigger."

"Actually do it. I was as far down the line as having the red dot on some sod in Margate, with an axe and his missus in an armlock – shouted top of my voice. He did it, dropped the axe, lay down

good as gold, closest I've been ... But for real, see him drop –
better, I'll bet, than any shag."

Which was not as Jonas intended and not as he planned it. He
did not move, did not break his breathing.

"What he asked for . . .?"

"Asked for a dog lead."

"What does he want a dog lead for?"

"Not a clue. Suppose I'd better go and get one. What do I say,
that I want it for?"

"Suppose you had. You . . . think of something – good luck."

He did not think it would be difficult, finding a dog lead. Didn't
matter if it could restrain a Rottweiler or a toy poodle. On an
estate like this, there would be dogs two a penny. He felt rested.
Very soon he would play-act his waking and then would start, in
earnest, the business of putting Cameron Jilkes in a cage and
denying him the sweet-scented last thought of martyrdom, the
Valhalla final moment of a *jihadi* life. All about encouraging others,
and nothing encouraged less – in Jonas's opinion – than sitting in
a cage for days and weeks and months and years and knowing the
key was lost.

11

Time drifted for Jonas.

By now had he been at home, he would have been overseeing the cat's last visit to the flower beds, then checking the locks, front and back, and he would already have folded away the maps on which they based their vacations ... He had not yet advised Vera that, all being properly in place, they would have done the journey by this time the next day and would be tucked up in the caravan: she might have had a celebratory sherry and he might have opened a beer, low alcohol. Liked that route past Stonehenge: it was always best when the sun was about to set and the stones were in silhouette, or dramatic when the sun had gone and the moon had risen ... He allowed himself to grin, no mirth, because if the weather stayed as now – steady rain – there would be no setting sun and no rising moon.

His phone beeped in his pocket. The American from that base in the Gulf. Appreciated the call but had imagined it would come when the matter in hand was settled. He did not gush thanks, never did, seldom thanked those who came back to him, but it would have been deep into the small hours where he was soldiering and likely he had been up all night annotating the information ... more pegs going into the holes and the picture gaining greater focus ... Kami al-Britani had been coded as Kilo Bravo One. A German woman was listed as Kilo Bravo Two, and an Estonian was Kilo Bravo Three. There had been a South African and a Ukrainian, four and five. The Canadian national was Kilo Bravo Six, and there was a Belorussian who the intelligence analysts had labelled as Kilo Bravo Seven. He listened carefully to the distant voice, did not interrupt.

"So, Kilo Bravo One was the focus point of the group and the others were his shock force, his inner circle. They would have seen themselves as brothers – yes, we did that at military college, your King Harry and the "band of brothers", élite and special. Grand while it lasted, and what I've dug out has them in retreat from Barghuz and probably with the intention of disappearing, heading off to new territory, then hunting down another enemy to scrap with. Trouble was the "disappearing" and the "heading off" failed. Began to be degraded. The file says that Kilo Bravo One lost all his siblings, one after the other. By the time he quit the scene and went off our radar he was alone, our assessment . . . You got a feed on him, Mr Merrick?"

"Just sniffing for him. I'll call you if it becomes pungent. Please, some guidance."

"Shoot, Mr Merrick."

"I believe I already have the answer but what annoyed them most?"

"Made them mess their pants? It's the eye in the sky. They even started buying up big quantities of kitchen tin-foil, what the lady back home wraps meat in before it goes in the oven. Could not get their hands on the big sheets that they drape over marathon runners at the final line. They thought that the foil would deflect the heat-seeking kit on either the camera lens or on the Hellfire guidance, would shield them. They learned otherwise . . . That eye up there and the soft sound drove them fair to distraction. The top weapon we had. The Russians just dropped heavy ordnance, and the Syrians put barrel bombs out of choppers. Both were Stone Age compared to what we and your people used. Answered?"

"Very clearly. Good night."

No small talk, nothing about the weather down in Qatar, about the state of the beach and whether the sharks were friendly. He switched off. He did not do a running commentary and would only call the AssDepDG when he had something to tell him: not his concern if the man sweated.

Footsteps approached. Not the ones he expected, but a lurching, stumbling giant. A guy making it back from the pub down in the village and he paused behind them. Pissed against a tree, finished and grunted and struggled to get his zip back up, and then must have realised that the car had folk in it. Would have had a good evening in the pub and was everybody's friend. Jonas did not do enough stints outside, and was ignorant of how to send an unwelcome visitor on his way. The man was at the driver's window, belched and then tapped it. The window came down and he must have thought that his luck was in place and chat would be good. An armed cop wearing a bulletproof vest and with heavy stuff on his lap . . . Could he be of any assistance?

The answer came "Just fuck off, and fuck off fast."

A response that Jonas thought appropriate, and more footsteps. The drunk stumbled away, and the policewoman returned. She settled in her seat. Turned. Passed him a dog lead. He heard panting, then saw a lolling tongue over her shoulder and smelled its foul breath. He thought it was a spaniel.

Jonas said, "I suppose they thought we needed a dog as well as a lead. Not true. Only need a lead. If we have use for a dog it will be later, not now . . ."

She said, "Disabled owner, needs two sticks for walking. She's Rosie, that's the dog. Doesn't get the exercise it should. And a thermos, tea without sugar, and a half pack of biscuits."

He had the lead and opened the door. The dog was settled on her thighs and wriggled and must have found it uncomfortable to share her lap with an H&K assault weapon. He stretched, asked that they save some tea for him. He held the lead, let it dangle and swing, kept it prominent, and started to walk towards the second turning on to the right, a cul-de-sac, where Cameron Jilkes had once lived. He looked around him, and he whistled sharply.

She came down the stairs. A light was on on the landing above her.

Cammy had waited, waited some more, had considered whether to turn and head away, and had rung the bell again.

A man walked along the road towards him. He wondered if that were her husband. Had kept walking and had ducked his head so that his expression could not be seen: none of his business if

Victoria, number 8, had a visitor on a wet night at that late hour. Cammy had not hidden, had no longer cared whether he was seen or not. Another man had brought a dog out, last comfort stop for the night, and Cammy had seen the animal oblige and it had crossed the concrete strips where the car was parked and had gone on to next door's handkerchief of grass and had squatted there. All that while he was waiting. He saw her shape. Heard her voice.

A whisper, hissed and barely audible, "All right, all right, I'm coming. Leave your key somewhere? Don't ring it again."

A bolt drawn back, a key turned. His mum locked the front door, and the back door, only from habit: used to say, "Nothing in here worth pinching so I'm not making this into Fort Knox." Vicky had the full works on the door. It was opened. She looked into his face. She wore an ankle-length nightdress, prim and too old for her, had a robe over her shoulders but hanging open. Her hair fell loose on to her shoulders. No recognition but not much light was on his features. Modesty made her clutch at the robe and pull it across her.

A nervy frown and a sharp query, "Yes?"

Cammy did not answer her but did the smile. What had won him through bad times, what had left Vicky – years before – chasing after him. Did it slow and measured and he saw the realisation dawn on her. A hand up to her mouth and a little squeal and her eyes widening. Another frown as if indicating that her memory of an old face, one from a few years ago, might deceive her. A blink, because she might have been already asleep, and one hand still over her mouth and the other dropping its grip on the robe and wiping at her eyes, and her face all clean and shiny, her make-up washed off. He tried to recall how it had been, the last time he had seen her . . . remembered his excuses, a headache, an early start at work. And in his room, under the mattress were his airline ticket and enough cash, US dollars, for the one-way trip, and his passport. Probably he'd have said, "See you, love, I'll call you." Left it vague, but didn't have the recall.

Her mouth was wider and her hand no longer covered it and the robe sagged open.

Gasped, "Fuck me, fucking hell. Cammy . . ."

And his smile grew because in this street, in this house, he doubted she ever used that language. Wouldn't have done "dirty talk" here, the way they had. Not that he did dirty talk where he'd been. The guys would not have liked it and Ulrike would have hissed that the language was "out of order" . . . Then anger on her face, her lips pouting and accusation welling. And she had cause to bawl at him, even if she woke the baby, took a foot back, no slippers, bare feet, burgundy-painted nails, and kick him hard in the shin, to turn him around and shove him through the door, and slam it, bolt and lock it. The anger faded, and she must have been deluged with questions she wanted to ask, and then – perhaps – thought, "Fucking inquest, what for?" Cammy had not touched a woman in the years since he had taken the train out of Canterbury and gone to the airport, and had never thought he needed to because he was with his brothers, was never alone. The rain fell on him, and the wind blustered around him and through the door and cannoned into her and flattened her nightdress across her chest and waist and thighs.

Did not know what to say, so said nothing.

Her call. Stay or go? He did the smile, and she went through the emotions, then jerked her head. Two steps forward. She closed the door behind him. Seemed to quiz him; How long? Mouthed an answer; A couple of hours. Standing there, facing each other was time wasted.

She said, "Fuck, and I've missed you, you bastard."

There were prints on the wall of the hallway, and he stepped around a buggy, and carpet on the stairs, and a pseudo antique table with a phone on it. If she had stayed with him, if he had not taken the ride to the airport four years before, if they had shacked up together, then it would have been in a couple of rooms, a bed-sit, and a kitchen in the corner, poky space, and watching the pennies let alone the pounds. Now she had a tidy home, and she had done well if that was what mattered to her . . . She had his anorak off, dropped it on the mat. Then had his jacket off.

Extraordinary how Cammy made it up the stairs because by

the time he reached the last step, his clothing was scattered. All he'd done was the laces of the brogues, and her fingers had careered over his body. Belt loose and trousers dropped, and the shirt heaved off and two buttons broken, and his T-shirt and him kissing her, full on. He finished it, took off his own socks . . . she said, an afterthought and not important, that her husband was on a work thing, staying over. Into the marital bedroom and the robe dropped and the nightdress over her shoulders.

As good as he had remembered her, and then the gasp.

"Are those wounds? Is that what happened to you? How many holes? How did you live through . . ."

And he kissed her harder, covered her mouth, and they fell together and the bed heaved.

"What do you want?" the man had asked and had stood suspicious and defiant on the mat in the hall.

"Very sorry to disturb you," Izzy had said.

"Could we please come in?" Tristram had asked.

No outside porch to give them shelter. They'd have looked half drowned, her hair would have been flattened on her head and the rain would have been running off his nose. They were probationers, trying to make their way in the covert and complicated world of the Security Service. And they had been scared and had walked along the cul-de-sac and had identified the house where Jonas Merrick had told them to be . . . Didn't know whether their target – Jilkes, Cameron – was already at the location, didn't know whether he was armed. Nor did they know how this family home, chosen by Merrick, would react. The curtains drawn, no lights on in the room and there would have been a view of the end of the road, the top, where it widened to make a better turning space, and where the semi-detached brick-built home stood, dark and lifeless.

"Who are you?"

"We are actually a government agency and . . ."

"Don't piss about, Tris – we are from the Security Service. May we please come in. If you didn't know it, sir, it's raining out here."

One thing to be scared and coming up a road, not knowing where a *jihadi* might be, and no weapon to hand, and they were a boy and a girl, and they had held hands, and had arrived on a neighbour's doorstep. Needed to produce identification. She had to open her shoulder bag, dig inside and produce the wallet, and flash the card embedded under a cellophane cover. He had to take his plastic card from the zipped internal jacket pocket where he thought it was safe. Both needed spare hands, and they were held, and she might have blushed scarlet and might have groaned, and the man saw it. Cards produced, and shown and him peering at them and wanting to take them and move away to the light and neither permitting him to handle them. And then a woman in a dressing-gown at the top of the stairs and demanding to know who visited them, that time of night. Then two kids behind their mother, and them wanting to know too.

The man had said, "Any conman could rig up that card. No thank you, on your way and . . ."

Tristram had had his foot in the door, could take the weight of it. "This is a matter of importance. We are not here without reason."

Izzy had her weight against Tristram's back so he'd not shift. They should have been smiling and oiling their way forward, and giving all the shit about "national security", then been honoured guests. "I think if we could just come in and explain, we'd . . ."

The man had said, "I think not. I am not obligated to open my house up, no warning and no clarification and no verification. Just get on your way."

"Not a helpful attitude."

"Not intended as a threat but failure to cooperate could rebound severely against you."

The man was pushing harder and it was the fiasco moment, and Tristram had the flash thought in his mind that he'd be phoning up old Jonas, the crocodile hunter, and saying they'd failed to get past the lowest level of base camp, and it was the boy at the top of the stairs who saved the day.

"Steady, Dad. Of course it's genuine. Think about it, Dad, where we are. Opposite Sadie. We can see her front door. It'll be about that bastard ... Let them in, Dad, it'll be about Sadie's bastard. Do it, Dad."

And they had been let inside, had been economic with the facts, but the boy had smoothed their path. They sat in the Hunters' front room and watched, sat close to each other ... aware that it was comfortable when they held each other's hands. Sat watching the front door of the house where Jonas Merrick was certain the target would show. And, the house into which they had intruded was quiet, no creaking boards above them, no movement. And they watched.

He said, "I keep seeing that picture, the one Merrick stuck on his wall. The still water, looks calm, looks safe, but that bloody thing is there. Can't see him, but you can sense him. If he shows, a little ripple, tiny ... but what *we're* looking for – if it does, what do we do?"

She said, "Not a fucking idea, not one. Know nothing except that he'll have decent sized teeth if he cares to use them."

Two aircraft landed, a minute between them, and both touching down smoothly on the runway. They needed a fraction of the space required for the fast jets with which they shared USAF-administered space on a Turkish military airfield.

Both had flown a few minutes short of eleven hours, so landed well within the safety limits that permitted them to be airborne when carrying the maximum armament of two 500lb GBU-12 laser-guided bombs along with four AGM-114 Hellfire missiles. In darkness, identifiable only by navigation lights, the aircraft taxied.

On a busy airstrip, which this was, and one used principally by the strike aircraft, the sight of these drones still raised an eyebrow. Impossible that they would not. They were designated as MQ-9A Reapers, built by the American company General Atomics Aeronautical Systems. They had a wingspan of 70 feet, a length of only 36 feet, a flying ceiling of 30,000 feet. They always aroused interest from the technicians at the base because the Reapers, moving carefully at slow speed across the aprons towards the hangers where their maintenance team waited, had no pilots on board. The personnel who had flown them over Syrian airspace that day and into the evening were some 2,600 miles away. Past them, on the centre of the runway which they had just vacated, a pair of F-22 Raptors gathered speed, went to flaming after-burn, were deafeningly loud . . . Not so the Reapers, which flew with a dulled murmur, a noise similar to that made by a household lawn-mower not in the next road but the one beyond.

Their pilots, far away, brought them home for refuelling and maintenance, sometimes still carrying their weapons. The drones were now coming back more frequently carrying bombs and Hellfires, but at the peak of the war against the black flag *jihadis* they usually returned with empty pods. They had been a powerful weapon in the war – in fact a game changer. That evening, a Public Affairs Department officer, briefing a friendly hack said, "They are terrific, whether they're ours or those the Brits have. The camera can give us a hawk-eye view of the ground – the street, individual cars and individual people. They can loiter for hours and give a continuous feed, and if they identify a target then we have the capability from the weapons platform to obliterate our enemy. And, important, they create fear. They cannot be seen – they are too high, the sound is minimal, and the target has no idea he is being watched, tracked, is about to be killed. It's why we love them. They are lethal, which is why the other crowd hate them."

Up in the Kirkstall part of the city, at a lock-up garage behind a terrace of weathered old brick houses, Farouk – in his mode as Wolfboy – knocked gently on a door.

He was asked to identify himself. Told them Wolfboy had come.

Heard nervous laughter, then the noise of bolts being drawn back. They were justified, those who worked there, late into the night, in being both cautious and anxious. The men inside all came originally from the Shah Zaman Road district of Quetta city in that part of Pakistan close to the remote tribal homeland; if they were arrested during this enterprise, they would spend decades in gaol. They were good at secrecy, trusted only a very few outside their inter-related family, and obeyed the instructions they received from those they regarded as of higher authority. It had been an interesting project that Wolfboy had delivered to them. The steel sheeting had been obtained from a scrapyard in Dewsbury and the vehicle the sheets would protect had come from an auction, cash only, in Barnsley. They had converted a van, the sort used by a small jobbing handyman, and for much of the journey from here to Lincolnshire, the plates would be carried out of sight. At some time in the late morning or early afternoon of the following day, the plates would be fastened to the sides of the vehicle and the driver given protection, and the tyres, and the engine. As an armoured vehicle it needed only to achieve surprise and then be proof against erratic small arms fire. It was rated as satisfactory, and also as secure, and they believed the trail to their garage was comprehensively disguised. The man who drove the van, who would burst through a perimeter fence and close on a complex of buildings, would not survive the attack: that they had been guaranteed. Wolfboy had promised it.

The closed area of the garage stank from the oxyacetylene cutters as the final adjustments were made. Wolfboy was hugged and his cheeks were kissed. The men in the garage would be huddled close to radio sets the following afternoon. They drank coffee, celebrated, and were ripped by excitement – and each agreed that prayers should be spoken for the success of the man who would drive the van into the fence and beyond.

Jonas whistled. Not a tune, not a cheerful serenade to the cul-de-sac, but a piercing whistle more like a sports referee's . . . also like that of the dog walkers who took their animals out on the Civil Service recreation ground near where he and Vera lived. He looked around him as he walked.

The lead dangled from his hand. He would stop, turn a full revolution, would hesitate, let time pass, then would march forward again and whistle once more, and anyone seeing him would note his agitation.

Not Jonas Merrick from the third floor of Thames House, south aspect, and working in Room 12, but a rather stooped elderly man, dressed respectably but shabbily, and out in the rain when he should have been in his bed. His precious dog had gone walk-about, and needed to be found. He was unknown in the cul-de-sac, which mattered not at all. He was old, distressed. He looked in gardens and peered over fences. Those who had seen him might have said: "Poor old beggar, should be tucked up by now, but the dog's gone and lost itself, he can't do anything else . . ." He passed a smarter looking property, same structure as all the rest, but well looked after and the garden tended; saw an upstairs light on a landing, and a curtain flickered in the front. Below was the living-room and he noted, would have expected nothing else, that the room was dark and the curtains a little ajar, so he did another whistle, and moved on.

Jonas came to the end of the cul-de-sac. A cat came to greet him. He showed it his toecap, had no need of its attention. He was outside the house in which Cameron Jilkes had grown up, gone from choirboy to a *jihadi* fighter: had enlisted in the all-star cast of choirboys at the most prestigious religious building in the country and moved on to acquire a reputation, a dose of notoriety, as a member of the *muhajireen*, the most valued foreign fighters. The curtains were drawn, and no light burned inside. The grass at the front was long, and the flower beds beside the hard standing were weeded up. A gutter dripped. A street light showed where paint had come off the window frames. Easy and appropriate for him to go up the side of the house and peer over the gate that shut off the back, and he skirted the rubbish bins and looked down that part of the garden – and whistled some more. He was satisfied and turned to retrace his steps, all the time holding the lead in readiness should his dog, whatever its size or breed, reappear. He did the part well and quite enjoyed himself.

Jonas was not a man who cared greatly for the status of rank. He had never, in his many years with the Security Service, put in for promotion, had made no effort to advance himself up the civil service grades. He belonged to no club – other than one repre-senting caravan owners in Raynes Park and Merton and Motspur

Park. He never wore the medal awarded to him, nor used the initials it bestowed.

He was pleased that he had achieved the reconnaissance without jeopardising his cover. Another curtain was momentarily flicked sideways. He imagined a whispered remark: "Poor old bugger, still hasn't found it." He wondered if he was being watched.

Could have already been at his mother's home. Her birthday that day, his files had told him, or the next. Would want to be there for that. Might already have come. If he was not yet there then he would be soon, in an hour or two. Had no doubt of it. He started back up the cul-de-sac . . . Funny old place to fight a war . . . Not with any of the drama, not the location that his High Value Target, young Cameron, would have wanted . . . But the right sort of place for Jonas Merrick to be deployed – good ground for him, wrong for Cameron.

He swung the lead and whistled.

The picture was beside the bed, her side. Ornate frame of painted flowers, showed a guy who grinned proudly and wore shorts with a crease in them and a works T-shirt, and there was a space where in girly handwriting was written, "My darling Gavin, from Victoria", and the table on the other side had a matching frame and her picture and "My wonderful Victoria, from Gavin". The ceiling light was on and she had not bothered to pull the duvet over them. Had done it, and afterwards they'd talked a bit and then started again, her on top.

He might have asked her how she was. Might have said that she looked brilliant. Might have said that the lines her nails had made on his back, where one of the bullet holes was and where Ulrike had done some stitching on a shrapnel gash, had felt great. Might have said that he had missed her, which would have been a lie.

She might have asked what he planned, why he had come looking for her after four years with no contact, and where he was headed. She might have told him that most days she had forgotten he ever existed, which would have been good because then he wouldn't need to feel guilty about leaving her with no explanation. Might have told him her baby's name, and who from school she still saw. Might have told him that the worst day in her life had been when she had realised that he had gone, and had heard that his mum had no clue about his whereabouts, he'd vanished, done a runner. Might have questioned him about what he was going to do, when he would be moving on ... Where to? Why?

She rode him. He thought they were both animals, like the dogs that roamed the streets of Raqqa, scavenging for scraps, or the ones that brazenly hunted in the flattened shallow bunkers at Barghuz. However bad life was for the dogs, ribcages prominent because they were more than half starved, the dogs would break off from searching for food if there was a bitch on heat. It took priority ... not about love, but need.

She could have refused to let him in, been aggressive or coldly indifferent. Could have let him do it out of sympathy. Could have bombarded him with questions. Could have prattled about himself.

She helped him through the second time, went slower and took control of him. He had run the lives of his brothers, had taken only nominal advice from them, and they had been happy enough to follow him and, until the break-out and the crossing of the Euphrates in the darkness, it had worked well – better than well. Now he was alone, and needed her, and she needed him.

The second time, her eyes watching him for his response and his breathing starting to quicken, he had realised the folly of it ... Had been to the cathedral and had looked back in time to when he had been a star in the firmament ... would be going to his mum because any man approaching death would want that blessing, that love that did not question. He felt Vicky's warmth over him, her nails seeking out the lines of the two shrapnel wounds on his chest, and her fingers pressing into the ugly hole where the flesh had failed to fold over neatly. Being with her, under her or over her, walking in the street with her, her hand tucked in the crook of his arm, shopping with her, eating with her, and laughing with her, had never seemed as important before he had gone – or while he was away, a fighting man – as now. Realised that his anger had drained. If it ran dry then he would fail the next day. Realised the mistake.

Had not considered it possible that Vicky, a little fuller in the breasts and a little thicker around the hips, would seduce him. He was always in control. No longer.

Had been in control of his emotions and actions when they had been together the first time. Had never lost control when he was with the brothers. Had managed to control the great journey he had made, from the frontier he had crossed, another solitary fighter who had somehow survived, and had a reservoir of lapping hatred. Had made the new journey with the Iranian Christian family, the nightmare of the storm in the Channel. And then he had diverted from his plan and had come to this street and had pressed that doorbell. He thought she made a trophy of him. Perhaps, in the morning, long after he was gone, she would take a pair of nail scissors and would make a small scratch on the varnished wood of the bedpost, where she could see it. Would remember him, and how she had screwed the anger out of him.

Coming faster, breath quickening, her eyes still open. Like it had never been before, left him helpless – and weakened. He could not see the face of his watch, did not care. And yelled out, she was grinning at him and the ceiling light burned bright above them. Cammy clung to her, could not help himself, and tears welled in his eyes.

"Did you have a girl there?"

"No."

"Not one of those little black crows out from school in London? Did you go without?"

"Didn't have a girl."

"You weren't as good at it. Not special like you used to be . . ."

Just wanted to sleep, hold her and sleep.

She asked him, "I suppose you were killing people. Too busy to shack up. You kill plenty?"

He wiped his eyes.

"Are you done with killing? Or have you come back to kill some more?"

She did not break away, snuggled closer, and he held her tighter.

She said, "You used to make me laugh, Cammy. I'm not laughing now. Wish I was."

"The fact is that it is a bloody liberty. I'm not saying we're perfect neighbours, but we care. We don't turn our backs on any of them, and especially not on Sadie. Those two come into our house, try to give us a bit of soft soap and then switch double fast to intimidation. I should have put them out on the street."

Dave and Trace were wide awake and his words hissed in her ear. Quiet now beyond their window and the floral curtains were not quite closed; they could hear the rain but the whistling had stopped. Some old guy who had lost his dog and had been poking around looking for it. Dave had a tough day and an early start tomorrow and Trace was always stretched at work and both needed their rest but weren't getting it. Did not help that Karen had gone into Bradley's room and they could hear them talking.

Trace might have cried but was over that now, and she whispered at Dave, "What shames me is that we're providing the base, from which *they* can spy on Sadie. We gave in too fast. Not blaming you, they bounced you. I suppose they're trained to do that, take advantage of people. We're talking about Sadie, not about a war thousands of miles away, not about something her boy might or might not have done. I regard her as a friend, and she's our neighbour – and that counts. You saw the way they looked at us, them downstairs, looked at us like we're just 'peasants', should do as we're told and take them on trust. It's wrong. We're betraying her."

"But if it's terrorism. I mean, where does that put us?"

"We don't know what he's done, or not done. We're not judge and jury . . . Sorry, Dave, but I feel ashamed, them being in here, under our roof . . . Know what I mean?"

Dave would have admitted that his own thoughts were garbled. Trace would have agreed that what she dripped in his ear might have over-egged their situation. But both were rock solid that a friend, someone whose trust they appreciated, was being violated, was being watched in secrecy . . . Like a woman standing in her bathroom, drying herself after a shower, and a pervert stood outside and was hidden in shadow, and watched. He tapped on the common wall. The kids came in . . . Sadie had babysat, had minded them. Had not seen as much of her in the last few years as they should have but here was a way of appeasing guilt. Trace told the kids what they were going to do. No dissent.

At the bus-stop with a few other late workers and a few revellers, she waited beside the overflowing rubbish bin, smelled the shelter, accepted that this was part of her life.

By the time she reached home, had grabbed a piece of toast and gulped weak tea, had got undressed and gone to bed, she might have five hours' sleep, no more.

Sadie's phone rang. She saw that it was Dave Hunter's number.

Wondered what he wanted at that time of night. Used to look after their kids, snotty and superior and looking down on Cameron, but had hardly seen them after the police raid. She remembered coming out of her house after the counter-terror search and loading the bins with all the broken stuff from the rest of her house but not from his bedroom and she'd seen the Hunter family come out of their house and they'd not looked at her. All she'd bloody done for them . . . They had seen her come out of her front door, lugging a sack and none of them had come to help. Pretended they hadn't seen her, like she had the plague.

She answered. Had to listen hard because the bloody man spoke in a whisper.

"Sadie, thought you ought to know. We have the security police, whatever they are. They're here, in the front room. They're watching your house. We're thinking that means your boy is coming home, they're expecting him, your Cameron. We thought you should know. We reckoned calling you was the proper thing to do. We're always here for you, Sadie."

The bus came. She'd always assumed that, if he lived, he would try to get back to her, had readied her mind for it for months, years. Knew that if he returned, came back to the village, contacted her, that a net would close on him . . . Would she help him, her son, to evade it? Knew the answer.

Izzy's head was on his shoulder. Tristram had his arm draped over her.

Not quite a sleep but almost. Izzy snored softly and Tristram faded in and out of awareness and time slipped . . . An old man had been looking for a lost dog, and that was clever of Merrick, Wise Old Bird, but then he would need to be clever if he was going to catch a crocodile. Gustave, who had killed, eaten, was it 300? God knows how many – African villagers. Actually, who cared how many it had eaten? Not Tristram, not Izzy.

Had never had a bolt on the kitchen outer door.

Just had a lock, and the key was never left in it so he could get into the house if he were out late, coming back from work when she and the baby would be asleep. Came in, eased the door shut and locked it again. Well oiled and quiet. The light was on in the hall and threw a beam on to the kitchen table. The day's post was there. He tiptoed into the hall, left his jacket and overnight bag at the bottom of the stairs. Saw the trail of clothes from the front door, across the hall, and up the stairs to the landing. A mist went over his eyes.

He took the stairs two, or three, at a time and burst into the bedroom. Half-asleep, Cammy jackknifed.

The man was frozen in the doorway, his expression one of disbelief. Tried to speak but had not found his voice, wore a suit and a loosened tie. He held the door open and gawped.

Cammy heard little gagging noises from deep in Vicky's throat and she had slid away from him and had the duvet up to hide her body, and her head was down and . . . Bit late for regrets, darling, he might have said.

But not much to say, Cammy reckoned, and wondered if the explosion – the poor sod was building for it – would be incoherent sobbing or violence.

She had grabbed too much of the duvet. Had exposed him. He was staring at Cammy's body – where he was limp, and where the hair was and the scars of two shrapnel wounds, both highlighted by ragged stitching, and where there was a bullet wound, would have had an eyeful of it.

He swung his legs off the bed. There was a chair beside the door, covered with Vicky's clothes. Tried a smile, nothing much else to offer, would have to come around the end of the bed. Nothing to say that needed saying. The guy, Gavin, grabbed the chair, spilled Vicky's stuff to the floor.

Back at the car, Jonas attached the lead to the dog's collar. Dominic asked him how he had done.

"Not bad, had a good look around. Saw pretty much what I wanted to see."

Babs asked why he had needed a dog's lead.

"Pretty basic. A dog has gone for a run, and he's not come back. The owner cannot leave it out for the night so he goes to find it. Consider the time. Close on midnight . . . I reckon that half the street looked out of an upstairs window and saw me and hoped that the 'poor old sod' would find his animal and get back to the warm and dry. Clear to you?"

Was asked what they should do with the dog now.

"Don't know. Have to see how things pan out."

And now?

"I am expecting a lady to pass. I'm assuming on foot. Mrs Sadie Jilkes and it is her house we are interested in. It's her son who we regard as a High Value Target. I suppose that with all those toys you have you are wondering if, when, you are going to be unleashed. First things first. You will follow my instructions to the letter. If I tell you to sit then you sit. If I tell you to keep your Safety on, then you keep your Safety on. I don't argue and don't negotiate . . . You do as I tell you or you take back the dog to its owner and you drive off and go back where you came from. Because if you dispute those instructions then you are of no use to me. Should this progress to the conclusion

I believe will be the outcome, then a champagne moment in your police careers beckons. Even a dog biscuit would be welcome, I am famished."

He sat in his place and the dog clambered over to settle on his lap.

12

In the front passenger seat, the policeman slept.

Jonas was on his phone, had the ability to go into secure networks and chased for more on the destruction of the brothers, the group led by Kami al-Britani . . . Ironic because the stereotype would have had them drawn from refugee camps and the *madrassas* where kids learned by heart serious lengths of the Book, and the reality was this housing estate on the hill above a traditional village in the Garden of England. The others, he now knew, were from Europe and southern Africa and the north of the American continent. Which went to show that gobbling down easy interpretations was seldom sensible. Now he had a pecking order for the deaths. The dog on his lap sometimes broke wind, occasionally snored and wriggled to make itself more comfortable. He believed his overview was becoming clearer, as if he gazed through the prism of a glass of water that was gradually losing its cloudiness. The policewoman, behind the wheel, turned to him.

"You all right, Mr Merrick?"

"Couldn't be better," drily said.

She persisted. "Anything we can do for you?"

"Very kind, I don't think so."

"What we say, if you can't catnap in a car then don't do this job. You used to it? Sleeping on the floor or in cars?"

"First time, actually."

"I'd have thought . . ."

"My experience, boxes are not often satisfactorily ticked. Conventional images usually lead us off-track. Anyway, I've been catching up on sleep."

"But, sleep or not, you are backing yourself?"

"Have to. It's where we are."

"Where I'm from, Mr Merrick, faced with this sort of threat – potentially big, possibly non-existent – we'd have a committee sitting in and a Gold commander. Down here at ground level we'd be the pawns and shunted round the board. Does that make you a big player, maybe a bishop, if you call it yourself?"

"I do. I try to anticipate events."

"That's it, *try to*, and that's the best you can do?"

"And it's the best your Gold commander can do, try to anticipate."

"If you try to, and you screw up – excuse my language, Mr Merrick – get it wrong . . ."

"I believe I have anticipated well. I'm confident. What if my picture of the boy, his character, his psychology, his plans, are wrong?"

"That is my question, Mr Merrick. No impertinence intended."

"None taken. My humble opinion is that I know pretty much where he will be, and what target he will think he is moving towards tomorrow."

"If you are wrong?"

"If I am wrong, the people I seek to protect become defenceless. If I am wrong, then many who could be innocent of blame for this long-running fiasco in the Middle East will have a very bad day. If I am right, then those same innocents will go about their usual business. And those who I claim are the boy's targets will stay in ignorance. It is the way life runs."

"We take responsibility."

"Yes, a weighty responsibility."

"And live with it."

"We all do, and accept realities. I offer you a confidence, officer: we are stretched to snapping point. That everyone can sleep safe in their beds demands that resources are managed with the acceptance of a gamble. Of course it is a gamble. Life is a gamble."

"Makes for a lonely old world, Mr Merrick."

"Indeed. I don't complain. Lonely also for him. We must not forget him. I have to say that I find excessive examination of the prospects of failure and the ethics of responsibility tend to get in the way of doing the job, straightforward or not. Nice dog, this Rosie, well mannered. Last word on the subject, I imagine it's not all milk and honey for our boy."

He was gathering up his clothing, the last pieces that had come off and were lying on the landing.

"You bastard, pig – get the hell out of my house."

Then the scream from inside the bedroom: Cammy thought Vicky and Gavin would have been hanging on to each other, strangers, but recognising the need to stay close. They'd sort it out . . . Did he care? Not greatly.

"Get out . . . Go, go to hell."

Cammy could not imagine the reaction he'd have had if he had come back to wherever – his mum's home, or the first hostel in Raqqa, or the old army camp in Deir Ezzor – and his girl had been on her back with her legs splayed and a bloke beside her, bollock naked. Had never been a girl who had mattered enough to him.

To begin with, Gavin – husband and supposed "hunter gatherer" – had gone quiet, like he'd swallowed his tongue.

"Get out of my house. Do you know what you've done? Does it matter to you?"

Had an anguish to it. As if he believed a wrong had been done that could never be righted. Well, their business, not Cammy's. He had reached the hall, had his underwear and socks on and retrieved the rest of his clothes.

"I suppose where you were, you thought yourself something special. People bowed and scraped – not because of who you were but because you had a bloody weapon. Means all you were is a bully. Pity is you weren't killed there. You will be, though. You will be killed."

Gavin had picked up the chair where Vicky's clothes had been, and was framed in the bedroom doorway. He was yelling and Vicky had now chimed in, and was sobbing. Predictably, the baby had woken, and now chimed in. Would wake next door, would rouse half the street. All of them blubbering ... Gavin, wronged and humiliated, was coming down the stairs with the chair raised.

"Decent people will finish you off. Decent people don't have a rifle, but that doesn't make them frightened of you."

Cammy was dragging on his trousers. The chair was swung high and dislodged the light shade on the hall ceiling, then broke the bulb and Gavin was huge against the wall and flailed again with the chair, and caught Cammy. The blow took him across the side of the face, a chair leg whacking his cheek, and his ear. Another blow came. Cammy ignored it, had the trousers on, was fastening his belt.

"People are decent and ordinary ... they will finish you, believe it."

Cammy was defenceless. More blows with the chair. Twisted his head in time to avoid the tip of the chair leg that might have caught his eye, instead the impact was against his lip. Tasted blood, his own blood. Her sobbing was louder and the baby screamed fit to bust, and the noise of it dinned around him. He saw a savagery in Gavin's face. When was the last time that the guy had ever racked up such anger? Ever? His own blood was in his mouth and he was now fastening his shirt, and blood was on his hands and on his shirt front.

"You know what 'ordinary' is? One day you will look at those around you and realise they have control of you. The ordinary people."

His brothers had never seen Kami al-Britani cower. Never seen him show fear. Vicky was on the landing, had the baby at her shoulder and was patting its back. It yelled, she yelled, and her man still came after Cammy.

"Victoria said you were a shit and dangerous. Your Ma must be ashamed of you, her son. Bastard, weren't you? One-night stand and she ended up with you."

At the first camp, where the foreign fighters were housed, they had been taught self-defence, unarmed combat stuff, all the moves that would show the *emirs* which of the newcomers were worth spending time on, and which could be dumped into administration or could just be fed into the front line, human wave and all that crap. Cammy could have taken two steps up the stairs, could have deflected the swing of the chair, pushing it aside. He could have chopped at the husband's throat with the heel of his hand and seen him drop dead on the carpet. Or put two fingers into his eyes which would have blinded him. Cracked his forehead against the man's nose and he'd go down sobbing at the pain. Could have put a knee into the man's groin and done it hard enough so that the will to fight would leave him and he would be lying on the floor, moaning – and the chance of a sibling for the baby would be out the window. He did not do any of them, just finished dressing and took the blows.

"You think your Ma will welcome you? Well, you're wrong. Nobody wants you. You're on your own. Was it like that where you were? Filling in time between wrecking places, wrecking people? You're a freak, that's all you are."

Because he did not flinch, nor duck his head away, but rode the blows and let the cuts bleed on his face, he could see Vicky. She had retrieved the robe, not that it hid much of her, and he saw the dull death in her eyes, and she could not silence her own crying nor her baby's. Cammy could have stopped the attack on him at any moment but didn't. He picked up his jacket and anorak and was tying his shoe laces. And said nothing.

"Just get out."

He opened the front door. Thought the rain was slackening. Turned to face the guy at the bottom of the stairs . . . and Cammy feinted, as if to go forward, as if to retaliate. Gavin stumbled back and slipped, caught himself in the chair, and went over, and Cammy smiled softly at him; had let him know what might have been and he'd carry that to his grave, the memory of that moment . . . No room for fear in the last few hours available to Cammy.

He went out, leaving the door to swing in the wind, walked down the path to the pavement. Could have killed him . . . felt the blood on his face . . . Could have killed him and thought as little of it as if Vicky's husband had been a Syrian, an Iranian, a Russian.

Could have closed him down. She would read about him, would see his picture in the paper, on the TV. Would know he had shown no fear. And it was time to get up the hill above Sturry village and find his mum.

Her voice was strident in the night. "They were here. Same people as when you went, the Security Service. They're expecting you, waiting for you. Did you think you could slink back and not be noticed? They're looking for you. Tracking you. I hope you're cowering in a ditch, pissing yourself, when they get you. Fuck you for coming here."

They walked in a small phalanx into the Officers' Mess. It was a traditional RAF Station building: a wide hallway, walls covered with paintings – some good, some less so – of the aircraft that, over the years, had flown from the long runway on the east side of the village. They were in the flat lands of Lincolnshire, in the heart of the East Midlands surrounded by prosperous farms. They need not have stayed so late in the prefabricated buildings in which, at least four days a week, they went to war. Well before their weapons platforms had landed at a Turkish-administered airfield, the two Reapers had been handed over to local ground control for the process of bringing them in and lining them up and dropping them down. But a bond existed between the mainstream crews that operated the unmanned machines, and the guys stayed in their padded seats, watching, almost as friends, until they had landed.

Now they came to the Mess for a late-night drink. They had families scattered on the base who might have been waiting up for them, wanting to talk about bills, or school reports . . . a host of matters that had nothing to do with the testing, taxing business of flying the platforms – burdened by bombs and lethal missiles – over the war zone. They went for a last drink in the Mess, still wearing their flying kit overalls with rank insignia on the shoulders and with the bright colours of the Union flag sewn on to the upper arms. It was necessary for these modern-day warriors, whose craft sneaked silently and unseen over a distant battlefield, to wind down after a day in the comfort of their ergonomic chairs. Truth was, the strains on their minds of this "removed" form of warfare had the potential to play merry hell with their family lives. They had all spent the day, the pilot and the sensor operator and the mission intelligence goon assigned to each Reaper, watching the sectors awarded them: one had had a wadi and the other a village community, and they had overflown both sites and had looked for the High Value Targets that the intelligence fed them, and for individual vehicles. Twice that day, one had gone to the state of readiness before releasing a Hellfire, then had backed off from firing, and the other had done great figure of eight patterns in the high skies and had not prepared to shoot. The crews would never have admitted that spending those hours in the negative state – no explosion to watch on the screen, no plume of smoke rising, no clearance of the cloud when the debris fell back to the ground, no bodies to count – left them taut and frustrated. They had done their debrief and had walked to the Mess and would try to relax and talk about holidays, barmaids in the surrounding villages, vehicle showrooms, and football. Would try to wind down and then would go home. Would all tiptoe into the kids' bedrooms and see a sleeping child and ease out, then would go down to the kitchen where the wife might be watching a TV show, flicking the pages of a magazine, wrestling with a tax form, and there would be the brief exchange that was possible if the anxiety, the tension, of the day had been successfully degraded in the Mess.

"Hi, love, day go all right?"

"Bit knackered, but good – thanks."

And "good" meant that they had not done a "splash" on a flat-roofed building and taken down three or four *jihadis* who intelligence reckoned to be prime targets, and then found it was a place where their version of the Mothers' Union was chatting. Had not hit a gathering of supposed fighters, and learned – too late – that they had "rifled" a wedding party with a Hellfire. "Good" meant there had been no cluster-fuck moments, and they had not needed to choose which little grey shadow on the ground went quickly to Paradise and which lived until the next day's Reaper patrol.

★   ★   ★

Sitting on the lower bunk in their cabin, Baz and Mags had a good view of the quayside.

The last vehicles had gone through the parking lot before driving on board. The sounds of the big doors rising and then clamping tight shut. Men on the quayside dangling huge ropes and then dragging them on board after they had been freed. The shake in the ferry from the surge of the engines. It went out slowly. Baz had the trained eye and Mags had the nose for what was unusual. Neither his eye or her nose had warned them. Baz thought it was all as he had predicted. The camper was a deck below them. Stowed away in the van was the package . . . sure as God spoke if Baz had had to lift it clear he'd have done himself a hernia. A hell of a weight. He knew about the Russian built RPG-7 launcher and about the armour-piercing capabilities of the projectiles that were effective at least up to 400 yards. Not much, but enough. A tidy weapon, he'd have said.

As they had gone on board, him driving and her beside him, and the platform had shaken under them, Baz had said, "You all right for this, last time of asking?"

She had said, "Never better, feeling good."

He had reflected, "Because, if they nick us with it or, worse, if they get us after it's been fired and with that payload, we're for the high jump."

"We're doing all right, you old bugger – in fact, doing well."

Clear water now between them and the quay. She kissed him on the cheek and grinned. It was not a long crossing and they would need to get on with it – as she said, and did, and he assumed that was why she had taken up the offer of a cabin. Used it well, and sweated in the heated cabin and not yet past the harbour groyne, and did not think of consequences. Out into the Channel and a fair swell shaking them – which seemed to add to the experience.

Dominic and Babs had changed places; Babs had stretched out and tilted back her seat so that Jonas's knees compressed: he made no complaint, nor did the dog.

"Mr Merrick, can I ask you . . .?"

He shut down his phone. He had been living – as far as he could – the last days, hours, of the brotherhood. He believed his assessment had been reinforced. He had been into the loop of the 24/7 intelligence dispersal of facts, conjectures, analyses. Had enjoyed the company of the dog, and when he was home the next day he would tell Vera some of it.

"How near do you think we are?"

"The first eyeballs and footprints? An hour, two at the most."

"So, why is this area not saturated? Why not a cordon?"

"To do what, Dominic?"

"Box him in, close him down, and . . ."

"Somebody coughs at the wrong moment, Dominic, somebody kicks over a rubbish bin, somebody steps on a piece of dried wood and it snaps, somebody is confronted by a dog as he slips through a back garden and the animal goes berserk; somebody has a radio that comes alive with a prattle of police *patois*. And what happens? Our target fades into the night and whatever plan has been in place is ditched. I prefer to stay quiet and have the pair of you."

He stroked the dog's head. The Norwegian Forest cat might have allowed such familiarity, and might not.

"Understood, but your way, Mr Merrick, you take the full weight of the responsibility. If you cock it up then they, the bosses, will hang you out to dry. They won't stand by you. Ours wouldn't. You're on your own."

"As I prefer it."

"The chap you're hunting, do you hate him?"

"Not really."

"After what he's done, where he's been?"

"I'm not a crusader, Dominic. I'm a lowly functionary. In the benighted period of recent German history I would have been the sort of man who kept the trains running on time, made sure that the ones feeding Treblinka, Sobibor, Stutthof were on schedule and not subservient to Auschwitz-Birkenau. Just do the job and make sure, as best I can, that it all runs smoothly."

"Not saving society." The young man's irony rang through.

"Doing a job, and doing it well, is satisfactory. Doing it poorly is disappointing. But there's none of this Queen and country stuff. No, like I said, I'm the man who knows the railway timetable and keeps the programme running . . . I also like to watch for crocodiles, if you know what I mean."

Cammy did not take the road that led to Sturry. He went through trees and along a track that kids had made over the years. He had been one of them. In those days, nights, he would have needed a torch to guide him, and he'd have been hurrying because he had missed the last bus home and was cold and probably wet.

Now, Cammy was skilled at travelling fast and in darkness. He would have led and the brothers would have followed and they would have crossed the supposed front lines held by the government troops, would have gone in and reached the point behind their bunkers and tent camps where they could create chaos among Syrians or Hezbollah or Iranian paramilitary troops, and then the main force with suiciders would have swarmed towards the enemy's front. Had been the leader, and not known fear. The worm had turned, the worm was doubt, failure. In the wake of failure he had made promises . . . they would be honoured.

No moon because of the density of the low rain clouds. No light other than that little filtered from the street lamps, edging through the trees to his left.

It was good to have made those promises; it tightened his resolve. Would see his mum, would be welcomed – would be fed, given money. He would slip away in the night, well before dawn . . . be on the first train of the morning. Knew the route he would take . . . Would take the fight to them. It had been his promise.

Saw again his lowest point . . . near to the Egyptian border with Libya. Footsore, tired, hungry. Had crossed Jordanian territory and hitched a ride on a dhow that would take him from Aqaba and into the Sinai sands. Had hidden in a lorry that had traversed the Suez Canal north of Ismailia. Had used Bedouin travellers to guide him over the desert dunes. His goal was Libya and then a

Mediterranean crossing and into Europe. Had reached the border, far from the main highway, and had slept in the dirt with a blanket wrapping him, and the promise sustaining him. Had woken with the first light of dawn, a little golden segment of sun rising behind him on a distant horizon, but a strong enough light to throw shadows. Two of those shadows had fallen across his body and he had registered the men and the weapons they aimed at him. Blinking as they looked into the sun were three others, all armed and all wary of him. Could they have known? Would have been smugglers bringing weapons and ammunition and narcotics and spare parts for Mercedes and BMW cars across the border – just a fallen strand of barbed wire – and feeding off refugees. Perhaps they had identified him as a straggler from the war in Syria, perhaps even had a slight respect for him. Could have shot him dead and the sound would have echoed into the distance and gone unnoticed. Perhaps they had not thought him worth the waste of a single bullet. If he died there, or was left maimed – and would be a carcase in a few hours under the force of the sun – he would not fulfil his promise. He had eased his hands away from his body as if that were a satisfactory gesture of surrender. One set of hands, gnarled and roughened and with bitten-down nails, had reached forward and had started to strip away his clothing. The barrels of five Kalashnikovs, weapon of choice, were aimed at him. His body was exposed and they would have seen the mark of the bullet's entry, crudely healed, and seen also where Ulrike had stitched up the shrapnel wounds – no anaesthetic – cleaned them as best she could. No gratuitous violence shown him, but no charity. They had taken his pistol, and the spare magazines. A travel document and an ID card had been examined, then pocketed; he had bought both for cash, way over the odds, from a trader west of the Canal. A small knife was produced, was handed to the man who searched him, and the blade snaked down against his skin and might have been used to puncture his stomach wall, to disembowel him, but instead had carefully, precisely, been used to cut through the cotton straps of the money belt he wore knotted across his abdomen. All the wealth he possessed was inside the zipped flap.

The belt was not examined, was thrown from one to another. It was a small gesture but one that emphasised the depths of his failure. The one who had searched him had taken the hem of Cammy's blanket and had covered his nakedness. He was not jeered at and was not abused. Nothing said – like it was an everyday transaction, and he was an everyday unfortunate, a loser . . . If he had resisted them, he would not have had the chance to fulfil a promise.

That had been the lowest point. Cammy believed the promise had sustained him.

Brambles and thorny branches caught his clothing, and scratched his face, bruised from the beating with the chair and still bleeding from the cuts. All unimportant because his promise had been given.

That day, Stanislau had carried more than his share.

Was always the way with him. He had the big machine-gun on one shoulder and swathes of ammunition for it, and had the mortar tube and half a dozen bombs.

They had stopped at dusk. Pieter and Cammy had made the camouflaged bivouac and they were sheltered between great rounded stones that had been scattered in some earthquake millennia before, and Ulrike was checking what food they could eat later, how to ration it. Cammy ought to have been ruthless and downsized the kit they took with them. They had talked among themselves about abandoning gear – weapons and ammunition – but always Stanislau had waved dismissively, and muttered though his misshapen mouth that the rest of them were weak as babies and that he could carry more. His great fists had thwacked together and the discussion was ended.

He could have been a wrestler in a booth, touring with circuses travelling through Belarus. Now, as they flopped under the camouflage awning, smoked and talked in low voices about where they were and where they hoped to be, Stanislau wandered away, saying he wanted a better view of the sunset. "I want to snatch the sunset and hold it." They never laughed when he tried. They would see him standing motionless in a field or beside a track and his hand, soup plate size, would be stretched out. Then, it would lunge forward, the speed of a snake strike, and would clamp. They never teased him or mocked him, never queried whether his fingers really had closed on a sunset.

From the capital of Belarus, from Minsk, he had been rejected for army conscription for alleged flat feet. With the group, he was without fear, would be watching Cammy's back, and following him as faithfully as a dog. The sun was near to setting and it had been a good tramp, but there had been no opportunity to steal a pick-up and ride with wheels. They were in an empty wilderness of territory where few herdsmen sought forage for their goats, but the stones made a useful bivouac. All of them kept an eye on Stanislau, as if all of them prayed that one day he would achieve the snatch. He was with them because of an incident three years before in a bar on the north side of Minsk. Drink taken, probably excessive drink taken. As he told it, it would have been vodka made with cranberries, and he was starting to wreck the bar because most of his drinking had been on tab, and now they were closing and he had no money, and an argument started. Stanislau hit a priggy little bastard hard enough to require a rewiring of the jaw in the Minsk Regional Clinical Hospital. The kid was admitted there because of his father – a Russian embassy official ... a price to pay for the punch. Stanislau was worked over for many minutes when the city police located and arrested him. He hated Russians, as much as Mikki, fought them and killed them.

They lounged under the camouflage canopy and watched him. The low sunlight threw great shadows from the rocks where they sheltered.

They saw him move. Saw his right arm jerk up and all of them at that moment thought he had achieved it, had snatched the sunset, and the tired faces of Pieter and Ulrike and Cammy were wreathed in a smile of pleasure. Then realised he was collapsing, then heard the crack.

A single shot. A sniper.

A head shot. Expert work. Stanislau went down on to his knees and his right arm sagged beside him, then he fell. Pieter said that, from the sound of the bullet's carry, he thought the marksman was about a thousand yards from his target. The man would have seen them trudging along open ground on the track, would have watched them reach the bivouac. Would have seen Stanislau set off to find the open space where

he could better see the sunset.Would have tracked him with the magni-
fication of the telescopic lens, and would have picked his moment. It
was a good shot, admitted.

When it was darker, Cammy left Pieter and Ulrike. Both would
scan the ground from which it was estimated the bullet had come.
Cammy took with him the one entrenching tool they had salvaged from
the last pick-up. He worked till his muscles seized and his throat was
parched and his guts ground in pain, then worked some more.When he
deemed the pit deep enough, the limit of what he could achieve, he rolled
Stanislau's body with the broken head into it. He stood for a moment,
at the very last moment of light, and remembered the first lines of Jesus
Came when the Doors were Shut and for a few seconds his voice would
have carried over the grit and sand.

They were gone, the survivors, before dawn, and in all of them a
greater anger burned. And his promise was given, again in silence –
given to Tomas and Mikki and to Dwayne, given to Stanislau – given
to them all.

Bradley said, "I've thought about it, thought about it some more.
Have to say, whatever he was looking for, wherever he went, I
never experienced anything vicious in Cameron."

They were gathered in their hallway, huddled under the central
ceiling light, and faced the closed door of their sitting-room.

Dave said, "What gets me in the throat, bloody near chokes me,
is that we're permitting people to spy on Sadie, use our home as a
viewing gallery. Didn't see anything that wrong with Cameron."

They stood in their nightclothes and the heating was off and
their teeth chattered and they hugged their dressing-gowns around
their bodies.

Karen said, "After all that Sadie has been through, we are sort
of piling it on, aren't we? We're part of the *deceit*. She deserves
better from us."

And none of the family knew what they should do, and their
voices became louder and more confused.

Trace said, "We did what we could, didn't we? Phoned her . . .
What about now? Very soon, she'll be in that house. There's

probably a cordon of police around us, and guns. They're going to go in there after him and . . ."

The door to their living-room opened. The woman faced them and the guy was close behind her.

The woman hissed, "Just switch that fucking light out, and go back to your fucking beds, and leave us to do our job."

The guy snarled, "You know bugger all of what happens in this world, the real one. Don't come to us now, bleeding your consciences off your sleeves . . . If we lose him, don't for a moment think that you will not be paraded at the inquests. There *will* be inquests, which means fatalities, if we lose him. Get upstairs and get into your bloody beds."

A bit pathetic, no fight left in them. Switched off the light and groped their way back up the stairs.

Tristram closed the door behind him, and said, "I have never in my short life felt so inadequate, said anything so pitifully pompous. They hate us."

"We were asleep. Which was dereliction, first degree."

"I feel inadequate, total."

"Me too. Inadequate and incompetent."

Izzy took his hand, held it loosely, could make out the shape of his long, almost delicate fingers. They shared an armchair, had a clear view of the front door of the house they were charged to watch. The house was darkened. "At least, small mercies, we didn't miss her return . . ."

He kissed her gently on the lips. Thought that both of them would still be asleep, nestled against each other, had it not been for the family's voices behind the door. They watched the shadows, waited, and somewhere in the house a clock ticked.

He went by the old and trusted route.

Cammy had been the chorister kid. His half-brother had been out on a day/night release scheme, and wearing an electronic ankle bracelet. He would take him down to the city and would sit him outside the pub, would give him shandy and roll-ups. He'd thought the shandy foul and the cigarettes made him cough, but he'd sat there. There was a way up from the centre of Sturry that went north which was the direction of home. Mum would have been at work and his half-brother, on pain of death, was supposed to mind him . . . except that he had learned in HMP Maidstone how to hack into the system of the ankle tags and wipe them out. This was the route by which his half-brother had taken him out and had brought him home. And a few months earlier, when the filth had come sniffing, it was the way that his half-brother had done a runner and been at liberty for four days before being hauled out of a girl's bed. Anyway . . . it was the way that Cammy approached his home.

Out up the road towards the estuary and Herne Bay. Hugging darkness, and making sure that his back turned when rare headlights lit him. Going fast and tiredness settling in his legs and his chest hurting. And off the main road short of Broad Oak and crossing the fields and skirting the farm, then taking the dog walkers' track in woodland, doing three sides of the square, the long way around, and every few minutes he would stop and listen. There would be traffic behind him, and sometimes birds would clatter out of a tree and owls would screech. Cammy had no fear of the dark, regarded it as a friend . . . Went around the school's football pitch and could see a near perfect wall of lights ahead of him, and they led all the way down to the outskirts of Canterbury, except for one gap, like a missing tooth, and it was that section of darkness that he headed for. Would have taken him an extra hour, and would have pushed hard at the limits of his endurance, but he was pulled there. He took a risk but could not escape it. He stopped more often now, listened harder.

When he reached that section, black in the depths of the night and the rain still falling, he would be close to his mum – would not fulfil the promise made to his brothers until he had seen her, taken strength from her love . . . Would be good to see her, have her smile break on her face. Each day that he had been away, in Syria and on his journey back, he had taken a moment, like it was a prayer, to be alone and to fish her photograph out of his money belt, and speak softly to her: the photograph had gone when the smuggler gang had taken his belt, his pistol, his cash and his papers.

Ears pricked, the dog stiffened as it lay on Jonas Merrick's lap, and a low growl came from somewhere deep in its throat.

The windscreen wipers cleared the view ahead, but not from the side windows or behind them. Jonas had a hand on the dog and was restraining it from leaping at the window. They heard slow steps, seemed to slap reluctantly on the wet pavement. They came up the hill, paused for a moment at the bend. A woman paused, leaned for a moment on the street sign then seemed to suck air into her lungs and straighten her back, and set off again.

Babs whispered, "Is that her?"

Jonas waited until the woman approached a street light. With his sleeve he rubbed a small section of his window. She wore flat shoes, her ankles were wet from the rain – she would have been splashed by passing vehicles as she had trudged up the hill from the bus-stop. She wore an old-fashioned raincoat that reached below her knees, and a headscarf, and on her arm was a shopping bag. He did not think she noticed their car.

"That is her. That is Sadie Jilkes."

"What do we do?"

"I go and have a brief word with her. We live off hunches and instincts and more often they direct you, me, towards the correct destination. *A tide in the affairs of men that taken at the flood leads on to fortune.* Anyway, something like that."

He passed the dog to Babs, opened his door quietly, then leaned back inside.

Jonas said, voice little more than a murmur, "They have excellent capabilities of disguise. They can lie in the water, still as a floating log, only showing a tip of a nostril or glint of an eye. I do not locate it by hiding on the bank. Nor do I find it by wading out and splashing around. Much better to take advantage of the crocodile's intent. Might be a wildebeest at a water-hole, or a young deer that is alone, naive, does not read the danger signs, or even a goat tethered by a shoreline and enabling hunter, possibly, to confront the crocodile . . . A useful image, the tethered goat. Mrs Jilkes is acting out the part of the goat. I'm sure you follow me. Get the brute out of its cover and then, chuck a big net over it, subdue it, negate the power of the gnashers, cart it off to a zoo and put it in a cage. That's my idea of the best place for crocodiles . . . and I'll be fine."

He stepped out from the car. Hardly wanted two tooled-up young police officers, pumping adrenaline, accompanying him. Heard the dog scratching at the window behind him and thought it could probably do with a square of grass and a gulp of fresh air. Mrs Jilkes was in front of him, walking slowly into the darkness beyond the street light. He accepted that, in his dealings with the young officers, he posed as an expert and a man with a well-full of experience. Was in fact a novice. Had spent his working life corralled in an office, his attention on screens and his card index system and a phone clamped to his ear. It was an inexact science. He thought of the coming contact with the mother of a man subsumed with loathing, with anger. She might spit in his face.

"Mrs Jilkes? Mrs Sadie Jilkes? A moment, please."

She stopped, turned. Jonas stopped beneath the street light. She would have seen him clearly, his face and his clothing, should have been reassured. No preamble, no messing with her, no soft soaping. Jonas looked into her face. Her eyes quizzed him, her jaw set in defiance. A tough woman who did not need a bouquet of gilded lilies, and whose life was hard . . . He ducked his head as if respect were owed her.

"We believe, Mrs Jilkes, that he is very close. If I am wrong, as I may be, then we face a time of maximum danger. But I believe my assessment is correct – that he is here to see you. You are, of course, at liberty to reject my request but you would then have to live with the consequences . . . It would help me greatly if . . ."

He told her what would help him greatly, and looked for a reaction and did not get one, saw only the weariness in her face. She said nothing: did not agree and did not reject. She walked away. He thought she might have started to limp as if a blister or a bunion pained her. He was confident. Had to be. Stayed in the darkness until she had turned the corner and was on her way to the last home in the cul-de-sac.

He went back to the car and the dog jumped across the back seat at the pleasure of reunion.

Babs asked, "How did it go?"

"Time will tell."

Dominic said, "Difficult to subdue the brute, that crocodile, even when netted. Why not just shoot it? Turn it into handbags and dog food?"

"And then it is in the territory of mythology and legend. A glorious death at the hands of the tyrants, bullies, despots. I prefer the cage. Endless days without hope turning into months, then years. How did it go? Not long until we find out."

He settled in the back seat. He felt old and tired, clung to his instinct that seemed – now – fragile.

13

The phone beeped. The dog grunted as if annoyed.

Jonas heard the voice of the AssDepDG, clipped and well-schooled, clear but with an undisguised hint of nerves. "Just going to bring you up to speed."

"All quiet at this end – but not for long if I am correct in the assessment."

"Like a morgue here, all except for the control areas. Everybody we can turf out and put in the field is now assigned."

"We are waiting. I remain confident."

"What would you like first? The almost bad news, or the definite bad news?"

"I'll take 'almost'. Is it relevant to me?"

"Perhaps, perhaps not. We are operating in a fog. One of those where you hold your hand out in front of your face and cannot see it. We have a target in Leeds who should be doing the washing up in an internet café, except he is not. He is off the radar. We reckon he's the facilitator . . . You want the second option, 'definite'?"

"I'm listening."

Jonas could picture the man alone in the pint-sized office awarded to an AssDepDG, all the rooms around him silent and empty, no footsteps in the corridors, and no voices around the coffee machine. Maybe he would go outside, using the side door and stride around the perimeter fence of the gardens, letting rain drip on him smoking a cigarette. Jonas imagined the AssDepDG dragging a filter-tip, then tossing it in a gutter, then returning to the building, checking the control area: his reward would have been shaken heads, no change of situation.

"The courier I told you about . . . the Germans have lost him, and the Dutch and the Belgians have not picked him up, and the French are still checking. Actually, it's a couple, and mislaid with them is this bloody missile launcher. It makes for a difficult situation, Jonas."

"If you say so. They'll be picked up at a port."

"You show, Jonas, very tolerable optimism. We are going through the protocols, procedures of notification for an automatic stop . . . God, Jonas, you should know that. Matters of that type take time, take fucking authorisation. I *hope* that we have the necessary in place."

"At my end, I remain confident."

"Your boy down there, he will need – if your prediction is correct, Jonas – a facilitator. Whom we have lost. He will also need a weapon with guaranteed hitting power. And that is also lost. Is your target, locating him, our best chance?"

"I think so."

A pause on the line, an intake of breath, a moment of consideration. Then the reason for the call. "Jonas, I value your judgement, but . . ."

"If you value it then you will ride with it."

"He was, in that theatre, a formidable fighter and a very fair tactician."

"So we are told."

"Quite a reputation in the combat zones."

"Which means that the next few hours offer the best chance of taking him down."

"I am saying, Jonas that I am forced to believe this is the moment to beef up where you are. I've gone along with you, your concept, but I am – sorry to say this – puking at the risk involved. 'Beef up' means putting in some serious resources, but police resources in the main part. By dawn, I can have a couple of hundred officers there, at least five more gun teams, can close off the whole bloody place. Should he be there. That's the other side of the coin. Is he actually there, actually coming, actually prepared to risk his neck on a visit to his mother, actually going to present this opportunity to us? It is what I want to do now, Jonas. Saturate the place."

"Put in the Parachute Regiment, maybe a Commando of Marines, rustle up a company of Gurkhas. Excellent idea, but wait until dawn, otherwise they'll be blundering around and we're bound to have some 'blue on blue' casualties . . . Yes, saturate the place. First class."

Why? Why had he praised the idea that was anathema to him? Unmarked vans loaded with H&K armed cops, roadblocks materialising, and all looking for a skilled and practised expert in evasion. Cameron Jilkes, as Jonas believed, had exfiltrated the Syrian battlefield, had worked his way across an Arab land mass, had crossed Europe, had traversed the Channel in an open dinghy, had probably reached the city he had adorned as a chorister, would see his mum and sign off his life. He had a target that he would walk through Hell – had already done so – to reach. Obvious to Jonas that the man would identify the cordon, turn and slip away.

"Pleased to have you on board, Jonas. Hoped you would not challenge it, the concept . . . If he's there."

"I think he'll come. If he does, then his mother will feed him. He will be anxious and exhausted and will crash out. Probably sleep till midday, flop about for a bit, then think of moving on. He will be in a comfort zone – and you will have organised a perimeter, put it in place, but not early."

"First class. Thank you, Jonas."

The call ended. He thought the AssDepDG a good man, well stacked with dignity and humility, and right now likely to fill his pants under the weight of the stresses challenging him. If the blood started to flow, if the *triage* doctors were casting around for guidance on who was worth spending time on and who was already on a death conveyor belt, if the nation was gawping at TV images of stricken buildings, weeping families, then a gale of accusations would buffet the AssDepDG: ". . . You followed the assessments of one Jonas Merrick, a junior member of staff, and with no command experience; followed his advice without any examination . . ." He shivered, pocketed his phone and the dog settled. It would be all over, well before any ring of steel was in place.

"You feeling all right, sir?" Babs asked.

"Never better," Jonas answered her, grimly.

They'd exchanged glances. It had surprised them that there had been no attempt from the back seat to keep the conversation private – "need to know" – and both would now have accepted that they had grandstand seats, a privileged view, of what *might* or *might not* happen. They were, Dominic and Babs, going to be a part of the end-game, simple enough and easy to understand – but scary. She eased out of the car, said something about the need to get in the dark among the bushes.

She had her phone. The H&K bounced on her chest, hurt the flesh under the bullet-stopping vest. Sent a text message. Thought they were entitled to know the rank of this guy in the back of their car, and seemed to have too many answers.

Back in the car, she turned to him and smiled. "You still feeling all right, sir?"

"About the same as the last time you asked me ... Difficult, isn't it, the waiting?"

Cammy had reached the cemetery behind his home.

He threaded through the first line of gravestones.

He walked on grass, took care he did not trip on fallen stones or vases or flower holders. As he remembered, it was the older graves that he would find first, those with the higher and more ornamental crosses and angel figures with the drooped heads of the dead. He would have to head for the far side. His shoes were leaden and he would have left a trail of mud from the field. Not that it mattered.

Could have been a century of the dead lying here, and supposedly at peace, at rest, the pain of living taken from them. He knew where he would pause. Although darkness was around him, he seemed to remember where he should be, had recall of the sights and the silences of the cemetery. There were men who kept the place tidy with petrol-powered strimmers and rakes and shears and wheelbarrows: like it mattered, was important, how the dead should be left. Not in Syria ... not when the corpses were from outside the ranks of his battalion, the foreign fighters, and absolutely not when the bodies had been of their enemy; they were left for the vultures – flying nearly as high as the cursed drone planes – and the wolves and the feral dogs, and even for villagers who would creep out from holes under their buildings and strip anything of value worn on a wrist or around a neck, or secreted in a wallet. Cammy felt the pain of leaving shallow scraped graves for Mikki and for Tomas, and for Dwayne. Each more hurried than the last, and no time for respect or for anything that was sombre and marked the farewell to a good friend, a brother. Raw hands, bleeding, after wrenching at stones, or sharp flint rock to cover their bodies. No foragers, no wolves or dogs and no vultures over the Sturry cemetery.

He assumed that his mum still came to the grave. Cammy remembered that she would go into the back bedroom, stand on tiptoe, look out over the little garden at the rear of the house and might see the raised earth and the wooden cross. By now the earth would have sunk and there might be a proper stone in place; likely that Cammy's half-brother would have paid for it.

He went towards the grave. Bats flew around him. His half-sister was a few places to the left, and a couple of rows behind a big stone on which was the carved message that for years had made Mum need to wipe her eyes: *If tears could build a stairway And memories build a lane We'd walk right up to Heaven And bring you home again.* Not that Mum would have allowed anyone to see a single tear, would turn away to hide it. He did the counting, to the left of a child's grave and paused, then went right ... There was now a stone but only a few inches high and the earth had settled and grass grew, and one rose was fresh in a vase. Must have been cut and placed within the last 72 hours because it had not drooped and the petals were still tightly bound. Not that his half-sister had meant much to Cammy. But she had been Mum's favourite child. He stood there in the darkness and the rain was on his face and his ankles were sodden and the stubble was growing fast on his cheeks . . . And himself? By the next evening, he would be – whatever was left of him – on a mortuary slab and the *post mortem* would take place the following morning. And when they had finished chopping at him and slicing him, they would order a cremation and the ashes would not be given to his mum. They would be frightened, after what he'd achieved in the morning, that his name would become a rallying cry and his grave become a shrine. Needed to be certain of that because it would be hard in the last moments.

He supposed that his footprints would be clear in the muddy grass around his half-sister's grave. Not important. He stood and listened. As the leader of the brothers he had always preached the need for moments of quiet, for time spent hoovering up the sounds of the night: a dog might bark and should be avoided; a sentry might cough and should be approached from behind and speared with a knife; a twig might break, leaves might be scuffed as an enemy changed position, easing his weight from left foot to right; a weapon might be armed; or a match scraped and the flame hidden in cupped hands . . .

Vicky, good and warm and welcoming Vicky and all the crying and yelling had been fake and for her husband. Vicky had said that the spook people had been around to hers. He thought they would be crap, thought also that if they kept watch it would be from a car facing the front, and that the guns would be up the road. Not here . . . believed if they had been all around the house, telescopic sights on him and image-intensifier lenses picking him out, that he would have known it, sensed it. Good to have been with Vicky but the rainwater was stinging the scrapes on his face from the chair.

He mouthed something to the low stone and dropped his fingers on to it, traced the indentations, read her name, wished her well; had not much else to tell her.

Wondered what he would say to his mum, when they hugged, her warm and dry and him cold and wet . . . He reached the overgrown hedge at the back of the cemetery. Paused there, again, to listen.

*   *   *

Sadie Jilkes, home from work, would eat toast, drink tea, then sit in her chair looking out through the French windows into her back garden. It seemed that the rain eased and the panes no longer ran with falling streams . . . She knew which way he would come.

The plate was still on her lap and she could not be bothered to place it on the table, nor could she be bothered to put the empty mug there which was balanced on her thigh. There was a considerable amount that Sadie could no longer be bothered to do. There was an empty vase on the table; there were hardy annuals outside in the beds from which she could have cut flowers but had not. The grass outside was too long and she had a push mower in the garage but could not be bothered to use it. Weeds choked the beds – she had not cleared them for weeks . . . Funny that amongst the chaos of the garden the rose bush flourished. It had been a present from her elder son. Her elder son had formed an alliance with a guy who owned a market garden. He grew roses, legitimate, and also grew cannabis plants under glass or in plastic tunnels, and it had been thought a great wheeze, sure to be safe, overlooked. The guy was inside on a five-year stretch but, long before, her son had brought her the rose bush, had planted it himself, had shown an aptitude she'd not have acknowledged. Most weeks in the summer she would use kitchen scissors to cut a stem, lop off the leaves and then place it in the vase on the grave. That was the way her younger son would come, and she expected he would pause by his half-sister's stone.

As she looked out of the window and waited to see a shifting shadow, in her mind she played the image of the man who had stopped her as she had trudged up the hill from the bus-stop. Not a frightening man. Had he been, she would have hurried away.

A sort of guarantee had been given him. A price came with it. She had thought it a good deal and the best one likely to be offered.

He had seemed a man who could be trusted and had had a kindly tone in his voice . . . She thought that had her elder boy been with her, and not banged away in a cell, he would have warned her: "Beware the ones you think are sensitive, friendly. Sure as day follows night, they're the ones who'll screw you".

She watched the window. And knew what she would say. Had it clear in her mind.

Knew also that a young man and a young woman had taken over the front room of the Hunters' house. Knew also that in a few hours she would be up and dressed, clean clothes, washed but not ironed, and would be away down the hill to catch the bus at the Margate road stop and be taken into the city for her first shift. In a few hours it would be the start of another day for her, and her life would have moved on.

It had been a clipped and quick conversation, enough time to register what she presumed was the character of the man, and he had known what he had wanted and she had been determined on what best suited her. She had asked: "He is coming, you seem to know that, and he's been identified and is close?" His answer: "Not seen, nothing positive, but it is what I expect." And her next question: "And that is enough for you?" And his answer, after a thoughtful pause, "It's what I have."

She watched for him, and tiredness engulfed her. She struggled to stay awake, and the darkness outside stayed thick and she saw no movement.

Her final question: "How long will he be here?"

His answer, "Not long, just passing through."

"Going where?"

"Cannot answer that, not at liberty to."

Her eyelids became heavy and her breathing was soft and regular, and the view from the window faded.

He drove the van slowly, steadily, observed the speed limits though the route took him on side roads and away from dual carriage-ways. Wolfboy avoided, he believed, the vehicle registration cameras. At times he seemed to crawl but he thought it necessary to travel within the law.

His own city, Leeds, was now behind him and he had been around the outskirts of Dewsbury. He knew of homes in that community, now quiet and dark, where there would be an under-stated wave of triumph passing between activists, hidden, when the news was broadcast the next day. It would interrupt TV programmes, what they called "breaking news". If he had taken a direct route then he could have done the journey in under two hours, but he would take longer and would travel through the Peak District National Park on lonely narrow roads. He wanted to be at his destination by nine in the morning so it would be necessary for him to find a lay-by and rest up. He had gone so early from the makeshift garage where the conversion had been fashioned because the guys who had worked on the vehicle's armour-plating were trusted men, but were frightened men. He imagined by now, with him gone and Upper Heaton and Upper Hopton on his satnav phone screen, they would be scrubbing down the garage interior, working at it with bleach and scalding water and using a yard brush to clean the floor. They had helped, but not willingly, and arms had been twisted, and warnings given as to the fate of "touts". And a teenage boy, wearing Wolfboy's visored helmet, would be driving the scooter back to the internet café; that too would have been well cleaned, and the boy would be wearing a pair of thick, mass-produced gloves. A police car went by . . .

A moment of panic. Wide, staring eyes. His foot frozen on the pedal. Waiting for the indicator to wink at him and a uniformed arm to emerge from a window and wave him down. One of them advancing, cautious but threatening in the bulk of the yellow coat worn over the stab vest, and a torch beam in his face. Another hand close to a truncheon or a Taser weapon. Would he survive? Would he be able to resist the persistence of hostile questioning in a police cell? Would he betray all those who . . .? But the police car was disappearing into the distance and had not slowed. Heart beating faster, Wolfboy drove on.

Vigilance is paramount. You may just have a ripple to identify, like a fly lands on still water. Not a splash, nothing easy. Updates please. Jonas pressed Send.

Dominic and Babs talked quietly in the front, mostly in the shorthand of their jobs, about overtime rates and kit issue and duty rosters, and when was the next training day for marksmanship assessment ... Only the last seemed to concern them, and that would have been vital in their lives, Jonas assumed. Keep missing with the aimed shots and it would be the fast heave-out, and disappointment, and a glamour zone removed. Or they listened to their music – one ear for communications and one for jazz or hip-hop. The dog was comfortable. Jonas stroked its head every few minutes. He believed it a transitory friendship, and one that suited them both, but there would come a time when the little beggar decided that it wanted home, and its breakfast, and a crap and a pee, and the relationship would end. The dog suited him. There were times enough in caravan parks in the west country when – to please Vera – he could be everybody's chum and so helpful: plenty of advice on other sites, on tow-bar maintenance, on the best rates for gas cylinders. Then, time to pack up and go home and those who had thought him a new friend would find him cutting and uninterested. It was the common ground that sealed his relationship with the dog. He had plans for it, seemed to see the action playing out. He tapped his pocket, felt the angular shape, was satisfied.

Tristram came back into the front room.

He closed the door behind him, made more noise than he'd wanted, and there was the sound of a toilet flushing at the far end of the hall. She cursed. He groped his way across the dark room and flopped into the chair by the window and landed in her lap.

"What the hell am I supposed to do?" he snapped.

Izzy whispered, "I did not think, Tristram, that when I applied to join our glorious monarch's Security Service that an important factor would be the ability to control the bladder flow of a fellow officer while engaged in covert observation duties. That was not on my list. I thought intellect, ability to sponge up facts fast, to make human judgements, would all be top ranked. You?"

"Thought I would strut around, walk tall. Feel I was part of something special."

"For fuck's sake, not be in the élite! Most overworked word in the English language and I only slap it on the Islamic Revolutionary

Guard Corps and the Kazakhstan Presidential Protection Battalion, and the Democratic Congo parachute regiment . . ."

"This hardly fits the bill."

"Just heard from the Wise Old Bird. Needs our 'vigilance'. Back on the crocodile stuff, looking for ripples . . . Can I ask you something, Tristram?"

"Please."

"Do you have a girlfriend right now?"

"Is that a chat-up line?"

"It's not."

"I don't have a girlfriend right now. That good enough? I did, and I'd put my application in and I was going for a first interview the next day, and I told her that I'd got this appointment. Of course she asked where, who with, what was involved. I said to her that I couldn't say. That was the instruction, not to tell parents, wives, girlfriends or boyfriends. I didn't tell her. I thought the job more important than her – she walked out, kept walking. Not seen her since, nor heard from her . . . so, no girlfriend."

"It was not a chat-up line."

"Heavy stuff, Izzy. And you?"

"Haven't."

"Feeling a bit isolated?"

"You could say that."

The psychologists would have emphasised the dangers of inter-office romance. The induction courses warned of the loneliness of the work that pushed officers, under stress, into relationships. They were both staring out of the window, through the glass that was clear now that the rain storm had passed, and the house was quiet. He thought of the intrusion into the family's lives, down to using the downstairs toilet without asking. Could have shouted up the stairs that it was about "defence of the kingdom", keeping innocent people alive, or "the greater good of the greatest number, and cheap at the price of a few human rights violations". Both watched the house across the road, no new lights had come on, no shadows moved; there were no ripples in the water. Tristram knew what his future would be, doubted that it differed from Izzy's.

He kissed her gently on the fullness of her cheek.

And she kissed him . . . and both would have understood where that led.

They broke apart but were still close and kept watching the target house. Tried to maintain "vigilance", as demanded of them. Looked for any slight motion in the water.

Chicken wire divided the cemetery from his mum's garden, and the hedge of untrimmed conifers had grown through it, bent it and had broken it. He knew there was a gap where the wire could be lifted and a body could crawl under it. If *they* were there, then they could be in the kitchen, their feet under the table and their weapons across their thighs, or they could be in the sitting-room, near the doors that opened into the garden, or they could be in a van parked in the street in front. Or they could be in the kitchen *and* the sitting-room *and* in a van outside; *they* could be mob-handed and waiting.

Cammy had stood over the graves and felt the anger rip. When the last of the brothers were gone he had wept, had allowed tears to swell his eyes, and the promises had stacked up but not how to honour them. That had been Benghazi . . .

. . . a rubbish town. Parts of it as damaged as Aleppo or Raqqa or Kobane or Deir Ezzor. He had reached the city – no money, no food, no water – travelling courtesy of a tanker driver whose job was to clear cesspits, then take the tanker into the desert, squirt its contents, then go back for more. He had ridden into the city with the stink of the vehicle permeating him, and had been dumped, and had walked for no more than a quarter of an hour. And had been picked up. "Picked up" in Benghazi meant captured – blindfolds, wrists tied, face down in a pick-up. At first they might have seen him as worth something as ransom, or as a spy, or simply as useless shit, but had taken him to a leader. Had fallen on his feet, a black flag leader, an *emir* with control of a sector of the city. Cammy had said where he had come from, had told the guy where he had fought, had seen the cloud of doubt, suspicion, clear. Had told the guy his name. This *emir* was Egyptian, spoke perfect

English, had a brain, and had smiled, a little awe. "You are Kami al-Britani?" He had said he was. "You are the Kami al-Britani who punched the hole in the defence line at As Sukhnah on the Deir Ezzor road, that was you?"

A stalled attack, he and his brothers sent for. A coordination with two suiciders each in an armoured vehicle. The defenders had been Syrian government. Cammy and his brothers had not hung around to watch the show when the black flags had come into the salient and gone through the gap but it would have been bad for the boys who had taken Assad's pound, 500 to the US dollar. He was hugged, was a celebrity . . . Did he want to fight in Libya, would Benghazi be a new home? Spoke briefly, vaguely, of a promise . . . Was there for four days and was aware that, while he was fed and resting, messages were sent, and answers returned. Arrangements were made. They seemed disappointed that he would not be staying with them. There were scrawny Arab kids there and a couple of Chechens and a Russian deserter who kept a grenade attached to his shirt and swore he would pull the pin if there was any danger of capture and repatriation to Kremlin territory: they were not going to be his brothers. He had been sent on his way and a driver set him down at the Educational Hospital on the south side of the port city of Sirte, and a cargo tramper would give him a berth if he came on board in secret, at night. He carried money, and contact details for the French city of Marseilles – five days' sailing. The *emir* and his people knew him to be a "walking dead" and might have thought it a waste of a fighting man's talent, but accepted that a promise had been made, had shrugged, had told him he would be remembered in their prayers. That had been the start of his effort to fulfil the terms of the promise. This was a diversion but he was near the end.

He felt the stiffening wind drying his body.

Noted that a moon now showed through the surging cloud ceiling.

Stood motionless, listened, heard nothing. Would not hurry would wait until he was satisfied and beyond the hedge was the small back garden and beyond the garden was the little patio and the kitchen door, and alongside the door were the French windows opening out from the living-room. Felt good now, at peace, and his mum would hug him. He would wait a few more minutes, then move and find the place where the wire lifted in the depths of the hedge.

Only a brief diversion, then Cammy would again be on his way and would have his mum's money in his pocket and would start his last journey, where his promise would be kept, where people would be waiting for him.

Clothes straightened, buttons fastened. Neither Baz nor Mags did romantic kisses afterwards, but he gave her backside a smack. They were up and off the lower bunk because the engine pitch below them had changed and through the porthole they had seen that the ferry had started to manoeuvre, and in the far distance they could see the ribbon of lights at the port. No more talk of this being – yet again – a critical moment in the process of bringing an RPG-7 launcher and six projectiles into the country of their birth, their lives, their reluctant income tax payments when such had seemed unavoidable, into the country that would have believed it owned their loyalty. Done all that, been there, and both would have been bloody idiots to have doubted that the next few minutes would be hairy, arse-pucker time. He was straightening his hair, she was applying lipstick when the cabins erupted . . . Passengers were told that they were near to docking, were called to their vehicles. A matter-of-fact announcement boomed around them.

"You good, girl?"

"Course I'm fucking good – what else?"

They left the cabin, headed for the staircase that led steeply down to the vehicle deck, and immediately ahead of them would be the UK checks for passports and customs, and they could not know how it would be for them.

"Keep smiling, girl."

"Course I'm fucking smiling – what else?"

He held her hand as they waited at the tail of the queue above the staircase: another old couple coming back from a holiday.

*   *   *

He passed the rose bush. Came to the kitchen door, where he would have dumped his first tricycle and his first bicycle, and they'd have weathered in the rain and the wind. It was through the kitchen door that he had gone with his mum when he was first awarded the place at the college, wearing his new, laundered secondhand uniform. Had gone out of the back door and then had hurried around the side to where his half-brother waited in the car, engine going. Mum had not wanted him seen by the whole of the cul-de-sac in his new uniform, with his hair cut in the style they wanted it. His mum had thought it would seem ostentatious if he were paraded in their road, off to a school – with a scholarship taking care of the money – that no other parent nearby could even dream of.

The door needed paint and putty. There was enough thin light for him to see the bare wood around the glass, and the stains where it was rotten and needed chiselling out. His half-brother would have done it had he been there. He grasped the handle . . .

There were guys in the *Amn al-Kharji* part of the security units who were supposed to teach basic self-preservation as the black flag scene crumbled and men were drifting away, not deserting but looking for new combat theatres. They had not used him, but this guy had joined them and they'd escorted him into Barghuz, had him among them for two days and always kept Ulrike as far away from him as they could manage. He had been well wised up and had spoken of phone monitoring, about properties that would have had electronic beams around them or low-set tumbler wires, about bug mikes fastened in trees or against walls, and cameras. The whole lot of it . . . Cammy had crossed the rear garden, gone along the fence that was askew – probably had useless wet-rot posts – and every few paces had paused and listened some more. The guy from the *Amn al-Kharji* had liked to show off how well briefed he was – had a story from the UK: two Irish approach the remote house of a man on a death list and set off the electronics and show up on a screen, white shadows, two cops inside with weapons because an attack is expected. They see the pair of them coming forward but still well down the garden. The cops arm their weapons, metal scraping on metal, but do it slowly and quietly, but the Irish leg it, had heard it. They were caught weeks later and in their car was an old person's hearing aid, what you'd need in a care home to follow the soaps on the TV ... Cammy had no hearing aid, but he had patience.

The kitchen was in darkness but he could see that the door into the hall was open and the ceiling light was on. No sound of a radio or a TV. He eased his strength against the door handle but it held firm ... remembered. By his foot was the food box, went out each week for clearing with the bins. The key was always underneath. Bent, groped, found it. Cammy straightened, found a smile coming on to his face ... would be hugged, and she might cry a bit and he'd do the charm and the love – and would get her to cook, and get her to clear out her purse so that he could be on his way as dawn broke. He had the key in the lock.

The tramper he had boarded in the Libyan port had sailed west up the Mediterranean then had put in at the docks of Marseilles, and immigration procedures were crap and he had gone ashore on a deck-hand's papers and had a contact to make. Had expected a bigger welcome there, recognition of who he was, what he brought to the table, and to the level of anger he felt and the target he had chosen, and to hear of the promise he had made. The response had seemed distant. Like they regarded him as merely one more in a queue, and it had taken time, and messages had been exchanged between the Marseilles cell and those back in the old war zone. It had been sorted ... he had been hidden away in a housing project known as La Savine: narcotics sales were done there and gang warfare was rife and the police stayed away. The ones who had housed him had seemed reluctant to wave him on his way and he might have had a career extension as a gun for hire. Money was in his pocket, and some documents that might pass inspection if the light was poor, and he was to head to Bordeaux where he would receive instructions for the next stage of the journey. Had bought his ticket at the station, had it in his breast pocket, had the cash in his zipped-up hip pocket and a photo of his mum ... had been greeted, a long lost friend, by a man with outstretched arms – never seen him before – laughed about it and didn't feel the slightest pressure on his backside. Caught like a sucker, and he was Kami al-Britani, and a cheapskate gang from north Africa had done him over. By the time he had realised they were well clear and the bustle of the terminus flowed around him. His hip pocket had been cut open and hung loose. He had his rail ticket and the phone number for the contact in Bordeaux. He had cursed silently, and boarded the train – had only his promise to cling to.

He turned the key, opened the door a few inches, then paused again and listened. If there had been guns then torches would have speared him and shouting deafened him and he would have been flattened on the step. Heard nothing, held his patience.

Her phone pinged. A text message, sent by their boss. She glanced at it, and grimaced.

Passed her phone across to Dominic, and he had to lean forward to read it.

She said softly, "Bit of a turn up."

He murmured, "All part of life's rich tapestry."

Your passenger is a low-grade long-serving Fiver. Has few friends in-house but many admirers. My advice, don't pick a fight ... Keep calm, carry on. Bill. (Read and delete).

"Could be fun, being there at the end. Will know a whole heap that he isn't sharing."

"Breaking the duck and all that. Might get to squeeze the trigger."

She sent back a message. *Our guy is having a snooze and his best friend is a borrowed dog, kipping on his lap & (Delete – and go back to sleep).*

They heard quiet snoring behind them and did not know if it came from the passenger or the dog: it seemed of little importance.

Jonas dreamed.

On the A303 and approaching Stonehenge.

Had a clear road ahead. Kept his pace and observed the speed limit.

Felt the drag of the caravan he towed. Had a friendly dog on his lap.

Vera talked to her friend on her phone, the one who managed the art gallery, and explained why she would not be there the next day. They were past Middle Wallop and nearing Winterbourne Stoke, and the weather seemed to be brightening in the west, and . . .

His phone shook.

He read the message. *Maintaining vigilance.* More impertinence from them. He did not like them or dislike them, they were what he had been given. If they failed him then he would bollock them off the park, and if they did well for him then he would curtly acknowledge that they had done what they were paid to do. Too intelligent for this kind of work? Probably what they thought.

Closed his eyes again. Stroked the dog's head.

Saw the road stretching away in front of him and they would soon be at the junction for Codford St Mary and Fisherton de la Mere, and the weather improving.

But Jonas found it hard to sleep again. It came on him suddenly, seemed to crush him at the shoulders: his responsibility and the weight he carried. Saw the face, scarred and carrying stubble, aged from warfare. Blinked, saw it again and clearer – memorised it . . . Did not doubt that soon, he would look at the face, be close to it.

14

Midnight. A church clock struck in the distance.

The rain had stopped. Jonas lowered his window. He needed a break, and the dog did, and maybe Dominic too, and Babs. He assumed they would be expert in choosing the moment when it was suitable to duck into the bushes – and they might enjoy a cigarette: Jonas did not smoke, had not for years, but harboured none of the fascist tendencies against those who did. He had enjoyed a good journey down the A303, the chosen route for those with a dislike of the motorway, never fazed by the length of the queue behind him and his towed caravan. Had appreciated the recollection of the target's young face. An old picture, and the man would now show the wear and tear of warfare. Would have been a pretty bloody experience in Jonas's view. He had seen the arrest snaps of Provos in the net late in their conflict – never met with them face to face or sat in on interrogation – and had looked at the monochrome images of the faces and measured the extent of the pressure they had lived under . . . Did not mean he sympathised but he understood better.

"A comfort break, are we up for that?"

All out. He gave Dominic the dog. Babs went deep into shadow. Jonas thought it a caricature of a night operation. Was a little shy himself and stood apart from them, but could see that the dog did its business and so did Dominic, the assault weapon hanging awkwardly from the strap around his neck. Before he'd shaken, Babs was coming back, fastening her belt.

Jonas said, "I suppose it's something you want to do."

"What's that, Mr Merrick?"

"Get a chance to perform. To shoot."

"Is this conversation, Mr Merrick, or is this for a psychologist's assessment-of-mental-state report?"

Dominic said, "We had a bit of biography on you, Mr Merrick, but an economic one. Didn't say what you'd done that singled you."

Jonas said, "What I call a 'clear blue sky' moment. An impertinence on my part. Something happens in front of you, and sparks a reaction. You do something . . . cannot explain it. Didn't have a manual to leaf through, five hundred pages of regulations. Train and train and make ready, but how will it be? And – will you be up to it – all that palaver? Tonight all three of us are weighed down by responsibility. If I get it wrong, if you get it wrong, then we'll swing in the wind. Which I suppose is what responsibility is about."

"How are you feeling, Mr Merrick?"

"Rather tired. Will be glad when it's concluded."

"Not the most comfortable place, Mr Merrick, our back seat."

"But not for much longer. Very close, I'd say."

"We've rather taken you on trust, Mr Merrick."

"Appreciated."

"Where is he, Mr Merrick? Any idea?"

"Could already be there. Could be with his mother. Either there or very close. Not going to be fun for him. I think she is a woman of quite powerful resolve. He has put her through pain, some very acute, and she will not have appreciated the ripping apart of her life. He will get the book thrown at him, and maybe the kitchen sink as well. He will not have expected that. He'll be quite severely shaken. But that is only my assessment."

"If you are wrong, Mr Merrick?"

"Problem is, I am the only game in town."

"If he doesn't come, Mr Merrick?"

"That's beyond where I am prepared to go. Means he is loose . . . Sitting in your car, and with my new best friend, I was thinking of holidays. Always lightens the mood, don't you think, the thought of a holiday? Vera and I like to take our caravan down to the southwest. Some very pleasant sites in Devon, which is where we prefer to be, but the same is true of Cornwall. I don't know the Dorset coast, but I expect it's quite fun to be near Bridport and looking for those fossils on the beach, those ammonites. Yes, we should try that one day . . ."

He realised there was a quaver in his voice and that he rambled and that both of the police officers were staring at him and there was enough moonlight for him to see that both accepted that he had told the, as he saw it, the truth. He was, for the next few hours, "the only game in town".

The dog had started to drink from a puddle of rainwater.

He said boldly, "It is a crocodile we're looking for. When it moves, it shouldn't be too hard to spot."

He climbed back into the car and the dog nestled up close, and he held his phone, waited for the call.

He had used that back door, the one into the kitchen, when his mum had brought him back from the college. She had said there was no shame attached to a changed voice, but Cammy had bolted from her and had run around the side of the house, skipped past the bins and the rest of the dumped rubbish, and had waited for her at the kitchen door. Had left her to carry his bag, and not much in it. She had unlocked the door and let him in.

Same door, and he eased it shut behind him.

Sufficient light now for him to register that no furniture had been moved. The table where it always had been, and the four chairs around it, and the fridge in the same place, and the photograph in the frame . . . should have been on the window-ledge. The photograph had been of himself, aged twelve, wearing the full uniform of a cathedral chorister, in colour. His mum had paid £11.75 for the picture and then another £9 for the frame. It had stood on the window-ledge for the remaining year of his time with the choir and then while he was at the local school, and when he had drifted, and had still been there on the day he had slipped away, told his lie, gone. There was a plate in the sink, and a knife, and an empty mug.

Fighting, killing, air strikes, the loss of friends who he rated as brothers, wounds and gut rot. And he had come through and a source of strength had been home, the semi-detached home at the end of a cul-de-sac, and his mum living there, still giving him that same strength after his money had been taken – and her photograph – on the border with Libya. Now his faith was shaken and all because his picture was not where he had expected it to be.

He crossed the kitchen. The inner door was closed.

Cammy stood by it. Hesitated . . . Wondered if he should turn on his heel and go. Had been through barbed wire entanglements that were strewn with tin cans and would rattle if moved, and had crossed minefields and had gone on his stomach in darkness and had eased his elbows forward so that he could grope in the sand with his fingers and search for a jumping anti-personnel bastard . . . Needed her blessing: wanted food, wanted money, wanted her love. He pushed the door, slipped through, closed it after him. The hall light bathed him. The landing at the top of the stairs was dark and the door into the living-room was closed. Took the gamble, opened it. Did not know whether he would face black-clad men, cops, and weapon barrels, whether lights would blaze into his face. He eased the door closed and stifled the light he had momentarily admitted.

She was sitting in the wing-back chair. Had been her chair as long as he could remember, and next to the chair was a low chest, as there had always been, and on the chest were the zappers for the TV, and anything she was reading, and where there should have been a picture, framed, showing the choir going towards the cathedral's side door, robes flowing in a brisk wind and winter sun on their faces and their hair riffling.

He rounded the chair, knelt before it. Reached up, took her head in his hands, was resisted.

He leaned towards her. She twisted her head away. His kiss landed on the side of her head, his lips buried in her hair . . . And he had crossed the world for this moment. He let go of her head.

"I came back. Came back for you."

A small voice but clear. "You were neither expected nor wanted."

"I came back out of love for you, to see you."

"I didn't ask you to, didn't need you to."

"Had to see you."

She stared straight in front of her and did not look at Cammy. "Then hurry up. They're waiting for you. They're outside and watching for you. Your choice was to go. My choice was never to want to see you again."

Only a few at the Station were not asleep.

The Mess had cleared and the grille had been lowered on the bar and the glasses were in the washer, the machine going through its last rinses. In the canteen, lights were low and the only sound was the hum of a refrigerator where breakfast ingredients waited the arrival of the chefs who would serve up the first meal of the day to the early technical and flying staff.

Pilots and navigators slept, those who drove the big Sentry AEW1 and the Sentinel R1 which carried the high dome on its back, all part of the Intelligence Surveillance Target Acquisition and Reconnaissance hub, and their pint-sized army of communications experts who flew with them . . . those not based down in the Mediterranean and doing shifts over Syrian airspace. Also crashed out were the pilots and sensor operators and intelligence people who flew the Reaper drones, though their aircraft were 2,500 miles away, locked up in Turkish hangars. And the teams of maintenance men, and those who fed the raw data of the locations and identities of the remnants of the black flag groups into the systems. The Station was quiet. No night flights were scheduled.

The few who were awake manned a security control area and had responsibility for the protection of the Station, its equipment, planes and drones, and for those assigned to them. They were RAF Regiment and were armed in a way considered appropriate to deal with any potential threat, likely to come from a home-grown *jihadi* who would be categorised as a "lone wolf" and carrying an improvised explosive in a vest with crude wiring. The Regiment men whiled away a shift with coffee breaks and, on what had become routine timings, went out with their Land Rovers to patrol the perimeters, and might let their dogs have a run and give them a toy to chew on in place of a volunteer's padded arm as used in training.

The Station covered many acres, and some buildings included were recently erected and considered temporary, or were modern, and some had served a purpose in the last war when the runway had been used by heavy bombers flying night after night over Germany. The men and women of the Regiment, charged with guard duty, were at a normal level of preparedness: they had not received a threat assessment ratcheted up to levels of Amber, and no indication that might have put them up to Red. There was no intelligence that an attack was either "likely" or "imminent".

The light rain had moved on, and clearer skies were forecast, and a decent temperature was expected . . . Had information been received that an attack – from however an incompetent quarter – was likely that morning, then the Regiment personnel would have been placed on full alert, and the local police would have drafted in every firearm available. The Station would have resembled a well-defended fortress, would have gone into lockdown . . . But they were in ignorance of any risk, and life was lived as normal within the hours when the place slept, after a fashion.

"I promise, Pieter, you have my promise."

Fat good it would do Pieter to have Cammy's promise.

It had seemed, a little after dawn and with the sun not yet high, as if this was a moment hoped for, even – after a fashion – prayed for. They were on foot. The three of them, all that remained of the brothers, had been walking through the night and were nearing, they believed, the Jordanian border. Left behind them in scraped graves were Mikki and Tomas and Dwayne and Stanislau. Ulrike had been leading, and each of the trio was burdened with rucksacks that carried ammunition and grenades, but they had only the scrapings of old food from tins aban-doned by other personnel, and a few inches of bottled water between them. They had been looking for a place where they could shrug off the weight of the rucksacks, then hunker down in shade, each had and hope they didn't get the shits. There had seemed to be a dried river course ahead and some scrub, and what Pieter would have called a kopje, a little hill with substantial rocks. Ulrike had spotted a wisp of smoke climbing, separating, dispersing: Ulrike had the best eyes. She had whistled for their attention, then had crouched.

They had stayed hidden, had seen a small settlement established among rocky crags, well camouflaged. Under tarpaulins draped in scrub branches were two big pick-up vehicles. More tarpaulins over three crevices. There were armed men, black-clothed, squatting. They had also spotted a sentry posted on the summit of the kopje, Pieter identifying his position, but he had disappeared. They whispered among themselves: what had they blundered across? They needed food and water . . . most likely they had found the covert location of one of the big figures of the movement. Cammy had been told, had not known if it were true, that a price of $100,000 was offered for the capture or the corpse of Kami al-Britani. A big man in the black flag leadership would be worth $5 million. The remote countryside of this province, devoid of roads, towns, villages, where there were few farms and no grazing land, would likely be home to various remnant groups of fleeing men, those who had not gone in the net with the women and the kids when the perimeter at Barghuz had collapsed. Had they had food and water, enough for the three of them, then they would have turned away and skirted the small camp. But they would die without food or water.

He would go to them, his decision. Pieter and Ulrike would stay behind, a quarter of a mile back, but would make themselves visible. A brief hug, nothing important.

He had gone only a few paces when he spotted movements among the stones, heard calls, had seen the awkward shapes of rifle barrels peeping between rocks.

Cammy had kept walking, had shown no fear. He had covered half the distance when a tall rake of a man had appeared from beneath the cover disguising one of the vehicles. A hand was held up, he was to stop. Cammy ignored it. He heard the arming of at least two weapons. His own rifle, the trusted AK that had been with him all of the last year, was on his shoulder and held there with a strap. He made it clear that he posed no threat. Ulrike and Pieter would have been watching him, covering him, Ulrike with her rifle that she could fire – could strip as well – and Pieter with the Dragunov sniper weapon that he coveted.

The shouting in front of him rose in pitch. He was a hundred paces from his interrogator when he stopped.

Who was he? Who were they? What did he want?

He was Kami al-Britani. A foreign fighter in a unit led by the emir Ruhan. Wanted food and water and was headed towards a new battleground.

Was greeted as a friend, but told to stand where he was. He could smell meat cooking, would have been goat, giving off a rich scent. Only a man of importance, in flight, staying hidden and hoping to avoid the accursed drones, would have been fed on cooked meat. He saw four guards, big men and heavy-shouldered and all armed. A woman came. Head to toe in black, a pencil-wide slit for vision, no skin shown nor hair, and she came with a plastic bag and a plastic container. Cammy was being offered food and water.

The exhaustion was deep, hunger ached in his belly, and his throat was raw from lack of moisture. The woman, or she might have been a teenage girl, came towards him and four rifle barrels, at least, covered him.

He saw a face. Most of it was hidden behind a grey beard, loose below a sharp pointed nose, and deep-set eyes, and the hair scrambled around a small opening for the lips and his head was cloaked in a black hood. He recognised the man, had never seen him in the flesh. Cammy stared back at Abu Bakr al-Baghdadi, leader of the caliphate, ruler of a broken cause, architect of a thousand destroyed dreams. He thought the woman would have been a wife, a child bride, and probably the only "groupie" permitted to accompany them . . . Did their eyes meet? Might have . . . Were others aware that their eyes might have met? The woman brought him a plastic bag in which were husks of bread and apples, and her small body was bent under the weight of a couple of gallons of water. They were put down in front of Cammy.

He bowed his head. He showed respect and gratitude. He called back that they would remain in his prayers. He had the blessing of God given him. Cammy turned and took the water and the bag and walked back to Ulrike and Pieter. He knew they could have killed him, but could not have guaranteed dropping his brothers. He had locked eyes with the most hunted man in the region, the man who was at the apex of the High Value Target list now that Osama Bin Laden was dead, his corpse dropped from a helicopter into the sea. He had his back to them and kept moving, and gestured to Ulrike and Pieter that they should get the hell out and fast. Saw them hitch up their rucksacks and make his ready for him to shrug into. Did not look back, and did not hurry.

When he had almost reached his brothers, Cammy called out, "Don't look, show no interest. We have to move."

They went. Did not look at the food and did not drink from the plastic container. Might have gone half a mile. Were tramping on ground that had scant vegetation, no cover, was hard on their feet. Somewhere ahead they would find a place where they could lie up, rest, drink and eat, and then sleep through the heat of the day.

A pick-up came after them . . . To give them a ride, another gesture of hospitality? A moment of extreme danger? Had been too busy telling them to push ahead and make distance, had not shared with them – yet – that he had looked for a moment into the eyes of Abu Bakr al-Baghdadi, had not quipped with them that if they could but find a working phone box and have directory enquiries do the link through to US Central Command in Qatar, and give coordinates and pull in half a squadron of fighter jets and about every drone in the airspace then they could carry off – shared between them – $5 million. Sufficient for a neat little life on an Aegean island or off Australia's Queensland coast, might even throw in the whole island and . . . the pick-up came after them.

They went across the wilderness of dirt and the pick-up followed them and then accelerated and came alongside. The clatter of the machine-gun mounted on a pole behind the driver's cab was deafening. Cammy threw himself down. Saw most of his life and Ulrike was across him, and Pieter seemed to stumble and then fell backwards. More bullets were fired and, between those fleeting seconds when his eyes were tight shut, Cammy saw that Pieter's body was lifted, the proverbial rag doll, and dirt was spat around him. He lay motionless, stifled his own breathing. No sound and no movement from Ulrike. Had that funny fraction of time when he did not know, whether he lived or was dead. One of the guys came down from the pick-up, a pistol in his hand, and walked around them and would have used it if a sign of life had been offered. The plastic bag with the food was picked up, and the water container, and were taken back to the pick-up. It drove away.

Easy to understand. Simpler to have given them rubbish to eat and a minimum of water and let them go in innocence. Easier to kill them all together than when he had approached their hide and the other two had stayed back. He had supposed it a basic attitude of suspicion that would be harboured by any boss-man with $5 million resting on his life or his freedom. He had heaved her off, and she had sworn, rich and German. They were both untouched and Pieter was a colander from the machine-gun bullets.

They had not buried him, had only kicked some dirt on to his face and tried to hide his mouth and the shape of his nose. His saying had been "Never look back. Never chase the past". From the north-eastern Transvaal. Had a wife there and two small kids in a town called Warmbaths and had told them he was going for a drink in the hotel on the main street, and instead had taken a train to Jo'burg, then a flight out. He might have made an effort to get his hand into Ulrike's clothes, but not a big effort. He had been a good fighter and an expert sniper, and was used, he said, to dropping a gazelle or an impala at 800 yards. When Cammy had needed advice or wanted to shift the load of responsibility it was to Pieter that he'd turn. They made a poor job of covering him and then hoisted up their rucksacks and left his. Did not even take his wallet. Left the wallet and the photo of the blonde wife and the scrawny kids. Cammy's fault that Pieter had died because Cammy had locked eyes on the caliphate leader. They had hurried away. Last thing that Cammy had said to the failed grave was, "Yes, Pieter, you have my promise. Don't know how, when, or where, but my promise is my word."

He had given her time, had believed she would soften, just a few minutes before she would feel him close to her, then her hand would rest on his shoulder and her fingers would work inside his shirt, and she would touch the scars that had been stitched from the shrapnel and might even find the hole where the Iranian bullet had entered, had burst through tissue and exited, and the dirt had been minimal and the pain excruciating as Ulrike had probed for detritus and . . .

She would soften. Her hands were at her sides. He thought she would take him in her arms and their tears would run together.

"I came to see you."

"Better you hadn't."

"I need food, Mum."

"Then go somewhere you can buy it."

"I have no money, Mum."

"Sit on the street and beg for it."

A sort of wonderment. "No blessing, no food, no money, is that what you have to say to me?"

"You smell."

"I was in the sea. A boat in the sea and I fell off and . . ."

"You smell of perfume, of scent. Were you screwing someone before you came to see me?"

"I need food and money."

"With that Victoria girl? Married, I heard. Put you behind her?"

"You have to feed me. At least give me money."

"Go and rob someone. Mug them, threaten them, isn't that what you do?"

He pushed himself up, stood his full height. He remembered how it had been, when he had wanted something. They would have gone into a village and the original defenders would have quit, run at the sight of the pick-ups approaching, flying the black flag, and dust clouds spitting from their tyres. Just the civilians left, and if he, or any of his brothers, had gone into even the most wretched home, mud bricks or concrete or corrugated iron, and had demanded food then it would have been brought for them. A family would have gone without in order that the men with guns were fed.

"Something to eat and some money, then I'm gone."

"They're watching from the Hunters' place. They're waiting for you. Put on the lights in the house and you tell them you're here."

"You have bread? Fruit and cheese? I have to eat."

"I cooked your dinner that night, the night you were on a plane. I cooked it and waited for you. Then put it in the oven, then left it in the microwave, and you did not come, and your food went into the bin. You'll get no food here . . . Did the girl not feed you?"

"Thought you would."

"Thought wrong. You know where the knives are, there's some fruit, and some cheese in the fridge and a loaf. You know how to use a knife, I think. Did you cut throats with a knife? Did you have a knife in your belt, keep it handy so you could slit a throat when the opportunity came up? Cut many, did you? Get the taste for it, slitting and cutting?"

He said, weakly, "I didn't do that sort of thing. I was a fighter, was ahead, it was other people who . . ."

"Pass the parcel, don't take blame. So you were ahead of the throat cutters and that makes your war good? No, you just facilitated, were an accessory . . . Did you fight against our people, British people? Kill any of them when you were 'ahead'?"

"It wasn't one-sided."

"That's super, Cameron. Very good. What, you on the side of the good people?"

"Russians, Syrians, Iranians, the Shi'a fighters from Lebanon. What do you think they were like?"

"I don't have to listen to that. I don't want to hear your pathetic justification, your propaganda talk. I just want you to go. And don't take any of my kitchen knives with you."

"I need some money."

"And if I refuse?"

"You won't . . . I must have some money. You won't see me again, and that is my word."

"Important is it, your word? Do I swallow that . . . and keep your justification for others to hear? Don't want it . . . If I refuse you money will you come after me with your fists or with one of my knives? Just a monster, aren't you?"

"Money, then I'm gone."

"You don't understand, do you? Come on, I'll show you and then you'll have learned something. Why you are not welcome."

"The picture of me, where's that? My picture."

"Gone, had no use for it."

She stood, reached out and took his hand. Held his hand as if he were a stray child and needed taking back to a parent, not her.

Sadie took him out of the darkened sitting-room, led him into the hall, crossed it. Made him go in front of her and gave him a shove to get him started up the stairs.

She could only guess what could be seen from the Hunters' home: something or nothing. She remembered the brief exchange with the man who had spoken to her on the way home and the agreement, of sorts, she had accepted. Would she back track? She would not. Determined. Stood him in front of the door to what had been his room . . . Cameron had been awarded his own room, and her daughter had a room of her own, and most times when he was at home, and was not in one of Her Majesty's Prisons, her elder son slept on the settee downstairs. She stood him in front of the door. It would take him a few moments to become accustomed to the light in there, the lack of it. He was inside and she closed the door behind him. It was a matter of consequences, and he would learn what he had done to her: and many others would have learned what they had inflicted on their parents, their families . . . She went into her own room.

If she had been burgled then any self-respecting thief would have easily found her tin box. The bed had a drawer under the mattress. In the drawer were extra blankets for the winter, the lightweight duvets for the summer, and at the back of the drawer was the old tin box. It was there for "a rainy day", for more than a shower of rain but for a time when the heavens opened. Sadie had a bank account from which her basic bills were paid, but the box held the cash – £50 and £20 notes – for any catastrophe that confronted her. If the fridge packed up, or the boiler needed replacing, if the cooker failed or the washing machine, that was where the replacement would come from. She had not had a holiday, been away with a little packed bag and been a single occupant in a seaside guest-house, since he had gone. How much for him?

How much? After what he had served up for her was £200 right? Rejected. Was £100 suitable? Too much. Would £50 be acceptable, not missed? She thought so. Extracted one note from the folded wad ... in excess of £1,000 was left in the tin. He would have to make do with what she gave him. She replaced the box in the drawer, and pushed it shut under the mattress. It was an old bed and an old mattress and where he had been conceived: a one-night stand, a cheerful and convivial man whom she had met at the bus-stop, a commercial traveller. A diversion to a pub, and a couple of drinks, and then a taxi home, and of course he was coming in ... and long gone when the bump had started to grow. She had loved the boy, doted on him, had been awash with pride when he had sung as a lead chorister in the cathedral choir, with a scholarship to support him – all gone.

She went back on to the landing.

The door of his old bedroom remained closed.

She had forgotten what her elder son would have told her, and had thought the man in the road who had emerged from the shadows respectful and polite. He had not lectured her about "duty" and her obligations to "society", had given no guarantees nor had she asked for any. Had only made one request ... she would honour it. She thought she might have had a serious but pointless conversation with her other son were he not tossing on his mattress in his cell, would have discussed the matter of a family's loyalty to a felon and whether obligation ever ended ... How far down the road did a son have to go before he was turned in by his own mum. She went downstairs and sat again in her chair, lost in the darkness.

Jonas' phone beeped. He had to shift the dog's head to hold it against his ear.

"Yes?"

"Jonas. Just wanted to clarify our earlier conversation." The AssDepDG called him on a secure but tinny line.

"Seemed clear to me, thank you."

"I feel a sense of guilt, you stuck down there, without the resources. Still in the back of that car?"

"Very comfortable, but I'm grateful for your concern."

"Just wanted to confirm, Jonas, that we will have the bodies in place by seven-thirty this morning. I have a chief constable's guarantee. There will be a cordon in place, and the guns on hand. I have to say that we have allowed you too much slack, Jonas. That's down to me and should not have happened. Anyway, by that time I will have a full surveillance team on the ground. Around the Jilkes' house. I had to shake the tree but finally I have the numbers to put on the board. What we should have had as soon as the Deal news came through. Agnes Burns will be heading them up, first-class operator, as you know. Once they are there, Jonas, then you are free to get on back to London. We really appreciate what you have put in for us, and the weight you have taken on your shoulders – good man. I suppose it's because of that other business, what you achieved, that we take your skills for granted and also your endurance factor. We should not have. Anyway, you will, please, hold the fort for a few more hours and then we can stand you down . . . No sign of him yet, is there?"

"No, nothing – drawing a blank."

"Are you happy, Jonas, with where we are?"

"Happy? Yes, sounds a good plan."

"May I say this, Jonas? There have been times, to be very frank, when you might not have been the easiest colleague to work with. That is not meant to be offensive, but you can be sharp, have a reputation for abrasiveness . . . You have been, on this transfer of tactics, commendably cooperative. If I did not know you better, Jonas, I would say suspiciously cooperative. It's a sensible attitude and does you credit. Won't be long now till Agnes has her team in place. Will probably take over that house from your probationers, then you can get some well-deserved sleep. Thank you, Jonas."

The dog wriggled. In the front they grinned, would have heard every word exchanged.

He cleared his throat. Jonas said that he might have killed for a strong coffee, or a bar of chocolate, or a bacon sandwich of the sort that Vera made for him, and he explained. Told them, as if it were a bedtime story, of a young man who had gone away from his home,

shed comfort in the hope of finding adventure. Not an evil young
man but not one who gave credit to his family; just another who
looked around him and saw no satisfaction and moved on.
Adventure had clutched at him, and with it had come a group of
comrades, an alliance of brothers, and a sense of invincibility. He
spoke quietly and they listened to him with respect. But it was not a
fairy story, and no uplifting ending awaited the young man. The
adventure had gone sour, the colleagues – one by one – had been
cut down. He was alone and the driving force in his mind was one
of hatred against those responsible for fracturing the dream.

Told the two police in the front of their car that when the residents of the estate on the hill woke up, went to shower, shit and
shave, that the cordon would be in place, and the guns. Jonas
offered them two alternatives to the end-game. The young man,
inside or outside of it, would identify the cordon, would evade it
and disappear . . . Or would do the modern equivalent of falling
on a sword and would seem to offer a challenge to the firearms
and would be shot dead, would be the martyr, his name lit up in
lights. Said that either outcome would be "unsatisfactory".

"So, what are we, Mr Merrick?" she asked.

"Just a back-stop. A bit of 'just in case'."

"When might we shoot, Mr Merrick?" he asked.

"If I am wrong, then you shoot. A bad outcome."

She dug her fingers into a tight pocket of her vest, brought out
a short length of peppermints. Enough for one each.

The vehicle driven by Farouk – better known, only to himself, as
Wolfboy – reacted poorly to sharp bends or steep inclines.

The steering was heavy and the engine struggled. To be
expected. The inside of the van was filled with the sheets of plate
metal and it was Farouk's responsibility to screw them into place
when he reached his destination, where the van – newly protected
– would crash through wire fencing. Once the van had broken
past the initial defences and outstripped the first layer of security . . . what then? The man who was coming, who would shortly
be on his way to meet Wolfboy, would have to run, and on his

shoulder would be the weapon. A smile played broadly on Farouk's face. The road ahead was empty. The vehicle whined and strained but kept up its speed.

Wolfboy felt a sense of joy. He had been chosen. Had been nervous, but no longer. Stayed cautious. It would be a mark of the trust placed in him that it was he who had been chosen to meet the martyr, *shahid*, and he had been told that this heroic man had been a great fighter for the cause, in defence of Allah's will, in the time of the caliphate. He was honoured that he had been selected . . . and did not realise that those whom he had met – hurried conversations in moorland picnic areas, or among the trees of his city's parks – had furnished him with no information as to their own identities. He did not understand that he was a "cut off" in the conspiracy, and imagined that men would come to greet him when he was back in his room or in the café and would praise him to his face. It had happened fast, had been put together in a race against shrinking time.

The weapon would arrive first, then the man would come . . . and Wolfboy would be back on his own territory, at work in the café, but would keep close to a radio. He thought it the high moment of his life and was flattered to be so valued.

Tristram said, "There was something on the stairs, I thought."

Embarrassed, both of them, like a line had been crossed.

Izzy said, "There might have been, I couldn't swear."

From the darkened room they looked out through the window and down the length of the cul-de-sac, past a couple of parked cars and across the small square of derelict front garden and at a door with misted glass and behind that door a hall light burned.

"What shall we do, Izzy?"

"Nothing," she answered him. "What's on your phone?"

"The cavalry's coming. Aggie Burns's crowd."

"Can't be too soon . . . Is this how you're going to spend the rest of your working life?"

No answer given.

*   *   *

He came down the stairs, had taken them slowly, no sudden movement.

Cammy thought it would have been hard for a watcher, covert in the Hunters', to have identified him.

Time to move on. He went into the sitting-room.

It had seemed an age since he had been in his old bedroom. He had not needed a light, sufficient had come through the window, curtains opened, from the moon ... A little owl had shrieked from the trees around the cemetery, had seemed to warn him. He could see what had been done to the room, its contents, and could feel and touch the wreckage. He did not have to be told by his mum why the room had not been touched. She did not blame those who had wrecked the room and smashed his possessions. He assumed there would have been a gang of them, boot-faced, if not hiding a grin while they worked. There would have been nothing in the room for them to feast off. A couple of days before he had flown out, he had cleared all the paper he had printed off from the web, locations and travel ideas and the basics of the black flag movement, and had gone into the graveyard and had burned the paper in the bonfire heap that the workmen used who tidied the place. He supposed it "gratuitous", and knew about that word because it was what they had all of them, the brotherhood, used when talking of the violence inflicted by the men from the *Amn al-Dakhili* who did internal security in the towns and villages that had been overrun by the fighters. They came along behind, when it was safe and when the guns were quiet, and ... He felt a cut on the tips of two of his fingers. A bedside clock. A present given him when he had gone to the college, Mum's present. He had touched it and realised too late that the glass on the face was broken, a shard had lanced his fingertips.

"Do you want to know anything? Where I was? What I did? Anything?"

No answer given him.

"Who my brothers were? The guys I fought alongside?"

Silence.

"Is he still locked up, my loving brother? Do you still go to see him? Does he tell you how it was, is, how it will be? Do you talk?

Do you make a judgement on what *he* did, does, will do when the gate shuts behind his arse and he comes back here, and he'll start selling again? That all right, is it? I don't have any shame for what I did. Understand that . . .?"

She was hunched in a chair, did not move. He heard her breathing but she didn't speak.

"Are you going to do food for me? Do I have to do food for myself? I can cook, I cooked for my brothers. I can boil mutton, can grill goat meat. I can clean a chicken then put it on a wood spit over an open fire. Here, do I have to do that for myself?"

His voice had risen. He was still not answered.

"And money. I need money, and . . ."

Her hand was raised. He could make out the little roll held between her fingers. The length of a fag, and the thickness. He snatched it, could see the denomination.

"Is that all I get? Came home, came to see you . . . Never a day when I was there that I did not think of you, have love for you. All that and no food and next to no money."

He never lost his temper, abandoned self-control. Never screamed, shouted, yelled, never lashed out with his fists. Loss of control was weakness. Stayed calm. Not saints, any of the brothers, but not sinners. Could have ranted down the comms link when they were up and ready to spearhead an attack but the suiciders had not arrived to make the diversion: had been composed, ice-cold. Could have verbally thrashed Tomas when the little Estonian boy had lost the book in which the code frequencies for radio links were written, and the garbled words that would be used. The brothers had backtracked and had searched until the book was found – fallen from his pocket when he'd dropped his pants for a crap in the sand.

"Your call, Mum. I don't argue. You choose, Mum."

Might have had a knife stuck in his guts, and felt the pain of it around the blade, but his voice stayed steady. Would like to have thrown the money back into her lap, but needed it.

Now, she spoke, had a gentle lilt to her voice. She said, "I remember, Cameron, a service in the cathedral about two months after you had been welcomed to the choir. A Sunday service. Was so proud of you, and used to come to hear you sing and would sit somewhere you wouldn't notice me. There was a sermon, a dean or a bishop. I did not know the Bible before you went to the choir. Always remember the text. It was Luke fifteen, the prodigal's return. I thought it was rubbish. A kid goes away having badgered his father into forking out an advance on his inheritance. Spends it on tarts, comes home broke, but a softy father kills the fattened calf as celebration in spite of an elder brother bitching that it's a bad response. Dad said, 'We had to celebrate and be glad because this brother of yours was dead and is alive again. He was lost and is found . . .' Didn't hold with it then, and don't now."

"That it, Mum?"

"Play the prodigal if you want, but there'll be no welcome here. I want you gone."

Jonas might have dozed but the dog shifted and the movement alerted him . . . His phone screen was still blank. In the front they were both awake.

Dominic asked him, seemed genuinely concerned, "Hope you are surviving, Mr Merrick. We're not offering the best hospitality."

He grimaced, "Surviving well. Perfectly comfortable."

Babs said, wry smile, "Apologies there's no coffee, no *croissants*, nothing to offer."

"There'll be time enough for breakfast."

"After we're relieved, when the big battalions move in?"

"Time enough," Jonas said.

"When we're surplus?"

"It'll be a good breakfast, and we might try to find a biscuit for our friend before she goes home." Jonas patted the animal's head.

"If it's not impertinent, do you know the final target, Mr Merrick?"

"I think I do, cannot promise I do . . . Unless we lose him, the target is an irrelevance. If we lose him then I'm for the high jump. I think I do . . . Tough old world, isn't it?"

"One more question, Mr Merrick."

"One more."

A long time since Jonas had laughed out loud but he managed it and the dog started vigorously to scratch its ear.

15

The dog still scratched and Jonas soothed it, might have murmured something in the velvet-soft ear about patience, and it took a while for Dominic to work out how to pose the question.

"Would he know you, Mr Merrick?"

He chuckled. "We can call him 'he', or can identify him as Gustave. Gustave is a very large crocodile and lives in a steamy wide river, the Ruzizi which flows into Lake Tanganyika, and it is probable that he ate – or at least killed – some three hundred farmers snatched off the river's banks. Or we can call him Cameron Jilkes, one-time chorister with a voice like an angel's. So, is it 'he', or Gustave, or is it Cameron?"

"He, Mr Merrick . . . Does 'he' know of you?"

"Don't think so. Very much doubt it."

"Would he understand the structure of your organisation?"

"Most unlikely."

"And never heard of you?"

"They're mounting up, these questions. Not heard of me, a lowly bottle-washer in Thames House, and not heard the name of my superiors, or of the AssDepDG to whom I report. Ignorant of me, but not of the more immediate enemies who governed his life until his flight. He'll be familiar with Russian sector commanders and I assume with UK or US Special Forces units, and he'd know about the tactical habits of an Iranian officer from the Quds force. He would know of Syrian government commanders and Hezbollah leaders . . . But all such information is now useless to him. Not knowing of me, and I offer up no conceit, is a mistake on his part. It's the way these things happen. I don't usually talk much but sometimes it helps me to stay awake. The way these things happen is that a mistake is made. I'm rather good at spotting areas where mistakes may occur. You do not need a university degree, first class honours and a heap of plaudits. You have to appreciate the way in which a young man of humble education will respond when his life is being pulled apart by quite unimaginable stresses. It is not a matter of intellect, just common sense. I was averse to classrooms and lecture halls, and came into the Security Service at a lowly grade, very much at the bottom of the bucket. I don't need a string of letters after my name but I need a good nose. I return to my proposition, the need to recognise an opponent's mistake . . . by the by, he is an 'opponent', not a scumbag, not an 'enemy', is not somone I chuck names and obscenities at. He is an opponent and my job is to observe the mistakes he – or she, and they have lively members of the fairer sex – will assuredly make. They make mistakes, all of them do. And the likelihood of the mistake comes when he is angry. An interesting cliché but valid: Revenge is best served cold. With me? Anger means the dish is piping hot. The act will not be thought through, will be hurried, his mind will be clouded, and that is the ladder to a mistake."

His phone beeped.

He read Tristram's message.

He might have lulled them in the front and they might not have realised that he'd stopped speaking because his small screen had lit up with text.

Babs said, "You did not finish, Mr Merrick. All about a mistake. What was . . .?"

"Be quiet, can't you. Quiet."

He had just received the words to activate him. She flinched. He saw Dominic's face harden . . . and cared not a damn.

He spoke to them in the front room of the house overlooking the end of the cul-de-sac, found it difficult to get a coherent description out of them. Thought their response was poor. He told them what they should do. Jonas heard Tristram's voice in the background: "For fuck's sake, do we have to do that?" Repeated the instruction, not loudly but with an edge in his voice. Izzy sounded subdued, frightened even. He rang off. He gave Dominic's shoulder a nudge, said what he wanted on the screen ... their position, the estate, the clear ground of the cemetery, the road running down the hill. Said what speed they should go, and all lights killed. She drove.

Jonas said, "I never apologise and I never explain, which is why I am quite generally disliked. You were asking what was the mistake? Obvious ... along with the heat of anger goes loneliness on an intense scale. The mistake? Came to see his mother. Has been fighting someone else's war. A mercenary where he and the rest of gang of misfits were the useful idiots. Gets angry because of failure and offers up a promise, which is a hostage to fortune, and it will kill him, he hopes. To get over that hurdle he needs some loving support. Instead he'll find his mother was a snitch. Going to see his mother was the mistake."

The car was turning in the dimly lit road.

Babs said, "A mistake that will kill him?"

"I hope not, sincerely I do."

They edged down the hill towards the Margate road and loitered in the shadows, out of the light thrown down from the street lamps.

She did it a second time.

A confirmation from Sadie Jilkes that she was happy to betray her son. No love left for him. She pressed the switch by the front door, and the patch of garden in front of her house bathed in thin light.

She left the light on, counted through a half-minute, then switched if off. Street lamps down the cul-de-sac were sparse. But there was a security light under the eaves of the Hunters' house which came on when there was movement on their front path. Within seconds of her switching on her own light the Hunters' door had burst open and a young man and a young woman had run out, each carrying a coat and going too fast to shrug into it. Sadie had turned on the light within half a minute of Cameron leaving by the back door. He'd opened the fridge but could only have taken sliced bread and might have swigged from the milk carton. She had seen his shadow move over the grass that had needed a run with the mower, pass the rose bush that she loved, and launch at the fence, the divide between her property and the hedge ringing the cemetery. He had called from the kitchen door, "You'll miss me . . . You'll curse yourself for not caring about me . . . Can't wind back the clock but you'll wish you could . . . You'll read about me, then wish you'd loved me." She had not responded, and a gust of cool air had come into the sitting-room from the open door, and he'd been gone. The shadow cleared the fence and would have pitched down into the bramble and scrub in the cemetery.

They'd left the Hunters' front door open. They'd cut across the neck of the cul-de-sac and the woman had slipped on the kerb and almost fallen and Sadie had heard her swear, before they both disappeared.

Sadie thought she would sit a little longer, then would go back upstairs. Well after midnight now and she would be off out of her home in four hours. Go back up to her bedroom and take off her clothes and lie on her bed, best to get under the duvet, and make sure that the alarm was set. She hoped she would sleep. It was hard to do the early cleaning work if she did not sleep. She hoped that he had left sufficient bread in the fridge for her to make some toast before she went off to catch the bus into the city, the early one where each passenger looked half-dead. And hoped there would be enough milk for her to have a mug of tea. Wondered whether the state of his room, the shrine she had left to the collateral of what he had inflicted on her, had marked him. Did not really matter. What is done is done and cannot be undone, and she thought someone famous had said those words, but did not know who . . .

What would happen to him? She assumed that armed police would shoot him. What he deserved? Probably and . . . and would she be happy to have helped the armed police kill her son?

Which was the implication of what she had done when she had switched on her front light, given the signal as had been asked of her by the man who had approached her. A pleasant-spoken man, and with a kindness in his voice, but she had not seen his eyes. Could not forget her child as a chorister. Scrubbed and clean-faced, with tidy hair and in laundered robes, and singing to the great heights of the cathedral roof, and people all around her in raptures when he sang solo. She had seen his face in the gloom of the unlit sitting-room, had noted the sunken eyes and the gaunt cheeks and the thin lips and the blotches on his skin, and his tousled hair . . . Could erase that memory, not the choirboy.

She saw that the cul-de-sac was deserted, quiet, and the Hunters' front door had been closed . . . Perhaps nothing had happened and no one had visited. She went up the stairs and hoped to grab some sleep before the alarm claimed her.

Tristram led and Izzy kept up a volley of obscenity, complaint and interjected squeals of pain. Had gone across one set of back gardens, and she had tripped on a watering-can – "Who leaves a fucking watering-can in the middle of a fucking path . . .?" He had a good stride and wore lace-up shoes. She had struggled with a short cross-country run in the early stages of induction but had ticked enough boxes for the financially deprived background quota to cancel any failings. They were using the torches on their mobile phones.

He hissed back over his shoulder, "For God's sake, Izzy, shut up."

She snapped back at him, "I'm trying! Bloody shoes are a bloody nightmare."

The phones gave a bouncing light around their feet, they blundered forward. They saw a sign for a cemetery but the gate was along a feeder lane and they had to cross more fences and more back gardens. Tristram hit a poly-tunnel, might have had prize strawberries growing in there, or a first crop of protected lettuces, but was – thank the good Lord – plastic and not glass. He knew she was close behind because he heard her wheezing . . . thought her a great girl, a top girl, and thought . . . They were on the next street down from the cul-de-sac, and he had fucking nearly impaled himself on a kid's scooter and he had a view of a road in front, the main drag. Paused for that moment, then looked up. Saw him.

Tristram reached back, caught Izzy's arm and pointed.

"Him, the Tango, see him."

"Got him. Tommy Tango. I'll buy that."

They were 150 yards from the main road. Had seen him because a lorry had come around a corner, monster lights on the front, and would have surprised him. He'd paused on the pavement and had let it pass, then had loped across the width of the road and it had been harder to see him except for the street light further up the hill. There seemed to be an alley between two small terraces of houses, might have led to lock-ups or to back gardens . . . No one, at that time of the morning, the small hours when doctors said old people died, opened a door and looked around, wary. He ran bent head and shoulders, and disappeared. Right height, right build but perhaps thinner, right hair colour but might have been blonder which was what prolonged exposure to the sun did.

Tristram called Jonas. Said where they were and what he had seen . . . had no thanks given him, was told to stay in touch. No fucking appreciation, like praise would have stuck in the old bastard's throat.

She said, a gasp for breath, "That was just brilliant, to see the shite, bloody brilliant."

Cammy ran.

The path was a familiar one. Used as the cut into the city when he had no money for a bus, or the way home when the last of the public transport had gone. It would take him down to the river, the minor one that had a separate channel to the Stour, and there was – as he remembered it – a track alongside. It would be slippery, and there was a fair drop into the water, but it would be nothing that taxed him after where he had been – drainage and irrigation ditches, paths that might have been strewn with anti-personnel mines sown by the Russians. He ran well, and had eaten two of the slices of bread that he had stuffed into his pocket.

Too late for regrets. He put the diversion to his mum's house

and to his sister's grave, and to his own wrecked room, behind
him. Like it had never happened. Was done, and in his mind he
had moved on, and his breathing was even and he kept up a good
pace. On a descending cinder track, he kicked aside fallen branches
but who was out that early in the morning to have heard? Maybe
a cat, possibly rats, and could have been a fox whose eyes he saw.
He focused on his promise, would get his strength from what he
had shouted at the skies, and at that brief flicker of light from the
undercarriage some 20,000 feet above him.

*It should have been the day when, finally, something worked for him
and for her, his last brother. Had started well.*

*They had been intercepted. The group came from their right side
emerged from the wreckage of a village that looked to have been pounded
by air strikes, and the flies were still thick in the air which meant the
killing was recent. There had been the stink of the dead that ran well
with the stench of failure. The two of them, Cammy and Ulrike, had
been threading their way up what was once a main street and had
picked their way past corpses and had shouted at the feral dog pack,
and the group had materialised, had challenged them. Seven or eight of
them and leaderless, and not knowing where they went, only interested
in flight, distance, getting the hell out. And they had some food, and
water, but enough to share. Ulrike's decision. She said he would take
them, and under his wing – had made the clucking noise of a chicken
and had gained ribald laughter.*

*They had moved on, and Cammy had been harsh, had insisted on a
fast pace although the sun was climbing, but then had started to sing,
none of them any the wiser of the meaning and the relevance of his
words. Not for days had he seen Ulrike smile.*

Cammy felt strong, went well, thought his resolve healed.

*He thought she was 41 years old, almost twice his own age. The
previous two nights they had slept together, fully clothed, but arms
around each other's backs, just for comfort. She had told him more in
those 48 hours about herself than he had learned in their months together
in the gang of brothers. From Rostock on the Baltic. A child when the
regime had collapsed and her father, who had been an official in the*

security police, was out of work, out of fashion and hiding out of sight, and a mob baying at the front door and occasional stone hitting the family's home. Had been smuggled out and sent to her grandmother's for safety and her parents had fled, had never sent for her, had disappeared from her life. Had gone to school, had flunked a university course, had taken a job in the Rathaus, number crunching. Had lived alone and never used cosmetics or wore jewellery. And the day after her 35th birthday she had signed up for a course in advanced first aid: learned about car accident injuries, bullet and knife wounds, third world sickness and infection problems, and had passed with an alpha grade and had been expected to join an ambulance crew in Rostock ... Had taken a plane to Istanbul, had gone across the Turkish frontier.

Cammy came off the track, went across a field and ripped his trousers and his anorak on a barbed wire fence and had not slowed to unpick himself, had torn the material free.

She had been attached to a casualty station and worn the niqab. Then had bought forged black flag papers, taken a man's name, covered her face and put a growl in her voice, and had met the brothers of Kami al-Britani. Became part of the brotherhood from the first day she marched with them; she rode with them, fought with them, and no allowances were made for her, and she would have spat in anger at any who short-changed her efforts. Calm under extreme pressure. Used to say: "Stay calm. It is never a crisis". Could fight in the front line, strip and reassemble an AK or an M16, a Barrett Browning or a Dragunov and could prime mortar bombs ...

Cammy scattered sheep, sent them bleating into the darkness and the wind was blustering into his face ... If it had not been for Ulrike he might have manufactured a fudge for the promise given for the deaths of Mikki and Tomas and Pieter and Dwayne and Stanislau ... If there had been a chance that he and Ulrike could have gone somewhere – and somewhere was anywhere – and been at peace, with no weapons, no ammunition and no enemy ... If ... then he might have evaded the promise. It stood, was locked in his mind. Would be honoured.

The night before they had clung to each other and weakness had consumed both of them, and he had wept and she had sobbed, and they had clung close. And then she had told him a story, a folk story of the forests of Germany, and had calmed them both, and finally they had slept. Now they walked well and they were around three miles short of a wadi, and there would be cover there, and it was late in the morning to be in the open . . . And his bowels broke, the Damascus Revenge came on suddenly. Cammy had ducked to the side of the road, and there was a ditch to take water when the heavens opened, and he was down into it and dumped his rucksack and his rifle and had his belt loose and his trousers down.

Cammy found himself trapped in a hedge. He had remembered a gap, but a pallet had been wired into the space. Stopped for a moment and heard only distant traffic – no sirens and no dogs. Worked himself loose, and went on. He thought the first train would go at about six that morning with the first of the London commuters surging forward for seats. He had expected to be longer at his mother's, not have time to kill, again.

It might have been the noise their boots made on the dried track, kicking at dust and stones. Might have been the humming in their heads of the music they remembered, might have been the clatter of their weapons against ammunition pouches and . . . from the ditch Cammy heard the sound of the drone's purring engine, but could not see it. They lived with the sound of the drones. Many attempts had been made, many theories offered, as to how they should be avoided. He listened. The one answer seemed to be that if a man was in a field surrounded by women and children, then sometimes they would not shoot. He heard it and thought it banked to turn. He might have been 200 yards from Ulrike . . . He thought it sounded like an express train hurtling through the closed space of a tunnel, and saw the light flash and his shout of warning was too late and too soft, and with the thunder of the detonation came the dust cloud which was followed by the blast of the air and then by the pitter-patter noise of the fragments landing, and from the few pieces of the missile's broken casing came the whine of shrapnel.

Cammy felt, quite suddenly, that his strength – not his resolve – weakened, as if the bank of it was emptying, and he was slowing and the ground here was boggy and his feet sank. His mind screamed with the promise given and he had to drag his feet, mud sticking to the brogues.

He had found a leg. Only a leg. He put it in the pit of the crater and threw dirt down on it ... Good if he could have found wild flowers. There were none. Good if he could have heard small birds making melancholy or chirruping songs, but heard only the soft drone of the engine. Looked up often enough. Once only, saw a light flash in the quiet blue of the sky. Just a leg, nothing more of her, and he did not bother with making a pretence of burying it. His trousers sagged at his knees and he had no paper to clean himself. He hitched his trousers, raised his rifle, pointed the barrel into the skies, let go the entire magazine. Pointless and stupid and all he was capable of. They might see on their screens, wherever they flew the drone from, a lone figure who fired at them and had no relevance. Cammy clenched his fist, shook it at the unseen lens and screamed his promise. They would see him, might chuckle, would not hear him.

His promise, "I will come. I will find you. I will hunt you down. Wherever you are, however safe you think yourselves, I will find you and will come for you ... That is my promise, believe it."

Cammy heard the flow of the river. Two years before he had left, a tree trunk had fallen across it and made a dam where a waterfall tumbled. Heard it and knew it. He was stumbling, as he had been at the end of his solitary march, when he had crossed a single strand of wire, in the cover of darkness, and had left Syria, and had started out on the next stage of the journey to fulfil the promise, honour his word. So tired, and his strength leaking.

Past five, and sunrise due in fourteen minutes and the Station came reluctantly to life.

Arc lights coming on. The first vehicles of the day moving into the heavily guarded area of the main gates.

The rush would come soon, and passes would be flashed irritably into the faces of the guards from the Regiment. And off the Station, in scores of homes, alarms would ring out for air crew and ground crew, and the technicians who did the repairs or maintenance and fine-tuned the electronics, and in the bedrooms of those who cleaned the toilets, hoovered the carpets in the Officers' Mess, those who would soon get the gas burning under the frying pans, would valet the uniforms of senior officers who that day were expecting a Civil Service delegation looking into cost cutting . . . A myriad of alarms, and a cacophony of grumbling as feet slipped out from under duvets.

But, for all the congenital moans – force of habit – there would be relief amongst many that the Station was a place of safety: rather serve here, the chime would have been, where security was pretty much guaranteed than in the arsehole corners of the Middle East . . . And soon the nurseries would be opening for the day's business, and the museum, and the centre where the spooks ruled in Intelligence Surveillance Target Acquisition and Reconnaissance. Just the start of another day in the Station's life. In some electronic archive, tucked away, out of sight and out of mind, would have been the video record of a drone strike that had been launched from Syrian airspace close to the Jordanian border. Not remarkable and not unremarkable, a minor moment in unmanned aerial vehicle warfare. The recording showed, as the Reaper loitered, scattered debris and body parts and a crater. Showed also a single detached leg that had been tossed to the side of the track – and it had showed a guy in a ditch who had had his pants down, and who seemed to fire an entire magazine into the sky, and who had then clenched a fist and punched at nothing.

"Never in doubt," Baz chuckled and took a hand off the wheel and squeezed Mags' knee.

"Piece of cake, big boy," she answered him.

The ferry port was behind them, and so were the banks of arc lights that highlighted the customs area. They had headed through, had waved at a tired-looking woman in uniform, and he had blown her a kiss which was cheeky and probably sealed her belief that too many old people had too much time on their hands, and should get off their backsides and . . . she had given them in return a flutter of her hand. They had not accelerated, had not shown impatience, but had kept their place in the queue of vehicles as they came out of the ferry area and started on the feeder road to the main route north. Very soon, he would turn off, following her directions, and take the B roads that would keep them clear of tracking and surveillance cameras and recognition systems, and they would round the capital by the west side and then drive cross-country back to the east for the last stages of their journey.

"Gone well."

"Gone a treat."

"Can I give you a thought, Mags?"

"Give it me."

Baz said, "Like it's certainty, I'll tell you what'll happen in the next hour. I'm telling you that we were just lucky – two pigs on a dry day finding some mud to roll in. In an hour, might be an hour and a half but not more, they'll start getting their act together, and the messages that clogged up overnight will unscramble, and they'll be looking for our wheels, might even have the phoney plate details. Bet your knickers on it, Mags. That dozy cow who waved us through, she'll be sitting with her head in her hands, and in front of her on a laptop screen will be the picture of our wheels. And the balloon will be up, except – if our luck holds – they'll not know where to look . . . The schedule's good, and . . . You all right, Mags?"

"Just gone a bit serious, but all right." Her head was down on her chest, lips pursed and a frown on her forehead.

"Tell me."

"It's powerful kit in the back there. Do some damage. Hasn't bothered me before . . . You thinking about it?"

"No, what I'm thinking about is the bonanza coming our way. Tell you something . . . it'll go, whatever it is, to some lunatic who'll probably shove it under his bed and keep it there for a rainy day, know what I mean? And if he ever did arm it up he'd end up shooting his foot off. Just an idiot from Bradford or Luton who wants to feel he's the top cat and has a loud enough shout to have brought it into the country. The chance of it going to a guy who knows what it's about, how to use it, has the training, is less than nil. Believe me, Mags."

"And that's not all shit?"

"You worry too much. An idiot, a lunatic, what he'll be, just a dreamer . . . And when they do get their act together, Mags, we'll be at home but the camper won't be. And you remember those pleasant lads we gave a ride to, who sat in the back with all their bags? How were we to know what they left in – after we dropped them off?"

"Smart thinking."

"Just a pair of old folks, aren't we? A bit simple and a bit naive . . . and ahead of the game. Give us a kiss, love."

Cammy reached the river.

Did not stop, did not break his stride. A short steep slope marked the path down to the river's bank, and Cammy fell there and pitched forward and was spread-eagled on the path. He dug in an elbow and plunged his fingers into the mud, so he did not go into the water.

He had used the path from the age of eight or nine, had never tripped and fallen. He was exhausted and his feet were painful, and the bread he had wolfed, only half of what he had snatched, ached in his gut. Had to get to Canterbury, then have to find somewhere to rest, then would head for the station and would need to buy a ticket. Mud smeared his clothes and likely there was some on his face, and he was unshaven, and had the scars where Vicky's guy had hit him with the chair. The wind rattled in the tops of the trees on either side of the river, coming in erratic gusts. It would be quiet, then without warning the branches would clatter and the trunks rub together and scream, and twice rotten branches had broken off and come down, made a whip-crack sound. He knelt, trying to recreate the professionalism that his brothers had trusted in. Listened. Heard the water's fall and the song of the wind and the breaking of more branches. Waited long enough to know that he was not followed.

He remembered the police who had been in the house when they were searching for his brother, and those who had come when his sister had been killed. He had thought them unimaginative and seeming to speak from a script and they would have been of the same standard as those who his mum had said were camped in the Hunters' home. Had no doubt that he had fooled them, would be far gone by the time that the first light of the sun popped up over the Margate road and came on to the cul-de-sac and fell on the front of his mum's house, and the Hunters' . . . because he was clever, they were not.

"Just keep going," Jonas said into his phone. "Enjoy the spirit of the chase."

The boy had been puffing and gasping, like he was a marathon runner and short of training, and he could hear the girl behind him, whining and whingeing and struggling to keep up. He had his torch on, and was tracing the route of a stream that ran adjacent to the river. All making sense, all satisfactory. He saw where the stream came out of a ribbon of woodland, and a stretch of open ground. He stabbed that point on the map and the policeman shrugged, accepted.

A few minutes before, they had been edging their way down the Margate road and Jonas had laughed. Tristram and Izzy had come at a gangling run from someone's garden and a cat had fled in front of them. They had been holding hands. He did not assess that as anything romantic, more in the interests of self-preservation: they needed each other and would have been frightened if separated, him fearful of losing her and her unwilling to take responsibility for leading. The policewoman had looked around at him and he had read her, had nodded. She had flashed them. Two flicks on the headlights and they had stopped, nearly piled into each other and would have looked up the road and not seen, in the gloom, the cause of it, and Tristram had yanked her after him . . . Now they had called him, had reported where they thought they might be. Very near to the end.

It seemed to Jonas that the dog had also appreciated that matters now moved at pace. It sat upright on his lap and peered through the window, raked eyes over dark pavements, unlit homes and gardens, and a growl was in its throat when they passed two women, trudging along the pavement towards the main road.

His hand went into his jacket pocket, and unzipped a small compartment, a place where a railway ticket could have been stored safely, or coins for a parking meter, or in this instance, or for a key. Attached to the key was a length of pink ribbon. He had asked Vera for some ribbon from her work-basket and she had produced this piece, around a foot long, and he had looped it through and had knotted it securely to the key. For weeks, months, getting on for years, it had remained in his desk drawer. Had been there ever since he had been allocated that small area in 3/S/12 and the desk had been moved in.

They had come on to the main road, the direct route into Canterbury. He checked the time, getting close to five o'clock, and they dawdled, allowing vehicles to power past them. He asked for the time of the first fast train to London: a few minutes before 0630. And what time would the sun rise? More clicking on the young man's phone. Sunrise was scheduled for 0543 that day . . . what he liked most about both of them, and he thought of them now as Dominic and as Babs, not as police officers but as colleagues, was that they no longer badgered him for answers. Truth was that both could have done the work of Tristram and Izzy for all that they probably had no degrees. Also a truth that neither Tristram nor Izzy could have done their work, carried a Heckler & Koch on a strap around the neck, and the Glock, and the grenades and the Tasers. He offered the key on the pink ribbon to Dominic.

"Just something for your safekeeping, young man. Keep it handy and don't lose it."

Closing the front door behind her, Sadie Jilkes looked back at her house, checked that only the hall light was on.

She stepped off her path and on to the pavement and turned towards the mouth of the cul-de-sac, and light flooded across her. The Hunters' door was open, and they came spilling out. The security light under their eaves shone bright. They were already, unusually, dressed for the day.

The whole family came across the road. Strange, she would reflect afterwards, that it was not the parents who spoke but their children. Nice enough kids and polite, but what would they know?

What business was it of theirs? They stood in front of her, blocked her.

"Did he come, Mrs Jilkes?" asked Bradley.

"If it's any of your concern – came and went."

"And your front light went on and those beggars in our front room went charging out," said Karen.

"Did they?"

The boy asked, "Was that a signal for them to come running?"

The girl asked, "At school we called that a snitch. Did you snitch on Cameron?"

"I've work to go to." No way past them, her way ahead blocked. The parents stood behind their kids, quiet but showing their emotions.

From the boy, "You did the signal so they could get him?"

From the girl, "Told on your son? They'll shoot him, won't they?"

"We wanted to help you. Don't you understand?" Bradley spat.

"Get him away, not have him shot. He's Cameron, just a silly kid who took a wrong path. And you are his mother," Karen hissed.

She pushed past them. Her world and no room for them inside it. Sadie Jilkes had a long walk to the bus-stop, but all downhill.

"I have him, I saw him. Straight ahead . . ."

A fleeting glimpse where the path beside the river ran straight, and across the river was a street of houses and a light pierced the trees, and Tristram had seen the movement in front of him.

"Just up there. Definite. I saw him."

Behind him he heard a bubbling gulp. He halted and almost fell but kept his balance and saw Izzy a yard clear of the bank, in the stream. He imagined that in a moment, as if a dam broke, she would scream. He took a few paces back, bent and reached down, his arm snaking between stinging nettles and across smooth mud, and his hand took Izzy's. He dragged her up. Tristram fancied that it would have been Izzy's dignity that was the casualty. She came up easily enough. Nothing broken except pride and nothing bruised except esteem. He put an arm around her shoulder, and brushed a kiss on her forehead.

"We have to move it. I saw him."

"It's in the water, my fucking shoe. One of my shoes is."

"Just manage, do the best you can."

The path was narrow and slippery, like they trod on ice, and Tristram called in and said where they were and what he had seen, and said that Izzy had fallen in the stream but was now with him and ... A curt response, no praise and no sympathy ... How would it end? This was the first time either of them had been out of Thames House on an operation, come down from the third floor and become part of an arrest mission unit. Had seen it often enough in the shaky, bouncing images that came off the body cameras – some little sod spread-eagled down on the ground and the guns and voices around him. Did not think it would end as the body cameras showed it. If only half of what they had been told of Cameron Jilkes was true, if he had only a small part of the capabilities awarded him, then he would try to break away in the darkness. Not that darkness would be with them much longer. It would be a shooting job, if they were lucky. Would be a manhunt job if it fouled. Would be a shambles. He stumbled along the path and Izzy followed him as best she could: plucky girl and there were little squeals from her, there might be stones on the path or glass or brambles, and he remembered she had pink toenails, shoes off in the house and almost asleep ... and there was a new factor in the way it would play out.

"We're following him, Izzy, and what that means is that we are giving the guns a better chance."

"Something like that."

"I don't see myself in that garb."

"Nor me. Not running after a fugitive in the middle of the night, not going without a shoe and not slopping around in a stream. And not barging into people's houses, and not lying, and lording it over them, and tricking that kid with a fucking ice-cream. Not right for me."

"Nor me."

"But I'm frightened, Tristram, frightened it'll be down to us, that he gets through."

"Just keep going."

Had his hand behind him, and one of hers slotted into his. They did not hear the sounds of flight ahead of them, and did not see any movement, but thought the light was breaking, with a soft grey smear.

Wolfboy had gone west of the Peak District National Park, and had no need to hurry, and his tank had sufficient fuel.

It was a meandering route but each time he looked at his watch, and checked the satnav, he believed he had the schedule set correctly.

He wondered how he would be treated, afterwards, by the people who had recruited him, who knew what part he had played. With respect, he believed. His destination was Grantham, the town in Lincolnshire where a former Prime Minister had been brought up. Out by the crematorium was a car park that had, he was told, minimal camera surveillance.

The vehicle handled reasonably and he had become used to the vagaries imposed by the new weight it carried . . . It would be a fine man he gave the cargo to, a man to be admired.

Cammy came out of the trees beside the stream. He passed the back of a new housing development: a pristine collection of town-houses and apartments, rows of parked cars, and lights above the parking areas. They had been building it when he had gone away. Beyond was the park, and benches down by the stream. So tired. Needed to rest and to wash his face and hands, clean the mud off his clothes . . . Then would walk to the station and buy the ticket with his mother's money, and would sit or stand on the train, and would be rushed to London . . . Then? It would be good to feel the weight of the launcher in his hands, and all fast and all finished quick. Driving the vehicle through the fence and then the chase, and maybe having to cross the full width of a concrete runway, shouting behind him and occasional shots that would be aimed too high, too low or too wide. They would give him – when he took possession of the weapon and the vehicle – pictures of the buildings that were his target. He would not actually get up to them, certainly not into them, but if he were within 200 yards of them, probably single storey, prefabricated and without windows, he could crouch and aim the launcher, go through the sights and lock on the target and squeeze the trigger and feel the thunder blow and the flash of the flame from its exhaust. Could follow the flight of it, track it until it hit – then load the next, and fire, and load again. Might let go four of them, even five, if the couriers had managed to bring that many bombs for the thing. That, Cammy estimated, was when the first of their bullets might hit him. Not likely, with the first one, to be a killing shot. Many more would follow. Might fire 25 into him, might creep close, and him long gone, and fire shots into his head … as it would have been at Flores off the Azores, the Atlantic islands.

A master who taught English at the college had been there. He'd had a fine voice, and had made the poetry alive. A ship in Elizabethan times, Sir Richard Grenville its master, 53 Spanish galleons and the *Revenge* alone, a day-long savage fight and a final capitulation and the buccaneer carried aboard the enemy flagship, mortally wounded, and them still cautious, fearful of him, even as death came. Remembered the teacher's ringing voice: *Was he devil or man? He was devil for aught they knew, But they sank his body with honour down into the deep.* They would stand around him, wary long after life had gone, and there would be a sort of awe, and … That was how it would be – and his promise had been given.

He was staggering. The strength bled from his legs.

The wind blustered, and the sun would soon show. Remembered what Stanislau liked to say: *I want to snatch the sunset and hold it.* Cammy would see a sunrise, not a sunset.

It was Kingsmead Park. His mind on *Nunc Dimittis*, and challenging were the verses of "*The snares of Hell*", and others were starting to compete, and his head rolled and his walk was feeble. Ahead of him he saw a bench.

*   *   *

They had parked. They had their weapons. They stood by the car, Jonas at the front.

Beside the parking area was the gateway to a nursery school, and a well-equipped play area.

The dog strained on the lead, was probably hungry. Well, the dog would have to wait for its breakfast.

The place, Dominic told him, was Kingsmead Park. Babs had it on her phone and said it was considered a precious place by the locals because it had been saved from developers by public clamour.

Jonas said, "Time to get this show on the road."

They had been in the car park a full five minutes when the lone figure emerged from a track beside the new housing development. Babs had let loose a sharp short whistle between her teeth, but quiet, and done it as a mark of admiration, something like that, and there had been a half-smile on Dominic's face. The figure had passed beneath a street lamp and had been lit well, and had not hurried. Dominic said that the target man, their Tango, was "knackered". Babs thought he was "about all in". Jonas thought appearances, in the grey and difficult light of dawn with the first sunlight not yet falling on the open spaces of the park, could lie.

The dog tugged on the lead. Would have wanted the grass.

Dominic cradled his H&K across his vest. Might have dropped the man at this range and in that light, might not. Across the stream were bungalows with pretty gardens, and trees with a flurry of blossom in their branches, and then a main road, a bus passing along it, the first of the day. Babs was doing a fast checklist of her kit, and they armed their weapons. Jonas supposed that was necessary – they had sufficient distance from the target and he would not have heard the sounds. He told them where they should be, what they should do, and listed eventualities, and gave them one of his better smiles. The park was deserted . . . but not for long because the early joggers and dog walkers would be out soon.

Dominic said, "What you ask of us, Mr Merrick, is against all the training we have gone through."

Babs said, "This is the tipping point, and we are supposed to have primacy."

Dominic said, "Something we were told when our group was qualifying. The last viceroy of India was Mountbatten, a top wartime commander, huge clout, and he told his personal protection that he was going down to the bazaar in Delhi that morning, needed to calm fears as independence and separation came nearer. His officer said he should not, he would not permit it. Mountbatten pulled rank on him. The policeman said that he was not going there, final. 'I couldn't care, sir, whether you get assassinated or not, but I do care about my reputation when I am responsible for you . . .' He did not go. That argument clinched it."

They watched as Cameron Jilkes made his way across the open park.

Jonas said, "Tough on your reputation if this goes sour . . . Don't like repeating myself. Wasting breath, but time to get the show on the road."

16

He jerked the lead, and the dog fell in beside him. Jonas and Vera had never owned a dog, so he had no experience of how to walk one, but this seemed a decently trained little thing.

Spring was coming. Would be earlier here than in London. The cherry blossom was not yet out at home. Ahead of him were some early flowers, and in the gardens of the bungalows the colours were starting to brighten. The sun was rising, good as gold and prompt. It was 0543. Would have been a problem, a greater problem than all of those others that queued up to attempt to frustrate him, had it been pitch dark, or had the rain not lifted.

He felt only a minimal sense of pleasure as he set off across the damp grass that had been recently cut and looked a picture. Early on he had to stop because the dog needed the moment for a break, then they were on the move again. It would be the matter of an interception ... Easy for Jonas because the young man came slowly, each step an effort. That was merely an observation in Jonas's mind because he had no feeling for Cameron Jilkes, was neither hostile nor sympathetic. He thought that the opponent – the correct description for a young man sitting across a chess board from him – would not have eaten hot food, had had little to drink, had likely lain up and taken cover since coming ashore on the coast at Deal, and his head would have been ringing from the denunciation meted to him when he had crawled in through the back garden and come into his old home. Obvious that it had been a pitifully bad welcome he'd faced or his mother would not have flicked switches, done the signal.

A hard all-weather path led from the housing development along the river; it cut across the grass and exited the park in a corner, opposite a leisure centre. On the far side of the path were simple, basic benches and around them the daffodils were coming to an end: Vera would have liked it here, would have settled comfortably with a book and would have had the sounds of the stream as company . . . The route that Jonas and the dog took meant, all things being equal, that he would reach the path at a point about level with the bungalows on the stream's far side, and he would be just a few paces in front of Cameron Jilkes. He held the lead firmly in one hand, and the other went into his pocket. A few quick movements and he had successfully slipped his right wrist into one of the open cuffs, then he dropped the lead on to the dog's back, had fastened the cuff, locked it, and had retrieved the lead. Rather self-conscious, because he did not know what language was appropriate for a dog, but he muttered something about good behaviour, and "well done". They were walking again and the interception point seemed right. He had his right hand in his coat pocket and could feel the other open cuff, and the fastening on his right wrist was hidden by his sleeve. He did not hurry and the dog sniffed consistently but did not drag him.

He had glanced to his right, not often, but had managed to check out the appearance of Cameron Jilkes. Would have been a fine looking boy had it not been for the ravages of Syria: eyes, mouth, cheeks, posture and laboured walk, all reflecting where he had been and the cost paid. And how different, where he was now. A world away. Jonas assumed that every corner of a village or a town in Syria had been a battlefield and carried the wounds of the fighting in demolished structures, and in every oasis out in the deserts most of the trees would have been snapped off by the blast from bombs and missiles. Jonas had never been to Ireland but was an encyclopaedia on its tragedies, deaths, scars, and reckoned that in each community, at every crossroads, there had been a killing – a Paddy O'Rawe or a Billy Wilson . . .

Here, the ground where Jonas would make his move, he assumed, and smiled at the thought, that little had happened other than a Mrs Smith managing some knitting while she passed time, where a Mr Jones planned better feed for his under-performing marrows ... those sort of pastimes. Good territory for Jonas because an opponent's guard would be down. He noted that Cameron wore an old man's clothing. Conventional trousers, a shirt with a check in it, a tie that was loosened and hung askew, and a jacket that might have been a genuine Harris tweed or at least an imitation. He assessed the former owner was now deceased, and that a house clearance had put the garments into a charity shop, assessed again that the charity shop would have been close to where the young man had come ashore: he'd have arrived wet and shivering, at the door of a Deal charity shop and the staff would have taken pity on him, would have kitted him out, and done it carefully because the clothing hung well on him. He would have every charity outlet in the town of Deal checked out, and their casual volunteer workers identified. Their time, the staff's time, would come, and he made a note of it. Maybe that afternoon, if all went well, maybe the next morning, they would be interrogated – would probably face charges.

Cameron Jilkes sagged down on to one of the rough wood benches. Seemed to flop, then checked his watch, would have been satisfied that he had time for a brief rest before moving on to the railway station.

The dog was allowed to sniff some more, and Jonas guided it with fractional flicks of the wrist. It was an obedient little soul and did as it was directed.

Aching in his back, and in his legs, and aching because of the welcome he had failed to receive back home, Cammy slumped.

Saw an old man meandering towards him, a dog on a lead. Just an old man out early with his dog ...

He would sit here for five minutes or ten, not more. Would draw the air down into his lungs, take strength from it. The first layer of sunshine came over the grass and nestled on his face. In five minutes or ten, no more, he would go down to the stream and crouch and wash his hands and see how much mud was on his jacket, and might dump it and might not ...

The old man followed the dog. Seemed to talk to the dog but Cammy could not hear what he said. He had glanced around, had done a full rotation before sitting on the bench. If there had been police, he would have seen them. They'd have been in black dungarees and would have had German Shepherds, and they'd have had firearms. He had looked, not an idiot, far from it, had seen nothing . . . A couple came from the path beside the housing estate but they veered away, went towards the Leisure Centre – would have been shagging and would have come across country because they were too early for the buses. He'd seen them, checked them, and they held hands. It was a pretty little dog. His mum would have liked a dog like that. His mum could not have a dog because she was out too early in the morning and back too late in the evening, and slept when she could. He did not want to think of his mother, and whether she had a dog, or did not . . . hurt him to think of her.

The old man came closer, had not looked up and their eyes had not met, but the dog gazed at him, seemed to interrogate Cammy.

Cammy would be a suicider. Had seen them often enough. All boys, thin as rakes and murmuring to themselves, and might have been dosed up, fidgeting. All had handlers who spoke for them and received the instructions on where in the line they were to run to, at what moment they should reach the checkpoint they would demolish, when they should go forward in the armoured vehicle. Cammy was sitting in Kingsmead Park, close to the Leisure Centre where he had learned to swim, was among the late daffodils, and a river, clean and fresh, flowed ahead of him, and he reflected on suiciders. He had thought most of them dosed up because they had no conversation, just nodded in rhythm, and most – God's truth – were useless. They seemed to have no names and were given no respect. Were just detritus and might achieve a moment of advantage in a fire-fight and might not . . . If they wore vests or drove an armoured vehicle then there was a second detonation system programmed in, and should the suicide funk out then the big man, far back and safe, could press a button and do the job the kid had failed to carry out. They would have made promises, the would-be suiciders. All about promises ... would have made promises and would not be able to renege on what they said. Were committed, could not back down. Himself? Neither could he back down ... Could not consider it ... One option was to go home, go in by the front door, sit in a chair and wait for the police to come. Another – to go into the city, through the old gate, and give some flannel as to his business and then sit in the area reserved for the choir and look to see if the priest came back, or had already shopped him. Have himself carted out of the cathedral, marched past the tomb of the Black Prince – the warrior. And another – could go into the city and past the Miller's pub and on to St Peter's Street, over the bridge and on to the High Street, out past the city walls and turn up at the police station: "Had enough, was scared, want to jack it in, and promises mean nothing". He laughed out loud. The thought of it ... and saw the faces of his brothers. Laughed some more at the thought of ditching his word ... How would it be? Would be fast. What would he feel? Nothing.

Would have been his laugh that attracted the dog. Just a few yards away now ... The old man seemed dressed in clothing similar to his. The sun warmed him. He arched his back, stretched, felt joints creak. They'd say his name, wouldn't they? Say it at the Station where they flew the drones from, and say it back in Syria where people who had known him in the fighting days would learn it from their texts, and there would have been guys who had reached as far as Afghanistan or were in the Benghazi enclave of Libya, they would all hear his name and rejoice in him. Would know his name in the Choir School and in the big comprehensive he had ended up in, and would speak his name and see his picture all the way down the cul-de-sac and to his mum's house, and she'd hear his name. It was a promise ... the sun was warming the back of his head and the side of his face.

The old man ambled nearer, led by the dog.

It was how it would be, his mum would hear his name.

* * *

The bus was on time.

She had a window seat and a view of the park. It was cold enough outside and warm enough with the bus heaters on for the windows to have misted, but she'd used her sleeve to wipe the glass and had a view of the park and the distant play area.

Sadie saw her son. Saw the man who had stopped and spoken to her, who had brought her, and saw what she thought was the dog from the next road up to hers. Saw her son, certain of it, sitting on a bench and arching his back like he was trying to get stiffness out of it, and he'd have walked, or run, from Sturry village. It was all clear to Sadie, clear as the first fierce peep of the sun that came up over the river and topped the trees and lit the park. Everyone around here loved the park because it was claimed that developers would have built over it if ordinary people had not protested. No fool, Sadie, she understood. She could see a uniformed man and woman standing beside a car, the sun catching the metal of their weapons. Understood that the dog was the trick the man used to get close to her son, to Cameron.

She reached up, rang the bell. Twice. Not a designated bus-stop, but maybe the driver was in a good humour. The bus braked. A door opened. What to say? Could not say, "My boy's down there and the security police are up close to him, and might call up the firearms and they might shoot him dead, my son." She hopped down from the bus. As she started to track back along the hedge bordering the stream, she called back.

"Thanks, pet, just forgotten something."

She would stand and watch, see how it played out on this day, her unsung anniversary. And thought of him as a stranger. Would not interfere, would be late for work, would watch.

Jonas sidled to the bench.

He dripped an image of a harmless old fool, out early because he could not sleep, had brought the dog with him, probably his best friend. Lonely and harmless, searching out company. Would talk the hind leg off a donkey, that sort of man – tedious but without malice, no threat.

Quietly, little soft words, Jonas urged the dog forward: a cheery enough little soul. The lead went taut: he smiled at the young man and pleaded that the dog had a mind of its own. And came closer.

"Lovely morning."

The sort of anodyne greeting, common courtesy, that he might have employed in a caravan park.

"She's a right rascal, no harm to her, love you to bits."

Jonas thought he barely registered with Cameron Jilkes. Had death in his eyes and his chin trembled, and his eyes were blood-shot. His tie hung sideways but the collar button on the shirt was fastened. Filthy shoes and mud splattered up to his thighs. Jonas reckoned it a good a time to make his approach.

"Rough old night? Been on the bottle, have we? Wish I still could, but the bladder prevents it. Moving through, are you?" Innocent and pseudo-friendly and playing the game of the bus-stop bore, doing it well, and the dog was now against Cameron Jilkes' knee, and nuzzled against him.

"Little terror, she certainly is." Jonas gazed down at the dog, and let his eyes move across Cameron. There was, of course, another way. He could have backed off and waved Dominic and Babs forward and they'd have come at a fast jog and would have been bellowing to their target to freeze and submit, would have demanded he went down on his face, his hands away from his body, and the target might be intimidated and go to surrender-mode . . . Or might leap up, kick the dog clear and lunge a swinging arm at Jonas if he were idiotic enough to intervene. And he'd be down and into the stream and across it and then lost in the next street or the one going off to the right, then a left turn . . . he'd know them all. It was his home city. Cameron Jilkes free and running, and the forces required for a manhunt and a lockdown were not yet in place . . . He took his time.

"Don't mind her, do you? Course you don't. Don't mind me, do you? Just stopping for a moment, taking the weight off the knees." Jonas sat on the bench, not too close, not yet.

Jonas thought the young man beside him was outside the limits of his experience . . . quite dissimilar to Winston Gunn. That boy would have been a reluctant volunteer, had had his brain rinsed, washed, tumble-dried, was frightened and missed his mother, and would not have known how to back out. In the months ahead would he thank his God that Jonas Merrick, peeved at compulsory retire-ment and a token drink in the atrium of Thames House – at the end of a lifetime of hard graft – had sat beside him. Unplanned, unex-pected, and Jonas had needed to make few considered actions, all done by instinct – which was why the Health and Safety gurus in the building had given him the mother and father of bollockings for endangering himself. Rather liked the boy, Winston Gunn, now alert and alive with his assumed identity and liable to throw his arms around Jonas Merrick's neck, hug him as if that were the best gratitude he could offer. And visits to "neutral locations" to see his mother, and . . . Nothing was the same, no factor matched.

"Little terror, always hungry. Never has enough to eat. You've stuff in your pocket, haven't you?" The dog strained closer to Cameron Jilkes and its nose snuffed and pressed against the young man's pocket. Jonas sensed annoyance, but needed the dog close up and causing distraction . . . If the one-time fighter ran and failed to get clear, if the guns came after him, then he would have the chance to steel himself and would go for the old one, the tried and tested solution, that of "suicide by cop". Could fake the sudden movement that seemed to be going after a weapon hidden inside his jacket. Could appear to be reaching into a pocket where there might well be an explosive vest's contact device, and might be in a bus-stop queue or outside a primary school gate just as the mums and kids were gathering. This parcel of parkland, here, would be the first opportunity for a "safe" shot, no ricochets and no collateral, and might be the last. Not how he wanted it to end. Jonas could be stubborn, rarely changed his mind when an inten-tion was fixed. Did not want him dead, too easy for him.

"Won't be long. Couple of minutes, then I'd better be pressing on." He sat on the bench. Let loose a little sigh of relief as if it was welcome to get the weight off his knees. He played the part well, feeble and without malice. He could smell him. It was that rank odour of a body coated in sweat and grime.

"Don't mind me, will you." Jonas sat upright, seemed relaxed and was not, and the dog pressed its snout against Cameron's pocket.

"Bloody hell, Dad, look."

Trace driving, Dave beside her, and their kids in the back. Instead of heading straight into town, where they'd get a parking space at that hour, she'd knocked the schedule back a few minutes to go by the Leisure Centre and drop Karen off for a fast hard swim to get the night's events out of her system.

"It's them, Ma, isn't it?"

Karen had seen them first, and Bradley followed the line of her arm, and Trace had slowed to get into the lane that would take them to the Centre's drop-off bay.

Like the nightmare of the night was resurrected. Dave had them. He said, "Kids are right, it's them. Don't know where she's been, but it was wet – snooty bitch – and he's there large as life. They're with cops. See them."

Trace pulled in, went up on to the pavement, ignored the traffic offence, pretty rare for her. "Got it, cops and guns . . . There's an old guy over by the benches and he's got a dog with him. See it?"

"On the bench, you reckon that's Cameron, love?"

"Could be . . ." and Trace came off the pavement, and did a U turn and drove into the car park and reckoned, rightly, that if they took a space at the back then they'd not be noticed.

"We just keep our heads down," Dave said. "I mean, we're sort of part of it. Didn't want to be but are. We've the right to be here, see it finish."

Not a great view from their car, but adequate. They could see the saloon car in front of them and a woman cop, black overalls, kneeling by the front fender, a rifle at her shoulder, and another cop, a young guy using the roof of their car as a resting place for his rifle, his eye in the sight. Sitting on the tarmacadam beside the front of their car were the couple that had been in their home, mud-spattered, wet, quiet, as if unwilling to distract in any way as a crisis moment approached. Beyond the car was open grass and sunlight and fading daffodils, and the bench. Sure enough, Cameron sat there. Sure enough also that some old idiot had wandered into the middle of a police operation, might blow it.

They'd never had a dog. Cammy could remember the dogs at the gaol on the other side of the city that patrolled the outside wall, big bastards with bared teeth and straining at their lead. The dogs in Syria were as adept as the vultures in clearing up carcases: they did the job in the towns and the high-flier birds did it in the desert. Nobody in Syria kept a dog as a pet and any of them that hung around where there was food would have been carpeted in fleas, and showing their ribs . . . They were just foul and when there were too many the recruits would be sent out with rifles to improve their shooting skills.

This dog had started to irritate Cammy. It had already pulled a slice of bread from his pocket. This time he had been transferring it to his mouth when the dog had slobbered over his trousers: he had given the bread to the dog which had been dumb because that only further encouraged it . . . He supposed the old beggar next to him was gagging for some meaningless conversation. He might have said, "Good to meet you, old boy. My name is Cammy, and I was once from Sturry, just up the hill from here. Right now, to those that matter in my life, I'm Kami al-Britani. I was in Syria. They had the *muhajireen*, the foreign fighters, the ones that did the hard yards. I was in that lot and with some great guys, my brothers. We didn't take any of that religious shit, nor any of the political crap – just did fighting. Doubt you'd know, old boy, about an adrenaline surge, but believe me it's what gets in your system when you've a weapon on automatic and hammering your shoulder. We were in a crack *katiba*, that's a battalion, and we had a quality *emir*. All of us had a reputation as the best. It all went arse-up . . . you following me, old boy? The tide turned and we were bombed and had missiles coming after us. It failed. We quit. Went on the road, looked to get out. I lost my brothers, each last one of them. The best of my brothers was a German girl, and she was the last to buy it. A drone took her.

Know what a drone is, old boy? It's a weapon platform, flown by some bastard thousands of miles away. When it's hot outside, the bastard has air-conditioning in his make-believe cockpit. When it's snow, fog or ice, the bastard has central heating . . . There's an RPG-7 launcher being brought into the UK, and the bombs for it, and a vehicle's been armoured up for me. In a few hours, I'm going to drive it, with the launcher across my legs, and I'm going into that place where the bastards fly the drones. Am going to take them down . . . So why don't you just piss off and take your dog with you, and leave me to get on the road?" Could have said that, and doubted the old boy would have known what he was talking about. The irritation grew.

The man said, "Yes, better be on my way. Going to be a lovely day."

The dog was still at Cammy's pocket. He checked his watch. Trouble was that Cammy found an odd form of comfort from having the man next to him, felt safer, and he reached down and ruffled the dog's coat. Would allow a few more minutes to slide – but not many.

Tristram said, "It's not for me."

Izzy said, "Am thinking the same, not my life."

"See it through, and . . ."

"See it through, finish the day."

"I didn't think that . . ."

"Nor me. I didn't think it would be like this."

"They need a different animal. It's not what I am."

Her clothing hugged her body, and she knew she stank, and her trousers were drying slowly and her skin was cold, like she was a fish on a slab, and he looked half out, concentration blown away, and the confidence seemed to have peeled away from him. He thought that they'd write the same letter and . . . The target had turned, looked straight into Jonas Merrick's face, and he thought the guns in front of them were readied, eyes at the sights, and the barrels still, and the fingers hovering on the triggers' guards.

She said, "I have no idea what will happen. Am just so fucking frightened."

Cammy looked at his watch. Did the calculations. How long to walk to the station, how long to buy his ticket, and then how long on the platform. Stretched again, and thought of the back street route he would take to get to Canterbury West.

The dog sat in front of him.

Thought of his brothers. Was on a park bench with an old boy beside him who seemed lonely as hell, except for a dog. Wondered if the old boy had had brothers. Remembered all of them . . . Ulrike who used to say *Stay calm. It is never a crisis.* Could feel her body against his when they slept in the dirt together. Pieter, who he always went to for advice and who he loved and who would say *Never look back. Never chase the past.* And Tomas who would grin, try to laugh and then mutter, *Better to hang together, not separately.* And Dwayne from the Canadian outback with the heavy-lidded miserable eyes who would tell them, *Things are going to get a lot worse before they get worse.* Mikki who would clap his hands when their mood was down, and punch their shoulders and shout at them, *Life is short. Live it.* And Stanislau from the city of Minsk who liked to say, *I want to snatch the sunset and hold it.* Loved them all . . . wondered if he could snatch a sunrise and hold it, clasp it in his fist.

From where Cammy sat, he could see the Bell Harry Tower.

Words came to his mind, lodged in his throat. *Be thou my guardian and my guide, And hear me when I call: Let not my slippery footsteps slide, And hold me lest I fall.* Good words. He soaked up the quiet around him where most of the daffodils were almost spent, and the sun was warm on his back. *The world, the flesh and Satan dwell Around the path I tread: Oh save me from the snares of Hell, Thou quickener of the dead* . . . He flexed himself to stand.

"What a very decent voice you have," the old boy said, and smiled into his face.

He pushed himself up, felt the wobble in his legs, stood still and stretched some more. He had not realised he had been singing.

*   *   *

From Dominic, "I've a bad angle. You?"

From Babs, "Difficult. Not one I'd choose."

Both had the target standing and immediately in front of the target was Merrick, who had shared so little with them. He stood, and Jonas obscured the aim they had on the chest of Cameron Jilkes.

"Sorry, but it's gotten worse."

"Correct, gotten a whole lot worse."

"Like we're out of the game."

"What a man once said, 'They also serve who only stand and wait'. Talking about us. But it's all about to happen and – Sod's Law – we've rotten angles."

Jonas said, "It's been really nice to meet you."

He was not answered.

"I think we'll have a decent day, good sunshine."

He won a limp smile . . . It was that moment. Recognised it.

"What's that over there . . .?"

Jonas screwed up his eyes, squinted into the middle distance, and his upper teeth bit on his lower lip as if he faced something that puzzled him. He pointed and there was a place on the far bank of the stream where a garden went down to the bank, where already some of the blossom from a tree had been stripped by the night's rain and the wind.

"You'll have better eyes than me, young fellow. What is it?"

Would have seemed so banal, so ordinary. He thought he'd done it well. Had indeed done it well. Cameron Jilkes had the line of Jonas's arm to guide him and he had turned his head away – might have reckoned to humour an old fool – and looked, and would not have seen.

Jonas removed his hand from his pocket, a fast crabbing movement and dropped the dog's lead at his feet and the dog looked up, confused.

His right hand came from his pocket and there would have been a flash of light as the sunlight caught the chrome. His left hand snaked across his body and took the open side of the hand-cuffs. Jonas glanced down, located the wrist, and Cameron's head was still turned away, wondering what the hell it was that the old fool had noticed, what needed identifying.

Done rather expertly.

If anyone had seen the procedure they might have wondered if it were something that Jonas practised. Might have spent hours making sure that it worked as intended, might have . . . He closed the two bars over the wrist and squeezed.

There was a look, first of astonishment, then confusion. Confusion changing to clarity. Jonas saw that Cameron Jilkes understood that he had a closed manacle on his wrist but did not appreciate that he was now fastened to the elderly man who seemed concerned only about the weather that day and the welfare of a small dog. His head had turned, twisted, and his eyes had come alive and blazed anger at Jonas.

Jonas was heaved off his feet. Cameron's arm swung away as if the speed of its movement would break the irritation of the hold, and Jonas's arm went with it. Jonas lost balance. He toppled and fell across the bench. He heard the first bellow of fury. No question now that Cameron Jilkes, front line fighter, survivor in a hostile world, had started to appreciate that he had been – stick with the vernacular, Jonas – conned rotten, been taken for a ride and a half by a man he had assumed was no more than a lonely pensioner. He was across the bench then was dragged further forward and his face went down and hit grass and his legs came loosely after him. Had the feeling that if subjected to another such lurch, full force used, his arm would pop from the shoulder joint . . . Not possible that Cameron Jilkes would break free of him. He was dead weight and the lad could not run. A savage kick was aimed at his head and caught Jonas a glancing blow and he felt blood welling in his nostrils. The dog jumped up and down and barked hysterically. More blood seeped in his mouth from a split lip.

Jonas tried to shout, "Thought better of you, Cameron. You disappoint me."

Thought that Cameron Jilkes was a man held with a ball and chain, dragging it, scraping it along. Still he was pulled, and again he twisted his head too late and only minimised the kick, and Cameron was still moving, but slower.

Jonas called out, "What do you think you'll do, Cameron? You going to drag me into Canterbury, up the High Street, wait outside a butcher shop . . ."

Felt old and weak.

". . . hang on there until the big man comes and raises the grille, and you pull me inside and demand he lend you a cleaver . . ."

Jonas had never been more determined, and his voice lost its quaver and he shouted as he was bumped over the grass.

". . . Then off to the station, with a handcuff on your wrist and my arm hanging down from it. Make you popular on a crowded train . . . It's all over, Cameron, accept it. All over."

The guns were approaching. Jonas Merrick saw them and so did Cameron Jilkes.

17

Jonas was tugged, shaken, punched.

Not a youngster and probably carrying a few pounds too many, and not particularly fit. Had he merely held onto a rope fastened to Cameron Jilkes, he would have let it go. A sense of survival would have kicked in. He could not, and the handcuff fastened to his wrist had seared the skin and blood ran down the sides of his hand. No possibility of freeing himself – had given away the only key.

He was soaking punishment and Cameron was dishing it, and the level of engagement was such that neither now had the breath or the energy to speak. It could not last much longer. The guns were closing on them. They did not come with a sprint but with what seemed to Jonas to be a lethargic jog; would have said in a manual that it was best to stay back, conserve breath and concentration, be able to think clearly. It would not last much longer because he could sense that Cameron's attack was becoming frantic. His free hand had already gone deep into Jonas's pockets, trousers and jacket, and his handkerchief was on the grass and the few coins that he carried and his wallet with the ID behind the plastic cover, and his phone, and no key had been found. Poor old Cameron, learning the hard way, that Christmas only came but once a year and this was not the day that he would find a shiny little key fastened to a length of pink ribbon knotted to a ring. He took a beating and did not know how much of it he could endure but the guns were still not near and their control was not yet exercised . . .

They had come to the last moment of the last effort and the anger still ran riot in Cameron, and Jonas was hurt in too many places to feel pain, then . . . hands on his throat. On his wind-pipe, pressure grew. He heard the dog yelp. Harder to breathe and the force of the fingers tightening . . . remember the damn crocodile, that sort of strength. His eyes misted over and he could no longer see how far away were Dominic and Babs and their rifles. Might have croaked, had he been able to, something about them not shooting, not committing the soul of Cameron Jilkes to the apple orchards in Paradise and the 72 virgins, and all the rest of that stuff – what had been fed into the mind of little Winston Gunn. Failing to breathe and choking . . . He heard the dog growl deep in its throat, like it was gargling medicine, then a squeaky snarl, then a howl from Cameron. The hands came away, the weight was taken off Jonas's neck. Blinked hard, and looked, and the dog, the dear little dog that had shown it liked little more than to sit on a warm lap, had its teeth tight on Cameron's ankle.

Dominic hit him, not hard, but sufficient, on the shoulder. An adequate blow and using the extended length of a police truncheon.

Babs had Cameron covered and peered over the sights of her rifle.

And still, Jonas reckoned, a last chance for that Valhalla moment, one more lunge might square it, be good enough for her to say from behind a screen at an inquest that she believed her life, Dominic's life, and the life of Jonas Merrick, to be in the gravest danger – enough to justify giving him the Paradise ticket.

Jonas exerted himself, found – a miracle – the necessary energy. He rolled. He used his body to cover Cameron Jilkes and he put his hands, one handcuffed to Cameron, over his opponent's face. He gave her no target.

He sucked air into his lungs and spat and heaved and coughed, spread the phlegm around, and found a hoarse voice.

"What he wants is for you to shoot him. He does not get what he wants. You do not shoot."

Her finger seemed to be a quarter of an inch from the trigger. It did not move, no flickering movement. He thought the control

she exercised was remarkable . . . Dominic flashed the pink ribbon
from his pocket. Had his own cuffs off his belt, and yanked
Cameron's arms so that his prisoner would have replacement
restraints and Jonas could be freed.

He eased away. He sat on his haunches and rubbed his neck
and the dog came up close.

"It would have been what he wanted. A bullet would breed a
legend, he would have thought. Quick way out and no pain . . . A
martyr is a hero in the minds of enough of them who look for an
example to follow . . ."

To Cameron had said, "You will go to prison and you will sit
there for days and then for weeks, months, years, and you will be
there for the rest of your life . . . No kid is going to take you as an
example of how the life of a hero fighter might end."

Jonas rolled away, and pushed the dog clear of him because its
usefulness was over. His phone rang. He reached for it on the
grass, picked it up.

The AssDepDG told him, a little breathlessly, that the full
surveillance team was now moving out of the police station and
would take up position in the housing estate within a quarter of an
hour.

His answer, "It is dealt with." And ended the call.

The phone rang again. Aggie Burns telling him to get to the
police station where she was going to do a joint Gold Commander
with a police boss.

His answer, "Go back to your breakfast."

He switched off the phone.

Jonas Merrick took little enjoyment from exercising authority.
He did it in a staccato burst of speech. Tristram and Izzy would
have liked to fuss around him but were waved away and were told
where they should take the dog, find its owner's number on the
collar, should thank them, should return it.

Told Dominic and Babs what they were to do, authorised the
action they should take. Did not thank them, not a habit of his –
wished them well, but gruffly. He stood up, retrieved the items
rifled from his pockets and walked, briskly, to their car to take out

his bag: then he would walk to the station. Would rather not accept a lift?

Cammy shouted, "You bastard."

Jonas did not turn.

Cammy saw the man lift a bag from the police car before heading away and across the road in front of the Leisure Centre.

Cammy told the policeman who had hit him, then handcuffed him, that his shoulder hurt.

"I expect you'll live."

Told the policewoman, who had the rifle, that his ankle hurt from the dog's bite.

"Maybe you'll get rabies. But that'll be the least of your problems."

They had him on his feet. He looked back at the stream and the bench, he *thought* he saw his mother on the pavement on the far side of the stream and beyond the line of bungalows, going slowly towards a bus-stop.

And looked forward where a car was parked and a young pair, a guy and a girl, stood with the dog, and *thought* that he saw the Hunter family, the mother and the father and the two kids, and none of them would have known what it had been like to run in the Syrian heat, with the whip-crack of incoming fire around him: all in ignorance – and scared of him because they all looked away as soon as they realised he had locked eyes on them.

He was put in the back seat of the police car. The handcuffs were adjusted so that his wrists, still pinching, were in the small of his spine. The seatbelt was fastened for him.

Babs said, "You give me grief, Mr Jilkes, and I'll fucking belt you with my stick."

And Dominic said, "And, along with it, Mr Jilkes, you'll get a dose of pepper spray."

They told him that he'd be going for a ride now, courtesy of the gentleman's instructions and that he should sit tight, and enjoy it. The siren went on and they were both laughing. They passed the front of the Leisure Centre, and Cameron saw them. They stopped and turned and she was carrying the baby, and her husband had his arm around her shoulder – Vicky and Gavin. The siren was deafening. They came to a junction, and then a roundabout and again the driver needed to slow.

He saw the old man. He was walking quickly, short steps, and the car's siren would have blasted his ears. Didn't turn, didn't acknowledge it.

"Really sorry, was held up. Buses were a nightmare this morning," Sadie Jilkes said to her supervisor.

Dave Hunter said, "I don't want to remember any of that. It's gone and should be forgotten . . . it's like somewhere and something far away and outside our experience. We're safe, and that's the end of it."

At the side door of Thames House, each holding a plastic container of coffee were Tristram and Izzy.

It did not have to be said, but Tristram did. "That's that, then."

He did not have to be answered, but Izzy said, "Gone, swallowed into that great electronic mouth – good riddance."

They had talked it through all the way back to London. Had taken a taxi, with the dog, had argued with the driver about his willingness to ferry it, and had given him both barrels. Had dropped it off, no word of explanation and left the string of questions hanging . . . Had turned their backs on Sturry after collecting the office car from down the road from the Hunters' house. Had driven back to London and had chewed it.

He'd said, "No way I'm suited to it – tried it and failed it."

She'd said, "A war without end and I haven't the stamina to go the course."

"Takes people of a sort to fight that war, Izzy, and I don't want to be like them."

"Good for him, though – for old Merrick, Eternal Flame, Wobby and all that crap. Not for me."

Two armed police sidled up to them, would have come from

the back entrance on Thorney Street. Said they were Kev and
Leroy, said they had been told to be here, at around this time,
not given an explanation: had weapons hanging from their
shoulders and belts. Tristram shrugged, Izzy grimaced, no
answers offered . . . They had each written a letter of resignation,
identical. Had offered their judgements that they were not suited
for the work involved. Each had pressed Send. *Alea iacta est*, he
had said, and she'd replied that he could be a pompous prat,
then had kissed his cheek: they were an item. They would confirm
that status as soon as they could get the paperwork done and be
clear of the building: might be at her place or on the bed in his
flat. And they'd also had time, coming into London, to take the
first steps in future planning: maybe health and safety in the
private sector, maybe social work . . . where victories could be
counted.

The car arrived, lights flashing behind the front grille, and another
had been at a crazy angle on the roof, and they had the siren blasting.
Tristram took her mug and walked the few paces to the café and
dumped his and hers on a table: rude, but it did not matter; he could
not imagine they would use the place again. He told Kev and Leroy
that he was taking charge of a prisoner who was being brought up in
police custody from Kent, and what their role would be.

The car pulled up on a double yellow.

The AssDepDG had materialised behind them.

In the car, sunk on the back seat, his hands awkwardly fastened
behind him, was Cameron Jilkes. Tristram thought it hardly a
glorious end to the man's work. Like the defiance was knocked out
of him, like the fight had already been crushed. Threatening?
Hardly. A hazard to public safety? Did not seem to be.

He heard a murmured voice behind him, "Not much to write
home about, is he? Bit of a let-down, I'd say. But that's how they
all are when their ego takes a dive. Well done, both of you. I expect
you've enjoyed it, being alongside old Jonas, my Wise Old Bird.
Quite a privilege. You're very lucky."

And he was gone. Tristram wondered how far Jonas Merrick,
Wobby, had travelled on the train, whether he was into London

yet, and how his face was, and his bruises. Izzy had the paperwork on a clipboard.

Cameron was helped from the car. New handcuffs were put on him, and the original pair were handed back to the policewoman. There was a moment when the prisoner seemed to lift his head, look up at the sky above Horseferry Road, then tilt and look further and see scudding clouds over Lambeth Bridge, and might have sniffed at that air. Then Kev had a hold of one arm and Leroy had the other.

Leroy's question, "Is this down to old Merrick? Bet it is. He's a fucking guy, that one. Proper special."

Kev quipped, "Amazing guy. Like the man said, 'You're very lucky'. Too right."

Izzy had them sign for delivery, and added her own signature, handed it over. What to say? Nothing. The car drove away. The prisoner would be held in a waiting area until the anti-terror police arrived and he could be taken into orthodox custody.

There would be a brief interview with each of them by Human Resources. Would admit that they did not feel suited, would be shown the door and have their ID cards mangled. Would go to find a bed somewhere, his or hers, and would accept that they had failed the career test.

She said, "Didn't much look like a crocodile, that Jilkes, did he?"

He said, "Nor would Merrick seem to fit the bill for an intrepid crocodile hunter."

On the east side of Grantham is the local crematorium. Good car parking available, and minimal camera surveillance at the extremes of the site.

Wolfboy parked his van under trees. He had come in with a convoy of mourners, would not have been noticed, had attracted no attention ... He should have had a call by now ...

He waited.

Two funerals later – and no call on his phone – a camper appeared. Wolfboy saw the couple in the front, and a woman was pointing at him and directing the old guy beside her.

Wolfboy had walked around that part of the parking area and there had been no suspected surveillance vehicles and no one loitering and smoking, no one with a wheelbarrow and broom endlessly sweeping the same ground. He met their eyes. For a couple of minutes, the guy ignored him, looked the other way, and the woman took out a thermos. No call came on his phone. Should have been told that the link guy, the one referred to as Kami al-Britani, was off the train at St Pancras station in London, had crossed to Kings Cross, was on the fast train, a 67-minute journey. A dicker should have identified him, tracked him to the platform, seen him board, then called.

A quarter of an hour passed. Maybe it was the woman in the camper who thought time was up. She climbed out of the front and dragged open the side door, and started to raise the bench seat. The man gave a peremptory wave and Wolfboy was summoned. No pleasantries, no introductions, no laughs. A package was manoeuvred clear of the space under the seating. They heaved and gasped to shift it, and Wolfboy had his rear door open. There was enough floor space for the package and it would fit alongside the customised sheets of metal, what should have been the necessary armour-plating. He saw that both the man and the woman wore gloves, professional. Imagined there would be a place far away where they could dump their vehicle, load what little they had into another car, then torch the camper.

Wolfboy might wait an hour, not longer. Might wait an hour . . . If no call were received, if the schedule were broken, Wolfboy would leave the keys in the ignition, then would walk smartly, purposefully, past the entrance to the crematorium and would head for the bus-stop, and would be on his way home. *If* no call reached him, *if* the man who intended to die for the cause had in fact been arrested, *if* he were now in a bleak interrogation room, then the likelihood, Wolfboy had been told, was that he would talk: it was said that very few resisted questioning.

Just another day at the Station.

Two Reaper drones were flown that day and they quartered the airspace above deserted villages north of the Syrian town of Deir Ezzor and over a desert area close to the ruins of Palmyra.

The nursery on the Station was open, and the canteen staff were busy and lunch was about to be served in the Officers' Mess. Technical teams worked hard at the maintenance of the electronics required to keep the birds airborne some 2,500 miles away, and pilots flew and sensor operators checked their payload of munitions, and the intelligence people sifted what was passed them . . . Twice that morning the Reaper lenses had fastened on to, focused and made sharp, the whitened bones uncovered by the weather from shallow graves, but that was not unusual. They were seen and noted and then the cameras had moved on.

On the south side of Thames House, Jonas took the lift to the third floor, then set off down the familiar corridor which would take him beyond the coffee machines and the confectionery dispenser to Room 12. He had been via the room occupied by the resident nurse, and his face had been cleaned and the scars covered in Elastoplast strips, and his broken lip had been stitched, which was painful. And had been to see the AssDepDG: no inquests and no hindsight examination, and he had been asked what he intended to do in the immediate future, and had answered. Then had been asked what route he planned to take, and had said what road he had chosen. Must have looked a bit of a sight: the mud had dried on his trousers and their creases were long gone and his jacket buttons were torn loose and his shirt was covered in dirt stains and his tie was crumpled, and he had neither shaved nor been able to polish his shoes. He carried his bag, and arrived at the door of 3/S/12 and opened it. The noise stopped. No conversation, no clicking at a keyboard, and no talking into a phone. Action suspended. All eyes were on him, and they tried to strip into his mind and to read him – might not have liked him nor enjoyed his company – but seemed to want to understand him better. No applause and no congratulations. He saw Tristram and Izzy sitting at the central table, already their resignation letters had been copied to him. He acknowledged none of them but went into his private area. The bag would go back in the cupboard, with the sponge bag, the clean socks and the fresh shirt, and pyjamas. All was as he had left it. He did not have time to waste . . . He reached up and unfastened the two pictures. First off the wall was the view of the stagnant pool where two inked circles showed the tip of a nostril and the narrowed eye. He pulled it off the wall, but carefully so that it did not tear. Next, the original picture was taken down, the beast with the horrid set of irregular teeth. He looked around him, was satisfied and went back into the main area. Jonas made a point of first going to where Izzy sat and he dropped in front of her the portrait of the crocodile's head, and then allowed that of the water expanse to flutter into Tristram's place. He said nothing. He could have wished them well, could have urged that they think again on their futures and might contemplate withdrawing their resignations. He did not look back and went out through the door and closed it after him. They would have heard his footsteps going away down the corridor.

A cell door slammed. Keys rattled, footsteps retreated, a distant voice yelled abuse at an unnamed target. He sat on the bed, had nowhere else to sit and he gazed at the tiled floor, had nowhere else to look.

Sitting opposite each other at a canteen table, foreswearing the senior dining-room were the AssDepDG and the DepDG.

"He's gone off home now. He'll take a week's leave: can't say that he'll use it all but at least some of it. It has actually been a rather extraordinary few hours. For us, because we are used to confronting home-grown fighters who have limited experience in weapons and tactics, though still danerous. For him, he will have come from a war zone and will be looking into the skies for fixed-wing fast jets and for missile-carrying drones, and expecting to have close-quarter fighting with top-drawer Special Forces and going right down the scales to Syrian press-ganged recruits but also with plenty of firepower. The ground chosen for our operation was wonderfully banal – a little corner of east Kent, and the most famous cathedral city in the Anglican world. Jilkes would have been awarded a 'best in show' rosette where he had been, whereas down there, Canterbury, he'd have been floundering like a bird with a broken wing. Jonas recognised it, and went for the boy's jugular. Takes all sorts, and thank the good Lord we still have room for him, our Eternal Flame, our Wobby. An unsung hero, the best type . . . So good, these sausages, aren't they?"

Other than the motor cycle in front of them, the road ahead was clear.

When he had reached the front step, had been fiddling for the key, Vera had opened the door.

"What's this, some sort of scarecrow?"

He had grinned, a little sheepishly, had said something about needing a bath and a brush-up.

"I suppose you walked into a door."

A bit of a shrug. He had stood in the hall and had eased out of his coat, then had discarded the stained jacket, had dropped his trousers, then had taken off his shirt and tie.

"Clever door, if it could make those bruises on your throat."

He had given her a rueful kiss on the cheek, and she had pulled a face, then had gathered up his clothing and he had padded off up the stairs to run the bath, and in the mirror while the water cascaded from the taps he could see the damage on his face that the in-house nurse had sealed. He had called down his hope for a departure time, and she had started to prepare the necessary food, and what else they took, and had gone to the garage to find the cat's basket. While he lay in the bath she would also have been around to the back door of their neighbour and warned her they'd be away a few days. Might have been asked for how long – might have said she had not been told, and grimaced.

The motorcycle took them at a steady pace, one that recognised without quibble the speed limit for that section of road.

He had come down the stairs and the cat had been shouting abuse from the cage. She had asked, "Not my business, Jonas, but what's the state of the door?"

He'd said, "The door came off badly. The door's shoulder took a whack from a truncheon which would have hurt, and the door's ankle ended up with a dog bite, only a spaniel but done with vigour. And the door won't be going off to the country for some quiet walks because it will be under lock and key. The best place for a door – be there for a bit, quite a bit."

Which at the time was enough of an explanation. He was pleased with the expertise he'd shown when he hooked up the caravan to the tow-bar, then bringing it out of the parking area in front of their house, then beginning the journey from the tree-lined road in Raynes Park, where very soon the blossom would make a show. Vera had made a suggestion for a minor diversion as they had headed west. Had shown him a destination on the map, and he had agreed. There was a gin factory in a building once used as a printing works, and the Test river ran through an historic mill beside the factory. He had walked around the site, had seen brown trout from a footbridge, and had stayed close to his wife and had learned about the production of the drink and how the flavours were added from hothouse-grown plants – and then had had a sample, non-alcoholic, in their bar. He had permitted her all the time she might have wanted as if he had no distractions and his scabbing wounds gave no irritation. The place was crowded and several of the other visitors peered at him. At Vera's guidance, Jonas had wrapped a loose scarf around his throat and it hid the flesh around his windpipe, but he heard her say to a woman who had shown particular interest that he'd "had a fight with a door, quite a rough door." And while Jonas learned about the production of "mothers' ruin", he could reflect – briefly – that his opponent would by now have been marched out of the holding cell and would be in an interrogation suite. A relay of questioners would be forming an orderly queue and waiting to get at him and prise open his secrets' box, which would be the interesting bit for Cameron Jilkes and would keep him alert; more interesting than the following months and years in the cell when no one would come to visit. No one would bother.

They had joined the A303 at the Beacon Hill roundabout,

where the motorcycle had awaited their arrival. Jonas flashed his lights and received an acknowledging wave and the rider had pulled out ahead of him, and the rotating blue light on a pole at the back of the bike had been activated. That had been good of the AssDepDG, fixing it with a county's traffic division, had been appreciated.

"Is that for us?" Vera had asked.

He chirped, "Must have the wrong vehicle to escort, but we'll not deny a gift horse."

The road in front stayed clear. Behind Jonas and Vera would have been a convoy of motorists going puce with frustration. He and Vera, and the constabulary, would have been subject to violent abuse, and a few tried to take the matter into their own hands and accelerated up the road in an attempt to pass the caravan, then had found the centre of the road occupied by a police motorcyclist. No overtaking was permitted. They passed Stonehenge. It looked spectacular that late afternoon. Clean sunshine fell on the stones and the lichen was highlighted and the sky was scoured by the winds so the clouds moved fast. Very pretty . . .

Not so in the interview suite. He imagined an atmosphere of scrupulous politeness directed toward Cameron Jilkes, and they would have been beavering to locate the weapon he would have used . . . By now, but for the scrap in that Canterbury park, it would all have been over at the Station that Jonas assumed would have been the target. Blood and guts and smoke and sirens, and recriminations on a grand scale. They would want to find that weapon and quickly, and learn about the contacts in this country and abroad. Would want to exploit that window of opportunity when the prisoner had so recently gone into the net.

After Stonehenge and Winterbourne Stoke, the A303 widened to dual carriageway. Not that it would help the grumbling convoy in their wake. Nothing passed him. Jonas reckoned the motorcyclist might have been the most perverse character in that force's traffic section. The rider was out in the fast lane, and brooked no overtaking. After Wylye, and after Chicklade, were steep hills where Jonas needed to drop his speed below the limit, and then the rest of his following log-jam had to ape him. So pleasant, Vera remarked, not to have the hassle of traffic. It was good not to speed and the cat in its basket would not be thrown around on the back seat of their car. By the time they reached the turning for Wolverton Oak, Jonas imagined that the cars and lorries and vans behind him stretched all the way back to the Keysley Down crossroads. He thought himself richly rewarded for his encounter in the park.

Coming towards the junction for Stoke Trister to the south or Stoney Stoke to the north, he flashed his headlights, and the rider acknowledged him, gave a gloved salute. He indicated left ... There was a small site they had heard of at the pub in Stourton Caundle, a Dorset village. He swung the wheel, waved to the motorcyclist, and he was gone and the traffic squashed behind was in racing mood. He felt quite tired. Not as tired as his opponent would be. The questioning would be remorseless and, from what Jonas had read, they would exact every possible advantage from the early sessions because opened windows should always be used to maximum effect.

They were now on narrow B roads and she called out the directions from her phone. There were cows grazing beyond neat hedgerows, and sheep, and a tractor was shifting silage on a trailer. Jonas felt the stress drip off him and Vera had looped her arm around his, and he thought he might sleep many hours when he had parked the caravan, hooked up the power and the water, and stretched and walked around the site as dusk fell. Cameron Jilkes was unlikely to see any cows or sheep for twenty years, and no country dusk to watch as the sun dipped through the trellis shapes of leafless old trees.

She gave him good warning of the turning out of Stalbridge Weston to Stourton Caundle, and said, "Jonas, I suppose I ought to know ... what sort of day was it for you?"

He pondered for a moment and a low branch scraped the caravan's side. They would be working hard on Cameron Jilkes, bleeding him, and unlikely he would hold out much longer, would want a bed and food and to lie in darkness and contemplate his misery. He deliberated on what he should say. Took a deep breath.

"A near-run thing. That sort of day. Could have been worse – yes, quite a bit worse."

"Are you finished with it, Jonas, or not finished?"

"The cat will be glad when we get there. Trouble is that those sort of near-run things keep coming along, without an end in sight. Probably, sorry and all that, not finished . . . The cat's been very good . . . No, not finished if they sniff out another crocodile."